THE NOISE REVEALED

Also by Ian Whates

The Gift of Joy
The Mammoth Book of Alternative History
(edited with Ian Watson)
The Bitten Word
City of Dreams and Nightmare
City of Hope and Despair
The Noise Within

THE NOISE REVEALED

By Ian Whates

SOLARIS

First published 2011 by Solaris
an imprint of Rebellion Publishing Ltd,
Riverside House, Osney Mead,
Oxford, OX2 0ES, UK

www.solarisbooks.com

ISBN: 978 1 907519 53 6

10 9 8 7 6 5 4 3 2 1

A CIP catalogue record for this book is available from the
British Library.

Designed & typeset by Rebellion Publishing

Printed in the UK by CPI Bookmarque, Croydon

For Margo Whates, my mother,
who doesn't read my work
so may never realise this book is dedicated to her.

PART ONE

CHAPTER ONE

Joss Brennan stared at the screen, trying to decide why she wasn't more delighted at what she saw there. After all, wasn't this every tramp miner's dream – the pot of gold at the end of the celestial rainbow? Yet she felt more nervous than excited.

"Has to be a ship," she muttered.

"Yeah, but what kind of ship?" replied Crane, who, in the absence of anyone else, was the nobody in question.

She could feel him at her shoulder, a too-close presence nearly as irritating as the sweat that prickled her short-cropped scalp. More than that, she could *smell* him – none of them had washed in more days than she cared to remember; there were too many other priorities out here. Personal hygiene tended to drop to the bottom of a long list. She knew without looking that he'd be clinging to the wires above his head with one hand and to a pipe to one side with the other, which was the only way two of them could fit into the cramped cabin unless she was willing to offer him her lap. And she wasn't, not Crane.

Joss grunted. "Beats the hell out of me."

Joss knew ships, but these readings didn't match any she'd ever heard of, even granting that this was a derelict and so likely to be an old model, almost certainly pre-War.

"Well," asked a voice made tinny by the ship's internal comms system, "are we going in or what?" Wicks, the engineering guru who kept them in space; third and final member of their merry little band.

"Patience, Wicksy, patience," Joss murmured in response.

She glanced around at Crane to gauge his thoughts, and found him trying to suppress a knowing grin, which disappeared the second her gaze fell upon him. Damn! He'd caught her playing with the bullet again, turning its familiar, machine-smoothed length between the tips of her stubby nail-bitten thumb and forefinger without her even realising.

It was a comfort thing, something she had a habit of doing when she was nervous or uncertain. Joss knew that, which was fine. So did Crane, which wasn't.

She dropped the bullet immediately, allowing it to dangle from her neck from its delicate gold chain, scowled at Crane and turned back to her screen. Screw his advice, whatever it might have been. *She* was captain of this ship and the decision was hers to make, no one else's. She looked at the readouts again, recognising what prompted her misgivings: life had taught her the hard way that when something looked too good to be true it probably was. But she also knew that if they turned away now without ever finding out what was down there, the wondering and the 'what ifs' would drive her nuts.

Joss took a deep breath. "Okay, people, we're going in."

"About time," Crane muttered, which, she guessed, told her where he stood on the issue.

"Wicksy, get kitted up. Crane, you're staying with the ship."

"But..."

"No buts. We don't know what's waiting for us down there. Somebody has to stay onboard *The Gold Digger* to monitor the situation and be ready for a quick lift-off if needed, and it's not as if I'm spoilt for choice here... That somebody is you."

She unbuckled and climbed out of the chair, legs aching a little from so long spent in the same position. Shit! When did she start getting old? "Take us in, close as you can," she said to Crane, who was forced to back out of the cramped cabin to let her past. "I'm gonna get ready."

At its heart, *The Gold Digger* was a decent little ship – had been when she took it over and would be again, if and when Joss ever got enough money behind her to take care of all the little jobs that credit flow had forced her to neglect – and Crane was a competent enough pilot. She had no qualms about leaving him to handle the landing while she suited up.

They were a long way from home, having been forced to go further afield than ever before by all the tension building up over mining rights. The loss of *The Polly Anna* was the final straw. She'd known that crew, had drunk with them often and even woken up with one of them after a particularly ribald night – not an incident she cared to dwell on. She wasn't about to let *The Gold Digger* be the next craft to suffer an 'accident.' So, after a hasty pow-wow with Wicksy and Crane, Joss had taken a gamble and brought *The Gold Digger* out here, way beyond what could even be viewed as the fringe of human space, to a virgin system whose asteroid belt held the promise of mineral treasures. They were far enough out that profit margins were tenuous at best, but if they *could* make enough just to tick over, at least until things settled down a little, the gamble would have been worth it.

Now this, first time out: a ship; a wreck; a God-only-knew-what. It was on the smaller moon of the first planet in-system from the belt. Pure luck they'd passed this way and seen it at all.

"Touchdown in one minute." Crane, suddenly turned all business now that he was in the chair.

"Anything on visual yet?"

"Dunno. There's a sort of hill where the readings are centred."

"Sort of?"

"Yeah."

She sighed. "It's buried then, whatever this is."

"Maybe."

"Crane!" The man really could be an asshole sometimes. She needed a break from this. Not only her, they all did – time spent somewhere that had a surfeit of bars where the three of them could vanish and get tanked up without having to look at each others' ugly faces for a while. Such a small group, cooped up together for days on end... minor irritations were bound to become big ones, and some of Crane's were never all that minor in the first place.

"Hey, don't yell, I'm doing my best here," he assured her. "This just... well, it looks too regular."

She stopped, in the last stages of sealing her suit. "Man-made, you mean?"

"Could be. You can make up your own mind in a bit."

Suit sealed, Joss hastily strapped herself to the wall beside Wicks, scant seconds before the whole ship vibrated and then bucked and jolted to the irregular rhythm of landing, a passably smooth one considering the lack of a proper landing field. Both she and Wicks were out of the airlock in quick order, striding through the swirls of dust kicked up by *The Gold Digger*'s arrival, until they were looking at... something. They stopped and simply stared.

"If that's natural," Wicks said, "then I'm a one-legged whore from a Frysworld cathouse."

"Better hop on over and take a closer look then," Crane quipped in their ears.

"Shut it, Crane," Joss growled, "and keep your eyes glued to those friggin' sensors."

"I'm on it, don't worry. Nothing moving out there 'cept you two little bunnies."

In front of them stood a vast dome. How it could ever have looked like anything natural as they came in was beyond her; it certainly didn't from down here, despite being the same basic colour as the surrounding rocks.

"Crane, any chance the dome itself is what we were picking up?"

"None. Whatever brought us here is inside."

Joss had known as much, really, but the confirmation left her facing the second major decision of the day. Obviously this wasn't some undiscovered wreck waiting to be unearthed and claimed for salvage. If it *was* a downed ship – and that still remained a big 'if,' given the readings – somebody had beaten them to it and invested a considerable amount of time, effort, and resources in building a shell around the damned thing, presumably intended to conceal it. And then, apparently, they'd gone away again. So where in Hades' name did the crew of *The Gold Digger* fit in? They didn't; not in any profitable way.

"What do you reckon, Joss?" Wicks asked. "Do we pull out now before someone notices we're here?"

"Could do, probably *should* do... but then we'd always wonder, wouldn't we?"

"Yeah," he sighed, "there is that."

"Don't see that we've got anything much to gain, way things look; but we're here now. So we might as well do what we came for. Come on." She started forward again.

It wasn't far. Crane had brought them down as close as he could, on a patch of ground more level than most. To their left, a ridge of rock paralleled their course, standing perhaps three times head height. To their right a vista of barren rock opened up. Joss barely paid attention; it was indistinguishable from a hundred similar places she'd been to. The dome – that was where her eyes focused. She couldn't help but think that anyone who'd gone to so much trouble should have done a better job of hiding whatever was contained here. There were ways of fooling sensors, of cloaking things far more effectively than this had been. Unless they were meant to notice; unless this was a trap, a honey pot to lure them in.

"I..." The unexpected voice in her ear startled her.

"Crane? You got something?"

"Not sure. For a minute there I thought... Oh, shit!"

"What?" She stopped dead in her tracks.

"Life signs, a dozen of them, on that ridge to your left."

"I thought you said there *weren't* any life signs."

"That's right, I did, because there weren't, but now there are."

Joss had already turned to face the ridge, and she could see them: identical figures, arrayed in a line along the ridge. Military, had to be, judging by their stance and the look of the guns they each hefted. They didn't approach, but just stood there, holding their positions.

"You want to hear the rest of the good news?" Crane asked.

"There's more? Go on."

"Three ships above us, came out of nowhere; small but heavily armed, and they've got weapons-lock on me."

She'd been right: a trap, of course it was. Ships and men camouflaged behind technical wizardry far too sophisticated for *The Gold Digger* or her crew to pierce, and she was willing to bet that the dome wasn't deserted either, whatever their sensors reported. Why couldn't she just have flown straight past this godforsaken rock?

At least Wicksy was experienced enough not to ask her what they should do next. He could calculate the odds as readily as she. The only thing they *could* do was wait and see what was required of them; thankfully, that didn't take long.

Sound doesn't travel in vacuum, so Joss didn't hear the canopy start to raise, but she felt it. Even through insulated boots the soles of her feet reported the rock trembling as the dome split at ground level; a horizontal seam which, bizarrely, reminded her of a grinning mouth as it grew ever wider. Light blazed from the expanding slit, causing Joss's faceplate to darken. After a fractional delay, the visor recalibrated and she could see again.

As the dome continued to open, three figures strode through the centre of the gap, their elongated shadows stretching out across the barren landscape to where she and Wicks waited – three fingers of darkness questing towards them. One stood slightly in front, flanked by the other two; guards, both carrying heavy guns in case anyone doubted their status. But it was what stood behind them that really caught Joss's attention.

The dome had lifted most of the way now, the side closest to her sliding back until it presented a half-dome, which in turn provided a backdrop to one of the most astonishing things Joss had ever seen.

"Holy mother of God," Wicks murmured from beside her.

She knew what he meant. Joss never had been a believer in much beyond her own capabilities, but this was enough to have a person invoking any deity they'd ever heard of. It was a ship all right, and a derelict one, an ancient wreck, just as their initial readings had suggested; but now that she actually saw the thing, Joss could understand why those readings had been so confused. What stood framed within this half-dome, like some giant hatchling breaking free of its egg, was jarringly different from any ship Joss had heard of. Not just cosmetically different, but conceptually, philosophically so. She saw thrusting bulks that looked more organic, or perhaps geological, than anything shaped by intelligence – huge splinters of rock fused together by a flow of lava; yet clearly they weren't, and somehow these bizarre formations combined to form the hull of a ship, or perhaps multiple hulls congealed into one. Broken, with what she took to be the front section shattered against the moon's surface while the aft pointed skyward like a handful of clutching fingers, or the frozen tendrils of some grounded cephalopod reaching for the stars. The structure was impressive, if shockingly different.

One thing was certain: nothing human had built this ship.

"Captain Brennan," a voice said smoothly. No surprise that their comms had been compromised, though the quality and speed of the newcomers' intelligence was a little unnerving. No one ever called her 'Captain Brennan' over the comms. The foremost of the three figures raised an arm, presumably to identify himself as the speaker. "My name is Hawkins. One of my men is going to board your ship and bring her into the dome. I presume we all realise the futility of resistance?"

No argument there, and they were all still alive, which she took as a good sign. "Crane, do as he says."

"No kidding," the familiar voice came back. "You really think I *wasn't* going to?"

She ignored him. Who were these people? ULAW, had to be; some secret government installation set up to glean all they could from the derelict alien ship. How long had they been here? What the hell had she got herself and her crew into?

The men on the ridge were still there, but at least the guns weren't pointing in their direction any more. She started forward again. "Come on, Wicksy, no point in standing around out here until our air runs out."

The closer they came to the dome and the unlikely structure it housed, the more awed Joss felt. There was something beautiful about the strange ship, for all that it wasn't whole. Trelliswork, looking like rusted filigree from this distance, jutted from the hull at irregular intervals, though whether this was part of the original design or some form of scaffolding erected since the craft's demise, Joss wasn't sure, although she suspected the latter.

They'd reached the dome's perimeter, where Hawkins and his two goons waited, and her attention switched reluctantly from the derelict. She refused to kowtow by acting either guilty or apologetic, but instead marched straight up to the man.

"Thank you for co-operating," he said as she stopped before him. As if he'd left her with any choice.

"So, what happens to me and my crew now?"

"That rather depends. Let's go inside."

She and Wicks followed as he walked the short distance back into the dome, the two guards bringing up the rear. If anyone there *wasn't* thinking about the alien craft, then it was someone other than her.

"What... what is that thing?"

Joss would have happily kicked Wicks all around the perimeter and back for that. She'd been determined not to ask; didn't want to give this Hawkins the satisfaction.

"Ah, yes... the reason we're here, obviously." He stopped walking. They all did. "Spectacular, isn't she?"

She. Why were ships always 'she'? Joss would have been hard pressed to think of anything more phallicly masculine than the thrusting hull components of the derelict, yet still it was referred to as a 'she.'

"This single ship has yielded more insights and revelations than... well, more of that later." Which struck her as a good sign – the fact that there was going to *be* a 'later.'

They resumed walking, Joss deep in thought. She realised they'd stumbled on a secret. She wasn't entirely sure *whose* secret, but it didn't take a genius to realise that this was a big one. A universal truth about secrets in general and big ones in particular was that people tended to want to keep them. If she followed the logic too much further it was going to lead to some very depressing conclusions. Her only comfort, the thing she clung to, was the fact that none of them were dead yet.

"You were unlucky," Hawkins explained. "Normally this place is so tightly shielded you could have passed directly overhead without the faintest notion we were here. But we suffered a systems glitch just as you were approaching. As I say, bad luck."

"Funnily enough, that's exactly what I've been thinking of renaming the ship of late."

Hawkins didn't comment.

They entered an airlock built into the dome's inner skin. Big enough to take the five of them and more without crowding, she noted. Presumably built that way to accommodate work crews and equipment.

On the far side, Joss got to see Hawkins's face clearly for the first time as he removed his helmet. Older than her, but not by much; ten years at the most. Although several shades darker, his hair was as close-cropped as hers – a habit common among those who frequently wore space suits – and he wasn't unhandsome in a clean-cut sort of way, but incredibly pale-skinned, as if sunlight was something he'd vaguely heard about but never experienced.

One thing she'd grown increasingly convinced of. "You're not ULAW, are you?"

He chuckled, "No, we're definitely not ULAW. We're the habitat."

The *habitat*? Who the hell were they when they were at home?

He was still smiling. "Welcome to Far Flung, Captain Brennan."

CHAPTER TWO

MANNY OUSAKA HAD a nose for trouble, a keen sense which he'd developed as a survival mechanism over many years of dealing with the unsavoury and the downright vicious. He clocked the woman as soon as she came in. Tall, slim, but looking as if she worked out, with a narrow waist and an insignificant chest but well defined arms and legs, a body that looked equally capable of delivering pleasure or pain. As for the face, it was slightly too angular to be called pretty, boasting high cheek bones and pleasant enough features, but with eyes a little too close together and a slightly darker brown than her fashionably close-cropped hair. *Handsome* was the word that sprung to mind. Manny was not in the least surprised when the screen built into his side of the counter – out of the customers' line of sight – flashed up a negative, indicating that the state of the art facial recognition programme he'd installed at great expense had drawn a blank. This didn't strike him as the sort of woman whose face appeared on any database. While studiously rearranging the bric-a-brac on the counter before him, he watched her from the corner of his eye as she sauntered around the shop, picking up a piece of ethnic pottery here and a colourful knickknack there, with interest so feigned that it was almost insulting in its shallowness. What was she waiting for? The shop to be empty, he guessed.

There were only two other customers at that time: a Mr and Mrs Loudon Kerchenko from Sigma III. Their profiles were nowhere near as elusive as the woman's. Mr Kerchenko had grown prosperous as part-owner of a mining concern, before going on to become extremely wealthy via some shrewd dealings in tangential futures. Slightly overweight and well past the first flush of youth, there was still a keen intelligence behind his eyes and an aura of success and power about the man which explained why women found him attractive. He was currently rumoured to be having affairs with both his wife's sister and, a more recent development, the sister's daughter. For her part, Mrs Kerchenko had been a minor celebrity in her youth, a star turn in a long-running holo-drama. She remained glamorous despite having put on a few extra pounds, and liked to think of herself as an altruist. She was a vocal supporter of the underprivileged and in recent years had become patron to several humanitarian charities. Perfect, just the sort of individual Manny loved to welcome to his little emporium.

He didn't want to leave the counter untended, not with Ms Anonymous prowling the aisles, so he signalled for one of the twins to take over. The girl dutifully shuffled out from the backroom, disturbing the fly curtain in the process so that its beads clicked together like the chirping of irritated insects. He had no idea which one this was – never had bothered learning to tell them apart. Lanky, languid, painfully thin, with an androgynous figure and a face that might have qualified as pretty had it been more animated, she had sandy blonde hair which fell long and straight past the shoulders, with enough split ends to have any hairdresser twitching and reaching for the cutters and conditioner.

The twin sisters provided perfect accompaniment to the downbeat ambience of the charity store. So emaciated were their frames that they could easily have appeared in one of the displays occupying half the front window, featuring a revolving parade of images to pull at even the tautest of heartstrings. Orphaned children, tattered clothes that hung from wasted limbs, arid landscape and poverty, skeletal ribcages, tears and forlorn expressions, all tailored to persuade the observer how essential it was that they should give freely of their own abundance to help these less-privileged souls.

There was nothing in the twins' appearance to hint at their augmented nature; nothing to suggest the speed with which they could move or the lethal strength they could bring to bear in a single punch should the need arise. No, the upgrades were all hidden beneath very ordinary seeming, if somewhat listless, skin – the alloy-sheathed bones and powered joints that made his girls so deceptively deadly. They'd have one hell of a time passing spaceport security checks should they ever choose to travel off world, but that was hardly Manny's problem.

Satisfied that the counter and its sophisticated equipment were well guarded, he moved across to where Mr and Mrs Kerchenko were currently pawing at a woollen garment mass-produced in the sweat shops of Kaitu City. Manny considered the item – a hooded top with wooden peg-buttons stitched on – to be one of the ugliest things he had ever seen, but its bold designs had exactly the right ethnic feel: stylised crosses, walking birds and bow-legged stick-figure men, all depicted in chocolate brown against a pale tan background.

"Beautiful, isn't it?" he said as he joined the couple. "Hand knitted by the children of Saratoga from wool gathered off the backs of their own sheep. These clothes are the only source of income for the entire region since the ilenium mine collapse which killed so many of their menfolk."

"How awful," Mrs Kerchenko said on cue.

"A great tragedy," Manny agreed, making it up as he went along and enjoying himself immensely. "If our sourcing agents hadn't found them and established routes and systems through which they can export and sell these exquisite handmade clothes, I shudder to think what would have become of them by now."

"How many of these do you have?" Mrs Kerchenko asked, batting her long, spidery eyelashes.

"Only what you see here," he replied, indicating the stack of half a dozen neatly folded and identical garments from which she'd taken the top one. "There's a limit to how many the children can actually produce."

"Of course, I understand. We'll take the lot, won't we, Lou?"

"Hmm? Sure. Whatever you say, my love."

Impulsively, she reached out to grip Manny's hand. "I want to thank you for all you're doing to help these poor children."

Was it his imagination or did her hand linger a fraction longer than it needed to? No, not his imagination; he felt her well-manicured thumbnail very deliberately caress his palm as she let go. A little startled, he glanced up and caught her fleeting smile. It was enough to make him wonder exactly how much she knew or suspected about her husband's playing around, and what she did to compensate. Manny had no illusion about being god's gift to women, but he knew that his dark features and twinkling eyes leant him a certain rakish charm. Trouble wasn't the only thing he had a nose for – albeit a slightly crooked one, the result of a long-ago fist fight which he'd failed to correct in his youth, misguidedly retaining the defect as if it were some badge of honour. He sensed that this glamorous if slightly plastic-looking woman, with her arm draped so casually through that of her husband's, was his for the taking.

"I just wish there was more we could do to help," she said.

"Well, if you'll trust me with your wric details, I could always put you in touch with our agent who handles the Saratoga account, see if there's anything that could be sorted out."

"Really?" she gushed. "Oh, that would be so wonderful."

Wonderful indeed, if he could screw her both physically and financially. "How much longer are you going to be in town for?"

"Another week or so. That's right, isn't it, Lou?"

"Yeah, something like that."

"My husband has a little business to attend to while we're here."

Leaving her alone for long periods, no doubt. An invitation

if ever he'd heard one. Manny realised he hadn't even bothered checking her first name. A fine looking woman, no question. Her forehead might be as immobile as her elegantly curled golden hair, but he bet those full, plump lips could suck life back into the dead.

Moments later the couple breezed out of the shop, secure in the knowledge that the precious garments would be delivered to their hotel later that day, while Manny's credit account had swollen a fraction and his WRist Information Centre pulsed with a little green envelope signifying the arrival of Mrs Loudon Kerchenko's contact details, squirted across from her own wric. Maybe now he'd get to learn her first name.

All in all, a highly satisfactory interlude, which held the promise of even greater satisfaction to come.

The rattle of something crockery-based being placed carelessly back onto a shelf reminded him that the shop still had one other customer.

He glanced across at her, to find a hint of amusement in the eyes that looked back. Abandoning all pretence of examining the merchandise, the woman started towards him. The way she advanced brought to mind a predator stalking its prey, and Manny was glad to have Sia or Maisie – whichever one of the twins this was – just a few steps away. Sia, he belatedly realised. She was the one who'd come in that morning with a white-headed zit ready to erupt from the centre of her forehead. The spot was now gone, but a livid red mark bore witness to its recent passing.

The security scans hadn't shown any obvious weapons on the woman, but there was a blank patch where her belt bag sat against her hip that had him worried – something the scans couldn't penetrate.

"Manny Ousaka?" she asked.

"Who wants to know?"

The smile didn't fool him for a second. It never reached her eyes. "The name's Boulton."

"All right, Boulton, I'm guessing you're not really interested in helping our society's forgotten poor by buying any of my stock, so what exactly *do* you want?"

"Information."

"Ah." That word was music to Manny's ears. Perhaps he'd misjudged this ice-cold woman and the day was going to keep getting better after all. Information, was it? Manny's life-blood, what he lived and breathed. The shop was more than just a front, more a hobby he indulged himself. It brought in a few bucks and let him keep his hand in at dealing with the great unwashed. His *real* business was that of listening, finding, enabling, procuring – all for a price, of course. Manny was a fixer, a facilitator, the man with one ear to the ground and the other to the gods. You wanted to know what was going down before it actually went down, you came to Manny. You wanted a particular piece of kit for a particular job which the law said you couldn't have, Manny was your man. If you had a hankering for the latest synthetic narcotic or contraband tech, Manny was your first, your *only* port of call. 'As long as you can pay, I'll find a way,' was his proud motto.

He stood straight, feeling taller and more important in the process. "Information, you say... about what, exactly?"

"An old friend of yours, a mutual acquaintance; one Jim Leyton."

The smile died. He could taste its bitter corpse on his lips. "Leyton? Sorry, never heard of the man." As lies went, this was a poor one. It didn't even convince him.

The woman sighed. "Manny, Manny, I'm disappointed." She wrinkled her nose and shook her head. "You don't want to play that sort of game with me, I promise you."

Manny flicked a quick glance towards the nearby twin, reassured by her presence. This Boulton might think she had the upper hand, but he still had a pair of aces up his sleeve.

"Look, lady..."

"Let's cut the bullshit." The woman actually had the audacity to get bolshie with him, here, in his own place. "You're Leyton's principle contact in this sector, someone he meets with regularly."

'Meet' wasn't exactly the word Manny would have used. The man dropped in from time to time – in the same way that a bomb might drop through the ceiling. An alarm flashed red on Manny's screen. It meant that somebody was mounting a concerted effort to hack his systems. "What the…?" He glared at the woman. "Are you doing this? Get the hell out of my systems!"

Sia started forward, but in the blink of an eye Boulton whipped out a gun – damned hidden compartment. Manny knew that gun. Either this was the same weapon Leyton habitually carried, or his bodyguard wasn't the only twin in the room. Shit! Don't tell him this Boulton was some kind of female equivalent of that bastard Leyton.

Before he could react, before he could think to say anything, there came a muffled *whumpf*. The gun was clearly silenced. The bullet punched into Sia's forehead, right where the zit had been, and exploded from the back of her skull in a shower of shattered bone, blood and gore which smacked against the wall behind her.

The twin's body had not even had a chance to fully crumple to the floor before the gun swivelled towards Manny, centring between his eyes.

"Unless you want your other dolly guard to be the *third* person I kill here today, I suggest you tell her to come out now with her hands raised and empty."

"You heard the woman," Manny called. "Get your ass out here."

The second twin, Maisie, emerged; hands held level with her ears as instructed but eyes burning with defiance. Boulton must have spotted the latter too and decided she didn't need the potential complication, because, after a brief frown as if she were weighing up the options, she brought the gun smartly around and shot the second girl as cleanly and finally as she had the first. Two bloody splatters now decorated the wall.

So much for augmentation.

Manny swallowed on a sand-dry throat as the gun returned to cover him. He made certain to stand very, very still.

"That's better. Just you and me now." Her smile sent a chill sliding down the length of his spine. "You were about to tell me everything you know about Jim Leyton."

"Yeah, sure, anything you say."

"Oh, and while we're having our little chat, you won't mind opening up your systems, will you? Just to confirm there's nothing you've... forgotten."

"Ehm, sure, of course not."

"Good, only that's an impressive security system you've got there, and while I'm sure we could hack it eventually, everything will be so much quicker if you invite us in."

Manny hurried to comply.

"Perfect. Now, for openers, when was the last time you saw our dear friend Leyton?"

Manny took a deep breath. He had a feeling that Boulton wasn't going to like the answer, that he hadn't seen Leyton in a while – never mind that it was the truth; this was one woman that he really *really* didn't want to disappoint.

SHE WOKE WITH a bitter taste at the back of the throat and mucous clogging her mouth. She tried to swallow but was interrupted as somebody grabbed hold of her and attempted to pull her upright. Her eyes shot open and harsh facts tumbled into place: guards, prison, Sheol Station.

"Get up!" Wisely, the man had stood back.

Prisoner 516 did as instructed.

"Arms!" She dutifully brought both behind her back to be cuffed. It was then a case of shuffling out of her cell and trudging between the two guards – one in front and one behind.

Neither of them touched her, not now she was awake. They'd learnt that lesson. Besides, the cuffs now securing her wrists were capable of delivering a surge of pain enough to ensure obedience. The guards remained wary though, she could sense it. Small satisfaction perhaps, but that was all they'd left her.

The catcalls and wolf whistles that trailed her passage were irrelevances she barely noticed anymore, as were the shouted promises of what her fellow inmates would do to her given half a chance, and how they'd have her moaning for more. Given that chance, she'd break every bone in their bodies, leaving them even limper than their dicks, but such defiance echoed only in her head these days; she could no longer spare the energy to vocalise it. She knew that elsewhere on the station there were political prisoners, subversives, cybercrime kingpins, industrial fraudsters, and assorted intellectual giants whose genius refused to conform and who, therefore, were too dangerous to remain at large. Not here, not on this landing. She shared this level with the thugs and the psychopaths, the perverted bullies and the sadistic murderers, those whose crimes might embarrass the government and so would never be allowed to come to trial. She was the only woman on the entire corridor.

They had put her here to intimidate her. It didn't.

Her current destination, on the other hand, did. She knew precisely where they were taking her: to the clinic. Such a deceptively innocent-sounding name for such an evil place. It was a bland oblong box, as were all rooms in this facility, which had once been a starship – a vessel which official records cited as decommissioned and broken down for scrap more than a decade ago. The clinic was the modern, civilised face of an institution that reached back into man's darker, cruder past: the torture chamber. The functional angles of the room's walls and ceilings and the clinical brightness of its surfaces presented a misleading veneer. Strip them away and beneath you would find ancient brick walls damp with subterranean moisture and oil-drenched torches that guttered in wall brackets, while the black upholstered chair which formed the room's centrepiece hid within its depths a set of iron wall manacles and the wooden frame of a rack. The attempt at innocence didn't fool her for a second.

The bald-pated round-shouldered Dr Etherington, whose name slipped so readily into 'Deathrington,' looked down his prominent Roman nose as she entered. "Ah, 516. How nice to see you again."

She trusted that her answering glower was eloquence enough. The orderly who hovered behind the good doctor was an inconsequence, but Deathrington she would deal with, somehow, some day.

One guard took station by the door, the other behind the chair. Both had drawn their shockclubs. This was the moment they would expect her to try something, when the manacles came off – she had done so before, but not this time. She wouldn't give them the satisfaction. So the prisoner stood docilely as the cuffs sprang open, flexing her wrists for the all too brief seconds of freedom before a smiling Deathrington motioned her to sit down. She did as instructed, silently vowing that her next attempt at escape would be when they *didn't* expect it, and that she would succeed.

Steel bands closed around her ankles and wrists, holding her firm, and she braced herself for what was to come. Method, that was the only difference between this place and its ancient counterparts. Torture had evolved, although the intentions were certainly the same – to break a person's will and loosen the tongue, to unlock their most guarded secrets. Nor had the chief tool – pain – changed, though the way it was administered certainly had.

What need did the torturer have for flails and forks and thumbscrews when his victim could be primed with a drug that made receptors so sensitive that the movement of air against the skin induced a sharp intake of breath, an involuntary wince of pain? Prisoner 516 felt a telltale tingle at her wrist as the micro-spray permeated her skin.

What need of heated irons or dripping water when the body's nerves could be isolated and stimulated at will and impulses targeted at specific areas of the brain?

No, a medieval torturer might see nothing familiar in the clinic at first glance, but only because he lacked the understanding to interpret the modern world. Once all was explained to him, he'd doubtless feel right at home.

A further tingling, this time in her other wrist, told the prisoner that the second drug had been administered, the one designed to break down resistance. She knew the drill, had been trained to hold out against such things, but training only carried you so far and reserves of strength had their limits. She felt herself relax and tried desperately to cling onto her resolve, even as it slipped inexorably away. After a moment, Deathrington came forward to peer into her eyes. She stared back, trying to focus on one of his brown, flecked orbs and its black-hole centre, imagining herself plunging something sharp into that eye and twisting, rummaging around in the soft tissue beneath.

Evidently satisfied with whatever he saw, Deathrington grunted and stepped back. The rest of the room had lost focus. All she saw was the distorted oval of his face.

"I think we're ready. Do you feel ready, 516?"

No! she screamed in her head, but, "M – yes," her treacherous mouth mumbled.

"Good. Now, I want you to tell me something; I want you to tell me all you can about a man you know well, a man called Jim Leyton."

Leyton? That was new. Why did they suddenly want to know about Leyton?

"We'll start with how you met him, shall we?"

Somewhere deep inside, a lingering shadow of the person she'd once been quailed, but it was only a tiny scrap of character, easy to ignore. Prisoner 516 began to speak and knew that once she started there would be no holding back. She prepared to lay bare her soul.

CHAPTER THREE

A FIGURE STOOD in the shadows, biding his time, waiting for the moment to kill. Sheol Station. Hell in space. The last place Jim Leyton had ever expected to find himself.

When he and several other eyegees had been assigned to hunt down the crew of *The Noise Within*, Leyton questioned the wisdom of devoting so many key resources to deal with a mere pirate, little realising there was nothing 'mere' about this particular vessel. Clearly somebody in authority *had* realised, and while, admittedly, superiors were supposed to be privy to information you weren't, in this particular instance the implications were profoundly disturbing. *The Noise Within* had quite literally changed the world, *all* human worlds. How could anyone have known that was going to happen?

Conspiracy theories had been around forever. Leyton had even helped to fan the flames of one or two in his time – misdirection, smoke and mirrors. Most were preposterous nonsense perpetrated by crazies with a skewed sense of reality but, even granting that, some still held at least a kernel of truth, as he well knew. The perpetrators of such things were currently having a field day, convinced that the 'first contact' represented by *The Noise Within* was anything *but* the first. Leyton had seen smear campaigns, cover-ups and hoaxes, knew how ULAW en-masse and officials individually reacted to given situations, and the longer he watched what was going on right now, the firmer his conviction became that this time the crazies might just be on to something.

All of which went a long way to explaining why he was here now, breaking into a facility operated by the United League of Allied Worlds, who, until recently, he had served faithfully and unreservedly. Yes, *The Noise Within* had changed worlds all right; his more than most.

Such musings weren't like him, not once a mission was underway; another indicator that something was wrong with his mindset. Not that he needed the benefit of any clues – he knew exactly what was wrong.

They'd taken away his gun.

Leyton felt naked. He could understand the logic, even if he didn't entirely accept it. The explanation that the gun's AI was slavishly loyal to his former masters and would inevitably betray him to ULAW sounded all too plausible. Then again, a really good lie generally did. He might have argued more forcefully were it not for the way the gun had deceived him aboard *The Noise Within*. That incident had shaken him all the way down to the soles of his boots, and ultimately was the reason he'd relinquished the weapon with such minimal fuss. But understanding that did nothing to assuage his sense of... loneliness? He could think of no better word.

Nor was he oblivious to the fact that depriving him of the gun made him that little bit less formidable and all the more reliant on these newfound allies, these people who called themselves 'the habitat.'

Kethi was the key. The beautiful, enigmatic girl had been the bait that lured him here with her casual reference to Mya, the woman he'd never really stopped loving. Could he trust her? The jury was still out on that one, but the longer he remained in this company the more limited his options became.

So the gun stayed behind, its AI brain deactivated, essentially useless until someone figured out a convenient way of switching between the weapon's various functions without AI supervision.

This shouldn't have been a problem. After all, as he kept

reminding himself, most of his career had been spent without the gun; just not recently.

Old habits die hard. Leyton trusted that the same held true for old skills. He'd killed with his bare hands often enough of late but this was different: no gun to back him up this time, no voice whispering in his ear and relaying information about concealed defences or how far away any other guards might be. He was on his own.

Nor had the significance of the moment escaped him. Currently ULAW would have him listed as absent; suspiciously so, granted, after he disappeared from New Paris without a word. Doubtless there would have been a fair bit of fuss at the time – eyegees, those elite agents trusted with Intelligent Guns, were few and far between – but he'd always been confident that he could go back if he chose to, could explain his actions and be welcomed into the ULAW fold once more. Not after this. He was about to cross a line. Killing a ULAW officer, no matter how minor their status, would change everything. What he was about to do represented a firm commitment to a cause he had yet to be convinced by. It would mark him as a rebel through and through.

Too late for misgivings. The target was an arm's length away.

Everyone who is ever likely to be called upon to kill – be it soldier, assassin, terrorist or ship's gunnery officer – should be made to do so with their bare hands at least once. Such intimacy is the only way to truly experience the act, to appreciate that when they pressed that button, pulled that trigger, detonated their bomb or released their pathogen, they were putting an end to something precious.

Leyton reached forward, clamped his right hand firmly around the guard's jaw – covering the mouth – while his left arm wrapped around the man's torso, pinning both arms to his side. He gave the guard no opportunity to react, no time for defensive reflexes to kick in, but immediately pulled the hapless victim back against his own chest, while at the same time pulling forcefully with his right hand. He heard the snap of bones and felt the neck break, felt the life slip away.

Few things were more final than snuffing out a life and removing an individual from the tapestry of the universe. It was an act that merited respect. Not that Leyton saw himself as a killer with a conscience or any such sentimental twaddle. He never questioned his own actions, never doubted they were necessary, but nor did he underestimate their impact.

He eased the lifeless body to the floor. There was nowhere to conceal it and, in any case, no need to do so if their timing was right. They should be done and gone long before anyone ventured down this particular corridor again. Eight shimmer-suited figures ran past, his own suit's visor enabling him to see them.

He stood up and followed, focussing on one person in particular. To his practiced eye, Kethi's tall, lithe form and her effortless gait were unmistakeable, even in the all-encompassing suit.

Almost at once he was acutely aware of a void where there ought to have been a reasoned voice calmly providing information about enemy deployment and potential threats.

Leyton had always prided himself on being a loner, particularly once he was chosen to be an eyegee. Members of the elite unit were a caste apart within the military hierarchy. Not for them the discipline of fighting in formation or partaking in massed troop movements, nor the *esprit de corps* of a platoon. The eyegees were the cutting edge of ULAW authority, sent to those hotspots where a problem might be solved more readily with a swift clinical incision than with the bludgeoning of a military sledge hammer.

He was coming to realise, however, that he'd been kidding himself. He'd never been a loner at all, but had still been part of a team: him and the gun. The weapon's silence was now a constant absence. An acute lack that gnawed at his concentration and left him straining to hear, *wanting* to hear its reassuring presence, even though he knew the voice was gone forever.

They ran through dimly-lit passageways of dull grey functionality, defined by pipes and turbines and humming machinery. Members of their small party split off in ones and twos, peeling away to left and right at intersecting corridors, each with an allotted task to perform, until only he and Kethi remained.

Their point of entry had been carefully calculated, allowing them to spread quickly through the bowels of the station like an infestation of vermin, with a minimum of human contact. So far, so good – just the one guard, not even an engineer or maintenance man to deal with. That couldn't last, though. There had to come a point where they were forced to step out into the densely populated areas of the station proper, and, as far as he and Kethi were concerned, that point had just been reached.

They stopped before an oval metal slab standing slightly proud of the wall; a bulkhead door, the demarcation between habitation and the network of supporting machinery. Without hesitating, Kethi slapped a gelatinous patch against the door seal. Nothing to do now but wait. Neither spoke. Words would have been redundant, reassurance and banter an unnecessary distraction.

Beyond that door lay the beginning of Sheol Station itself – one of ULAW's darkest secrets, a place that appeared on no official record and was claimed to exist only in whispered rumour and unsubstantiated tales of torture and terror.

Minutes dragged and Kethi began to fidget, as if worried that something might have gone wrong. Leyton stayed still, having learned the value of patience long ago. Then he felt it: the sudden absence of a subtle vibration, accompanied by a sudden sense of lightness. The station's gravity field had gone. They both stood firm, anchored to the floor by their smartboots, which clung resolutely to any surface until the foot lifted in just the right way. As soon as the weight of gravity left them, Kethi pressed her thumb into the centre of the gelatinous device. For a couple of agonised seconds nothing happened at all, but then the door sprang ponderously open with a hiss, and they were able to step out into the ominously dark corridors of ULAW's least talked about prison ship.

SOMETHING WAS WRONG. The first clue came when the lights dimmed. Time was a difficult thing to keep track of in here, but prisoner 516 knew enough to realise that the next night cycle was a long way off yet, and the lights only ever dipped in the final few minutes before total darkness descended.

The dimming became a flickering, which heralded the lights failing entirely – everything went out, even the pale 'nightlights' that provided the grey-green glow at either end of the corridor during night cycles. The reaction was as immediate and forceful as it was predictable. Angry voices rose from the stygian blackness all around in query and outrage. Chains were rattled and walls and bars beaten, punctuating the roars of consternation and the mock-screams and hoots of derision. During the brief period of darkness the crescendo of noise reached a peak which threatened to be self-sustaining, especially when the lights only came back on after a fashion – the twilight radiance of a back-up system kicking in. Thankfully, after a while, being able to see again seemed to mollify the inmates and the noise started to subside, but the respite was to be short-lived.

The gravity failed.

She fought to focus, battling against the residue of drugs that still lingered in her system. She had been trained and conditioned to resist such methods, but the authorities knew that. After all, they'd been the ones who trained her. They also knew that her mind would collapse entirely before it yielded anything to the more invasive mental probing of AIs, so they persisted with the drugs and the nerve stimulation, wearing her down by degrees. They could afford to be patient. She wasn't going anywhere.

But this might just be her chance, so she did her best to rally her fractured thoughts and her abused body, anchoring the latter to the bed by hooking her feet beneath its frame. Secure for the moment, she strained to hear beyond the surrounding cacophony, to seek clues as to what was going on.

The dim light began to pulse rhythmically; among the shouting and the yelling, she detected the blaring of an alarm. She felt, rather than heard, a faint vibration which seemed to course through everything and then cease. That had to have been an explosion. Whatever was happening here, it was more than simple equipment malfunction. A breakout, she guessed, or perhaps a raid to free a particular prisoner. Whatever the specifics, it provided a potential opening, an opportunity she intended to seize. With the station's systems disrupted, the physical confines of her cell looked to be the greatest and most immediate obstacle. No chance of escape if she couldn't even get out of the cubicle.

She pushed off from the bed and floated across to the front of the cell. As suspected, the energy fields that normally hemmed each prisoner in were gone, but the solid metal bars remained. Nor had the loss of power shorted out the door locks; that would have been too much to hope for, but it never hurt to test the obvious. A wave of nausea swept through her, causing her to cling to the metal bars and breathe deeply as it passed. *Concentrate!* There had to be a way she could exploit what was happening here.

A pair of guards clanked along the corridor, their movements awkward in the unfamiliar lack of gravity. Magnetised boots anchored them to the 'ground' and provided a sense of normal perspective. The boots were cumbersome, intended for emergency use only, and lent the proceedings a surreally comic edge – the two guards having to exaggerate every move and gesture. They wore white and blue armour – not the full protection of a military battlesuit but the lightweight half-armour designed for riots and civil disturbances. The combination of costume and inhibited movement gave them a mechanical, robotic semblance.

Some bright sparks in neighbouring cells tried to spit at them, producing stringy globules of viscous fluid that floated out into the corridor, invariably missing their moving targets. One lucky shot splattered against the shoulder of the second guard, attaching itself and trailing in his wake like some nebulous tattered banner.

Other than that, the globules of saliva presented more of a threat to fellow inmates on the opposite side of the corridor than they did to the guards. A spitting war started, as indignant prisoners retaliated at their neighbours opposite.

She ignored all of this and doggedly clung on to her fractured thoughts, holding things together by sheer force of will. She was determined to be ready for whatever came next, anxious not to miss a fleeting opportunity because her mind or body was too flaky to respond.

Another explosion, unmistakable this time and sounding a good deal closer. It even caused a brief lull in the spitting and shouting and the rattling of plastic cups on bars. The noise returned with added impetus, perhaps fuelled by an edge of panic, but at least the spitting seemed to have been forgotten for now.

She examined the cell door, knowing that with the right equipment she could have it open in seconds.

How? What needed to be done? She might not have the necessary tools but if she could remember the process, perhaps she could improvise? *Improvise?* With what, for God's sake? This was a prison, a cramped cell – a featureless box.

Panic welled up; she was in danger of losing it, could feel her precious grip on sanity slipping away. She *had* to stay focused, *had* to be ready to seize that one chance if and when it presented itself.

"Go on, you can do it." Louis's voice. She turned to find him smiling at her. They sat on a hillside covered in grass and wild flowers, the sun beating down. They were both little more than kids. "You can do anything," he told her.

Something floated past, banishing the vision. Vomit. Somebody had thrown up in the zero g. She watched, mesmerised, as strands of semi-digested food and bile drifted past, none of it coming too close, thank heavens.

Another guard came clanking along the corridor, this one with shockclub drawn. The deceptively elegant baton of polished white ceramic could deliver a jolt of electricity, via its metal tip, graduated from mild to near-lethal, sufficient to incapacitate even the most formidable of drug-crazed prisoners.

She watched his approach with a predatory intensity, willing him to stray just a little bit too close, but he didn't. He stuck rigidly to the very centre of the corridor, out of reach of any arms that might stretch towards him from either side. He was almost past her cell when the third explosion came. The whole world lurched. Caught in mid-step, the guard tottered and stumbled, but not towards her. Instead he staggered in the opposite direction, nearer the opposing row of cells. She watched in despair as a pair of strong, hairy arms reached through the bars and grappled with the hapless guard. *No!* Did she shout that out loud or only in her thoughts?

Even as cruel fate seemed determined to rob her of the very opportunity she'd been waiting for, hope was resurrected. In his desperate, futile attempts to free himself, the guard let go of his shockclub. It floated away from the struggle, spinning languidly as it drifted across the corridor towards her. No, not quite towards her. As the spinning stick drew nearer she realised, with sinking heart, that it was actually heading for the cell beside hers. Salvation was going to evade her again.

She pulled herself frantically along, squeezing into the corner, cheek pressed against the bars, and thrust an arm out towards the white baton. Her shoulder burned as she stretched desperately and she was shocked to find herself sobbing from the effort and the frustration. Her fingers brushed against something and she closed them quickly, too quickly. They grasped only empty air. That touch, however, was enough to deflect the shockclub, to divert it in her direction.

"Hey, you bitch, what d'ya think you're doing?" snarled a voice from the neighbouring cell. "That stick was mine!"

A hand shot out, narrowly missing hers and, in the process, losing whatever chance it might have had of grasping the shockclub.

Reaching out to grab the smooth white baton was now simplicity itself. She drew the weapon into her cell and clasped it firmly to her chest, trembling with relief, cuddling it like some newborn babe. Next door the thwarted oaf was still ranting and screaming, shaking the bars of his cell, but the sound washed over her unheeded.

She was getting out.

The shockclub might have been unfamiliar, at least the end with the controls, but it was hardly the most complex weapon in the world. She thumbed the charge to maximum and pressed the metal plate of its business end to the cell's lock mechanism, dreading that nothing would happen and the door would remain firmly locked. Her hands were trembling and she felt her concentration drifting away. She squeezed her eyes shut, gritting her teeth and dragging her thoughts back where they belonged. Nothing mattered more than getting out of here. This *had* to work.

No point in delaying. She squeezed the trigger, sending a surge of power coursing through the lock. The club didn't tremble or warm up in her grasp, there were no sparks, no dramatic indication that anything at all had happened, except for the fact that her cell door swung slowly outward.

Still clutching the shockclub, prisoner 516 pulled herself out of the cell – the first time she'd ever passed through that door unsupervised. This wasn't yet freedom, but it was a huge step in the right direction and it felt *good*.

There was a knack to moving in zero g, one she'd been required to master a long time ago, though it wasn't a skill she'd needed to call on in a while. For long seconds prisoner 516 simply clung to the bars of her cell, anchoring herself while she marshalled her dwindling energy and shattered nerves. The jeers and screams of her fellow prisoners rose to new heights as they saw her escape into the corridor, and fresh gobbets of spit sailed towards her, but these were all easily ignored. At least nobody had thought to try and piss at her as yet, or worse.

She was going to have to traverse the length of the corridor while staying as far away as possible from the cells on either side and the clutching hands of the inmates, but push off from her current position and, whatever her trajectory, she would eventually end up against the opposite row of cells. That was by no means the only obstacle lying between her and ultimate freedom, but it was the most immediate. One at a time, that was all she could aspire to – cope with each new challenge as it arose.

She never once considered trying to free anyone else. Most of them deserved to be where they were, in this forgotten corner of human space – a former colony ship whose engines were disabled when they turned her into a prison satellite, the small cubicle-like rooms easily converted into cells. This was where the government sent their worst offenders, the dangerous ones. Her, for example.

The floor was unremittingly smooth. Nothing there she could grasp hold of and use. The ceiling, though, boasted a series of light fittings; shallow, elongated blisters, out of anyone's reach in normal circumstances, but not in zero g.

She'd need both hands for this, so hung the shockclub around one wrist via its strap loop and then pushed off from the bars, angling towards one of the light fittings. Not too hard – she didn't want to overshoot. The nearer she came, the more her concerns grew. The lights were pretty well sunk into the ceiling, leaving little to grasp, but she was committed now. Catcalls and whistles accompanied her move; a reminder of exactly what kind of a reception she could expect if she messed this up.

Her fingers reached for the nearest fitting, immediately slipping off its smooth curved surface. She fought to stay calm and tried again, cracked and broken fingernails scratching for purchase at the edges, where the light met the ceiling. All the while her body continued to drift towards an inevitable, if soft, collision with the ceiling which would bounce her ever so gently towards the nearest waiting thug. She had to twist around, the light fitting no longer in front but slightly behind her legs and body. Then she had it, the fingers of one hand fastening tenuously to a solid ridge at the fitting's rim, those of her other hand joining them a second later. It wasn't much, but proved enough to absorb her momentum, enabling her to stop herself. For precious seconds she rested there, crouching on the ceiling at the corridor's very centre, focusing her mind, zeroing in on the door at the far end, which represented the next step towards freedom.

"You can do anything," Louis whispered.

She pushed off, using her finger tips as the fulcrum. Progress was frustratingly slow, a mere drift in the right direction, but she daren't try for more momentum by pushing off with her feet; that would only send her legs away from the ceiling and her head towards it; a spin that could easily become uncontrollable and lead to disaster. Even so, there *had* to be a way of speeding things up. More guards could appear at any time, and with every passing second her chances of escape narrowed.

Time seemed to stretch and drag at her with the cloying grip of softened toffee, and her frustration built rapidly towards panic. This was hopeless. She was going to have to risk kicking off to achieve a more practical speed, but had missed any chance of doing so immediately. Drift had taken her steadily away from the ceiling and she was now out of reach of any surface.

She passed unheeding through globules of spittle and other less identifiable things, her concentration centred on the steadily approaching floor and her chance to gain some momentum. Mess this up and all her efforts would have been for nothing.

With the floor agonisingly close, her worst nightmare was realised. The door she had been focussing on slid open.

She strained to see, twisting around for a better look, expecting to hear the heavy tread of magnetised boots at any second, followed by rough hands dragging her back to her cell. Yet, despite the doorway gaping wide for several seconds before it closed again, the entrance remained empty. Nobody had come in. Then she caught a slight distortion; nothing much, just a quick stretching of details in the corner of her eye, readily dismissed as an after-effect of the drugs still flowing though her veins, but she knew better. She recognised that effect. Shimmer suit. Somebody had entered after all, but why would anyone be wearing eye foxing shimmer suits here? In order to rescue somebody. This was the raid she'd suspected. It was happening *here*, on her landing. How were these would-be rescuers going to react to finding someone in the middle of the corridor, clearly intent on their own escape? Kill or ignore; these seemed the most likely options and there was little she could do now to influence which they chose.

Of course she prayed for the latter, yet it seemed those prayers were to go unanswered as an unseen hand grabbed her arm, stopping her.

"This her?" A woman's voice, rich-toned and self-assured.

She tried to struggle but was easily subdued and held.

"Yeah." A man's reply.

Something stung her arm, lightly, no more than a lover's kiss compared with much that she had endured of late.

"DNA match," the woman said. "It's definitely her."

Me? A corner of her thoughts queried. *They're here for me?* Impossible. She wasn't important enough for all this effort, not to anyone.

Somebody grabbed her arm. Instinctively she lashed out.

"For pity's sake, Mya, stop fighting us will you? We're here to get you out."

She knew that voice. "Louis?" Her brother, come to the rescue, here to keep her safe. Joy swept through her.

"No, Mya... not Louis. You know it's not Louis."

Not Louis? No, of course not; she realised that now. Another image formed in her mind. A man's face: a large, oval face, but strong and ruggedly handsome with intense eyes. Memories washed over her in a wave, and recollection brought with it hope, gratitude, joy, and even the echo of love. Yet it also brought with it crushing disappointment that this wasn't her brother, that it would never be her brother. The torrent of feelings swept through her, as the final barriers collapsed and all the things she had deliberately walled away, never expecting to need them again, were freed.

Correction; perhaps there was one person to whom she meant this much after all.

"Jim?" *Jim Leyton?* Her former lover. The man she once believed she would spend the rest of her life with. That was before, of course. Before Louis died and the ability to love deserted her forever.

She recalled the recent interrogation and for a bizarre moment was convinced that the session, that constant thinking about this man and the repetition of his name spoken out loud, had somehow conspired to bring him here, as if summoned via some arcane ritual. Ridiculous, of course, but she couldn't escape the conviction that it was true.

She felt the need to reassure him, to let him know that this really was her, to make sure he wouldn't abandon her here. "What took you so long?" she asked and tried to smile.

Prisoner 516 stopped resisting, allowed the two ghosts to lead her along what remained of the corridor and through the door that, mere seconds ago, had seemed so far away. Beyond was a space which, though still cramped, was at least free of clutching arms and free-floating liquids. She stood docile as her rescuers pulled a shimmer suit up over her body and sealed it, and revelled in being in her own space, cocooned and protected from Sheol Station, no longer a part of that vile place. The hated number had been left behind forever. Mya knew they were still exposed and that speed would undoubtedly be of the essence, but at that instant she didn't care. Sobs started to wrack her chest and tears rolled free to wet her cheeks. Her eyes screwed up as her face contorted and she collapsed against Leyton, clinging to him as, in another life, she had clutched him so hungrily in the throes of passion and body-jarring ecstasy. She drank in the solid fact of him, while memory of the lust and the love that had once burned so fiercely between them took her breath away. Crying suddenly became the easiest thing in the world.

CHAPTER FOUR

SPECULATION ABOUT 'FIRST Contact' was nothing new. Such things pre-dated space flight and became all the more popular once mankind had spread to the stars. Most people took it for granted that there were sentient aliens out there somewhere, particularly when a handful of simpler, non-sentient ones were encountered on various worlds. General consensus seemed to be, "Well if we've done it, why can't they?"

In a poll conducted a score or so years before the Great War, 87% of people were found to believe in sentient aliens. Admittedly, in a similar poll taken ten years after the War, that figure had dropped to 74%, but everyone agreed that the dip was only to be expected. Naturally, they failed to agree on *why* this was expected – some experts argued it was due to the general exhaustion and depression of a populace subjected to a century and a half of constant warfare, while others put it down to the opposite, claiming that optimism and high spirits resulting from the War's end meant that less people yearned for the psychological crutch of technologically-superior aliens and were more confident of humanity's ability to forge their own future.

What no poll managed to predict was how slight the impact on everyday life of mankind's first meeting with another civilisation would prove to be. People heard about the Byrzaens, talked about them, speculated, offered their opinions, and then went on with their daily routines as if nothing had happened. After all, work was still there the next day, their boss was still the same old cranky self-serving bastard he'd always been, food still needed to be paid for, and energy prices continued to creep inexorably upwards at every turn. What had changed?

Not that this was a one-off headline soon to be forgotten, of course; the Byrzaens were here to stay and the media went out of their way to ensure the story remained fresh and bright. The public were bombarded with images, analysis and comment on the minutest of developments and with the views of a succession of experts (though many a cynic questioned how humanity could possibly have experts on the subject). Then there were the learned debates and panel discussions that did little but rehash the limited material available, though frequently spicing it with a liberal helping of unfounded conjecture. None of which amounted to anything more than a series of fanciful diversions for the ordinary person in the street, of marginal relevance at best.

As far as Philip could see, those most directly affected by the Byrzaens' arrival were the celebrities of the hour. They weren't any more, at least not to the same extent.

The normality of it all left Philip bemused. He found his native world Home *post* first contact to be pretty much identical to Home *before* first contact. Philip and his father returned there sooner than either of them had anticipated. Once the initial excitement caused by the Byrzaens settled down a little and matters on New Paris began to take on a semblance of order, somebody found time to notice the presence of the two enhanced partials, and nobody seemed to have the foggiest idea what to do with them. In the end, rather than use them as a resource as Malcolm stridently argued, the ULAW officials decided to pack them off back to Home.

"But my help could be invaluable," an exasperated Malcolm had argued. "I built *The Noise Within* for goodness sake!"

"Yes, we're aware of that, Dr Kaufman, but matters have moved on, and the pirate ship is no longer our primary concern," a smiling ULAW official explained. Of course not, top priority would be the Byrzaens themselves – a subject

Malcolm also had some unique firsthand experience of, though he seemed reluctant to advertise as much. Still in the process of finding his virtual feet, Philip was happy to accept parental guidance on such things for the moment.

"Thank you for your offer. We know where to find you should we need to," was ULAW's final brush off.

Personally, Philip suspected that those government officials onsite saw shipping the two transhumans out as the quickest and most convenient means of removing an unknown factor from the equation. He toyed with the idea of cloning himself and leaving a version behind on New Paris to see what could be uncovered about the Byrzaens, but supporting a virtual personality as complex as he'd now become required a lot of power and it was bound to be noticed. The only person he'd trust to cover for him on something like this was Leyton, the government agent who'd been present at his corporeal 'murder' and, indeed, had hunted down his killer. Unfortunately, Leyton – one of ULAW's elite force of Intelligent Gun wielders, or eyegees – had dropped off the radar somewhere along the line, presumably assigned elsewhere to some other covert project.

Besides, the prospect of having two versions of himself running around was strangely unsettling for Philip, who was still coming to terms with having one virtual version of himself, so he shelved the idea.

Philip was still testing the boundaries of this new existence. In theory, he could simultaneously occupy all of a given system, but in practice that proved a disturbing experience when he tried it. Even within the comparatively limited confines of the New Paris' stationwide net, he felt his sense of self, his very identity, slipping away and quickly pulled himself back into a centred node of awareness which he knew to be Philip.

"That's a dangerous game," Malcolm told him.

"You've tried it, then?"

"Of course, when I first uploaded. But I don't intend to try it again in a hurry."

Philip could understand why. He had a feeling that if he'd stayed that thinly spread for any length of time, all sense of who he was would have evaporated with little chance of its ever returning.

The two of them hitched a ride back to Home aboard a ULAW ship, travelling officially within the ship's systems rather than stowing away as Malcolm had on the outward trip.

Once underway, Malcolm seemed to accept the return to Home with remarkable good grace. Indeed he seemed almost eager to do so, his anger at being prised away from New Paris quickly forgotten. Philip knew his father too well and was determined to work out what the wily old goat was up to before being told.

"What's the rush?" he asked,

"You tell me."

Philip thought for a split second. "Money." He'd been concentrating too firmly on what they were leaving behind and not paying attention to what awaited them.

"Exactly."

Philip Kaufman was now officially dead. The funds he'd always taken so much for granted were no longer his but now formed part of an estate, to be distributed according to his officially recorded will. Theoretically, in the absence of objections, that could all take as little as a matter of days. In Philip's case it would inevitably be longer, due to both his prominence and the complexity of his financial affairs, but, even so, the process of freezing accounts and valuing assets would have already begun. Living on as a transhuman would cost money that was swiftly slipping from Phillip's grasp.

"You've taken contingencies, I assume?" Malcolm asked.

"Of course." Funds tucked away in hidden accounts, investments which didn't appear in any official record – reserves against unforeseeable circumstance. "They won't amount to much, though, not in the long term."

"We might have to be a little loose and free with the law."

"You mean tamper with my will." To create a provision, to ensure sufficient funds were in place to support his virtual self in perpetuity.

"Something like that."

"I didn't think that was possible." Wills were supposed to be sacrosanct, heavily encrypted with such sophistication that they were beyond the reach of hackers and would-be thieves.

"It isn't," Malcolm confirmed, "which is why it's so expensive. Impossible things always are."

A further reminder that Philip was still a babe in virtual terms, reliant on his father's experience.

As soon as they reached Home they paid a visit to Catherine Chzyski, acting CEO of Kaufman Industries following Philip's demise and almost certain to be confirmed in the role once the board got their act together. The transfer from the spaceport to Catherine's office was all but instantaneous, a feat Philip only wished he could have managed in his former corporeal life. Catherine accepted their call without hesitation. He didn't think he'd ever been happier to see the severe features of his former colleague and sometime boardroom adversary than he was at that moment, though it was a little strange being greeted as a visitor in an office he'd occupied for so long.

He could see instantly that she'd made changes – the mobile photos, or moties, of him meeting various dignitaries were gone from the wall (though Catherine hadn't yet chosen to replace them with any of her own) and she'd installed a large multi-shelved cabinet filled with books; genuine bound paper, a luxury he had never acquired a taste for. The desk remained the same but his chair had gone. None of the changes were a surprise, which didn't prevent them from being a shock. He tried to ignore the emotional baggage the moment brought with it and concentrate on what Catherine was saying.

"Philip, very sorry to hear about what happened to you on New Paris," which was a neat way of referring to his assassination without actually mentioning it, "but delighted to learn you took the decision to ascend." Typical of Catherine; efficiency in all things.

Malcolm fell into conversation with the shrewd old crow like the two long-term collaborators they were, and Philip couldn't help but wonder how much interaction there'd been between the pair even while he was still alive. Fortunately, Catherine didn't seem to share Philip's prejudice against enhanced partials, and declared she was happy to accept the input of both generations of Kaufman in an advisory capacity. "There'll be a suitable retainer, of course," she added, in a way that suggested she understood exactly what financial burdens were involved in living on after death.

Perhaps she did. Perhaps Catherine was intending to join them after *she* passed away. Now there was an interesting prospect. Had Malcolm started a whole new trend among the wealthy and powerful rather than merely performing a rebellious, maverick act as Philip had always assumed? He was still determined to uncover what prompted Malcolm's change of heart over leaving New Paris, convinced the old man was hiding something. Malcolm had used the issue of funds to divert him just as he'd used the fuss over leaving New Paris as a smokescreen for something, Philip was sure of it.

Then he remembered his own temptations before leaving the space station and things fell into place.

He waited until they'd left the meeting with Catherine and were ensconced in a trendy bar somewhere within Home's Virtuality – all clean lines, subdued lighting and gleaming surfaces – before saying casually, "How do you intend communicating with him?"

"With whom, exactly?"

"The clone you left on New Paris."

"Ah, that."

"How are you going to support it?"

"Assuming I *did* leave such a clone in place, I wouldn't need to, not for any length of time anyway. Its only purpose would be to find out what it could about the Byrzaens, and, while ULAW might prefer to keep our new alien friends isolated at New Paris for now, that situation won't last forever. Were I to consider such a course, in order to cover the short term energy requirements, I might have, oh, I don't know... invested in a small generator and perhaps even some specialist hardware as soon as I reached New Paris, just in case."

Philip had to admire the old man's foresight. "I didn't even consider doing anything like that until we were on the verge of leaving."

"Don't beat yourself up about it. After all, I've been doing this for a hell of a lot longer than you have."

True enough. Presumably, Malcolm's clone would have to be abandoned once it had served its purpose and left to simply fade away. Philip considered the implications of that and wondered whether any version of him would willingly accept such a limited existence. Somehow he doubted it, but then wasn't that exactly what normal partials were expected to do? Fade away once their human original died and their purpose had been served. How aware were partials of their finite lives, and did they mind? The new perspective gained from this side of the virtual fence was highlighting moral issues Philip had previously never even realised existed.

"Your clone's all right with this?" he asked.

"What clone?" Malcolm grinned and winked, then added, "Don't worry, I've done this sort of thing before."

Really? When and why? Philip was quickly coming to appreciate how seriously he'd underestimated both this transhuman version of his father and the implications of the virtual world as a whole.

"It seems I've still got a lot to learn."

"That's where I come in."

"Are there any others like us?"

"No," Malcolm assured him, "not yet."

The audience with Catherine appeared to have solved one

problem, at least. "I guess there'll be no need to tamper with my will now that we both have an income."

"Don't be so naïve, Philip. We can't rely on Catherine's successor or the one after that being so generous. You've got to start thinking long term. We're here for the duration."

A sobering thought, one which highlighted yet again how different this new life truly was.

A little later, Malcolm turned to him and said, "By the way, congratulations on having such foresight."

Philip stared, assessing possible meanings and settling on one. "The will?" He had no idea what Malcolm had done, or how much it had cost him, but he could think of nothing else which would prompt such a comment.

"A sizeable and highly sensible provision I'd say. Well done." Malcolm grinned.

Philip felt torn between conflicting reactions, emotions which felt just as strong as any he'd experienced in corporeal life. "Thank you," he said, giving voice to the more generous first. "They're going to think I'm a complete hypocrite," he then added, expressing the second. Philip had spoken out so vehemently and publicly against his father's decision to enhance his partial and live on in the virtual state, declaring it 'an egotistical abomination.' Yet now it would seem to everyone that all the while he had been planning to do exactly the same thing himself.

"Let them," Malcolm advised. "What difference is that going to make to you?"

"You're right. Force of habit." Another aspect of this new existence he would have to get used to. Public image had been so important to him for so long, whereas now, of course, it didn't really matter at all.

They were served by an improbably pretty waitress with black bobbed hair, a cute, upturned nose and dark bright eyes that gazed at him from beneath long, fluttering lashes.

Philip savoured a mouthful of the cold beer she'd brought;

gently effervescent without being too gassy, while the aftertaste was malty without being too bitter.

"Good?" his father, asked.

"Yes," he conceded, "very good."

"I meant the beer, not the waitress," Malcolm said quietly.

"So did I," Philip assured him, which didn't prevent his gaze following her progress back to the bar and noting when she briefly glanced back to smile at him. That smile and the way she wiggled her perfectly rounded hips which developed from the narrowest of waists prompted Philip to wonder for the first time what sex was like here, but he decided that was one question he probably wouldn't ask his father.

When Philip first encountered the virtual bar known as The Death Wish, he'd assumed it to be unique, or at least reasonably so. Faced with the prospect of actually living here in Virtuality, he was quickly coming to appreciate just how wrong he'd been. The place was vast, and far more extensively developed than he had ever dreamed it could be.

Without Malcolm to act as guide, introducing him to this new, virtual existence, he would have been lost.

"The original programs, the foundations if you will, were written by humans," his father explained. "Many brilliant men and women contributed, but the AIs took it from there, building on all that we'd done, extending and enhancing, and then knitting all the fragments together. Without them, Home's Virtuality would still be a series of isolated pockets. It's the AIs that have built the bridges and filled in the blank spaces, who have pulled everything together into a whole, knitting a patchwork quilt that matches seamlessly. It's impossible to say where human construction ends and that of the AIs takes over."

"I'd no idea," was all Phillip could say. He remembered the spiral of events that had led to his murder in the corporeal world, beginning with his joyriding through the computer systems of his neighbours on the back of addictive narcotics and pilfered equipment. Would any of that have been necessary had he paid more attention to the virtual world? More specifically, could all that followed have been avoided if he'd been more accepting of Mal, his father's lingering partial?

Regrets were pointless at this stage, but he couldn't help wondering just how costly his stubbornness back then had been.

"Few people of our generations have," Malcolm replied.

"Really?" So it wasn't just him.

"Think about it. How many times have you heard your friends, contemporaries, or even the media discuss Virtuality?"

"Never."

"Precisely. Oh, there are the geeks and the tech-heads, but they're the exceptions. It's the kids, the teens and those who were teens themselves a couple of years ago, who have embraced Virtuality. Their avatars are the ones you'll find walking the streets and packing out the clubs. The meek might have inherited the earth, but the emerging generation are claiming Virtuality all for themselves. They'll be the first to grow up with this place as a part of their culture. Your generation were born a little too early and mine missed the shuttle by a good few decades, but right here, right now, we're catching a glimpse of the future. You mark my words."

There was something infectious about Malcolm's enthusiasm – always had been; it was one of the man's greatest strengths while he was alive, so why shouldn't this virtual version be the same? Yet Philip suspected there might be an element of wish-fulfilment at work here as well, that his father was overstating the import of Virtuality because it was now very much his home. He *wanted* the virtual world to be as important as the real, because his own relevance would then be elevated accordingly.

Not that Malcolm hadn't given him plenty to think about. Philip savoured another mouthful of beer, wondering whether a human or an AI had written the program responsible for such an excellent brew. He watched a drip of condensation trickle slowly down the curves of his glass. Were beer glasses deliberately contoured to mimic the female form or was that merely his libido talking, courtesy of the bob-haired waitress?

He glanced across at his father. Malcolm looked much as Philip remembered from the days of his childhood; a face more rounded than his own but with the same dark eyes, though they lacked the laughter lines memory had etched at their corners. The hair was a little lighter than Philip's, though still a rich brown, showing just a touch of grey at the temples and above the ears. "Your father will never grow old, just more distinguished," he remembered his mother once saying. This wasn't Malcolm in his later years but a man still in his prime, when the vigour and enthusiasm of youth hadn't yet deserted him but was tempered with maturity and experience. It struck Philip as revealing in many ways that this was the face Malcolm had selected for his transcended self. Until Malcolm's death, the partial had reflected his actual age. Only when, against all etiquette and convention, that partial had been enhanced to contain as much of him as science allowed did Kaufman Senior tweak his outward appearance.

Philip wondered now why his father had done so. Vanity seemed too glib a response. Could it have been for his son's benefit? Had Malcolm chosen to live on in the virtual world wearing the face that he reasoned Philip would most associate with happy childhood memories? The explanation had never occurred to him before, but it felt right now that it had.

Philip hadn't even thought to tinker with his own partial when, on his deathbed, he'd been persuaded to enhance it in order to transcend to virtual life. Phil had always been a little younger and a little more handsome than reality, not to mention more confident. Vanity, it seemed, wasn't banished by transcendence but was merely granted greater scope.

Malcolm looked around, caught his son watching him. "What?"

"Nothing," said Philip, and he smiled. "Just glad you're here, that's all."

"Me too, son, me too."

*   *   *

SHE WAS BEING chased through a nightmare landscape of industrial equipment... she was led, stumbling through a dark and musty chamber of looming protrusions... was strapped to a chair, a needle embedded in each arm... floating in zero gravity in a featureless sphere that offered no point of reference... sitting in a field of wild flowers, laughing, Louis laughing with her... lying on her back with something cold and damp covering her eyes, water pummelling her face, unable to breathe... was lying on her back in a soft and divinely comfortable bed, her hands clutching black silk sheets while her lover's weight pressed against her, his manhood inside her. The woman on her right, who was supporting her, turned to offer words of encouragement, revealing the dispassionate face of her torturer, which swiftly morphed into her brother, Louis, and then again into Jim Leyton, who leered at her. She whimpered as the world shifted disconcertingly yet again, screamed as her veins burned with the searing invasion of some new agent, spluttered and gagged as the water entered her lungs, moaned in the throes of orgasm as her lover erupted inside her...

Throughout it all she could hear somewhere in the background a composed, detached voice delivering what she knew to be a monologue of advice, insight and instruction, although the individual words and their meaning slipped past, frustratingly just beyond her reach.

"Mya?" This voice was louder, closer, intrusive. It didn't belong. "Mya, can you hear me?"

A woman's voice. Why wouldn't it leave her alone?

Her eyes flickered open, smarting at the brightness around her. She screwed them shut again.

"Dim the lights," a perceptive soul instructed. "She's coming round."

This time the level was tolerable, and she was able to focus on a face, a stranger who was at the same time vaguely familiar.

Porcelain skin, dark eyes and delicate features which held a fragile yet exquisite beauty.

"Up the stimulants. Gradually." The same voice – a woman's – and it belonged to this familiar stranger.

She was aware of others in the room now, faceless people moving in the background.

"Thank you everyone, good job." The woman then sat back and the faceless folk departed.

Memories began to converge, knitting together sufficiently to present some clue to the recent past. She remembered the woman now, recalled being met by her as she tried to escape, features indistinct but recognisable beneath the visor of a shimmer suit, and there had been someone else: Jim – unless that last was another aspect of her delusions.

Somehow she'd managed to hold everything together as they ghosted through the bowels of Sheol Station, and she could even recall being hurried onto a shuttle. After that, nothing. Until she woke up here.

If that really had been Jim Leyton helping to rescue her, where was he now?

Strength started to return, her thoughts grew clearer. She struggled to sit up.

"Take it easy," the woman said, her face coming into view once more.

Mya ignored the advice and continued until she'd wrestled her body into a semblance of sitting. The other woman made no effort to help, for which she was grateful.

"I... I want to thank you." It felt strange to speak, to utter any sounds that were born of her own will and offered to another freely rather than being forced from her lips. She looked at this woman, who had saved her sanity if not her life. "But I don't even know your name."

The woman smiled. "Then let me introduce myself. Hello, Mya, I'm Kethi."

That rang a bell, but a distant one, and Mya was struggling

to recall *why* the name sounded so familiar. Then she had it. "Kethi?" She frowned, staring at her rescuer, trying to marry what memory told her with the reality of the slender, beautiful woman she saw before her.

"Yes. Why, is that a problem?"

"No, it's just that... I always thought K-E-T-H-I," she pronounced each letter individually, "was a project, not a person."

"Did you, now?" The girl's smile held more than a hint of bitterness. She seemed to consider the comment before saying, "Well, in a sense I suppose I am. To be honest, I'm a bit of both."

CHAPTER FIVE

PHILIP GAZED OUT on a dark city dominated by towering skyscrapers that rose up far above him. Some, he knew, were shells, created merely to provide an aesthetic skyline, while others were genuine places with substance here in Virtuality. He had no idea which were which. This was like the city he knew but in miniature, with every notable building and landmark condensed into one small area. To his left stood the Skyhall hotel, its distinctive twin glass spires emphasised even more dramatically here than in the original. Spires seemed popular in Virtuality.

The tapering nature of the building opposite, for example, leant it an eerie, gothic feel, as if this were a tower displaced from some ancient cathedral of old Earth – an impression reinforced by the vaguely green tint to the section directly level with his line of sight, presumably caused by some trick of the lights focused upon it. A huge billboard occupied a square section of the next building, covering several storeys. Philip knew that in the physical world the people in the apartments behind that 'billboard' wouldn't even know it was there. They'd look out from their windows over an unobstructed cityscape – the view perhaps marginally dimmer, but not enough to notice. Such boards were virtual. What did that make this one, a virtual *virtual* billboard? He had no idea what it was intended to advertise. The young blonde it currently portrayed, tossing her hair in slow-mo and smiling, could have been promoting anything.

The sky above the cityscape was a deep pink or perhaps even mauve, too dark to be the harbinger of any natural dawn. A sky like that in the real world would tempt him to think 'pollution.' He wondered what constituted pollution here in Virtuality – inefficient programming?

Malcolm came over to join him. Philip's education was set to continue even into the evening, it seemed. He felt obliged to question the process. "Couldn't this information simply be uploaded into me?"

"It could," Malcolm acknowledged, "but where would the fun be in that?"

Philip tried to recall if Malcolm had been this capricious before he died, but didn't think so.

"Yes, information can be supplied that way, but cold facts taken out of context are no substitute for those learned by experience," Malcolm explained. "Trust me, I've tried both methods and my way's better."

"Fair enough." Not that Philip was entirely convinced by his father's argument. He suspected the real reason for the hands-on approach was that his old man was actually enjoying the role of teacher.

"There are basically two types of citizen in Virtuality," Malcolm explained, "avatars and partials. The avatars are ephemeral, only here for as long as the corporeals who generate them are plugged in, whereas the partials are permanent residents. The majority you'll encounter here will be avatars, since partials are limited in many ways and generally slaved to specific tasks, but it would be a mistake to assume you're always dealing with an avatar.

"And then there's us.

"The avatars are the ones you have to watch for, especially the kids. To them this is a playground, a wonderland where anything's possible and nothing really counts. They see Virtuality as a version of the 'real' world but with the safety catches removed, somewhere they can get as wild and reckless as they like without the responsibilities and consequences that would normally apply. There are areas here best avoided, dangerous places where the kids let loose, where they try the things they'd never dare to do on the outside."

"How do you tell the difference between an avatar and a partial?"

"Attitude, mainly. The partials don't want to be damaged, the avatars don't care. That's a sweeping generalisation, but you'll find it holds true more often than not. Besides, partials don't tend to have fully rounded personalities. More often they're two- or even one-dimensional, depending on how much money's been invested and how much care has gone into their making. After chatting to one for a while you'll soon realise this isn't a whole persona you're dealing with."

"Avatars can't be hurt, then?" Philip said.

"Oh, they can feel pain all right, or rather the corporeal animating them can. Remember when you were at the Death Wish, you picked up a beer? You could feel the glass, right?"

"Yes."

"Same thing with pain; sensations are transmitted, but an avatar has an easy cop-out. He or she can simply disappear any time they want, stepping out of Virtuality and returning to the real world. Shoot an avatar and it vanishes. You've kicked it out of Virtuality, forcing its corp to reboot in order to come back and even then there'll be limits as to *where* the avatar can resume. Shoot a partial and you'll damage it, maybe enough that it has to go off and repair itself, maybe to the point where it *can't* be repaired and a new partial has to be uploaded."

"Shoot either of us..." Philip said.

"Exactly. Nothing left to upload. We're it. Shoot us often enough and accurately enough and we're dead."

Now there was a sobering thought.

"Don't get me wrong, a partial is a lot more difficult to damage than an avatar. After all, an avatar is just a quick imprint, not as deeply embedded in the programming. By the time I've finished with you, you'll be a lot more resilient than your average partial. It's not all doom and gloom."

"So we're tougher than the avatars but at the same time more vulnerable, because we have a lot more to lose."

"Now you're getting the hang of it."

Philip was forced to continually revise his perception of this place, expanding it to encompass each new gem of information Malcolm chose to reveal. He was desperate to learn all there was to know about this new existence, to familiarise himself with its limits and potential. "I want to see," he said.

"See what?"

"Everything, starting with one of these dangerous places, the ones where the kids go wild."

Malcolm looked at him for a moment, as if assessing how serious he was, and then said, "All right, if that's what you want. A club, I think. I'll take you to Bubbles."

THE THUD OF music struck him as soon as the doors parted. He expected pulsing lights but there weren't any, just a dim grey dinginess. They stood on a balcony – mesh flooring and metal rails which would have been more at home on a construction site than in a club.

A doll-cute blonde with raggedly chopped hair and vivid blue eyes framed by black eyeliner glanced up from where she leant against the railing and smiled at him, all invitation and provocation. He had time to wonder if she was this eye-catching in reality before Malcolm strode confidently past him. Philip tore his gaze away from the girl and followed. They walked along a narrow corridor, walls, floor and ceiling lined with steel mesh – a square cage tunnel. They emerged onto a terrace packed with people, and had to force their way through to reach a marginally less crowded space.

Dull golden spheres – small enough to fit into the palm of his hand – floated in the air, not in dense clouds, just dotted around in ones and twos, but they were everywhere, occupying the few spaces that people weren't. The balls were semi-transparent and reminded Philip of miniature balloons, though each was a perfect sphere, so, more appropriately, he should probably think 'bubble.' A neat gimmick. Philip casually warded one off with a hand as it drifted between him and Malcolm. It promptly burst and rewarded him with a flash of kaleidoscope fireworks. Another brushed his shoulder. No fireworks this time, but he felt a surge of euphoria sweep through his thoughts as the bauble disintegrated.

"What the f – ?"

Malcolm laughed. "Welcome to Bubbles."

Philip looked around and, now that he knew what to look for, could see the tiny globes disappearing in all directions as they came into contact with people. He didn't see flashes or fireworks any more than he felt the kick of pleasure, but guessed that each was delivering a shot of something to whoever it touched, and there were always more to replace the ones that burst, with no apparent end to the supply of little golden spheres.

"It's like free narcotics," he said, as another bubble-rush of happiness surged through him.

"I know, and not even on tap but floating around in the very air!"

Nodes of temporary code, Philip guessed, each primed to give a short term boost to specific areas of programming. Two or three varieties, constantly replicated – you wouldn't need any more. Ingenious. Philip had to admit that he was impressed.

A statuesque girl in a shimmering, figure-hugging dress, her bright red hair swept to one side so that it fell onto her right shoulder in a tumble of ringlets, caught his eye. She winked at him and, in doing so, changed – abruptly, as if a switch had been thrown – into a man wearing a shimmering vest, red hair combed into a lopsided peak above his right eye. In a split second *he* had become *she* again and then back, constantly

flickering from one gender to the other. Philip smiled at her/
him and nodded in appreciation at this novel approach to
transgender. Only then did he worry that his response might be
construed as an invitation. Very deliberately, he looked away,
shifting his attention to take in the rest of the room.

Beneath him was the dance floor, where a horde of youthful
forms gyrated to the bass-rich music. Wall panels pulsed in
time, though never straying from the silver, black and grey
that characterised the club's décor, contributing to the grungy,
edgy feel.

Philip had yet to see anything here that merited Malcolm's
ominous description of the place as 'dangerous, where the kids
let loose.' Maybe it was a generational thing. Easy to forget
sometimes that he and Malcolm had grown up in very different
eras. All Philip could see down there were people having fun.

"Shall we go down?" he said to his father.

"If we must."

They headed for the stairway.

Philip felt himself swaying to the mesmeric beat, itching to
hit the dance floor. When was the last time he'd had the chance
to dance? He couldn't remember; not recently at any rate, and
now seemed the perfect opportunity to make up for lost time.
With all due respect to Malcolm, his vote was with the kids.

In the very centre of the room stood the source of the bubbles,
an opaque column of light stretching from a low plinth on the
floor to the ceiling. It contained a core of what looked to be
thick, swirling smoke, which was spinning like a dervish – a
tamed whirlwind struggling to burst from its confinement.
The core was laced with silver flecks that flashed and winked
and dazzled as they reflected and magnified the surrounding
light. A stream of bubbles erupted from near the top of the
column, flung out by its spinning to float across the room in a
dispersing cloud.

They were halfway down the stairs when he felt Malcolm's
hand on his shoulder. He leaned in close so that Philip could

hear him above the music and warned, "Watch out for the black ones."

Philip laughed. "Why, what do they do?"

"They kill you."

Philip stopped and stared at the older Kaufman. "You're serious, aren't you?"

Before Malcolm had a chance to answer, things changed on the dance floor. The music stopped, cutting off in the mid-beat, leaving Philip's ears buzzing in its absence even after so short a time here. Everyone drew back from an abruptly isolated figure, like oil chased across the surface of water by a drop of soap. The figure, a willowy, dark-haired girl, stood encased in a block of light, which resembled a miniature version of the central column.

A man's voice boomed out across the suddenly music-free room. "We have a winner!"

All eyes were focused on the girl. People were whooping and cheering. Hands began to clap, picking up a constant rhythm.

"What's it to be, folks?" the amplified voice asked. "Remember, you decide."

"Fire, fire, fire..." Initially a few voices and then more and more picked up the chant, until the whole room was calling out the word in time to the clapping hands.

Inside her column of light the girl laughed, shook her hair, and lifted back her head to stare at the ceiling, as if waiting to receive some divine revelation.

"All right, I hear you," the voice declared. "You want fire? Let there *be* fire!"

A roar of approval rose from the crowd, many of whom started jumping up and down in their excitement. The rhythm of clapping faltered and collapsed into a rolling rumble of applause.

The girl abruptly screamed, her high-pitched agony cutting through the ambient noise, which dipped temporarily in response. Flames sprouted near her ankles, climbing and licking at her legs, tongues of blue radiance that quickly took hold. Her skin blistered and withered away at their touch. "Yes, oh God, yes!" she screamed in a semblance of ecstasy as the flames became a conflagration.

The cheering rose in renewed crescendo as those watching went wild, becoming a flailing, jostling mass of arms and kicking legs. The girl was now a pillar of flame, blazing brightly for a few seconds before collapsing to sputter and fade. With her demise the column of light disappeared and the music swelled up again, to drown out the sounds of celebration. The dancing resumed, if anything even more energetically than before, and the sea of people spread out to cover the spot where the girl had died, for all the world as if she had never been there at all.

Philip glanced at Malcolm. "A black bubble, I take it."

His father nodded, looking as shaken as Philip felt, and presumably he'd *known* what was coming. Philip turned and continued down the steps.

"You're not still going down there?" Malcolm called from behind him.

"Hell, yes!"

He understood. Even though his motivation was a little different, he *knew* why the kids did this. They wanted to play with the devil and court the ultimate danger, if only by proxy. They sought a taste of what it might be like to die, whereas he and death were already acquainted. They were there for the kick, the buzz, the thrill, while he merely wished to prove to himself that he wasn't afraid, that he could stare into the abyss without turning tail and running.

Malcolm hung back by the stairs. Philip didn't care. This was no longer about what his father could show him, but was one aspect of this new life that he preferred to embrace on his own.

He moved to the edge of the throng and danced. Nobody minded. There was no sense of proprietary resentment over floor space or dance partners. While a few couples had obviously paired off here and there, most people were dancing with anyone and everyone. He even began to enjoy the music, feeling himself relax and knowing that his dancing improved as a result.

Then he realised that somebody *was* dancing with him, or perhaps even *at* him. He gazed into piercing, black-rimmed eyes that looked up at him from beneath a shaggy fringe of blonde hair, and instantly recognised her as the girl who had been on the gantry as he and Malcolm first entered. She must have followed them.

She was shorter than him, barely reaching his chest, but perfectly formed, with a slender waist and gravity-defying bosom which her low-cut top made impossible to ignore. And, God, could she move.

Nobody here was ugly. The men either tended towards tall, muscular and media-gloss handsome or dark, brooding and dangerous, whereas any of the women could easily have featured in the various sexual fantasies he'd entertained over the years, but even in this company the girl stood out.

Philip noted the glances and outright stares of the men around them, and a good few of the women as well. There was something primitive and dirty in the thrust of her hip, the tilt of her head, the way her eyes never left his as she performed in front of him; and this *was* a performance, he was under no illusion about that, one which captivated him entirely. The woman simply oozed sex appeal in a way that no one he'd ever met in the real world had. That was it, of course. He wondered again whether she looked or behaved anything like this in reality, picturing a mouse-timid girl too shy to interact with boys, someone who could escape here and live out all the suppressed fantasies she was too insecure to act upon in the real world. The image was swept away and forgotten as the girl raised her arms, clasping her hands behind her head, jiggling her upper body rhythmically, hips swaying in counterpoint as she slowly turned around to rub against him. Then she had her back to him, her buttocks grinding into his thigh. Philip's hands moved almost of their own accord, reaching forward to grasp her hips, feeling her warmth, her movement, as he attempted to match her rhythm but instantly abandoned the idea, having failed dismally. His body reacted to this attention exactly as it would have done in the real world, and her smile as she drew away and spun back to face him suggested that she had felt his burgeoning erection rub against the top of her buttocks even as he had, and that this was exactly the effect she'd intended.

Philip felt a surge of lust course through him and knew that before the night was out he was going to fuck this woman. He *had* to have her. Even as reason receded, an analytical corner of his mind still functioned and that part couldn't wait to find out what sex here was like.

Only afterwards did he stop to wonder whether this aggressive surge of lust was entirely due to the girl – although he certainly wouldn't have ruled that out – or whether an unseen golden bubble had burst and delivered a jolt of stimulant programming.

He would never know.

In the club's dim lighting, the black bubbles were more difficult to spot than the golden ones. Philip only saw the one that struck his new friend the instant before it dipped down to burst on her head.

The music stopped instantly, as a cubicle column of light enveloped the girl.

Philip's heart sank. People were already drawing back and the clapping had begun.

"And we have another winner!" the voice boomed out. "What's it to be this time, folks?"

For a fleeting instant the girl's eyes sought his and he thought he saw in them frustration and disappointment, as if this was the last thing she'd wanted to happen, but then she spread her arms and thrust her chest forward, craning her neck and staring upward, lost in the moment, or perhaps the part.

"Slice, slice, slice…" the crowd chanted in time to the steady hand clapping.

"Okay, okay, I get the message. Here at Bubbles we always

give you what you want." Someone grabbed Philip by the arm, pulling at him. Malcolm. He shuffled backwards as directed.

"You want her sliced and diced, cut into wafer-thin ribbons, then so be it. Let the slicing begin!"

The crowd roared, the girl screamed – and now there was no question of her acting. A dozen toothed discs appeared in the air around her, circular saws supported by nothing obvious. They immediately became blurs of motion as they spun and converged on the girl, slicing across and around and up and down like some lethal mechanised production line gone rogue. Again the crowd went mad, closing in on the block of light even before it had faded and the girl's dismembered parts had finished falling to the floor. The music thumped out louder than ever and the crowd stamped and leapt and whooped like a mob of savages.

In a sense, that's precisely what they were, Philip realised. Savages. People robbed of constraint, reverting to something more primal and basic. Of the girl's remains there was no sign; no blood, no slippery gore to make footing treacherous for the dancers, who simply tramped and hoofed and cavorted over the spot where she'd been.

"Are you all right?" Malcolm asked.

"Yes, I'm fine," Philip assured him. She wasn't dead, he kept telling himself, just returned to the real world a little earlier than intended. As he gazed around the room, no longer feeling anything in common with these revellers, he noticed something. Built into the far wall beyond the central column of swirling smoke and light was a digital display, a clock which seemed to be running backwards. Currently it showed a little over three and a half hours.

"What's that?" he asked Malcolm.

"The countdown to night's end. When *all* the bubbles turn black."

Philip stared at him. "*All* of them?"

His father nodded. "Every night at Bubbles ends with a bang, though not of the kind you were hoping for."

This was what they were here for, all these kids, not merely to tempt fate as he'd assumed but to actually feel the Reaper's touch. Philip shook his head.

"Have you seen enough?"

"Definitely. Let's go."

As he turned away from the dance floor, Philip noticed a number of alcoves to either side of the stairs, built beneath the terrace he and Malcolm had stood on earlier. Something about them caused him to look more closely. The alcoves enjoyed a degree of separation from the rest of the room, courtesy of veils artistically draped and fixed around the entrances. Though they weren't drawn, the veils were cunningly arranged to break up the clean lines of the openings and give them a fluid, almost organic appearance.

A recent memory nagged at him, drawing him over to the nearest alcove. He fingered the corner of a veil thoughtfully, and then peered inside.

To his right a semi-naked trio – a woman and two men – were entangled in a writhing sexual embrace, legs lifting, bodies humping and hands reaching and caressing. Another woman, completely naked, stretched out along a bench directly in front of him, long dark hair tumbling down to cover her face – the only thing that was covered – while on his left a strikingly handsome woman clad from head to toe in black leather which had been slashed open to reveal apparently random strips of bare skin was busy carving motifs into the arm of a muscle-bound man using what looked to be a scalpel.

None of these people claimed more than his passing attention. It wasn't the booth's occupants that interested Philip. They weren't responsible for the sense of dread that tingled through his thoughts. It was the alcove itself. The theme set by the veils continued inside the small room. Nowhere was there a defined edge or corner. Instead the walls and floor and ceiling all curved into each other, flowing together to produce a very organic space. Even the seats and benches and the small table in the middle appeared to be an extension of this, a part of one whole, freshly emerged as if the room had somehow birthed them or grown them like fruit.

Beside him, Malcolm exclaimed, "Dear God."

Having seen enough, they stepped back, with none of the room's occupants having acknowledged, or perhaps even noticed, their presence.

The two stared at each other. Philip had seen something like this before. In fact he'd walked through spaces, rooms and corridors that were all but identical to the booth's interior just a short while ago, during his visit to the Byrzaen starship. He was one of the few humans privileged enough to have met the aliens and was certainly the only person on Home, real or virtual, who had ever been on board one of their vessels. So how did a perfect replica of an alien room, typical of humanity's newly encountered allies, come to exist in a place that had been a part of Home's Virtuality for years?

Philip stared at his father, the only guide he had here. "Well, how do you explain this?"

"I don't," Malcolm replied, shaking his head. "I can't even begin to. Not yet."

CHAPTER SIX

LEYTON HAD MET many of the most powerful members of the ULAW government in his time, and had stood toe to toc with some of the most dangerous criminals and jumped-up despots in the galaxy. So why was he finding it so difficult to talk to this woman whose face had appeared in his thoughts at some point virtually every day for as long as he could remember?

She stood before him now in a loose fitting pale blue smock, her small frame almost lost within its folds. The garment shouted 'institution,' even though he knew it would be fresh, supplied by habitat personnel after Mya had bathed and rested. A small irregularity at the base of her neck showed where the patch of skinfix was still settling after the removal of the tag ULAW routinely fired into each and every prisoner that came their way – tiny devices that would outlive their hosts and could be used to pinpoint and identify a former offender forever afterwards. The sight brought a subliminal itch to the recently-healed spot where his own tag had been removed. He might never have seen the inside of a ULAW prison but he *had* been an eyegee, which still qualified him as ULAW property.

"You're looking well," she said, into a silence that was threatening to become awkward. It was a remarkably neutral opening, bearing in mind the passion that suffused his and Mya's history. Disappointment struck like a blow and his spirit sagged under the weight of it.

"And you look beautiful," he countered, determined to up the ante before they became bogged down in a mire of polite inanity.

"Huh!" she barked. "No I don't. I look wasted... gaunt and malnourished... as if I've spent the last few months in prison getting the shit kicked out of me when I wasn't being tortured. Oh, wait a minute, I did, didn't I?"

Her dark skin had lost its lustre, looking almost sallow when compared with the image in his mind; her even darker hair —which he'd seen in so many styles, from cropped and spiky, to bobbed, to long and plaited into a ponytail – was a crudely chopped and tangled mess, the almost chubby cheeks were gone – as sunken as her eyes – while the sensual grace of her movements had been replaced by weary awkwardness... but she was still Mya. "Even so," he said, "you look beautiful."

Her face reflected a range of emotions, disbelief and exasperation chief among them, and for a moment he thought she was about to shout and rail against him, but in the end she laughed. It was a sound that welled up from somewhere deep within and shook her body in its escape. "Good God, Jim, how is it that you manage to perceive the rest of the world so clearly but always see me in pastel shades and soft focus?"

He shrugged. "I'm just talented like that."

She stepped forward, closing the distance between them, and suddenly they were hugging.

"I've missed you," she murmured.

"Me too." The words were wholly inadequate but all he could manage just then. Besides, he noted that her face was pressed to his chest. She didn't look up, didn't leave any opportunity for a kiss.

He still didn't know what had gone wrong between them. At some point the passion they'd shared became something she put up with, until she couldn't anymore. He had never understood why. Nor, deep down, had he ever accepted that she wouldn't return to him some day.

As their embrace lingered, there came a light knock on the door. They stepped back from each other and Leyton was far from surprised to see Kethi standing there. She looked at the two of them with... what? Not disapproval as such, or even surprise, merely with interest.

"Sorry to interrupt," she said, "but Nyles wants to see you, Mya."

Of course he did. Leyton wasn't naïve enough to believe that the habitat had gone to all the trouble of freeing Mya just for his sake. They wanted answers, to the same questions he did. For instance, what had brought about Mya's spectacular fall from grace? One minute a member of the elite eyegee unit, the next a prisoner aboard the orbiting cesspit that was Sheol Station, where ULAW tucked away those people they least wanted to hear from again. Torture wasn't something the government resorted to lightly. There'd be all hell to pay if the media ever got hold of the story, so presumably Mya knew something that ULAW wanted.

The invite hadn't included Leyton, but he was hanged if he was going to miss out on being there; besides, Kethi didn't object when he tagged along. He always had the impression that Nyles tolerated his presence aboard *The Rebellion* rather than welcomed it, that the habitat's leader put up with him for Kethi's sake and would never fully trust anyone who had spent so long as a ULAW agent. Leyton didn't mind; in fact, he privately applauded Nyles's cautious attitude. After all, at some point he might yet prove the man right.

ONE ASPECT OF Virtuality that would take some getting used to was the silence that reigned over the streets here. They weren't deserted, not quite, but there were many times when he alone, or he and Malcolm, were the only people in sight. On the rare occasions he did encounter others, they were generally in the distance and always in a hurry to be somewhere else. Kyle had yet to see a car.

"Of course," Malcolm replied when he raised the subject. "If you had a finite amount of time to spend in a virtual realm where all sorts of things are possible, would you squander it by piddling around in boring city streets? There will be the odd occasion when an avatar *has* to resort to the streets, but only in order to get from one place to another, and they won't want to dawdle."

"So why have the streets at all?

"Symmetry, credibility…"

"In other words you don't know."

"Not really, no. I didn't design the place."

Philip looked around. "And are all the streets here as deserted as this?"

"More or less."

Which definitely didn't constitute a 'yes.' "Oh?"

Malcolm sighed. "There is one section where the streets are anything *but* deserted, especially at night."

"I take it this is another of those places that are 'dangerous, where the kids go wild.'"

Malcolm favoured him with a sour smile, suggesting he was getting a little tired of the reference, but nodded. "And I suppose you want to see it?"

"Of course."

"All right, but there's something we have to do first."

Malcolm led the way through dark corridors that seemed to invite men in long coats with turned-up collars to stand in the shadows and peer at you from beneath the rim of their fedoras. In the event, they passed no one, but Philip found himself treading carefully, as if afraid that the slightest sound might attract unwelcome attention.

The final passageway ended in a plain unassuming door, which Malcolm flung open to reveal… nothing. Philip gazed out into a dark void that reached in every direction. Craning his neck a little, he could see the rough brick wall of the building disappear into the murk above and below; all else was blackness.

"I'm tempted to say the edge of Virtuality," he said slowly, "but it can't be, because Virtuality is continuous, like a Möbius strip. It doesn't have any edges."

"So?"

"This must be a glitch, a topographical bug in the programming."

"Good."

Philip stared for a further second and then felt obliged to shuffle back a step. He had never experienced anything so disturbing, so disorientating as this complete absence. It seemed to pull at him like some kind of black hole, tempting him forward.

Malcolm whistled; not a tune but a mere two notes, as if he were attempting to draw attention.

Incredibly, as in so many childhood stories, the whistle was answered. Not by a faithful hound or some powerful steed with wild eyes and a streaming mane, but by a steel walkway which appeared out of nowhere and extended towards them. It stopped a few metres short of their position and hung bizarrely in the void, as if reluctant to close the final gap.

"We have to leap across," Malcolm explained.

"You're kidding me."

"Not at all. Can't afford to let the walkway actually touch this side or it'll defeat the whole object. Come on, but be careful. There's no gravity in the glitch."

With that, he took a few steps back, ran forward, and flung himself into the darkness, seeming to float across the intervening space to land on the steel walkway with a clatter. It didn't sway, didn't budge. Nor did Philip, who stared after his father but made no move to follow.

"Your turn, Philip. Trust me."

Swallowing his doubts, Philip forced his feet to lift from the solid floor. Three long strides back, then a short run, before he hurled himself into the void. The sense of weightlessness was immediate and disorientating. He wondered fleetingly what would happen if he missed the walkway altogether. Would he be left floating in this topographical non-space for ever, unable to reach the resumption of programming in any direction?

He imagined himself stranded for eternity, or until Virtuality collapsed, which might just as well be the same thing. Then it was over. His hand brushed the railing and his feet impacted with metal, leading to a brief stumble forward to where Malcolm was waiting to steady him.

"Thank you," he said automatically.

The walkway was already retracting, carrying them away from the solid reassurance of the wall and into the blackness. He gripped the metal handrail tightly. Malcolm didn't look concerned and Philip resolved that he wouldn't either. He'd trusted the old man this far. Yet as the length of walkway continued to shorten, evidently disappearing into nothing and carrying them ever closer to it, Philip couldn't help wondering what the hell he was doing here. Before he knew it, his toes disappeared, crossing the unseen barrier, and in an instant the rest of him had followed. Weight returned immediately; a welcome touch of normality after the oddness of the space just departed.

He was in a room, stepping off the walkway with Malcolm still beside him.

"And we're now in…?"

"…Virtuality, of course, but a different part," Malcolm explained. "You mustn't keep thinking in linear terms. That was a break in the programming. We've jumped from one section to a completely different one without leaving a continuous history for anyone to follow, should they try to."

"All right, but why?"

"For protection," a new voice said.

Philip spun around, to see the silver haired figure of Kaufman Industries' latest CEO standing there. "Catherine?"

"Cath, Catherine's partial," the newcomer explained, "but close enough."

Of course, amazing how the distinction between person and partial seemed to be so much less important to him these days. His gaze switched between Malcolm and Cath. "Back ups," he guessed, "cloned programmes held in reserve in case one of us gets erased."

"There, you see? I knew some of your brains had to have come across when they uploaded you," his father quipped. "After what happened at Bubbles, there's no way I'm taking you to a street meet without a few precautions. Cath's going to update my own back up and create one of you. If something *does* ever take either of us out, there'll always be a cloned version stored and dormant, waiting as replacement. If we're taken out by anything malicious, it might be sophisticated enough to trace our back history, to pursue every programming path we've ever followed and erase all trace of us. The break we just leapt across means there's no direct trail leading here, which ought to keep the clones safe."

"Very ingenious," Philip conceded. "Does it work?"

"No idea, never been tested, but it should do."

"If you two have quite finished," Cath interrupted, "I do have other responsibilities. Shall we get this over with?"

Her presence intrigued Philip. He recalled what Malcolm had said about partials seeming incomplete, their personalities limited, but couldn't detect any such shortcomings where Cath was concerned. He wondered to what degree Catherine Chzyski had already enhanced her partial, which led him to ponder exactly what Malcolm might have started here. In another century, would Virtuality be crawling with enhanced transhumans and the avatars find themselves in the minority?

Now there was a prospect to conjure with.

THE INTERVIEW WITH Mya proved something of a disappointment, as Kethi had suspected it might. Leyton tagged along as she'd predicted. Nyles would have preferred to exclude the former government man, fearing his presence might inhibit Mya. Kethi accepted the possibility, but felt it more likely that his being there would reassure the new arrival. As usual, her opinion won the day. Nyles might be stubborn and even arrogant on occasion, but he of all people valued her capabilities.

Throughout the meeting, Nyles adopted what Kethi thought of as his 'professional warmth' persona, in which he smiled a lot and spoke in relaxed, sympathetic tones, while the words themselves were all business. He even managed to avoid anything more than the faintest hint of condescension when explaining to Mya that while he was delighted with her safe extraction from the prison station, he hoped she would repay their efforts by co-operating.

Kethi watched Mya intently, fully aware that, despite her current frail appearance, this was a highly trained government operative they were dealing with, but the woman's gratitude and willingness to help seemed entirely genuine.

"What were you doing there?" Nyles asked.

"Well, Sheol was one holiday destination I hadn't tried yet," Mya replied.

He smiled, though Kethi knew exactly how shallow that expression would be. This flippancy was a trait Leyton and Mya evidently shared. Perhaps it was drilled into ULAW operatives as a defence mechanism. "Did it live up to expectation?" Good grief, Nyles was even playing along. The man might not possess anything recognisable as a sense of humour, but clearly he'd learnt to feign one.

"And some." Mya grimaced and pushed a tense hand through her dark hair. Nyles stayed quiet, letting the silence draw her out. "I stumbled across something," she said at last. "Information I shouldn't have. I reported it. Next thing I knew they took my gun away, slammed me in there, and then set about torturing me to discover how much I knew."

"And did they succeed?"

"Oh, yes, but the problem was they couldn't know that, couldn't be certain I wasn't holding something back, so they kept digging even though there was nothing more to find. If you people hadn't come along, they'd have kept at it until not a scrap of me remained. As it is, I'm not sure how much longer my sanity would have lasted."

Nyles's thin smile came and went in a trice. "What did you find out that had ULAW so concerned?"

She took a deep breath and glanced towards where Leyton stood. "I learned... I *suspected* from what I uncovered while on a mission that there were elements within the ULAW government working to break up the union."

Really? That was interesting, though Mya seemed genuine enough. Kethi had picked up hints of dissension from time to time, but that was inevitable within a government as vast as ULAW's. She certainly hadn't seen anything on the scale suggested here.

"You mean determined to bring the government down?"

"Yes."

"What did you find?"

"I prevented an assassination. The target had been a woman, a planetary president within the ULAW government. I took the assassin alive. He begged me not to hand him in, claiming that he'd be killed if I did. He said that the man who'd hired him was a high-ranking ULAW official and that this assassination was just one part of a far wider plot. He also said that he could prove it."

"What did you do?"

"Took him in and reported his claims. Next thing I knew I was jumped by a squad of shimmer suited, very professional goons. I woke up in a cell on Sheol."

"Why?" Kethi interjected. "Surely they could simply have told you the assassin was lying and sent you off on the next assignment."

"Because they know me better than that, knew that I wouldn't have let the matter rest, but would have done some digging on my own. Presumably, they were afraid of what I might have found."

"How did these goons jump you?" Nyles wanted to know. "You're an eyegee. Surely your gun would have warned you."

Mya took her time in answering. "The gun stayed quiet," she

said finally, mumbling a little, as if she could hardly believe the words herself.

Kethi's attention switched briefly to Leyton, but he showed no sign of reaction. That didn't really matter. She was just glad he'd been there to hear Mya talk of her gun's complicity. It might help him accept the unpalatable truth of where his own weapon's loyalties lay.

"Who did you actually deliver the assassin to?"

"Pavel Benson, my boss, the head of the eyegee unit."

Now there was a name Kethi had heard before. "Wasn't he also the man they put in charge of operations at New Paris?" The man who had been responsible for ULAW's liaison with the Byrzaeans.

Mya merely looked puzzled, possibly she'd been out of the loop by then, but Leyton answered on her behalf, speaking for the first time. "Yes, he was."

Coincidence? An explanation Kethi tended to accept only once every other possibility had been eliminated. She determined to take a closer look at this Pavel Benson.

Mya said nothing else of interest and Nyles soon excused her, with a smile, an apology, and the advice to get some rest and rebuild her strength.

She left trailed by Leyton. Once they were out of the room, Nyles turned to Kethi. "Well?"

"She's holding something back."

"So she's giving us the truth but not necessarily the whole truth." He nodded. "Hardly surprising after all she's been through, I suppose. In her shoes I'd probably do the same, not wanting to reveal my whole hand straight away."

Maybe, but Kethi wasn't convinced it was that simple.

"We'll have to win her trust," Nyles concluded, closing the subject as far as he was concerned. "What do you make of her reaction to Leyton?"

"Interesting. She cares about him deeply."

"But she doesn't love him."

Kethi considered that for a heartbeat before replying, "No."

"That was my impression too. Do you think the rescue was worth it, given the likely cost once ULAW identifies who was responsible?"

"Yes." She answered without hesitation, determined that Nyles should hear no trace of doubt in her voice. She still remembered how crushed and defeated he'd been when they arrived at New Paris too late to influence events. Seeing him like that had been a tremendous shock. The habitat needed this man to be strong. "Planning for the attack on Sheol gave everyone a new impetus," she said. "Pulling off the snatch and grab without any casualties has boosted morale still further, and now Mya has provided us with a lead on a possible split within ULAW. That gives us renewed purpose, and she even provided a name for me to follow up on."

"Pavel Benson."

"Exactly. So, all in all, I'd say the mission was a roaring success."

"I hope you're right. I hope we both still think that when ULAW come knocking." Then he met her gaze and smiled. "Thank you, Kethi. That will be all."

Her thoughts as she left him were troubled. It was the first time she'd analysed the chemistry between Mya and Leyton. She didn't doubt for one minute the truth of what she'd said on the subject, but wasn't yet sure of her own reaction to that particular revelation.

AFTER THE INTERVIEW with Nyles, which Leyton had to admit was one of the more congenial debriefings he'd ever witnessed, he escorted Mya back to her quarters. She didn't invite him in, claiming weariness – something he could hardly argue with, given all that she'd been through. There were a hundred things he wanted to say to her, though perhaps they were merely a hundred different ways of saying the same thing. Either way, he felt he'd barely scratched the surface of what he needed to tell her. Mya had always been perceptive. The worry that gnawed at him deep down was that she probably didn't need him to say any of them, yet she hadn't responded as he'd hoped. Oh, there was closeness, they'd always had that, but he didn't sense in Mya anything to mirror what he still felt for her.

The Rebellion boasted a small but well-equipped gym – a sensible provision for any ship with a sizeable crew that was likely to be out of port for an extended period – and it was here that Leyton headed to work out his frustrations. For once, though, exercise wasn't enough, no matter how aggressively he threw himself into it, so he cut his routine short and headed for the rec room in search of more effective distraction.

Here was where the off-duty crew tended to congregate before, after, or instead of sleep. The place was busy without being crowded. Two faces stood out, both because he recognised them and because, well, they were different. Joss and Wicks were spacers recruited at some stage to the habitat's cause, their skin weathered and tanned from exposure to a score of different suns. They lacked the porcelain paleness of those native to the habitat, an environment without any sun.

Wicks beckoned him over, which was all the invitation Leyton needed. He took the empty seat next to Joss.

"Not often we see you in here," she commented.

True enough; he tended to prefer his own company, spending much of his downtime either in the gym or in his own quarters, but not today.

"He's had a busy day, Joss," Wicks suggested, "so feels the need to come and unwind with us commoners."

"You wonder why I don't come in here more often with a greeting like that?"

"Ignore Wicksy," Joss advised. "He's only happy when he's making someone else's life miserable. I hear the raid went well."

"Yes, it did." So much for his attempt to escape the day's events and relax for a while.

"Good, I'm glad. I just hope everyone realises that ULAW aren't going to take this lying down."

Leyton was quite sure that everyone fully appreciated as much. The government were bound to respond. In fact, he had the impression that a desire to be noticed was part of the reason Nyles had sanctioned the rescue in the first place, as if to deliberately tweak ULAW's collective nose. The habitat seemed desperate to be taken seriously. After this, they probably would be – assuming the authorities worked out who was behind the raid, and he was sure they would, eventually. There wouldn't be any half measures; the response would be swift and forceful. Leyton trusted Nyles and Kethi realised what they'd started here. Quite what ULAW would do in the face of such provocation remained to be seen, but he had a feeling his newfound allies' resolve was going to be tested to the limit. Not that this greatly bothered him at that particular moment, nothing did. After all, he had Mya back.

Almost as if she'd heard his thoughts, Kethi appeared, munching on a high energy ration bar and clutching a bulb of chilled water in her free hand. "Mind if I join you?" No one did, though Joss and Wicksy left soon after, leaving him alone with the enigmatic girl who had recruited him to the habitat's cause.

Never one to waste an opportunity, he asked about the men and women who'd founded the habitat, keen to learn more of his newly adopted home.

There was a brief pause while she squeezed some water into her mouth to wash down the ration bar, and then she replied. "William Anderson, the habitat's founder, was a genius and a visionary." Leyton made no comment. This sounded like something learned by rote rather than her own take on things, which didn't preclude its being true. "He attracted men and women of similar capabilities, and it's they and their descendents who form the core of our community."

He decided to change tack and hope for a less formal answer. "What about *The Rebellion*? Is this the habitat's only significant ship?"

"No, not at all. Four capital ships were built, powered by engines based upon the knowledge gleaned from the derelict alien vessel. Three were, in effect, mothballed – powered down and kept in orbit around the habitat, capable of being brought to full operational status within a matter of days, if not hours. This one, *The Rebellion*, has always been maintained at constant readiness with a skeleton crew on board, prepared to launch as soon as we received any news that hinted of alien incursion. Everyone in the habitat is trained as crew and between them the four ships have the capacity to carry almost all the habitat's population. Each of the four ships has a specific function. *The Rebellion* is the vanguard, our rapid response. *The Renegade* would have been next, brought online as soon as we left. Her job is to carry key personnel including senior scientists to a more secure secondary location..."

"Presumably the site of the alien derelict," Leyton guessed.

Kethi made no comment, but continued. "After that, *The Retribution*, tasked with providing support for *The Rebellion*, and finally *The Renaissance*, which by now would have replaced *The Rebellion* as the ship at constant readiness, prepared to defend the habitat or evacuate our remaining people, whichever seems the most appropriate."

Leyton was impressed. "Your whole society has been geared towards this, hasn't it?"

"It's why we exist," Kethi confirmed with evident pride. "And this is our time, the day William Anderson always knew would come and which we've been preparing for ever since the habitat was founded."

Leyton nodded. He knew full well that preparing for an event and confronting the reality were two entirely different things. He had to admit, however, from all that he'd seen so far, the habitat's personnel were coping pretty well despite their inexperience. He just hoped that continued to be the case once ULAW had noticed them.

CHAPTER SEVEN

THIS DIDN'T LOOK like anywhere in the real world Philip was familiar with, and he wondered whether it represented a part of the world he'd never visited or if this stark chunk of industrial urbanity had sprung complete from the imagination of some programmer. If the latter, he could only assume the imagination in question was limited. The buildings here were functional oblong blocks – soulless and ugly, with sharp corners and edges – arranged in repetitive rows of identical windows and tight-lipped doorways, while the roads were wide and straight, dividing lines burned in asphalt.

The high-pitched wail of a guitar clawed at the night, shredding the tranquillity into harried tatters, and the world resounded to the rhythm of a hundred drums.

They stood at the very edge of the developed area, with the boxlike buildings stretching away to their left and what looked to be open ground to their right, though Philip could only see a little way into the darkness. No streetlights were in evidence. A score of fires held the night at bay, some of them in braziers, others more haphazard – bonfires built of heaped-up rubbish and foraged sticks and undergrowth – while the largest of all had clearly been a car, now set ablaze. The fires dotted the pavements and side streets, and the fringe of the gently sloping wasteland beyond. People clustered around them, drinking, talking, laughing, and some even dancing to the all-pervading beat of the drums.

In front of one of the bonfires, a little way from where the road ended, strutted a long-haired youth, wearing tight black leather trousers and a black t-shirt emblazoned with a demon's smile. The eyes of the demon motif followed Philip as he moved, clearly designed to stare straight at the observer. The youth's fluid hands wielded the guitar – a slender instrument consisting of little more than a pole of polished ebony, one side flattened to support the frets while a slight bulge was all that suggested the body. There were no apparent tuning pegs, the strings simply disappeared over the abruptly truncated neck. The kid played with all the flair and arrogance of some rock god from a bygone era. Around him in a wide and irregular circle sat his disciples: the drummers. One or two huddled on stools behind small kits boasting bass, snares, tom-toms and high-hats, but most simply sat on the ground, playing a bewildering array of instruments. At a quick glance Philip saw several bodhráns, a couple of djembe, bongos, a few pairs of tabla, a number of synth-pads and several of the smaller finger-pad sets, even the odd unadulterated wooden box. All were being played with vigour, the skins, pads and boards beaten with stick, palm, fingers and tipper to produce a pulsating roar of rhythmic thunder over which the sweet notes of the guitar skipped and danced, one moment dipping beneath the rhythm, the next bursting through it to take flight.

Mankind had produced symphonies utilising such diverse elements as birdsong, the haunting sounds of ocean-roaming leviathans, the play of cosmic motes on far-flung gossamer receptors and the wind rushing through geographical formations from a dozen different worlds. Every type of noise imaginable had been synthesised, sampled, phased and blended to be labelled music, but to Philip's ear nothing had ever sounded sweeter than this simple lone electric guitar soaring above its accompanying orchestra of percussion. The very ground itself reverberated in time, as if determined to jog the idle feet of those listening into dance.

"So," he said to Malcolm as the two stood a little removed from the revelries, "this is a street meet."

"Indeed."

In many ways the scene before him was a long way removed from the nightclub, Bubbles, yet Philip couldn't help but draw a few comparisons – the energy, the vibrancy, the sense of something going on that was beyond normal constraint, these all struck him as similar.

They walked forward, coming closer to the fires, and he noticed one thing that was markedly different from the previous evening. At Bubbles, everyone, even the redhead who had flickered constantly between male and female, had been recognisably human – spectacularly so for the most part. Here, humanity wasn't always so obvious. As they reached the first fire a woman turned towards him, and he realised that the hood he had taken to be part of her costume – an extension of the sweeping emerald cloak she wore – was actually part of her head. Her face was covered in green scales. Seeing him stare, she opened her mouth and flicked out a long, thin tongue at him. Philip shied away. The snake woman's voluptuous companion opened her mouth to reveal well developed canines and laughed. She had the head of a tabby cat.

"Don't stare," Malcolm said, "or you're liable to offend somebody."

"I wouldn't have stared in the first place if you'd warned me."

As they walked past, Philip heard the two women exchange quick-fire comments in a language he recognised but couldn't speak – Sawal, a derivative of ancient Swahili, a minority language spoken in a few regions of Home. It was a timely reminder that Virtuality was a worldwide phenomenon, accessible to people from around the globe. He might not have understood the meaning of individual words, but the laughter that punctuated their comments left him in little doubt that the two women were enjoying themselves at his expense.

The further he and Malcolm went, the more bizarre and random the appearance of those around them became. Not everyone was outlandish; there were still some who had opted to appear completely human, but they were in the minority.

Philip saw werewolves, dragon ladies, a man whose face was invisible apart from his eyes, which hovered disconcertingly above a vacant collar, an ape-man, a figure of mist, a rubber-jointed woman who showed off by bending over backwards to bring her shoulders and head between her own splayed legs before turning to lick her own navel, a fully mobile statue cut from multi-faceted diamond, an iron man, a bronze woman, a trio of lizard people, a pair of centaurs, and a variety of imaginative and exotically realised bug-eyed alien caricatures. In some ways the scene reminded him of his visit to the Death Wish, but the more he thought about it the less the comparison satisfied. There the patrons had worn outlandish faces as a disguise, whereas here he sensed that people had designed theirs as a release, as if seeking to let an element of their inner selves out to breathe.

On the whole he was surrounded by unique avatars – individuals or, at most, pairs – but here and there knots of similarly styled folk had gathered together, forming gangs or small tribes. Around the burning car, for example, cavorted a group of cloven-hoofed fauns and human-toed satyrs. On the wall of the building behind them someone had daubed 'Faunication 4 Ever!' in stark black lettering. Philip wondered if this graffiti was set to be erased once the night's revelries came to an end or whether it would remain permanently as a rallying cry, something to mark the regular meeting point for these Pan-like avatars.

His attention was caught by a man who wandered past, between him and the frolicking fauns. He was juggling six balls in an intricate pattern with consummate ease, no doubt aided by the fact he had two sets of arms, one pair immediately beneath the other. Seeing this made Philip wonder why more people didn't choose to equip their avatars with additional limbs.

The answer occurred to him almost immediately, tripping over the heels of the question. It would be too much like hard work. Avatars were animated by the fully human brain of their corporeal self, and that brain was accustomed to doing things with just one pair of arms. Throw in an additional pair and you had a whole new set of skills to be learnt in the coordination department. Of course, there were always going to be those determined to master such skills simply because the challenge was there, but for the majority life was too short. Why bother going to all that trouble when you could do things the traditional way? It struck Philip that here was an endorsement of Malcolm's philosophy of experience over download. Without a person training their mind to coordinate four arms instead of two, he doubted a simple info-dump of juggling skills would be of much use.

A little further along from the fauns, a man stood with legs apart and right arm raised, in a pose that suggested he was challenging the wall to mortal combat. He sported the head and impressive mane of a male lion and was bare-chested, his torso and arms rippling with muscles and glistening as if oiled. As Philip watched, he roared and took a mighty swipe at the brickwork, utilising the raking claws that sprouted from the ends of his human-looking fingers. The attack left deep gouges in the wall. Presumably this was an attempt to impress the two women standing to one side and looking on. The nearest, who wore only the skimpiest of chocolate brown bikinis, had the head of a leopard, her slim body mottled in an intricate pattern of dark spots over tan-yellow, while the tip of a tail swished behind her heels – the whole ensemble was surprisingly sexy. The other, though fully human in body, boasted a head of flickering flame within which the shadowy suggestion of eyes and a mouth could vaguely be discerned.

"Ah good, we've timed it perfectly," Malcolm murmured. "The first race hasn't started yet."

"Race?"

"Yes, that's what draws the crowds."

His father nodded towards a group of people gathered a little further up the road. The two of them headed over, working their way towards the front of what proved to be a sizable throng. The greatest concentration clustered around what were clearly machines, half a dozen of them. They looked to be motorbikes of some sort, though Philip couldn't get close enough for a proper view.

"Come on, all you freaks and skike-heads," a voice boomed out. "Last chance to splash those credits and watch 'em soar. The road's about to burn!"

Initially Philip thought the speaker was talking through an old-fashioned megaphone, but then he realised that it was actually part of his face, with cheeks, chin and philtrum extending forward in a solid, fused funnel. The man's voice boomed out as if bolstered by the latest in hi-tech amplification. The crowd melted away as people drew back, giving Philip his first clear view of the machines. They *were* like motorbikes, if a little longer and lacking wheels.

"Skycycles, or skikes," Malcolm said.

Six figures stepped forward to take station by their respective machines.

"Give it up, boys and girls, for the jocks with the rocks!" the announcer called.

Each rider was clad from head to toe in glistening, figure-hugging black, as if oil had been poured over them from above. The black was unbroken even by mouth or eyes, apart from a coloured stripe that ran vertically from the crown of the head to the coccyx – gold, silver, red, blue, green and orange. Each rider's stripe matched the colour of the bodywork showing amongst the shining chrome of his or her skike.

People started calling support for this colour and that, or yelling out the names of individual riders. 'Randy' and 'Kensal' seemed the most popular. Philip realised that the drums and guitar had fallen silent for the first time since they arrived.

"Riders, mount!" the starter cried.

The sense of anticipation rose in proportion to the noise level, as the six jet figures slipped aboard their machines, lying forward along the skike's body, knees drawn up beneath the waist and legs extending behind them, hands clutching grips a little below and in advance of the head. The stance brought to mind a person caught in the process of leaping forward from a crouch, perhaps diving into a pool.

"Power up and lift those beauties!"

Fire ignited within the broad burners at the back of each skike, accompanied by the throaty growl of engines. Headlights shone forth from the noses of the six machines, which lifted into the air – a couple wobbling slightly as their riders adjusted position – to hover above the ground at around waist height. The air smelt abruptly of burnt oil, petrol fumes and ozone.

"And... go!"

The engine growl crescendoed to a deafening roar and flames flared from the rear of the six machines as they shot away at breakneck speed, heat washing over the assembled watchers, who shrieked their approval. In no time at all the roar dwindled to a distant buzz and the skikes were mere fiery dots vanishing into the distance along the improbably straight road, like a pack of ground-hugging comets.

Philip felt vaguely disappointed. As a spectacle, this had been impressive enough but much too brief. He'd hoped for more. The experience at Bubbles the previous evening had taught him not to judge events in Virtuality too soon, but so far the street meet struck him as lively up to a point but somewhat on the tame side. He was about to say as much to Malcolm when a 3D image formed in the air above the 'starting line', complete with sound. It showed the skikes racing towards the watcher before passing beneath, the viewpoint swivelling to follow their progress, enabling Philip to catch a bird's eye view of the riders' backs and then watch them shoot into the distance once more. The brief flash of coloured stripes as they tore past below revealed the current state of play.

"As you can see, Blue's forging ahead from the start, inviting the rest to suck his fumes. Green isn't about to take that lying down and is pushing him hard. Gold is boxed in behind them – he won't like that – with Orange to his right and Red on the left. Silver's playing a canny game, lagging behind the others and staying out of trouble. Still everything to play for."

Somebody poked Philip in the side. He looked around to find a pair of striking blue eyes staring at him from beneath a ragged blonde fringe.

"Are you following me?" asked the beautiful girl he'd danced with at Bubbles the previous evening, the same girl he'd watched being sliced apart by flying saws.

"No, I..."

Before he could say anymore, she reached up towards him, hand at the back of his neck, to draw him into a lingering kiss. Her lips were slightly sticky and tasted of strawberries.

"There," she said as they separated. "I wanted to make sure we at least did that much before anything happens to wrench us apart this time. I'm Tanya, by the way."

"Philip," he mumbled, still feeling the stickiness of her lips on his.

For a moment he'd forgotten about the race entirely, until she looked past his shoulder and said, "Who are you backing? My money's on the gold, Kensal – a real maniac. He'll either win or die trying."

"First time here," Philip said quickly, not wanting to look a complete idiot due to his lack of knowledge. "Still finding my feet."

"*Riiight*," she nodded, as if this explained a lot. "So you haven't placed a bet?"

"No." He didn't even know you could.

She laughed. "But that's half the fun. Don't worry, Tanya's here now." She slid her arm through his. He thrilled at her touch, her closeness, and flared his nostrils in anticipation of catching a whiff of her perfume but failed. Perhaps avatars didn't do scent? No, he'd smelt the sweetness of strawberries from her lip gloss. A detail overlooked, then. "We'll make sure you get fully involved before the next race."

Philip wondered what had become of Malcolm. He looked around to see the older man standing a little way off. Malcolm gave his son a knowing grin and winked.

Tanya fidgeted beside him. "First corner," she said, her gaze fixed on the projection.

Sure enough, the pack of skikes could be seen converging on a sharp left-hand turn. The vantage point was much lower this time and seemed to be trackside at the very apex of the corner. Little had changed in positional terms, except that Gold might perhaps have edged a quarter length ahead of Red to his left. If the riders made any concession for the approaching corner by slowing down, it was too marginal for Philip to notice. One, pushing hard – he thought it was Green – almost overshot. His skike skewed across the mouth of the turning sideways, heading for what looked to be certain catastrophe. At the last second, the rider banked his machine, so that whatever kept the skikes off the ground repelled him from the wall. The machine reared spectacularly in the foreground and almost hid the moment when Gold made his move and started to justify Tanya's dramatic build up.

Perspective switched at the vital instant, taking the watching crowd from skike-in-your-face dirtside to a loftier viewpoint once more. Gold cut the corner sharply, throwing his body into a precarious left-lean to drag his skike over. Even so, how he managed so tight a turn at such speed was beyond Philip. It caused Red, who was inside, to swerve, almost hitting the wall, and then to overcompensate, taking the corner far too wide in a repeat of Green's manoeuvre. This time, however, as the rider banked his machine, he overcooked it. The side of his mount scraped along the ground in a blaze of sparks and a screech of protesting metal. The oil-clad figure was thrown free as the skike bucked and cartwheeled. He hit the ground and rolled helplessly over and over as his machine crashed back to the road and disappeared in a spectacular bloom of fire and debris.

The other five racers were long gone by then.

The coverage continued to leapfrog the pack of four skikes as they jockeyed for position – Green now lagging some distance behind the others and unable to make up the deficit – showing them tear into a right-hand turn and then another. As they exited the second, Blue held a marginal lead over Gold.

"Final turn coming up," Tanya squeaked, squeezing his arm. "This is where things usually get *really* exciting."

No sooner had she spoken than Gold dived for the inside line again. He leant so far away from his machine that his back nearly touched the sharp brick corner. His bold attack forced Blue wide. Perhaps distracted by what was happening immediately in front of them, the two skikes at the rear of the group – Silver and Orange – touched, producing a spray of sparks like a saw cutting through metal sheeting. While Silver fought for control, Orange lost it completely, slamming into the wall of the nearest building. Rider and skike disappeared in a billowing fireball. Silver went down an instant later, skidding along the road in a trail of sparks. Something immediately below the projection caught Philip's eye; a blossoming of light as if a distant flare had gone off. He realised this was the explosion that marked Orange's demise, that he could see it with the naked eye. The combatants had returned to the road they'd started from, albeit they were still a long way off.

The calls of support and encouragement that had provided a constant background to the race now grew louder and more persistent, as others realised the skikes were on the home straight. The murmur of the surrounding crowd swelled to become a roar. Philip wasn't looking at the projection anymore. His attention was focused on the twin pinpricks of headlights growing steadily brighter and nearer.

Tanya, her arm still linked in his, was bobbing up and down, fist raised as she cheered Gold home. Her enthusiasm was infectious, and he found himself yelling along with her.

"Stand back, Jack, here comes the pack... and they're comin' in hot!" the announcer declared, his voice struggling to be heard despite the amplification. "Gold has his nose in front but Blue's pressing him hard. Green is still in the air but well out of the reckoning; it's between these two."

"Come on, Gold!" Tanya shrieked.

"Go, Gold... go, Gold... go, Gold..." a chant started up among the crowd.

Now redundant, the projection winked out as the headlights of the two contenders grew rapidly closer, larger, and more immediate.

"Shift your feet to the side of the street, people!" the announcer warned. "They're not stopping to watch you hoppin', it's pass the line in double-quick time, so clear the way or you're done for today!"

The man's slick rhythmic patter sounded as improvised as the construction of your average starship; it had to be scripted, or at least recycled and ingrained after constant repetition.

Nonetheless, feet shuffled in response and people started moving away to either side, clearing the road. Philip and Tanya moved with them and found themselves at the front of the rearranged cordon. Tanya had let go of his arm as they made their way across and was now jumping up and down beside him, clapping her hands and vociferously cheering on her favourite.

A finishing line appeared a little way up the street – a strip of lights embedded in the road, positioned roughly beneath where the projection had been. The thunder of the skikes' engines was now clearly audible even over the crowd noise, swelling until it threatened to drown out the watchers' rowdy excitement altogether. In the final few seconds the racers loomed out of the night with frightening speed – twin rockets with throttles wide open, neither giving any quarter and both hell-bent on crossing the line first.

As the pair shot over the all-important strip of lights they finally eased off, spinning their hurtling skikes around so that they faced back the way they'd come, their powerful engines now fighting against their own momentum.

It was then that disaster struck. One of the riders, Blue, overcooked the swivel, his skike continuing to turn and spin. Completely out of control, it flew at the crowd, heading directly towards where Philip was standing. At least the rider had the sense to cut his engines, but too late to prevent what was about to happen.

A detached part of Philip's mind heard the announcer calling out, "And the winner by half a length is... Gold!" Another registered that the screen had reappeared, to show a replay of the finish. None of him seemed inclined to move. He stood rooted to the spot, watching this increasingly huge machine slew towards him. In those last few seconds everything slowed, so that the skike appeared to be moving in slow motion while the screams of those around him came as if from a long way off. The tail of the skike swept unerringly at him and he knew there was no escape.

Something struck him in the side, hitting hard, knocking the wind from his body and sending him sprawling to the floor. Not the skike, however, which cut through the air an arm's length above his face as time resumed its normal flow. Heat and air washed over him as the machine struck the wall and bounced off, skidding along the pavement and scything down half a dozen bystanders who were too slow to react. The victims vanished, their avatars kicked out of Virtuality.

No, not the skike; a compact bundle of warm flesh and muscle. "Tanya?" She lay on top of him, her face glaring into his.

"Were you ever going to move?" Her expression matched the exasperation in her tone. "Or were you intending to just stand there and let that thing finish you off?"

"I..." Philip had always considered himself to be level headed in a crisis – hadn't he stayed calm and composed when that remote drone came to kill him in his own apartment? This time, though, he'd frozen to the spot. "Sorry." *Why was he apologising?*

She climbed off him and they both got to their feet. Philip found himself confronted by a blonde spitfire, anger still apparent in her face and in every line of her body. "There are no second chances in here you know, not for you. You *have* to start taking this life seriously."

She knew. Her words sent cold horror running through him. Somehow this girl he'd only just met had worked out that he wasn't simply another avatar. No, that was impossible, while her abrupt change from bubbly blonde thrill-seeker to angered professional was merely unlikely.

"Who are you?" he asked, though he already had a pretty good idea.

At which point Malcolm appeared, to pull his son around and hug him. "Philip, I thought I'd lost you again. Are you all right?"

"Yes, I'm fine, though only thanks to Tanya here."

He turned back but she'd gone, using the distraction of Malcolm's arrival to slip away into the milling crowd. That figured, but Philip wasn't concerned. She'd shown her hand and somehow he had a feeling he'd be seeing her again; far sooner than he might wish to.

CHAPTER EIGHT

THE WAY SHE heard it, even finding the habitat had been difficult. These people had very effectively cut themselves off from the rest of humanity and had then done an expert job of erasing their trail, though not quite expert enough. The amount of resources needed to build a place like this had to show up somewhere, and by searching hard enough and far enough back enough the ULAW AIs had identified traces of the habitat's construction and followed the tenuous trail to here. Everyone knew what this was about, although officially no one admitted as much. You couldn't stop rumours any more than you could hide something the size of the habitat from a concerted search. Sheol. Somebody had done the unthinkable and broken out of the notorious prison station that ULAW refused to admit existed. Yes, they'd had help, but even so the feat was impressive.

From what Boulton had been able to gather, there were only two groups reckoned to have the capabilities and the balls to attempt something like this, and favourite was the habitat. The authorities weren't taking any chances, though. Two task forces had been mobilised, set to strike both candidates simultaneously. She took it as a sign of her own personal progress that she'd been given command of the principle action in this one. On the far side of the station a second eyegee, Case, had two squads of marines under his command, tasked with taking control of the ship currently docked at the habitat –

large and of unfamiliar design, clearly a starship – but that was very much a secondary consideration. Hers was the mission that had brought them all here.

Even so, Alaine Boulton still felt she had a point to prove. To herself, to the smug bastard whose bed she'd so unwisely tumbled into one night after a particularly tense mission on a grotty little world called Holt, and maybe even to her ULAW overlords. This assignment was going to run like clockwork, it had to. She was one of the newest of the eyegees and that made her feel she had some catching up to do, particularly with the likes of Jim Leyton, a veritable legend within the whispered world of black ops. A man who owed her, big time.

His presence had haunted and tantalised her from the moment she first joined the service. Rumour of his ingenuity and near-superhuman deeds were everywhere, so she'd been a little in awe of his reputation long before they'd actually met. When ULAW had assigned her to the Holt mission, she could hardly believe her luck, knowing that she would be working alongside this living legend. Yet he'd all but dismissed her at first and then continually accused her of incompetence during the mission itself. He had humiliated her. Afterwards she'd sought him out, determined to tell him what a disappointment and a complete arsehole he was, and to convince him that she hadn't screwed up at all. Instead, he'd seduced her and used her body mercilessly. She'd left his room battered and bruised, feeling violated and more like the survivor of a vicious fight than a departing lover. The message she'd left about Mya – a woman she barely knew – had been a cheap shot, but the very least he deserved.

Now she learned that Leyton had gone rogue and was rumoured to have led the raid on Sheol. There was even talk that a guard had been killed. First this man she idolised had humiliated her, then he'd used her like some sexual object and now he'd betrayed everything she held dear. No question, Jim Leyton was going to pay.

Ian Whates

The mission briefing had been thorough, if a little hurried. There was a sense of urgency about the whole business. ULAW were hell bent on striking back swiftly and effectively, which suited Boulton fine. She was itching to get going. The habitat's carefully constructed isolation was about to be shattered once and for all.

"All units have confirmed they're in position," the marine sergeant beside her reported.

She nodded acknowledgement.

"No alarms have sounded," the measured voice of her gun spoke inside her head. "No one in the habitat is yet aware of our presence."

Perfect. "Engage," she ordered.

"Go," the marine sergeant said immediately. "All units go."

The airlock door in front of them sprung open and they poured through. Behind them, their own craft remained attached to the airlock, creating a seal against decompression now that both the lock's doors were open, their safety restrictions having been overridden. At all of the habitat's six main access points she knew the scene was being repeated. Heavily armed and armoured marines would be sweeping through the installation. No shimmer suits; the idea wasn't to sneak in this time around, but to intimidate, to overwhelm, to cow the population into submission.

Somebody screamed – a woman – clearly shocked by the sudden appearance of invaders. A young boy cried, clinging to his mother's legs. The screaming woman was useless, likewise the elderly man busy trying to comfort her. The mother of the small boy was too preoccupied and would only slow them down. Boulton ignored them and trotted past, into the habitat, a phalanx of marines surrounding her. Ahead of her, two dark figures crouched by the next corner, weapons levelled, ensuring the way was clear, although the gun would have warned her of anything threatening. Her visor remained blank, presumably an indication that the gun hadn't yet managed to fully penetrate the habitat's systems. Alarms were sounding now. Boulton would have been worried if they hadn't been at this point. Two more marines hurried past to secure the next junction.

"Turn right at the next corridor," the gun advised. "One lone male ten metres along; unarmed."

"Heading away or towards us?"

"Neither. He was coming this way but has stopped at the sound of our approach."

An orange dot appeared in her visor. At last. Boulton sprinted, reaching the corner at almost the same time as the two marines, much to their alarm.

"You!" She turned the corner and entered the next corridor with gun drawn, levelled at the young man, who was in the process of turning to run away. "Stop if you want to live." He froze in mid-step, adopting an almost comical pose.

She hadn't known what to expect from the habitat. Knowledge of its interior was almost non-existent, no schematics or plans had been uncovered and they hadn't wanted to probe too deeply during approach for fear of giving themselves away. So, initially at least, this would have to be played by ear.

"Sensible lad. What's your name?"

"Jason, ma'am."

Ma'am? So polite, even to an invader. "Now, Jason, I need to talk to whoever runs your community so that everything can be sorted out quickly. Would you mind leading us to your command centre?"

He looked to be no more than twenty, possibly less. The people here were so pale skinned, like ghouls, it made them seem younger somehow.

"Of course," she continued, "if you don't help us, I'll have no choice but to shoot you. Understood?"

His eyes widened and he nodded repeatedly.

"Good, and no heroics. I'll know if you mislead us."

He led them off at a brisk walk.

"Can you manage a jog, Jason? We're in a bit of a hurry."

He picked up the pace accordingly.

Whatever Boulton might have anticipated – perhaps dark corridors bored into bare rock, a community of mine shafts – the reality came as a surprise. The habitat was an enclosed environment. Too distant from their system's sun to reap any great benefit from its radiation, they had burrowed downward into the rock of the worldlet they claimed as home. Yet the corridors were wide, bright and clean, gravity was consistent and roughly Earth-normal – perhaps a smidgeon less but close enough. The whole place felt... *pleasant*.

One thing she had expected was a little more resistance. They'd ghosted into the system with their ships cloaked, slipping past a sophisticated network of sensors and automated defence platforms. ULAW had apparently stolen a march on both the Byrzaens and the habitat when it came to cloaking technology. After seeing such an obvious willingness to defend their home, she was vaguely disappointed not to have met with a little more spirit here. True, they'd taken the habitat by surprise, but you'd have thought somebody, somewhere might have grabbed a gun and at least attempted to fight back. Perhaps the populace were simply bowing to the inevitable and didn't want to throw away their lives in futile defiance.

Now that Boulton's task force had declared itself, they didn't need to be so coy about probing and systems hi-jacking.

"The command centre has been located," the gun reported.

"And you can lead us there?"

"Yes."

"Excellent." Without breaking stride she raised the weapon and shot their co-opted guide in the back of the head. Jason's head jerked forward, gouting blood and brains, and the rest of his body followed, collapsing to the floor. The sound of the gunshot echoed around the corridors. Good. Let people hear that and panic. It was all too quiet and orderly around here. She hurdled the body and continued, two marines coming forward to trot ahead once more, now that she'd lost her human shield.

"Door to the left, three people: man, woman and young female. No weapons," the gun told her, keeping up a constant stream of information as she jogged down another long, straight corridor. Orange dots appeared and slid past on her visor as they progressed.

"We've seized control of the habitat's operating systems. Doors to all residential units have been sealed shut."

Better and better. This should ensure there were even fewer people to get in the way.

Four staccato bangs sounded from somewhere over to their left, like a hammer repeatedly striking a nail. Gunshots. At last, somebody was showing a bit of spirit.

"Report," she intoned.

"A lone male with antiquated projectile handgun," the gun's calm voice responded. "One marine slightly injured. The gunman fled before the marines could return substantial fire."

Again, no bad thing. It would remind the troops not to take anything for granted.

"Turn left at the next corridor."

Boulton noticed that as well as boasting 'street names' – she was currently in Chandler's Walk and about to turn into Barrington Boulevard – the corridors were all colour coded. Narrow strips ran along the length of one wall close to the ceiling, on her right in this direction. Yellow marked their course through the last two turns. Whatever these habitat folk might be, they seemed well organised. One thing struck her; so far all they'd seen were uniformly bright, antiseptic thoroughfares like this. No sign of industry or manufacture. Was the whole habitat the same? "What do these people eat?" she wondered.

"Food," the gun supplied, helpfully. "Second level down is agricultural: hydroponics, high-protein fungus, arable crops and also some livestock. They appear to be self-sufficient."

She'd intended the question to be rhetorical, but it was interesting information anyway.

"Next right, then it's straight ahead, all the way to the hub."

"That's what they call their command centre?"

"The seat of government, yes."

She stopped at the next junction. This corridor seemed marginally wider than most and stretched to a distant wall on her left and an even more distant one to the right. The street name read: 'Spoke 1: Anderson's Way.' The whole place was laid out as a wheel, she realised, with central spokes leading to the hub.

"Schematic." The gun ought to be in a position to produce one now that it had infiltrated the local systems and established sufficient control to seal living quarters' doors.

An image duly appeared in the left upper side of her visor, showing a ragged ovoid, with six straight paths converging on a central hub with a jumbled network of interlinking corridors in between. Why the whole place hadn't been laid out more formally, in radiating rings or some such, was beyond her. Presumably it said something about these people.

"Direct all units to the spokes," she intoned.

"Done," the gun confirmed.

They hadn't encountered anyone in a while but Boulton could see a few figures running away from them in the distance, straight along the 'spoke' and towards the centre. Doubtless they were following standing instructions in the event of attack – make for the hub. Sensible, and it also made her job a good deal easier if everybody not already sealed in their quarters gathered in one place.

Boulton strode down the corridor in the wake of those fleeing – no point in running now that they could see their goal – her phalanx of marines keeping pace. They were sitting targets if the hub had anything worthwhile to throw at them, but she was counting on the gun to provide warning. In the meantime, their approach, their very attitude, was a blatant challenge, inviting attack, daring the habitat to unleash their worst. Boulton had complete confidence in her position and would actually welcome some genuine resistance.

The corridor echoed to the relentless tramp of booted feet. The scampering civilians had disappeared, having presumably arrived at wherever they were going, which left their party the spoke's only occupants. The end of the long stretch of bare passageway drew rapidly nearer.

"ULAW forces stand down." The voice, a woman's, seemed to come from nowhere and emanate from everywhere. "Your aggressive incursion is illegal."

At last, an official response. Boulton didn't deign to answer. She didn't see any point in doing so. She hadn't come here to debate the rights and wrongs of the situation.

"Concealed automatic weapon placements either side of the corridor," the gun informed her. Two wall panels, not directly opposite each other but diagonally staggered, lit up in red on her visor.

"Are they active?"

"Negative. I'm blocking their operation."

No point in worrying about them then. She strode past.

Seconds later the gun spoke again. "Automatic weapons placements have become active."

"What?"

The wall panels sprung open and energy cannons began firing immediately, tearing into the startled marines. Boulton threw herself to the floor, landing on her right shoulder, the gun already trained on the placement in the opposite wall behind her. A single cannon swivelled in its mounting, spitting death as it sought fresh targets. All was chaos: shouting, screaming, the rattle of gunfire. Several soldiers were down. Others were kneeling or prone, attempting to return fire. Bullets ricocheted off the cowlings protecting the weapons and she saw at least one man go down under what was referred to with such misleading coziness as 'friendly fire.' Boulton squeezed off a couple of rounds, realising belatedly that the gun was still set to projectile. "Energy!" She fired again, seeing her beam absorbed by the placement's armour, a broad patch of which bubbled and melted and dribbled down the plating like tears of liquid metal, but she wasn't penetrating as far as the weapon itself.

She rolled over and sat up, her back against the wall. This gave her a much clearer view of the cannon; it also put her directly in the weapon's line of fire should it turn her way, but no helping that. She took careful aim and squeezed, this time striking the barrel of the gun itself. It exploded. Her visor darkened instantly, protecting her eyes from the glare. The marines had succeeded in taking out the other placement, which led to an abrupt silence. After the violent cacophony, it seemed almost unnatural. The rattle of gunfire in the near distance brought the world back into focus and also told her that they weren't the only group subject to an ambush.

"I thought you'd taken control of their systems."

"I have," the gun replied. "Clearly there are overrides or perhaps even surrogate systems I've yet to identify."

"Clearly. Give me a status report."

"Simultaneous ambushes in three of the other spokes. Our forces in the remaining two are lagging slightly behind and haven't reached the corresponding positions yet, otherwise it seems likely the pattern would have repeated there as well. The two section leaders have been advised and are in the process of neutralising the placements in their respective corridors."

Judging by the cessation of gunfire, Boulton assumed the nearby skirmish had ended. She looked around at the order emerging from carnage as the marines regrouped. Four dead, three others too badly injured to continue, leaving her with the sergeant and a dozen men. There was still a fair length of corridor to go.

"Gun, I don't want any more surprises."

"There won't be. I'm consolidating my control all the time."

"Total number of casualties?" The other sections didn't have an eyegee with them.

"Including this platoon, twenty-four dead, thirteen incapacitated."

Which accounted for thirty-seven from her original force of a hundred and twenty – thirty per cent casualties after just one phase of skirmishes. There'd better not be any more like this.

"Patch me through to Case." The background noise told her that the gun had complied. "Case, what's your situation?"

"We're coming under sustained heavy fire," her fellow eyegee replied in his nasal, high-pitched voice "Nothing we can't handle. You?"

"We've just had our noses blooded. I'm about to begin final assault on their command centre."

"Happy hunting."

If the habitat had any further ambushes planned the gun's control forestalled them. Boulton and her party arrived at the end of the spoke without further incident. Ahead of them a curved passageway branched to the right and left, forming a circular corridor around the hub itself, which Boulton's visor showed to contain a sizeable group of people.

She didn't hesitate, but led the marines to the left, towards the nearest of the two opposing doorways opening into the hub. The door itself faced another of the six spokes, and as they approached they were met by a squad of around ten marines coming up that corridor.

The doors – larger if no more ornate than any others she'd seen here – were shut but proved not to be locked. At her signal, a pair of marines flung them open and the armoured troops poured in, guns at the ready and shouting orders, demanding that weapons be dropped and arms raised. A few disgruntled complaints greeted them but no resistance. Some of those in the vast auditorium – a good hundred or more – were armed, but all dropped their guns as instructed. A bit of an anti-climax, all in all, but at least it meant that they wouldn't be losing any more troops.

Boulton assessed the throng. The majority were standing, although a few had taken advantage of the seats ringing the auditorium. Most present were elderly, certainly more than she would expect if this were a cross-section of any sustainable society.

"Gun, excluding our own personnel, how many people are inside the habitat at present?"

"Four hundred and eighty seven."

"Would you say this place was designed for a larger populace?"

"Most certainly. Indications are that there were well in excess of two thousand here in the recent past."

"Where are they now?"

"Uncertain. Records have been doctored, information erased."

All well and good, but someone here would know. Boulton strode forward, onto a floor bearing an emblem she'd never expected to see outside of historical records – the sunburst and twinned planets of the Allied Worlds. Was that what the habitat were – a lingering afterthought of a war long settled? Surely there must be more to them than that.

As she stepped forward, Boulton kept an eye on her visor display. It showed a single smudge of red.

"Narrow focus," she intoned. The section of the throng she was gazing at jumped into higher definition, becoming individual dots, one of which shone red. Boulton snapped the gun up and found herself staring at a tall, elderly man standing towards the front of the gathering.

"You," she barked, "drop the weapon. I won't ask a second time."

"Do as she says, Art," a woman's voice said, managing to sound both reproachful and indulgent at the same time.

The man looked sideways towards the speaker, shrugged and pulled out a surprisingly pristine looking gun, which he tossed onto the floor between the marines and Boulton.

Only then did she switch her attention to the woman who had spoken. Tall, middle-aged, hair swept back from a face that glowed with an inherent beauty Boulton could only envy. "Are you in charge? Do you speak for these people?"

"We all speak for ourselves in the habitat, but yes, you might as well address me. Perhaps you could start by explaining the reason for this unlawful invasion of our home."

A number of responses flashed through Boulton's mind. She wanted to remember this woman, remember the tone that fell just short of patronising and a long way short of deferential. She would compare it to the tone the woman adopted *after* she had suffered Boulton's response.

"And your name would be?"

She smiled. "Kethi."

Kethi? That wasn't a name... unless...

Boulton stared at the woman, concluding that an example needed to be set. After all, that smile was just begging to be wiped away.

If anything was likely to provoke a reaction from this docile populace, this ought to. She took a step towards Kethi, who stared back at her, unflinching and apparently unconcerned, though she must have had at least an inkling of what was to come.

As Boulton adjusted her grip on the gun, the floor beneath her feet shuddered. This was no gentle vibration, such as you might feel when an engine started up, but something far more profound.

"Gun?"

"Checking."

People were restless; murmurs spread through the gathered locals. Clearly they were as surprised by this as she was. Well, she'd wanted to provoke a reaction.... There came a distant boom, a deep, sonorous sound that surely couldn't herald anything good.

"*Gun*?" Clearly something was up and the situation called for a reaction, but first she needed to know what to react to.

"The docked vessel has exploded, apparently an act of deliberate self-destruction," the gun finally explained.

"Case and his marines?"

"Dead, most likely. The explosion has ripped away a large section of the habitat. I suggest you hold onto something."

"Anchor yourselves!" That yell came from the marine sergeant, echoing the gun.

"Shit!" Boulton heard the rush of escaping air at the same instant and imagined she could already feel the tug of decompression. She twisted and lunged for the nearest wall, stretching out with her hands and feeling her fingers brush against it, which was all she needed. Instantly she activated the glove's smart skin, so that it melded with the substance of the wall itself. With her other hand she sealed the hood of her shimmer suit, before fastening her second hand beside the first.

"Trigger the retrieval beacon."

"Already done," the gun's dispassionate voice assured her. "Drones have been dispatched. I suggest you cease speaking. The air trapped within your suit is limited, and there's no guarantee that rescue can be effected in time."

If that was the AI attempting to calm her down so that she minimized use of her precious oxygen, it struck her as somewhat counterproductive.

Decompression hit and her entire body was yanked violently to one side.

She imagined this was akin to being caught in a tornado amplified to the nth degree. It felt as if the whole of existence wanted to move in the same direction, dragging the air with it. Her body stretched out, every sinew and joint complaining, her hands the only things keeping her in place. She cut the coms within her helmet, to distance the sounds of screaming. People were flying past her – a pair of marines, then a child, then a deluge of human forms, men and women in both military garb and civilian, many of their faces contorted in horror, as they clawed for non-existent purchase, all knowing that in seconds they would be dead. There were so many that they threatened to plug the door leading to the spokes, though without ever quite doing so. Nor was it just people. Anything not firmly fixed in place was plucked up and sucked towards the exit – chairs, tables, displays that had been wrenched from the walls; they all went tumbling past. She was off to one side and most things missed her by some distance, but not all. She watched dispassionately as an elderly woman brushed by her on the way to dying, and then someone, one of the habitat, tried to cling to her arm – grim-faced, desperate. His eyes sought hers and pleaded for help, for life, yet she could see in their depths that he already knew his own doom. Boulton shook the man off and struggled to bring her feet up, fighting against the inexorable draw of the escaping atmosphere. Finally she was able to bring one foot kicking against the same wall she clung to. The smart skin coating bit instantly into the wall and provided her with a third anchor point.

Through her hands and feet she felt a rumbling, a violent shaking that seemed more than even the venting atmosphere could account for. Dull thuds reverberated through the walls. Explosions, unless she missed her bet. They seemed to be growing closer and more extreme, shaking her whole body where she clung to the wall. Gravity had gone with the atmosphere, she suddenly realised. She'd been so wrapped up in hanging on and avoiding the passing soon-to-be-dead people that she hadn't even noticed its demise.

"The vessel's destruction appears to have set off a chain reaction," the gun calmly informed her, as if passing comment on an insignificant detail. "The whole habitat is coming apart."

Was it just her or were things getting hotter? Sweat trickled down her cheek. No, definitely warming up, which she suspected wasn't a good sign. Although whether this was due to her suit malfunctioning or her body, she couldn't begin to guess. At least the incessant tug of escaping air had ceased and no more bodies hurtled past her. The atmosphere had bled away.

"Gun, where's that retrieval?" If there was a risk in speaking, she didn't care anymore – she was desperate.

"Retrieval drones are almost here. They're currently negotiating the fringes of the habitat."

Thank God. She knew how quickly those things could move. One would reach her in time; it *had* to. Little more than mobile life support units, the coffin-like drones were designed for this very purpose: to snatch survivors from space following a disaster and ensure they *stayed* survivors.

Further rumblings shook her. Cracks started to appear in the walls. Great chunks of masonry drifted away from each other. They didn't fall, not in zero gravity. She was alone in a vast chamber which was steadily breaking apart.

"...although the drones' progress is not being helped by the habitat's fragmentation," the gun added, helpful as ever.

Shimmer suits weren't space suits. Hers had been designed with survival in mind, but Boulton had no idea how long the garment would hold its integrity in vacuum, nor how much oxygen had been trapped inside when she sealed it. Best guess: not long and not much. She could probably have asked the gun for more specific answers but she chose not to, her prospects were depressing enough for now.

She freed one hand and, without ever rising from a crouch, used it to gently ward off objects that threatened to come too close. Funny but, having accepted that the habitat itself was coming apart around her, she would have expected something more spectacular, more blatantly cataclysmic. In the event, there were no flames, no violent explosions – of course, vacuum might account for that – instead just a steady disintegration, a drifting apart that struck her as a bizarrely dignified, almost stately process, as if it were choreographed; a ballet of destruction. Something she might actually enjoy were it set to music and she wasn't caught in the middle, attached to a great slab of masonry like an insect stuck to flypaper.

Breathing was getting increasingly difficult. She felt lightheaded and her face continued to feel hotter, although, conversely, her limbs were now feeling cold. She was panting, as her lungs sieved the air for oxygen. She was dead. Her mind knew it, only her body refused to accept the inevitable and lie down, though biological process would soon put an end to such stubbornness. It was getting so hard to think, to concentrate. She felt tired, bone weary. The end would almost come as a relief.

Something nudged at her – part of the disintegrating habitat, no doubt. Then she felt herself grabbed and tugged. She turned her head to see what was happening, but doing so sent everything spinning. The drone, she realised. There was something she had to do... yes, of course, lift her feet and her still fastened hand – the drone couldn't accommodate her *and* the chunk of wall she was stuck to. Yet it all required so much effort and the world had already started to close in as consciousness faded. She tried, oh how she tried, but was left with no idea of whether or not she succeeded as perception slipped away completely.

CHAPTER NINE

"The habitat was founded by a man called William Anderson," Leyton told Mya. "Anderson seems to have been a big noise among the Allied Worlds during the early years of the War – an industrialist with his finger in many pies. One of his businesses dabbled in exploration and finding new worlds, new resources. It was a survey ship belonging to this company which stumbled on something unexpected in a supposedly virgin corner of the galaxy. A derelict alien space ship."

"You're kidding."

"No." He stared at Mya, a little surprised she'd even say that. She knew him better. "By all accounts, it was a Byrzaen ship."

"Fuck me! Does ULAW know about this?"

"Nope. Being a businessman, Anderson saw a chance of massive profits, so he kept the discovery to himself, put a lid on the whole matter, doubtless with ruthless application when required. You have to remember, too, that this all happened when the War was becoming increasingly intense and paranoia was rife. The last thing Anderson would have wanted was word of the derelict reaching the enemy.

"So he set about quietly recruiting scientists and spiriting them away to examine his treasure. After a while, though, the implications must have got him worried, because he began talking to politicians, urging them to seek peace with the United League of Allied Worlds as soon as possible, believing there to be a far greater threat waiting in the wings.

"He might have done a great job of keeping the derelict out of the news, but word of his political entreaties *did* get out, and you can imagine what the press would have done to someone whispering such treasonous, lily-livered suggestions when every self-respecting soul was howling for blood. They crucified him. Anderson found himself vilified and ridiculed, dubbed as everything from a naïve idealist to a traitor.

"His response was to build the habitat and withdraw to it, taking with him some of the best minds of the day and enough people to establish a viable community. They cut themselves off from the rest of humanity and went on their merry way, all but forgotten about."

"Until now."

"Precisely."

"And this ship, *The Rebellion*..."

"...is a marvel, drawing on both human and Byrzaen technology."

Leyton was glad of this opportunity to chat to Mya, delighted that she'd sought him out when she had questions that needed answering. The ship's database could probably have told her all of this in any case, which made him suspect that she needed the company as much as the information. His own knowledge of the habitat and its history had been gleaned largely from what Kethi told him during similar conversations, supplemented by what he'd discovered for himself.

Leyton didn't feel in any sense that Mya was avoiding him, but he'd seen less of her in the past few days than he'd have liked, less than he felt he would have done had she retained any real desire to pick up where they'd left off. He knew better than to crowd her and had done his best to give her space, throwing himself into his gym regime and even going to watch Kethi and others play z-ball a couple of times, despite having no great love for the sport. The presence of a z-ball court on what amounted to a military vessel struck him as a hell of an indulgence. Certainly you wouldn't have found anything like this on a ULAW fighting ship, or *any* vessel short of a luxury liner. Further proof, were it needed, of the differences between the habitat and the society he was used to.

"But what are they hoping to achieve by all this?" Mya asked.

"Ah, now there's a question. The habitat has been waiting for the Byrzaens to arrive, expecting to be at the vanguard of humanity's struggle against the alien aggressors."

"Are you serious?"

"*They* certainly are. It's what the whole culture's geared towards. Now that the Byrzaens are actually here and the anticipated conflict hasn't arisen, I think they're struggling a bit. The current game plan seems to be to unveil the Byrzaens as wolves in sheep's clothing, to reveal them as being far less benign than they're pretending."

She thought about that. "And do they have any real basis for that?"

"Not much," he admitted. "Prejudice mainly, as far as I can tell; but, having said that, I happen to believe they might just be right."

"More by luck than judgement, you mean."

Leyton grinned. "Let's just say good instincts."

"Okay, I'm willing to accept that *you* haven't succumbed to an outbreak of irrationality. What makes you suspicious?"

"Lots of things. Little things that come together in the shape of a big question mark. You and I have both seen enough ULAW spin-doctoring to recognise the signs, and this whole situation is being spun, big time. Not just PR-spin but covering-up-the-cracks spin. You heard about what went down at New Paris?"

She nodded.

"I was there. Trust me, something wasn't right about the whole set up."

"Are you saying you think the Byrzaen's appearance was stage managed?"

"Possibly. Hell of a coincidence the way they showed up out of nowhere just in the nick of time to save the day. Then there's the fact that Benson was put in charge of operations on New Paris. I mean, *Benson*, head of ULAW's black-ops, managing humankind's first contact with another species. *Why*?"

"Yeah, when you put it like that..."

"You know there are even rumours that the energy blast which wrecked the station's orbit wasn't a stray shot from the battle at all but a carefully aimed beam from *The Noise Within*?"

"Causing the problem which the Byrzaens then arrived to solve," Mya said, nodding slowly. "No, I hadn't heard that."

"And before you say it, yes, I'm sure there's enough telemetry to reconstruct the battle and trace the course of the stray beam, but if ULAW have ever troubled to do so, they haven't chosen to share their findings." He realised he was in danger of sounding fanatical, so consciously relaxed and grinned. "Don't you just love a good conspiracy theory?"

"Always." She smiled in response. "So, you've thrown in your lot with this habitat, then?"

His smile slipped away. "It... seemed like a good idea at the time." *To rescue you*, he thought but didn't say.

"I'm glad you did," she said quietly, evidently hearing the unspoken words in any case.

For now Mya seemed content to settle in with her new benefactors, the habitat, but Leyton knew her too well. Before long she'd grow restless and want answers, not to mention revenge. He was happy enough to wait until she felt sufficiently recovered to strike back at those who had imprisoned and tortured her. When she did, he'd be there at her side.

As for the habitat, at that moment gathering information seemed to be their priority. *The Rebellion* hopped from one pick up point to another, collecting parcels of data which Kethi devoured relentlessly. She wasn't the only analyst – there was a man called Morkel whose status Leyton wasn't entirely sure of, except that he didn't seem to like Kethi much – but she was the one Nyles listened to.

As something of an outsider, Leyton was able to observe all this and do some analysing of his own. There seemed to him an air of desperation about the whole process, hence his comments to Mya. He had a feeling that now the habitat had secured the services of one former eyegee and the freedom of another, they weren't too sure what to do with them. To justify all the planning and preparation they'd made for this moment, it would need to be something significant, or at least effective. They didn't need him to tell them that. The pressure on Kethi to come up with something was enormous, and a symptom of that was that she was spending less and less time at the z-ball courts or anywhere other than her work station.

Funny how often invention can spring phoenix-like from the ashes of adversity. Leyton had seen it more than once – a spark of inspiration flaring to life when spirits were at their lowest ebb. Just as well, since the crew of *The Rebellion* were about to suffer a hammer blow.

The Rebellion rendezvoused with another habitat vessel, *The Retribution*. The event instantly cheered up everyone on board and a welcome committee was quickly assembled, Mya and Leyton included. He'd never seen the habitat personnel in such high spirits. After so much time spent away from home, the prospect of catching up with friends and fellows must have seemed like a holiday. The sister ship's skipper, Captain Forster, came aboard with two adjutants. Tall, middle-aged, silver-haired, albeit with salt-and-pepper eyebrows, and stick rigid in both deportment and attitude, Forster struck Leyton as a military man through and through. Leyton couldn't be certain if his unyielding demeanour was due solely to the news the man carried, but he thought otherwise, suspecting that Captain Forster's character leant itself to that sort of thing in any case. Certainly he glared at the two former eyegees with mistrust bordering on hostility, clearly considering them vipers in *The Rebellion*'s bosom.

"The habitat's gone," he stated without preamble.

The smiles of greeting, of joy at seeing friends and fellows, died on the faces of the welcome party.

"Go on," Nyles said, sober and all business.

"ULAW attacked with a sizeable task force. Their ships were cloaked, evading our orbital defences. They sent in marines to take control of both the habitat and *The Renaissance*, then at dock. We believe Captain Gibson may have triggered the self destruct in both his ship and the habitat itself to prevent knowledge of our technology from falling into ULAW hands."

This news was greeted by a collective gasp from several, including Kethi, who looked stunned and lifted a hand to cover her mouth.

"Survivors?" Nyles asked.

"None that we're aware of."

"My aunt...?" Kethi's voice sounded small, strained.

"I'm sorry. The older Kethi was among those left to govern those few who remained at home. She was there at the end."

Kethi closed her eyes, tears gathering at their corners. Simon, never far away, put a comforting arm – his good one – around her shoulders and she leant into him. Leyton wasn't sure how he felt on seeing that. He turned his attention back to the ongoing conversation.

"Total number of casualties?" Nyles asked.

"We estimate around five hundred souls. Far Flung will have a more accurate count."

Nyles nodded.

Forster continued, still talking without any hint of emotion. "As the habitat died it squirted off a tight beam data package which ULAW failed to intercept in the confusion. For whatever it's worth, we believe government casualties were as comprehensive as ours. We also have some footage of the woman who led the attack... if I may?"

Nyles nodded assent. Forster's aide stepped forward, fiddling with something at his wrist that looked suspiciously like a wric. An image formed in the air. Leyton recognised the black cladding and armour of ULAW marines and, at the forefront, the unmistakable figure of an eyegee.

Breath hissed between his teeth as the facial features registered even through her visor. "Boulton!"

Nyles's head swivelled towards him. "You know this woman?"

"Oh yes, I know her all right." Not that he had the slightest intention of elaborating on exactly how well he knew her. Not now, not anytime, and especially not in front of Mya. "She's an eyegee, though God knows why."

PHILIP HAD DEVOTED his life to Kaufman Industries and was still having a few issues with accepting that he was no longer the company's CEO. Perhaps that went some way to explaining why this was the first time he'd been back to his successor's office since she so generously offered him a salaried position as a consultant; generous not because he wasn't worth the money but because, as yet, Catherine hadn't bothered to utilise him at all.

The thought that he and Malcolm must appear to her in much the same fashion that his own partial, Phil, had appeared to him in the past – a 3D image hovering somewhere towards the centre of the room – didn't help either. Most of the time he'd never even bothered ensuring Phil's feet touched the carpet. A trivial detail, one which hadn't seemed important then. It did now, but he dismissed the thought and concentrated on the purpose of the visit: Tanya.

"Why would you think I'd need a bodyguard, Catherine? What aren't you telling me?"

KI's longest serving director pursed her lips and studied him, no doubt weighing up how much to reveal. "Nothing sinister, I promise you. I would happily have shared all this before but thought you probably had enough to cope with simply coming to terms with your new status. I couldn't see anything to be gained by troubling you with additional concerns."

"*What* additional concerns?"

Again she took her time before replying, "It's probably nothing, but... Julia Cirese, the woman who killed you..."

Philip knew full well who she was. "What about her?"

"I don't suppose you ever bothered checking into her background?"

"No, why would I?" A contract had been issued against him; Julia had seen it posted in the Death Wish and had taken up the invitation. Eventually, on the space station called New Paris, she had succeeded in killing him. What else did he need to know? If the murderous bitch had suffered an unhappy childhood or been forced into a career as a hired killer by cruel misfortune, what did he care? *She'd killed him!*

"That's what I thought. Well I did – check up on her, I mean. Call me a pedantic old cynic, but I couldn't understand why she'd bothered to pursue you halfway across the galaxy like that, especially after the death wish had been lifted, or how she found you so quickly for that matter. So I did a little digging. Turns out she *was* a journalist just as she claimed, although clearly she was a good deal more than that as well. However, it seems Ms Cirese was posted to Home only a week before your Gügenhall lecture. We've cracked Universal News's systems and accessed her data records. What we found there was interesting. Julia Cirese began gathering information on you – your habits, preferences, and movements – from the moment she first arrived on Home."

"In other words she started researching me a week before the contract at the Death Wish was posted."

"Exactly."

"This doesn't prove anything. Julia was writing a piece on me and preparing for an interview; naturally she'd do some research."

"Except that the piece in question never really existed."

"So if the research was all part of her cover, why did she start all before the death wish was even issued?" Philip added.

The implications were unnerving. By the sound of things, Julia Cirese had been preparing to kill him before he'd ever made himself a target.

"It looks to me as if she was sent here specifically to assassinate you, Philip."

He nodded. "The death wish merely provided her with a convenient smokescreen. Which begs two complimentary questions: Who was she working for? And why did whoever it was want me dead?"

"Excellent questions both, neither of which I have an answer to as yet, which is why I assigned Tanya to watch your back. She's a martial arts expert in the real world, an experienced gamer and she's familiar with Virtuality. In addition to that, we've packed her avatar with a host of countermeasures."

"And her avatar was doubtless designed to appeal to my taste."

"We may have tweaked her appearance a little," Catherine conceded, "but the important thing here is that she's fit for purpose." Philip certainly wasn't about to argue with the 'fit' part. "Somebody powerful ordered your death, Philip. There's every chance they might decide to finish the job, even if that means following you into Virtuality. Tanya's there to ensure they don't succeed."

Despite his attempt at outward calm, Philip was shaken to the core. It had never occurred to him that his physical death was anything other than the work of an opportunist seeking to claim the price on his head. Who else could have been behind it? Someone who didn't want the project, the integration of human and AI minds, to succeed? That made no sense. The project was to the benefit of all humankind... unless those responsible didn't want humankind to benefit or to progress. He thought again about the Byrzaen infiltration of Virtuality, but instantly baulked at the thought that the aliens might be behind this. The concept seemed ridiculous to the point of paranoia.

His thoughts flipped back to Tanya. All right, so she was sent to protect him; her popping up in the right place at the right time not once but twice still represented a huge coincidence. Almost as if she knew exactly where to find him, as if Catherine had an accomplice in this little scheme.

He turned to Malcolm. "You were in on this, weren't you?"

Malcolm at least had the decency to look a little embarrassed. "Catherine did share her concerns, yes."

"No wonder Tanya was loitering by the door at Bubbles when we came in and then again at the street meet. You set it all up beforehand!"

Malcolm shrugged. "It was for your own good."

Philip was seething. They'd treated him like a child, both of them. "This stops now. Don't you ever, *ever*, hold out on me like that again, or how am I supposed to trust you?"

"Fair comment. I'm sorry."

Having said his piece, Philip's thoughts turned to recent events, seeing them in a new light. "Is there anything to suggest that what happened at the street meet was specifically targeted at me?"

"No," Catherine replied. "As far as we can tell, that was a genuine accident. A case of being in the wrong place at the wrong time."

"But you can't be certain?"

"Not entirely. Don't worry, we're still looking into it."

"There's no point in wasting Kaufman Industry resources on this..."

Catherine held up a hand, forestalling anything else he might have added. "First off, KI have the resources to spare now that the project's completed and the first needle ship squadron has been handed over to ULAW, and second, this isn't a waste. Stop with the false modesty. You're a valuable resource, Philip, an asset that's well worth our while protecting."

Strange to hear himself spoken about in such terms, but he supposed Catherine had a point.

*　　*　　*

KETHI FELT NUMBED by the news brought by *The Retribution*. Not merely because of her own personal loss, nor even at the thought of so many deaths. The habitat itself was the greatest loss, the only home she and most people aboard had ever known. With the utterance of a single sentence she had been transformed into a refugee; they all had.

Her response was to throw herself into her work in an effort to keep her mind busy. *The Retribution* had delivered several new data packages, collected from the network of beacon drops established by habitat sympathisers within ULAW's ranks. There was a wealth of new information here, which Kethi worked furiously to integrate with what she already had. Perhaps it was this new influx of data, or perhaps the renewed intensity she brought to the job, but she began to get a glimmer of something. There was a pattern here. Kethi could sense its presence even though the components of its design were scattered and buried deep beneath layers of apparently still unconnected data – a web of links so tenuous they barely existed; strands of the finest spider silk all but lost in the cracks between myriad blocks of solid fact and detail.

She continued to race through the accumulated reports, tagging incidents and then compiling a list of names, refining its composition all the while – adding this person but removing that one as more information came to light which perhaps eliminated one prospect by suggesting another. The framework of links Kethi could sense continued to grow. By the time the list numbered sixteen she felt able to take stock, and sensed immediately that there was something wrong. A few of the names didn't quite fit, though she felt certain they belonged to the pattern somewhere.

Tentatively, she drew one name out of the list and then another, moving them to one side, until she had two columns: five in the new list, leaving eleven in the original. Of course, it was obvious now. Two very similar interlinked groups which could easily be mistaken for one. She pushed the smaller list to the right-hand periphery of vision and the larger to the left, before continuing to work her way through the data, occasionally drawing out new names to add to one group or the other.

Finally she was satisfied. There was still some data to analyse, but this gave her more than enough to isolate and identify the nebulous pattern. What Kethi saw horrified her. She blinked, wiping the lenses and returning her awareness outward. Nyles and Leyton were still there, though neither was looking her way just then.

"Nyles," she said.

His head whipped around. "Anything?"

"Yes, and you're going to want to see this, both of you."

Kethi had wondered whether the shock would show on her face. Judging by the looks on theirs, it did.

She might have cleared her lenses, but Kethi possessed eidetic memory and was able to recall the two lists instantly, projecting them onto one of the virtual screens that surrounded the bridge. The longer list now held twenty names, the shorter eight. "Jim, do you recognise any of these?"

Leyton instantly fastened onto one name on the longer list. "Yes, I was with Philip Kaufman when he died, on New Paris... and these three in the smaller group," he highlighted the relevant names in red, "are all members of the eyegee squad."

"Were," Kethi corrected. "The larger group consists of politicians and corporate magnates. I'm pretty certain those in the smaller group are all ULAW operatives – though it's not always so easy to identify those for obvious reasons. Every one of these people has died by presumed accident in most cases, assassination in a couple, all within the last few weeks."

Nyles let out a hiss of breath. "Surely someone else has spotted this."

Kethi shook her head. "Group the names together this way and it looks significant, ominous even, but spread these across all of ULAW space and the result is well within statistical parameters, especially given that most of these are the victims of apparent accidents. No AI's going to pick up on it." She said the last with a degree of pride.

"Well done, Kethi, well done," Nyles said.

"Eyegees don't die easily or often," Leyton added.

"No," Kethi said, "I don't suppose they do."

"What's your reading of this, Kethi?" Nyles asked.

"That's simple. We're seeing here proof of what Mya warned us about. ULAW is in the process of tearing itself apart."

Nyles nodded. "All this at the same time the Byrzaens put in an appearance. It can't be simple coincidence."

"Agreed, and there's more."

"Go on."

"As I sift through the data and reports, one name has cropped up on several occasions, too often to dismiss as coincidence: Pavel Benson."

"The same Pavel Benson who runs the eyegee unit, the one Mya reported to?"

"Yes. He's involved in whatever's going on here, I'm sure of it."

"I *know* Benson," Leyton said. "I can't believe he'd be disloyal to the Union."

"Perhaps he isn't," Nyles replied carefully, as if testing the sound of the words even as he spoke them. "Perhaps it's simply a question of which version of the Union he's loyal to."

"That makes sense," Kethi agreed. "It might not be a matter of trying to bring down ULAW at all but rather a disagreement over which direction the Union should go in."

Leyton indicated the two lists of the dead, which still hovered in the air before them. "That's one hell of a policy dispute."

"People have been killed over a lot less, and I agree the theory has its appeal. It's certainly worth investigating." Nyles appeared to reach a decision. "Kethi, you take command of *The Rebellion* and continue to the next beacon. The more intel we can gather the better. I'll take *The Retribution* to New Paris. We need to confront Benson."

"He's no longer at New Paris," Kethi said. "He's returned to the honeycomb." It was the notorious headquarters of ULAW's intelligence operations.

"Getting in to see him there will be easier said than done," Leyton said, "but I'll go with you to handle that side of things."

"No," said a new voice. "I'll deal with this." Mya entered the bridge. "It's about time I contributed something. Besides which, Benson owes me an explanation or two."

"Very well," Nyles agreed. "We'll divide our forces. Leyton, you stay here with Kethi; Mya, you come with me on *The Retribution*."

Kethi watched Leyton carefully, curious to see his reaction to this enforced separation from the woman they'd all risked so much to rescue and whom he clearly still loved, but the former eyegee simply nodded, as if this were the most natural thing in the world. Privately she wanted to applaud Nyles. Decisive action was exactly what everyone needed. News of the habitat's fate had hit the crew hard. Anticipating the possible loss of their home was one thing, dealing with the fact as reality quite another. People would be looking for a continued purpose and Nyles was giving them just that. Nor was it an empty one – a goal set simply for the sake of having a goal. Kethi felt increasingly certain that Benson would prove the key to their discovering what was going on within ULAW, and that would put them one step closer to learning what part the Byrzaens played in all this.

CHAPTER TEN

JENNER NEITHER KNEW nor cared where the intel had come from. He was just relieved to confirm its accuracy. Finding the buoy had proved a time-consuming process, even though they'd been told where to look. Nothing stayed still out here. Things drifted, orbited, wandered off, so being assured that the object would be orbiting a given planetoid still left a pretty vast haystack in which to find their needle. Particularly when the needle in question was so small and completely dormant, primed to broadcast its location only once invited to do so by the appropriate trigger pulse from an approaching craft.

However, a systematic and meticulous search by nine ships, each housing a human/AI pairing operating in gestalt, eventually tracked down the innocuous-seeming beacon, allowing Jenner to set his trap.

He had at his disposal the bulk of ULAW's first ever needle ship squadron – still the only one of its kind until the Kaufman Industries advisors helped the government train and prepare another batch of pilots. Two of their number had been lost battling *The Noise Within*, while another, Fina, was still recovering from injuries sustained during that encounter, and three more had been co-opted for a separate mission, but that left him with eight ships in addition to his own. Twice as many as he'd commanded when taking down the pirate ship. For back-up, stationed a little further in-system and hidden in the shadow of the nearest planet, he had a ULAW dreadnought to call on. Not that Jenner expected to need it; he was fully confident of success.

He arranged his squadron precisely, so that the ships bracketed the buoy from every angle and were in position to engage an enemy caught between them no matter which way that enemy might turn. Now all they could do was wait.

Not long ago he would have dreaded the thought of such protracted inactivity, but that was before he'd taken a needle ship out for the first time – not in simulation but the real thing. He could never be bored, not now, not when there was so much continually going on in his own ship/body and, more especially, beyond.

As Jenner prepared to relax, he thought of Lara, the fiancée he hadn't seen since training ended, when the needle ship squadron had left Home bound for New Paris. At first their separation had been torture, but he'd been surprised at how quickly he'd adjusted. Not that he didn't miss her, not that he didn't still love her, but those absent pieces of his life were no longer the yearning pain they had been, more of a dull ache, one which gestalt with the ship could soon assuage. Most of the time that struck him as a good thing, since it removed a distraction and enabled him to work all the more efficiently, but on occasion he found this development disturbing and feared the implications, worried that it might mean he was becoming a little less human.

He dismissed such speculation; this wasn't the time. Instead he concentrated on relaxing.

Even in this enlightened age of interstellar travel there were still people who thought of space as being empty, which it isn't, not by a long shot. The interstellar medium is a tenuous but dynamic soup of dust, gasses, magnetic fields, and charged particles, specks of matter created and destroyed in an instant, echoes of cataclysmic events carried by microscopic debris. Jenner allowed his consciousness to be fully immersed within the body of his ship. Time ceased its relevance as he basked in the myriad sensations of the quantum foam that played against his hull – sensations which he knew no human had ever experienced before him. He might have been content to stay there forever if a sudden pulse of concerted energy hadn't drawn his awareness back into sharper focus. The trigger signal.

The beacon came to life, broadcasting its position, and the habitat ship made its approach. Big, that was Jenner's initial reaction; far larger than *The Noise Within*. Her design was unorthodox – bulkier than ULAW vessels, if far more elegant than the Byrzaen-modified pirate ship had been. She reminded him of a gigantic stylised teardrop with an extended, tapering neck, as if a glassblower had fashioned her but then had forgotten to properly crop the end. The position of her weapons placements was also far from obvious, and Jenner didn't want to risk probing for them any deeper for fear of prematurely revealing his presence. He'd simply have to be content with targeting the ship's drive for now. No doubt her armaments would become apparent soon enough, once the shooting started.

The ship stood some way off from the beacon, albeit still within the dispersed cordon of needle ships Jenner had established – merely closer to one edge of it than was ideal. This put his own vessel further away from the target than he'd have liked, but that couldn't be helped. He risked a very low level burst from the manoeuvring thrusters, which were specifically designed for stealth, and started to drift nearer, knowing that others in the squadron would be doing the same. The net was tightening. Presumably, the habitat wouldn't want to linger here. He detected a squirt of energy, very tight beam, projected from the beacon to the waiting ship. That was it, what the habitat were here for. They'd be leaving any moment now... just a little closer; another few seconds and he'd launch the attack.

* * *

"CAPTAIN."

Kethi looked up, still not fully accustomed to being called that. "Yes?" It was Simon who had spoken, from his station monitoring the sensors. She was grateful he'd remembered her rank this time, even though she nearly failed to.

"Nothing, sorry," he said with typical awkwardness. "I thought I saw... but it doesn't matter."

Simon had his faults, not least his forlorn devotion to her, but he wasn't stupid. "Thought you saw what?"

"A faint energy signal, but it was *really* faint, barely even there, and now it's gone completely, so probably no more than ambient..."

"Show me." She hurried over to where he sat staring at the projection hanging in the air in front of his station.

He moved his good hand deftly over the controls and Kethi saw it – a slight blip, too insignificant to be called a spike. But all sorts of energy and particles were floating around out here. She might just have caught a distant echo of a star's death or a planet's birth... or maybe not.

"Weaponry, prepare to bracket these co-ordinates with anything and everything you can bring to bear – a sustained burst in a wide fan. Acknowledge when ready. Helm, I want maximum acceleration on my mark."

There was no reason for them to hang around. The transmitter had sent them the data packages they'd come to retrieve scant seconds before. She hoped to goodness this wasn't what she thought it might be. If not, they'd have wasted a few munitions and everyone could laugh at her jumpiness; if so... embarrassment would be a small price to pay, given the alternative. Kethi remembered all too well what had happened to *The Noise Within.*

"Ready," the gunnery officer confirmed.

No point in delaying. "Fire."

The pulse and other energy weapons produced no recoil, of course, but she fancied she could feel through the soles of her feet the slight vibration of multiple missile launches and rail guns discharging.

All eyes were on the display floating centrally above the bridge, which showed the fan of their munitions spreading outwards from the ship's recently vacated position, a cone of death seeking a target. Nothing as yet, and Kethi dared hope that she'd been wrong and they would all soon be able to relax and laugh about the whole incident.

Five seconds, that was all she felt able to risk, counting them down in her head before calling, "Cease fire. Helm, go! Give me everything."

"Energy signatures," somebody yelled, an instant before the projections showed the same. "Multiple drives, all around us."

Damn! So much for hope. "How many?"

"Nine."

"Contact!" gunnery called out unnecessarily. Everybody could see the bright twinkle of something being hit which the monitors hadn't even known was there brief seconds before. "And another."

Two down, caught within their initial blind blanket burst. That still left seven, which was too many; far too many. "Stations, everyone," Kethi belatedly signalled the rest of the crew. "The ship is under attack."

LEYTON WAS SITTING and nattering with Joss and Wicks in the rec room when the announcement came. He'd been spending quite a bit of his spare time here since the raid on Sheol, almost as if he felt more able to relax once that was out of the way. He'd taken quite a liking to a thick, syrupy fruit drink they served at the bar. Doubtless reconstituted from stored pulps but it still tasted fresh and tangy with citrus and it wasn't too sweet. According to Wicksy the place also served a couple of decent beers but, though Leyton was more than capable of downing a few when in the mood, he'd never especially liked the taste of beer. In his youth he'd drunk because his friends did and because he enjoyed the bonding experience of getting hammered with them, but an implant kindly provided by Aunty ULAW when he'd first been selected for black-ops had put paid to that. It neutralised the alcohol before it had a chance to reach his bloodstream. After years of practice Leyton had imitating drunkenness down to a fine art, but inebriation itself was an escape forever denied him. So he now chose his drinks primarily on the basis of taste rather than their alcohol content, and went for fruit drinks more often than not.

Joss and Wicksy were good company. She had an acerbic wit when the mood took her, while he was a born storyteller who spun a seemingly endless stream of colourful yarns about his exploits both in port and in space. Joss, who presumably had been present for many of them, tended to give him the floor, looking on with a tolerant smile and a twinkle in her eye. Leyton couldn't quite figure out whether these two were a couple, really tight friends, or simply buddies who occasionally slept together, but there was a definite connection – the sort of thing he'd always believed that he and Mya shared. Unfortunately, recent events had convinced him that any link had disappeared long ago, at least as far as she was concerned. Not that they'd parted on bad terms, far from it – a hug, a smile, words of thanks – but her leaving aboard *The Retribution* had come as something of a relief, even if he'd never dream of admitting as much to anyone.

Perhaps this was what he'd needed. Perhaps now he could finally accept that it was over and move on, find somebody else.

"So there I was," Wicksy said, winding up to the punch line of another story, "with one arm around his girlfriend's shoulders and the other round his sister's waist, when…"

"Stations everyone," Kethi's crisp tones interrupted. "The ship is under attack."

All sound in the room ceased. For a frozen second everybody stared at everybody else; except for Leyton, who was first to his feet. His movement broke the spell and silence gave way to the sound of pounding feet hitting the floor as those present left their seats and headed for the door.

"Luck," Wicksy called over his shoulder as he turned left towards engineering. Leyton and Joss went in the opposite direction, making for the bridge. In theory, Leyton supposed he should head for his personal quarters, since he didn't have a station to report to, but he had to know what was going on.

The ship shuddered. Joss stumbled a little and turned towards him. "Hey, did the earth just move for you?" She looked nervous and it occurred to him that, as the captain of a tramp miner eking out a living from the scraps to be found around various asteroid belts, she might never have been in a real combat situation before. The odd bar room brawl perhaps, but nothing like this.

The next jolt hit them almost immediately and was far more violent; the whole ship seemed to spasm. It nearly knocked Leyton off his feet and was enough to send Joss staggering. She reached out, pressing one hand against the wall for support. No question this time; the ship was definitely taking a beating.

"Don't worry, this is a good ship," he felt compelled to say. "It'll take more than this to knock her down."

She didn't look convinced.

The bridge was built in one of the most heavily shielded parts of the vessel. This, the command centre of *The Rebellion*, consisted of a circular transparent disc that floated a little way off the floor, currently surrounded by an array of projected displays which undoubtedly meant something to the dozen men and women who occupied the work stations arranged around the disc's circumference. Each and every one of whom had their eyes glued to the images, the details of which were changing and evolving constantly.

"Any joy penetrating their cloaking?" Kethi asked.

"Negative." The answer came from a girl who didn't look or sound to be yet out of her teens. For all her youth she performed her duties with assurance and determination – her attention never wavered from the screens in front of her while her fingers darted across a light-display keyboard. "It's unlike anything I've seen before and I can't get a handle on it."

The off-duty bridge crew had started to arrive, strapping themselves into the upright crash couches that were arranged along the approach to the bridge, ready to step up if any of the currently active officers were incapacitated or killed. Joss already occupied the foremost. Not being part of the crew, Leyton didn't join them but instead stood at the foot of the half dozen stairs that led up to the bridge. He didn't go any further, appreciating the dedication and concentration of those involved and determined not to be a distraction. So he contended himself with hovering at the threshold.

Images appeared and disappeared in the air, while graphics scrolled across in front of one work station and then another. At the very hub of the disc stood the command chair, capable of swivelling through 360 degrees, but Kethi chose not to occupy the seat at present, instead prowling around the floor of the bridge, her eyes focused on a display projected onto the transparency beneath her feet.

"Another one down!" That from Simon, an individual Leyton would never have had on the crew in the first place, were it up to him. Nothing to do with the lad's crippled hand or his puppy-like devotion to their new captain, but everything to do with his flightiness and immaturity. In Leyton's opinion the combination made him unreliable and totally unsuited to a combat situation, as witness his triumphant call just now, compared with the professionalism of everyone else.

"It's working, bracketing the positions from which their fire originates *is* bringing results," a far calmer voice observed.

"Yes, but not quickly enough," Kethi responded. "Engine room, how soon before we're able to jump?"

There was no reply.

"The incoming attacks have been targeting the engines,"

another of the crew supplied. "That section of the ship has taken the heaviest fire and the worst damage."

"A new contact, ma'am, something big emerging from the shadow of the fourth planet. Looks like a ULAW warship."

"Helm, reroute everything to your board and give me a status report." Kethi snapped.

"Done, ma'am. Engines are not at full capacity but still functioning. We've got enough to jump."

"Good. Navigation, set coordinates for fallback point, and let's get the hell out of here."

Brief seconds later helm said calmly, "Jump initiated, ma'am."

Everything changed. The large projections which had surrounded the bridge during combat slowly winked out, all bar the main one, which displayed its usual blank serenity. The vibration of weapons discharge and the jolt of damage being sustained ceased, and Leyton could see the tension drain from the faces of the duty crew. Silence reined and had never felt richer or more welcome.

Then he remembered Joss. He glanced across to where she stood amongst the webbing of her crash couch. Some of the standby crew were beginning to release themselves, but not Joss. She stood transfixed, digesting what they'd just heard; fear and distress clouded her eyes. Engineering had taken the worst damage, which was where Wicksy had been heading when they last saw him.

JENNER WAS IN an excited state he could only equate with shock. This battle had been brutal and uncompromising – a far cry from the triumphant attack on *The Noise Within*, even though that had seemed tough enough at the time. On that occasion the element of surprise had worked, after which they'd always had the upper hand. This time it hadn't, and the result had been more in the nature of a disaster, with the rebel ship's captain continually one step ahead. At least, that was how it looked, but could the outcome have been avoided? And could events be presented any differently to his superiors? The last thing he wanted was for the importance of the needle ships and the human/AI gestalt they represented to be diminished. He replayed the brief encounter in his mind, reassessing his decisions and considering what might have been done differently. The rebel's concerted burst of fire that precipitated things had been completely unexpected. One of the unfortunate needle ships caught in the barrage could never have avoided that expanding field of mayhem even if he'd begun the attack immediately. So he'd waited. That was his assessment at the time and subsequent analysis now confirmed that decision. He would have expected the second ship to escape, however, and his review suggested that it could have done and should have done. *He* would certainly have retreated and avoided destruction. So the second needle ship's demise was due to a miscalculation by its pilot rather than any error on his part.

Two further ships had been lost, but that was to be expected in such a violent clash. No, it was the first two that had cost them, and he could hardly be blamed for those. Nor could he be held accountable for the habitat vessel's unexpected turn of speed, let alone its demonstrated ability to enter hyperspace without the need of an established wormhole. Only the Byrzaens were supposed to be able to do that. The fact that a section of humanity had also developed such technology would be of considerable interest to ULAW and that in itself would surely justify the mission and the casualties sustained.

Half the ships under his command had been lost in very short order, yet they'd managed to inflict significant damage on the rebel vessel before it disappeared and had learnt something vital about the habitat's technological capabilities. When viewed in that light, this was perhaps not the disaster it initially appeared to be.

Satisfied, he reformed what remained of the squadron and went to rendezvous with the ULAW dreadnought, which had never even had a chance to enter the fray. Yes, he now knew exactly how he was going to frame his report.

THE HOURS IMMEDIATELY following the ULAW ambush were the most difficult Kethi had ever faced, as she assessed the damage, monitored repairs and took count of the dead. In structural terms the damage to the ship was severe but not critical, and it was restricted almost entirely to a few key areas. The needle ships had known what they were after and two weapons batteries had been taken out, but most of the damage centred around the engines.

Engineering had been ripped open. Nobody from that section survived and there were no replacements for her to call on. Kethi remembered all too clearly her own command for all off-duty crew to report to stations. Standard procedure, but one she now had cause to question. The energy veils were damaged and the only people who might have an inkling what to do about that were dead.

Every child raised in the habitat learnt a few basic principles when it came to the veils – enough to know that they represented a flow of energy from another brane to this one, energy which fed the stardrives that powered their ships – but what she needed now went a little beyond the basic.

None the less, she scoured personnel records and identified the surviving crew member who knew the most about such things: one Emily Teifer.

"With all due respect, ma'am... are you serious?"

Kethi frowned. Teifer was two years older than her, broad shouldered and round faced, with hazel eyes and a wide-nostrilled, slightly squat nose. Kethi knew her in passing but little more than that. "You have the best grades in engineering of anyone aboard."

Teifer laughed. "At school, maybe." She licked her upper lip, suddenly serious. "Look, you know how basic all that stuff is.

Just because I can draw a decent picture of a cow doesn't mean I could perform open heart surgery on one, and that's what you're asking me to do here."

"No, you're wrong," Kethi assured her. "I'm not asking for miracles. There's a job to be done and you're the best qualified to do it. I just need someone to get engineering back into some sort of order now that the hull's sealed, and to give me their best assessment of where we stand with the engines. That's all."

"So, I do the house cleaning and keep things ticking over until a *real* engineer comes along?"

"In effect, yes."

"In that case, ma'am, you've got yourself a new chief engineer. I'll do whatever I can."

"Thank you."

She watched Teifer depart. One more thing to tick off the list, and the list was a long one.

"You look exhausted," Leyton told her as he entered the bridge a moment later. "Get some rest, for all our sakes. The ship doesn't need a commander who makes errors of judgement through tiredness."

"I will, I will," she promised. Yet an hour later found her still at at her station on the bridge, her thoughts grim. No sooner had Nyles left her in command of the ship than she led them straight into a ULAW ambush. Only their hybrid engines had enabled them to survive and those engines were now damaged. She felt confident Teifer would do what she could, but they both knew that wasn't much. Nobody aboard had the expertise to tell her how long the drive would hold out, how many more jumps it was good for and when exactly it was likely to fail completely and leave them all stranded. The situation was intolerable.

In truth, she knew they'd escaped the skirmish relatively lightly, having fled before ULAW could bring any heavier ships into play, but it had still happened on her watch, and after the news of the habitat's destruction even one more casualty was one too many. She scrolled down the list of the dead – twenty-three of them – and could put a face to every name. These were her friends, people she'd grown up with, folk she'd known all her life.

Realising that wallowing in her own hurt was a base form of procrastination and the very last thing that those relying on her leadership deserved, she blinked, wiping the list from her lenses. No point in putting things off any longer; a decision had to be made.

She felt as torn as the engines' energy fields. She was desperate to continue working, filled with the conviction that her own people's future and perhaps even that of all humankind might hinge on discovering what was really going on between ULAW and the Byrzaens. Yet in the current circumstances she didn't see how she could. She'd even contemplated jettisoning the data packages collected at the pickup point, afraid that they might be contaminated – one final trap set by the United League of Allied Worlds to snare them – but she rejected the idea. People had died to retrieve this information. How would those deaths make any sense if she didn't do her utmost to extract every iota of useful intel from these packages as possible? So they remained there, waiting for her to find the time to digest and analyse their content; which, unfortunately, was not now.

Kethi was self-reliant as a rule, but not to the point of believing that no one else ever had a valid viewpoint. Seeing no alternative herself, she called a meeting of the ship's officers in the hope that they might. Leyton was also included, almost as an afterthought, on the basis that he'd bring a different perspective and possessed knowledge that the habitat natives didn't.

Kethi spoke succinctly and dispassionately, outlining the situation before concluding, "So the most obvious course of action is for us to abandon our mission and go home, retreating to Far Flung, where the drives can be repaired and overhauled." She even managed to get past the word 'home' without stumbling. "If anyone has an alternative suggestion,

I'll be glad to hear from them, otherwise we'll set course for Far Flung within the hour."

She glanced around the small group, more in hope than expectation, and was only mildly disappointed by the silence.

"There might be one person who can help," Leyton said, just as she was about to call the meeting to a close. "A ship's engineer, said to be brilliant, name of Kyle."

"*The Rebellion*'s engines aren't exactly your standard Kaufman drive units..." Kethi said slowly, certain that Leyton already knew this and wondering what he was thinking.

"I know, Byrzaen hybrids; but, you see, Kyle was the first man recruited by *The Noise Within*, and he worked with *their* hybrid engines when they developed a hitch."

Of course, Kethi recalled the name now. The man had a first class record before jumping ship to join *The Noise Within*. She didn't realise he'd actually worked on the engines though. This opened up a whole new set of possibilities, though she foresaw one fairly major obstacle. "And how exactly would we go about finding this Kyle?"

"After *The Noise Within* was crippled, the surviving crew were arrested by ULAW for piracy. Kyle's out now, but..."

"The authorities would have tagged him!" Kethi suddenly realised.

Leyton grinned. "Exactly, just as they did Mya, just as they do with everyone who's passed through their penal system, however briefly."

Kethi found the corners of her own lips twitching upwards to mirror Leyton's expression. "Now that *is* interesting."

CHAPTER ELEVEN

PHILIP STILL FELT something of a novice when it came to Virtuality, but at least he was beginning to think of it as home rather than an exotic place he'd come to visit while on holiday. Tanya had turned up again. The meeting had been predictably awkward, at least for him; she seemed to take everything in her stride. She was as flirtatious as ever but he didn't feel able to respond, not now that he knew her real interest in him was business rather than pleasure. In fact, wounded pride made him positively frosty to begin with.

"Lighten up," had been her advice. "Who says we can't combine the two? It's not as if I'm going to fall pregnant... though that might be fun come to think of it. In Virtuality, I mean; wouldn't want a baby out *there*, far too much hassle."

Yet he remained resolutely formal in her presence, determined to treat her as a business associate rather than the sassy woman he fancied like mad, the only stiffness he now wanted in their relationship was in his attitude.

Their small cabal had gained another member. They'd been able to confirm straight away that the Byrzaen-inspired alcoves at Bubbles were not a recent addition to the nightclub. The relevant coding predated first contact at New Paris by at least a year, even if it wasn't part of the initial construct. The fact that the alcoves weren't an original feature wasn't significant in itself either, since add-ons and facelifts were frequent for establishments in Virtuality – such tinkering being a great deal swifter and cheaper than they would be in reality. Nor could they see anything strikingly unusual about the program written for the alcoves; there was nothing obvious to delineate it from the code sequences used to build everything else, but then neither Philip nor Malcolm were programming experts. They desperately needed the help of someone who was.

Catherine Chzyski came to their rescue. Lara Chinen was one of the best programmers Philip had ever worked with, and when the Kaufman Industry's CEO placed her expertise at their disposal he could not have been happier. Philip felt certain that if anyone could spot whatever he and Malcolm were missing, it would be Lara.

He remembered her as a quiet, petite young woman, an efficient worker who got on with the job with a minimum of fuss. What he'd forgotten, or perhaps had never before noticed, was how pretty she was – a delicate beauty courtesy of almond eyes and Asiatic features, a genetic trait that was rare on Home and so lent her an air of the exotic.

Lara had made a vital contribution to the Kaufman Industries 'project' which Philip had pursued relentlessly for so many years. That project resulted in the process of gestalt between human and AI minds enjoyed by the pilots of the needle ships that had defeated *The Noise Within*. Philip vaguely recalled that Lara had been involved with one of the potential pilots... Ah yes, Jenner, the cream of the crop. He wondered whether that emotional link persisted and, if so, how she was coping with her beau's protracted absence now that the needle ship squadron was seeing active service and found itself constantly in demand.

The logic chain his mind had constructed in the split second it took him to associate Lara to Jenner also intrigued him. This had been no intuitive leap instantly linking the pair, but instead a clear chain of connection leading from one to the other. Was that how all thinking worked for him now? Had he just caught a first glimpse of one of the fundamental differences between his past life and this new one – rigidity of thought?

He filed the matter away for further consideration later.

Lara produced results almost immediately. Tanya wasn't present at the meeting, evidently manifesting only for the virtual side of things. Philip still had no idea how closely her avatar mirrored her corporeal self's actual appearance, if at all, and determined to find out once this was all over.

"Of course, there are no telltale differences between the code underpinning your alcoves and anything else in Virtuality," Lara explained to them.

"Of course," Malcolm agreed, after they'd spent an age searching for just such differences.

"So what I've done is make a couple of assumptions. The first being that the date the alcoves were introduced is significant, that it represents the point where alien influence began to permeate Home's Virtuality."

Which made sense. Why hadn't they thought of that?

"The second is that any other objects showing Byrzaen influence would contain some similarities in the coding sequences to these alcoves of yours. To track that down, I've instigated multiple iterative searches running in parallel, beginning with one which looked for coding that's identical to the alcoves and then spawning search-trees from there, each dedicated to finding wider variation from the original than its predecessor."

"Told you she was good," Philip said to Malcolm.

"So this gives me two lists, one linked to the alcoves by date of origin and the other by some shared coding sequences." She gestured and two columns of numerical series appeared in the air. "I can't guarantee that either of these contains what you're looking for, but a comparison shows that two of the sequences appear in both sets." Another gesture and two lines of numbers in each column started to pulse, while a pair of red cords crossed the gap between columns, linking the identical sequences.

"Thanks, Lara," Philip said and meant it. "At least this gives us a good place to start."

"Two, to be precise," Malcolm said, "and this certainly beats the hell out of searching every nook and cranny in Virtuality."

"Let's go."

"Sure," Malcolm agreed. "As soon as Tanya can join us."

Great; that was all Philip wanted to hear.

IT LOOKED LIKE any street in a well-to-do part of some rural town. The only unusual aspect was its brevity – seven houses, three to either side with a sprawling manse at the far end; a cul-de-sac, giving the impression that the six smaller properties were attending on their more significant neighbour. Set against a background of gently sloping fields ripe with corn, and a small copse of tall trees at the crown of a low hill, this could easily have been many people's idyll. Not hers, though.

"Four hostiles in the first building to the left, three to the right," the gun informed her. At the same instant, red dots appeared in her visor.

Both houses looked quiet to the naked eye – the one to her right even boasted a low white picket fence. The two could have been mirror images of each other, with grand porches and a broad window to either side. Those windows were not smashed as yet and no one was shooting at her, but that would undoubtedly change as soon as she stepped between them and put herself in the crossfire. Boulton gathered herself. Had this been a holo-drama, she'd doubtless have strolled down the centre of the street, a gun in each hand, pumping bullets into the windows to either side as she went, taking out enemies with every stride. The whole set against a soundtrack of adrenaline-pumping music – something heavy, fast and edgy. What she was about to attempt seemed like hard work in comparison, and she bet holo-drama performers earned a hell of a lot more than she did as well.

"Sonic."

She lifted the gun's nozzle, squeezed the trigger and played the beam of high-frequency sound across the front of the building to her right. The two ground floor windows shattered spectacularly, razor-edged glass shards imploding into the building.

"Grenade." Already she was sprinting towards the opposite building, raising the gun and firing. One of the two explosive shells moulded to the gun's barrel flipped up and away, crashing through the nearest window.

"Projectile." Bullets tore past her and she could see shapes moving within the building.. The grenade exploded. Heat buffeted her and somebody inside screamed, and then she was leaping through the shattered window. Snatched impressions: a body sprawled on the floor by the window, another nearby, moving feebly; a settee on fire against the far wall, a table overturned, figures in motion to her right. She was firing even as she landed. One gunman went down, a second leapt to take cover behind the table. Bad move – he might as well have tried to hide behind a sheet of paper; the table was far too insubstantial to deter the bullets her gun fired. She held the trigger down and peppered the flimsy barrier, watching the wood as it was chewed to pieces and knowing that the man beyond would be faring no better. Her visor showed his red light wink out. She blinked away nascent tears – not for any sentimental reasons but because smoke from the burning settee was making her eyes water.

Movement at the periphery of her vision. Boulton whipped the gun around. The injured man, the one on the floor she'd discounted as being all-but-dead, had raised himself onto his elbows and produced a weapon from somewhere. His dot flared abruptly from dull orange to bright red. The two of them fired at virtually the same time, the sound of their twinned shots overlapping. Something struck her gun hand with jarring force – his bullet – no, not her hand but the gun itself; a glancing blow that reverberated through her wrist and forearm, almost pushing the weapon from her hand. Thankfully that was all his shot struck. The man's red dot had disappeared. Her own aim had been better, taking him in the chest and most likely the heart. No question of his rising from the dead a second time.

The fire from the settee was spreading. A curtain of flame crawled along the back wall, blistering floral wallpaper at its fringes as it was sucked upwards by the stairwell. Tendrils of fire crept along the ceiling, smoke filled the room despite the shattered windows and it was getting unbearably hot.

"Gun, are you damaged?"

Silence. Great, the impact had knocked out communications. *But had it done any more damage?* "Energy." She fired at the dead man. A bullet made a bloody mess of his right eye and everything beneath. Shit! The gun's AI was out of commission, which meant the weapon's various offensive options had just been kicked out of her reach. It was locked into 'projectile.' Nor did the bad news end there. Her visor was also dead; hardly a surprise since it relied on information supplied by the gun's AI, but still a handicap she could have done without while in the middle of hostile territory.

A shadow moved at the window she'd entered by. Boulton swivelled and squeezed off two rounds. A grunt of pain confirmed that she'd hit someone and she was on the move immediately, racing to press herself against the front wall. Her eyes stung and her lungs were filling with smoke. If these goons had any sense at all they'd simply stand back, make sure all the exits were covered and wait for the smoke and the flames to drive her out, but apparently they didn't. A snub-nosed machine pistol jabbed through the window and squirted a stream of bullets at the space where she'd been; presumably the weapon was fired blind. The flames lapped closer. Caution was no longer an option. Boulton ejected the nearly spent ammo clip, loaded a fresh one, and then stepped away from the wall. She thought about trying something clever – picking up a corpse and tossing it through one window before diving out the other, but there wasn't really the time. Besides, she'd always been an advocate of the simple approach. So she ran at the other window, the one through which no bullets had come as yet, lifted her arms to shield her face and dived.

Most of the glass had already gone, probably smashed so that the occupants could take pot-shots at her when she first approached the building, but shards still clung to the frame like teeth around a maw, tearing at her arms as she sailed through. The gun was clasped in her left hand and she had the trigger jammed down from the instant she felt the glassy daggers bite, firing back along the front of the building. No great surprise that she hadn't hit anything, but at least it kept them sufficiently occupied ducking bullets that they didn't have a chance to zero in on her. She rolled on landing, coming to her feet in a crouch. There were two of them. Whether these were from the other building – the one whose windows she'd blown in with the sonics – or newcomers to the party was hard to say. Her appearance, spitting bullets, had clearly startled them and they were slow to recover, one picking himself up from the ground where he'd dropped to, the other firing erratically and inaccurately. She dispatched them both clinically and efficiently – one bullet for each.

Behind her the fire still crackled as it greedily consumed the house, but other than that all was ominously quiet. Decisions: should she secure her back trail by checking out the opposite building – the gun had reported three gunmen in there, after all – or continue forward and get this over with as quickly as possible?

Onward; the sooner she was out of here the better. She ran, almost glad when the fragile silence was shattered by renewed gunfire. Bullets peppered the ground behind her and tore into the wall of the building she was running past. She fired back, at the windows of the second house opposite.

The throaty roar of a souped-up engine heralded the arrival of an outlandish vehicle, an armoured car sporting a rear-mounted machine gun. A trail of bullets churned up her footmarks as she dived behind the brick wall around the small front garden of the next house, death snapping at her heels. She raised her head and tried to shoot out the car's tires but to no avail. It tore down the street, turned and came back for another pass. The gun's AI brain might have been inactive but she still carried a spare clip of the barrel-mounted grenade shells. She clawed at her belt, freeing the clip even as she hunkered down, feeling shards of shattered brick sting her back as the machine gun chattered and chewed away at her hiding place. Somebody was laughing, enjoying himself – the bastard manning the gun.

As the jeep skidded around and leapt back for a third pass, she tossed the spare grenade clip into the road, directly into its path. She then slithered on her stomach so that when she popped her head up a few seconds later it was at a different spot, a little further along the wall. The car was almost on top of the clip. The machine gun chattered away but she ignored it, steadying her arm, focussing on the clip to the exclusion of all else. She gently squeezed the trigger, once, twice. The grenades exploded just as the car arrived, bouncing the vehicle into the air like some ungainly fish freshly landed and desperately seeking water, ripping open its front – the hood flying off in one sturdy sheet while the engine beneath flew apart in myriad fragments. Boulton ducked back behind her wall, hearing shrapnel ping against the outside, feeling the impact of a few heavier pieces through the bricks. So much for armour.

As soon as it stopped Boulton vaulted the wall and strode up to the smouldering wreck even as it rolled to a halt. The two men in the drivers' compartment looked dead, but she put a bullet in each of them to make sure. The pillock in the back – the one who'd taken such glee in shooting at her – had been thrown clear in the explosion and was crawling feebly along the ground; dazed and most likely injured. The two bullets she pumped into his head doubtless stopped the pain.

Boulton moved on, her target – the big house – directly ahead.

The gun's silence was uncanny, a prickling void, but not really a distraction. She was still new enough at being an eyegee to feel comfortable in its absence. In fact, she was almost glad to be free of the gun's presence for a while, that sense of something always watching over her shoulder. This was like getting her privacy back.

Something caught her attention, a sliding of detail in the corner of her eye, a bush and a flowerbed that seemed to flow fractionally to one side, as if viewed through a heat haze... *Shimmer suit.* On the other hand, the gun and visor combo could be fucking useful sometimes, especially when there were enemies around which the naked eye might not be able to see. She dropped to one knee and brought the gun up to spray a fan of bullets, centring on where she'd seen that patch of shimmer. Her reward was to hear a cry of surprise and pain and to watch an armed man collapse to the floor, his suit deactivating as its wearer died.

She was up and running immediately, crouching low, gun at the ready. Were there more of them? She cast her gaze about, not seeing any further tell-tale flicker of warped light, but then she wouldn't; not unless they moved. A single shot rang out and she felt a shaft of agony lance through her left arm. Drops of warm blood speckled her face as the bullet punched through her forearm. The shooter was behind her somewhere. Screw the idea of crouching low, the gunman clearly had her in his sights. She straightened and sprinted, ignoring her wound – that could wait – and using the pain as a goad. She ran at an angle, heading for the shimmer suited body, hoping walls and gardens might provide her with some protection, and even threw in a tight zigzag for good measure. A second shot rang out and she fancied she could feel the bullet's passage as it flew past her ear, but no fresh blossoming of pain resulted.

Then she was around the corner, at the side of the big house, with solid brick between her and the sniper. Her wound pulsed with pain and blood flowed freely down her left arm, its sticky warmth coating the back of her hand and running around to work into the creases of her palm, but she couldn't stop to patch the wound, not yet. A window. She fired three shots on the run and then leapt through the shower of shattering glass, bringing renewed agony to her already throbbing arm.

Beyond was a formal dining room which might have been lifted straight from some stately home. Very retro-classical – high ceilings and everything crafted out of polished rosewood, from the ornate round-cornered table that took centre stage to its attendant twelve disciples – the matching high-backed chairs that clustered around it – and the twin sideboards that stood against the walls. If that didn't provide enough of a clue, then the large heavy framed canvases above, depicting hunting scenes and the portrait of a regal-looking man, told you instantly that this was not your average slice of suburbia.

Boulton loaded a fresh clip of ammo and headed for the room's open doorway. Neither of the gun-toting goons beyond stood a chance, mown down in the hail of bullets that heralded her arrival. The sweeping stairway and the high-ceilinged entrance hall itself might have been impressive if she'd had the time to consider them properly. Instead her attention focussed unerringly on the solid wooden front door, which stood to her right as she burst from the dining room. Somebody yelled from behind her, words she didn't catch as she lunged at the door, her hands closing around its gleaming brass handle.

The instant her hand clasped the cold metal the simulation faded, winking out as if it had never been, to leave her standing in the vast warehouse-like space of the honeycomb's sim room. She was breathing heavily, having pushed her body hard in this one, but at least the agony of her injured arm faded with the rest.

Somebody clapped and a tall figure stepped forward from the shadows: Pavel Benson. "Very clever," he said, "coming at the door from the inside like that."

She shrugged. "You told me that reaching the door was the goal; nobody said anything about which *side* I had to reach. It struck me that you'd probably have some nasty surprises lying in wait if I'd gone for the direct approach."

"We did."

"Well" – now came the moment of truth – "did I pass?"

She had been exonerated of any blame for what went down at the habitat, at least officially, and nobody was referring to the operation as a fiasco, not in public. After all, the principle objective had been to eliminate the habitat as a threat, and they'd achieved that, no question. Yet when the specialists moved in to pick over the corpse of their enemy, they'd found hundreds of dead in a facility that was clearly capable of accommodating thousands, just as her gun had suggested, and the bald facts were that ULAW had lost one of its precious eyegees, while of the one hundred and eighty marines she and Case had led between them, only four had come back alive. Those four owed their survival not to any brilliance on her part but to the lightning-quick response of the retrieval drones, much as she herself did. No, nobody was calling this a debacle in public.

She'd gone through the mission a hundred times in her head, wondering if she could have done anything differently. The only thing she might have changed was the automated weapon placements. If she'd stopped to take them out when the gun first identified them, lives might have been saved there if not in the long run, but she'd counted on the gun's assurance that they weren't a threat. That was what this latest exercise was all about, she suddenly realised, to gauge just how dependant on the weapon and its guiding AI she'd become.

Benson was nodding and smiling. That had to be a good sign. "You did okay."

Coming from him, that was high praise indeed, and Boulton was amazed at quite how relieved she felt on hearing those words.

"Well enough that I'm sending you out again."

"Oh?" She hadn't expected a full reprieve *that* quickly.

"We've got a potential lead on Jim Leyton."

She stared into Benson's eyes, saw him smile and knew that her reaction had given her away. He now knew beyond any doubt how much she wanted this.

"The needle ship squadron recently engaged a habitat ship – the one we've identified as being responsible for the raid on Sheol, the one that Leyton is almost certainly on. After careful study of the intel gathered during the attack, we're confident that the rebel's engines took substantial damage. There was also a deal of collateral damage to the sections of the ship adjacent to the drive. Our best guess is that we've crippled her engines and taken out most if not all her engineering personnel."

"That's a heck of an assumption," Boulton couldn't help but comment.

"Taken on its own, perhaps, but hear me out. One of our monitoring stations picked up a hack into ULAW security systems. An apparently trivial thing that would normally have been noted and added to a list of thousands of things 'to be looked at later,' but some bright spark made a connection. The hack was designed to ferret out information on a particular individual, an ex-navy engineer by the name of Kyle, who happens to have been the first human recruited by *The Noise Within* and is, as far as we know, the *only* human to have ever worked with Byrzaen engines.

"Knowing my connection to the Byrzaen operation at New Paris, our friendly bright spark made sure the information was passed up the line to me.

"We're pretty sure that this hack was carried out by the habitat, and why else would they be interested in an engineer unless they needed someone who might just be able to fix their ship?"

Boulton frowned. There was a gaping hole at the heart of Benson's argument, and as far as she could see only one thing could fill it; something that made no sense at all. "All right," she said carefully, "but why? Are you trying to tell me that the habitat have Byrzaen technology?"

He shrugged. "Habitat ships can jump without using wormholes. So can the Byrzaens. Now somebody is trying to track down the only man in ULAW space with firsthand knowledge of alien engine systems at a time when we know the habitat needs a mechanic. You tell me."

Ian Whates

The bastard knew far more than he was saying. Benson had one of those faces that might as well have been carved from granite. He never gave anything away, but right now she knew he was holding out on her, despite his deadpan expression. He was also her boss, though, and after recent events she was walking on eggshells, which meant her options were pretty limited at present, so she turned her attention back to what he *had* said rather than what he'd so studiously left out.

"So *if* Leyton is on that ship, *if* its engines were sufficiently damaged, *if* enough of their specialists were killed and *if* they have a means of tracking down this engineer... they might be going after him."

Benson's smile had grown markedly thin-lipped. "I did stress that this was only a *potential* lead."

Sod the eggshells. She felt them grind to dust beneath her feet as she said, "Sounds like a long shot to me."

"Which is better than no shot at all."

Barely, in Boulton's opinion.

Benson was still speaking. "We've tracked down this 'Kyle.' He recently signed on as crew to an old trader-cum-smuggler called *The Peridon*. The ship's currently bound for a backwater planet called Arcadia. We've diverted a courier ship and have it waiting to take you directly there. If you leave now you should arrive a little ahead of *The Peridon*, and will have full authority to co-opt whatever local support you require."

Boulton knew she ought to feel delighted. After all, up until a few moments ago her very future as an eyegee had been in doubt, and now here she was being handed an assignment. Yet she couldn't escape the feeling that this was a wild goose chase, and that while she was dispatched to some forgotten corner of the galaxy on a pointless waste of time, a genuine lead would come in and be handed to somebody else. That was her greatest concern, that somebody other than her would be granted the pleasure of taking down that bastard Leyton. The prospect gnawed at her innards like a festering ulcer.

159

Not that she had a choice here, and the sooner she left the sooner she could be back. So Boulton made no further complaint but instead simply nodded and said, "Sir!" with only a hint of irony, before hurrying away to prepare for her imminent trip.

PART TWO

CHAPTER TWELVE

KYLE HAD VISITED a fair few worlds in his time but never Arcadia, as far as he could recall. Once, the prospect of landing on a new planet would have thrilled him, but not anymore. Too many new places had disappointed by being anything but. He might not know this particular town but he knew plenty like it. Cramped bars and narrow streets, cheap rooms, doss houses, narc-dens, quickthrill booths and seedy gaming halls, dealers on the prowl, whores on the hustle and bum-boys on the make; hawkers, fixers, pimps, thieves, contractors, pedlars and opportunists, all on the lookout for a mark. Spaceports attracted them like flies to a dung heap. All it took was for some forgotten patch of open ground to be designated a landing area and before you knew it a town sprung up, or existing, formerly-sleepy surburban streets would be overflowing with gaudy souvenirs, knocked-off cyber gadgets, cheap leather goods and sweat-shop clothing outlets sandwiched between fast food stalls and bootleg booze stands. Everything your average spacer, starved of life's little luxuries, could possibly wish for. Freshly released from the confinement of their star-flitting metal tubes with credits in their pockets – and even for those a little short on credit but still long on urges – this was exactly the sort of place most of them would be dreaming of.

Normally, you could have counted Kyle among them; this would have been home from home, but right now 'normal' didn't come into it. There'd been nothing normal about his life since he jumped ship to join a pirate crew, only to discover that he was the only human on board.

As far as he could determine, he'd barely escaped a lengthy stay in a ULAW jail following that fiasco, thanks to the intervention of the government man, Leyton; Jim, as he'd originally introduced himself. Since then, Kyle's life had gone into freefall, with one disaster following hot on the heels of another, this most recent career move merely the latest entry in a sorry catalogue of misfortunes.

Buchan had seemed a decent enough sort; Captain and owner of a small trade vessel, a scavenger, pootling around the fringes of ULAW space picking up cargo here and delivering it there – surviving on the jobs that were too small or where the margins were too tight to interest the corporate boys – and Buchan was short of an engineer. Perfect; the sort of venture which would never make you rich but where a decent living could be eked out, if you were savvy enough.

Kyle had taken the job with every expectation of revisiting his past. He'd assumed this would be much like life aboard *The Star Witch*, his first civilian position after leaving the navy – a period which he remembered with great fondness. However, he soon discovered that nostalgia wasn't all it's cracked up to be. True, *The Peridon* had seen better days, much like the earlier ship, but there all similarity ended. As soon as he stepped aboard *The Star Witch* he'd been welcomed with open arms, made to feel part of the family, and had soon found himself an accepted member of a tight-knit crew. *The Peridon*'s crew also seemed pretty tight, but they were far from welcoming. Instead, Kyle found himself excluded, treated with suspicion that fell just short of outright hostility. Conversations would stop as he entered a room, and smiles were few and far between. The longer this first trip went on, the firmer his conviction grew that the others were hiding something, that it was more than mere camaraderie that bound them together and cast him as the outsider, but rather a sense of shared guilt.

Kyle had never been so grateful to get off a ship in his life, not even *The Noise Within*. He determined to use the time in port to try and hustle up a berth on another ship as quickly as possible – on *any* other ship – and the scene that unfolded on the dockside as they disembarked did nothing to change his mind.

The five of them – with him lagging slightly behind the four regular crewmembers – were just leaving the docking arm when three figures came striding towards them.

"Buchan!" yelled the first – a short, grizzled man who was clearly livid and spoiling for a fight. The other three members of *The Peridon*'s crew tensed and drew a little closer to their captain. Hands strayed towards weapons.

"Heard you were coming in," the short man said, stopping before them an arm's reach away.

"Low, what a pleasure," Buchan replied. If a smile could ever imply a sneer, this was it.

"You owe me, you bastard." The pointed finger stabbed out, a hair's breadth away from Buchan's chest.

The Peridon's captain didn't flinch. From the look on his face and those of the other crew members, Kyle guessed he was finally catching a glimpse of whatever guilty secret they were hiding. At least, that was his hope.

"You weren't the only one to get burned, Low, we lost our engineer, remember?" Eyes flickered briefly in Kyle's direction, while he berated himself for not asking more about his predecessor. What had it been, this incident that had developed into a festering sore on the collective conscience of *The Peridon*'s crew? Robbery, smuggling, narcotics, illicit tech, passage for a wanted felon, what? Something high risk, high gain and highly illegal, that much was obvious.

"Your *engineer*? I lost my fucking *son*!"

"Yeah, I heard. Sorry and all that, but everybody knew the risks going in."

"What risks? There *were* no risks. Not until you tried to muscle in on my operation."

"Bullshit! The whole thing was obviously a scam from day one. Tech like that doesn't suddenly pop up out of nowhere onto the open market."

Ah, so that was it. Illicit tech; weapons system or AI interface, most likely. They seemed to be the two hot topics these days.

"No, no," Low was shaking his head, his fury unabated. "I'm not letting you slither out of it that easily. Everything was sweet as a nut until you came blundering in with your greed and your half-assed crew. Three men I lost, one of them Jamie; not to mention the damage to the ship." Low was literally shaking with anger, and Kyle wouldn't have been surprised to see the smaller man launch himself at Buchan there and then, but he controlled himself with evident difficulty, and actually took a step back. "And you're going to pay for what happened, all of you." He swept a pointed finger, taking in the group of them.

Kyle considered himself a bystander in this, no more than an interested observer, but of course he wasn't, he was a part of The Peridon's crew. He felt Low's glare sweep over him, and knew that in this man's eyes at least they were well and truly united. Low had clocked each and every one of them, as if to lodge their faces indelibly in his mind's eye. Kyle was now guilty by association and Low didn't seem the sort to concern himself with technicalities, such as the fact that all this had happened before Kyle even signed on.

"By the time I'm through with you, you'll wish you'd never even heard of The Peridon."

There was a flurry of movement behind Buchan. Kent, tall, swarthy Kent, moved more quickly than Kyle would have believed he could, sweeping up an arm and producing a gun from somewhere; a brutal looking rifle. Nothing fancy and all business, it pointed straight at Low.

The docks were quiet, at least this section was. Their altercation had drawn little attention and Kyle didn't imagine the presence of a gun was going to alter that. Somehow, he doubted this was the first weapon to ever be drawn here.

"Fuck off, Low," Buchan drawled. "You're beginning to annoy us."

Low didn't appear to be intimidated. In fact he guffawed, as if this was exactly the sort of contemptible response he'd expect from the likes of Buchan and his crew. "This isn't over. Don't think for one moment that it is." With a final glare, he swivelled around and stalked off, flanked by his two men.

A melodramatic oaf, no question, but that didn't mean he wasn't dangerous.

The gun disappeared back inside the long coat Kent was wearing. Buchan and his three cronies exchanged glances. Kyle didn't feel remotely reassured by the uncertainty he saw there.

"Don't take no notice," Cully, the navigator, advised, directing the comment at his captain. "Now that he's got that little outburst off his chest, he'll leave us alone."

Buchan grunted. "Yeah, most likely you're right." Although he sounded as if he were trying to convince himself rather than anyone else. "All the same, everyone watch your backs while we're here. There are a lot more of them than us."

Great. Just the sort of thing Kyle wanted to hear. "Is someone going to tell me what that was all about?" he ventured.

"No," Cully replied, which hardly came as a surprise.

"Best you don't know," Buchan added.

Perhaps he was right. Best for whom, though?

Kyle suspected that all those present realised he wasn't going to be around for much longer, one way or another.

They left the port facility without further challenge, and stepped forth into bedlam. The mass of people came as a shock after so long spent in an environment populated by just the five of them. Kids were the first thing, flocking to them the moment they emerged into the street, trying to tempt the new arrivals with everything from gaudy trinkets to guaranteed aphrodisiacs, from bootleg drugs to their own scrawny bodies.

They walked on unheeding, soon shedding the posse of young entrepreneurs, who slid away one by one, drifting back to haunt the port entrance, waiting for the next batch of freshly docked spacers. The kids were only the first irritation, though. Maybe this was Market Day, or even 'Get in the Way of a Spacer Day,' Kyle wasn't sure. All he knew was that the streets were heaving, with most folk evidently not in a hurry to be anywhere except in his path.

At least the crowds provided ample cover. He ducked away from the merry *Peridon* quartet as quickly as he could, no doubt in his mind that Low meant business. While the rest of them might be able to rely on each other in a scrap he didn't feel inclined to do so, which left him vulnerable – the one most likely to be picked off first. Therefore he removed himself, wishing Buchan and the crew a silent *bon voyage* as he slipped between two market stalls and headed off in a random direction. If nobody had noticed him slope off, this might even spook them a little and leave them wondering whether he'd gone of his own accord or been snatched by Low and his men. He hoped so. Petty, perhaps, but it was what he was reduced to.

They still owed him a bit of pay for the trip, but Kyle had always placed a higher value on his own skin than on his credit balance. Besides, slipping away for a little 'me' time while in port was hardly jumping ship, and he could always go back later if he changed his mind. Not that he expected to.

Finding a bar proved predictably easy. He strolled straight into a ramshackle place that didn't need a door – its entire front was open, the roof supported by slender metal pillars, half peeling white paint and half rust. The kid who served him seemed friendly enough, in a 'you-might-have-money' sort of way, and recommended a locally brewed beer. It turned out to be a little sour to Kyle's taste, but right then he'd have settled for anything cold with bubbles in it. Most of the urine-coloured liquid had disappeared before a plump middle-aged man in a blue and white hooped top decided to move on, enabling Kyle to claim a seat – one of the spindle-legged high stools clustered around the bar.

Drinking alone when he was already feeling lower than a midget stooping to tie his shoelaces probably wasn't the brightest of ideas. It set him thinking about his life and the choices he'd made. Truth was, he missed *The Lady J* – the luxury liner he'd been paid a small fortune to strut around, the ship he'd abandoned to go pirate. What was that old saying about the grass being greener? He hadn't appreciated how good things were back then. Returning to his roots, to working on rickety old rust-buckets three rivets away from the scrapheap wasn't as much fun as when he was fresh out of the navy. He'd been hungrier then, keener, with a flatter stomach and a less wrinkled visage. This was a young man's game and, much as he hated to admit it, he wasn't one, not any more. When had that changed? He thought back to *The Lady J* and the success he'd enjoyed with that cute little trolley dolly, what was her name? Marie, that was it. Marie and all the girls like her, always one to take the place of the last in a chain of casual encounters which he'd never expected to end. It hadn't been all that long ago, yet in those days doubt would never even have entered his mind. He'd taken for granted that he was charming, amusing, seductive and irresistible. So where had all that self-confidence gone?

The Noise Within, being arrested, his subsequent experiences in Virtuality – he shuddered at that one, and fervently hoped that the craze of establishing virtual worlds hadn't yet spread as far as Arcadia – all had eaten away at his arrogance, leaving a humbler, less cock-sure soul in their wake.

Perhaps someone was trying to tell him something. Perhaps it was time to get out and settle down, to find himself a nice little job fixing cars and tinkering with air scooters, a good wife to look after him in the kitchen and the bedroom, forget about the stars, new worlds and new partners. This Arcadia didn't seem such a bad place. Maybe he'd have a look around while he was here.

Kyle ordered another drink and fell into conversation with the man next to him, who had evidently been in the same spot for a good part of the day and was clearly a good few beverages ahead of him. The man had a balding pate above a wizened, weathered face, and was even older than Kyle, which reassured him. The fellow didn't need much prompting to share his memories and opinions. He could remember life during the war, when the spaceport had been under military control. What he had to say wasn't exactly as encouraging as Kyle might have hoped. "This was a decent neighbourhood in them days," the man insisted. "A real community, with shops – a greengrocer, bakers... even a butchers; 'Samuel J. Westerman and Sons.' Freshest cuts of meat you could wish for. Look at it now – cruddy arcades and knocking shops... No community left, that's for sure, nothing decent at all. There used to be fields, end of this road, believe it or not, trees beyond that and even a small lake..."

"A lake?" Kyle's ears pricked up. "Were there any swans?"

"Swans?" The fellow looked puzzled. "No, can't say as there were."

The man's brows furrowed, as if he wasn't entirely certain what a swan might be. Kyle took a deep breath, relishing the prospect of enlightening him, but it was at that moment he glanced past his new drinking buddy's shoulder and saw them. Two men, loitering by the door. They had drinks, though he couldn't recall seeing either come up to the bar. They were staring straight at him, and he recognised one of them; he'd seen him with Low at the docks an hour or so ago. He met Kyle's gaze and smiled. Kyle would have felt more comfortable had the goon snarled. That smile was one of the most chilling expressions Kyle had ever been subjected to. It seemed to say, "Got you!"

Kyle swallowed on a suddenly dry throat. So much for the idea that separating from *The Peridon*'s crew would take him away from the danger. It seemed that all he'd done was isolate himself, becoming all the more vulnerable in the process.

"Ducks, though," his drinking pal was saying. "I remember there was plenty of them."

"Sorry?" He wondered if there was a back way out of here.

"Ducks, on the lake. Shot a few in me time. Delicious roasted, I can tell you. Been years since I had some roasted duck."

Why would a place with a completely open front *need* a back exit? "Just going to the loo," Kyle said, standing up. Surely it had to have one of those at least.

He made a point of not looking in the two goons' direction, doing his best to saunter towards the back of the room; not bolting, no, definitely not bolting, just a man in need of a leak.

No back door, but he found the toilets; a cramped, tatty room in which the smell of disinfectant fought to hide other, more basic stinks. The place boasted a single window, high up but not as tiny as it might have been. He reckoned he could squeeze through. Bit of a cliché perhaps, escaping through the toilet window, but presumably something had to work in order to become a cliché in the first place. He stood on the loo pedestal, pushed the window open and pulled himself up, feet scrambling on the wall for purchase, conscious of brittle paint flaking off the brickwork beneath the toes of his boots and of the black iron window latch digging painfully into his stomach. God, he was getting too old for this sort of thing. For a moment he teetered, in danger of falling back inside, but he hauled and grunted and squirmed and after a few perilous seconds the balance tipped in his favour. He began to slide forward through the small gap. Momentum took care of the rest.

There's no elegant way to fall out of a window, or, if there is, Kyle had never learned it. He plummeted headfirst towards the ground, legs and feet pulling free of the window. His arms automatically came up to protect his face. Preoccupied with getting out, he only gained a fleeting impression of his surroundings – he was in a narrow alley, not one of the bustling thoroughfares, thank goodness. Even so, there were people here; briefly glimpsed shapes seen as he fell, legs and shoes being the first things to come into focus as his palms and forearms came to rest on the ground. The rest of him followed, and he landed a little painfully. Straight in front of him, a pair of boots, black leather with some fancy stitching on the sides, their pointed toes heavily scuffed.

Let them gawp, these passersby, let them laugh in astonishment at this mad spacer diving out of a window, let them think he was trying to evade paying a bar tab or whatever. He didn't care, so long as he escaped Low's men and the beating, or worse, they were doubtless waiting to administer.

The boots didn't move. In fact, more pairs of feet seemed to be clustering around him. Kyle pushed his face off the ground and sat up, to stare into the smiling faces of Low and three of his cronies. He recognised the two from the bar.

Shit! So much for relying on a cliché. An inherent characteristic of such things, of course, is that *everyone* has heard them before and knows what to expect. Something he'd try to bear in mind next time. Kyle instinctively pushed himself backwards, until his spine came up against the building he'd just vacated in such ignominious haste. Ludicrously, he brushed dirt from his arms, as if that was his greatest concern.

"If you were thinking of auditioning as a gymnast, I'd stick to the day job," Low advised.

"Look, I don't know what your problem is with Buchan and the others, but it's got nothing to do with me," Kyle said, or rather babbled, almost tripping over his words in the haste to get them out.

"Is that a fact?"

"Yeah, I'm new, not really part of the crew at all. Only signed up for this trip."

"That was your hard luck then, or rather your poor judgement, signing up with scum like that. Far as I'm concerned, you're *Peridon* crew, and that makes you fair game."

"But I don't even know what this is about, I wasn't even *there*!" That came out as a whine, even to Kyle's ears.

Low didn't deign to reply. Instead he glanced up and nodded to one of his men before stepping away, while the other three closed in. Kyle scrambled to his feet, back still pressed firmly to the wall. He'd considered staying where he was on the basis that if he stood up he'd probably just get knocked straight back down again, but a defiant part of him wanted to at least start this on his own two feet.

He saw the first punch coming and brought his arms up across his chest, leaning forward, almost hugging himself for protection, but the fist landed below the clumsy defence to sink into his solar plexus. It felt as if he'd been kicked by a mule. Pain exploded through his body, and he doubled up, gagging, wanting to throw up, gasping for breath. The second punch connected with his chin, jerking his head back so that it cracked against the wall. He suddenly realised that the first blow hadn't been so bad after all, not compared to the twin centres of agony that now blossomed in his skull. He slumped to the ground, onto his hands and knees. He knew he shouldn't have bothered getting up. No longer able to move or even focus on his surroundings, Kyle could do nothing but wait for the next blow. He screwed his eyes shut, braced himself and simply willed it to end as quickly as possible.

The sounds of violence continued. Shouts, curses, a scream, the rapid shuffle of feet, an *oomph* of expelled air as a blow connected and the sharp reports of fists on skin. It took Kyle a while to register that nothing more had struck him, that whatever was now going on seemed to be happening around him rather than being directed *at* him.

He risked opening his eyes, just in time to see a limp figure tossed against the far wall, to rebound and crumple to the ground. One of Low's men. The others, including the boss man himself, were already decorating the alley in horizontal fashion, clearly unconscious if not worse. A large, powerful figure stood over them, his back to Kyle, but the man's very posture spoke of violence barely contained.

What now? Some escaped lunatic intent on killing and maiming all he encountered? Was it Kyle's turn to be plucked up next and sent hurtling into a wall?

The breath caught in his throat as the figure began to turn towards him. Kyle squinted up and, when no immediate attack came, dared to hope that maybe this really was a rescue. He tried to see the man's face, wondering if this was someone he knew or just a passing good Samaritan, though he'd have been surprised if anyone would intentionally go to so much trouble on his behalf. Then the figure turned fully round and Kyle got a clear look at his saviour for the first time.

"Oh, hell, not you again!"

"Hello, Kyle. Long time no see," Leyton said, and smiled.

In principle, Kyle had faith in lady luck, had counted on her good grace too often at the gaming table not to, and on occasion he was even happy to accept coincidence at face value. This wasn't one of those.

"Just happened to be in the area, did you?"

"Something like that. How badly hurt are you?"

"I'll live." Kyle replied, gingerly feeling the back of his head and finding a lump already swelling there. His fingers came away sticky with his own blood.

"Good. Come on then." The big man took his arm and tried to pull him to his feet.

Kyle resisted. He wasn't sure he was ready to move just yet. He *hurt*, for goodness sake. Not to mention that he'd had a stomachful of taking orders in the navy and had never reacted well to being bossed around since. Besides, whatever reasons Leyton might have for being impatient, they weren't *his* reasons.

"Hey, what's the rush? Low won't be waking up for a while." He looked at the motionless form of the diminutive captain, reaching out a foot to prod him with the toe of his shoe.

"It's not this lot I'm worried about."

"Who then?"

"People that make your friend Low here look like a sedated kitten with its claws removed; people who wouldn't hesitate to take you apart from the inside outwards simply for talking to me. Now move!"

Kyle sensed that his supposed rescuer meant it and this time he didn't shake off the hand that reached down to help him, though he was still far from reassured.

He found himself stumbling behind the larger man, who led the way out of the alley and into the bustling streets of the market quarter.

"What the hell have you dragged me into, Leyton?"

"What, by saving your butt, you mean?"

"Thanks. That bit was good. It's the bit that comes afterwards I'm worried about."

"I'll explain later."

The streets were no less packed than Kyle remembered. Leyton's bulk forged a path through the crowd as they headed deeper into the market.

Kyle was feeling more and more resentful. "No!" he suddenly said, stopping dead in his tracks. His guts hurt, his head hurt, and he was sick and tired of people knowing more about what was going on than he did.

People stared, perhaps assuming this to be a lovers' spat. Leyton looked nervous, as if he'd prefer not to be drawing this sort of attention.

That gave Kyle some leverage, a bargaining chip. Presumably Leyton had gone to a fair bit of trouble to find him, so he was important for some reason, although he couldn't begin to imagine why. "If you seriously expect me to go with you, you're gonna have to give me more of a reason than that!"

Leyton glared, as if debating whether to simply walk on and leave Kyle to his fate, but instead he drew a long breath and said, "You want a reason? Okay, I'll give you one. You were in the forces, weren't you, during the war? So you must know that a moving target's more difficult to hit than one that stands obligingly still, especially in a busy and confused environment like this." He looked meaningfully around. "Reason enough?"

With that he turned and stalked off.

Kyle paused for a heartbeat before concluding *good point*,

and then hurried to catch up. He reassessed the value of his bargaining chip, and reckoned he might have used most of it up. "All right, but once we get to wherever it is we're going I want to know exactly what this is all about."

Leyton didn't answer.

Kyle struggled to keep pace, increasingly conscious of how on edge his companion was and how alert, eyes flicking from side to side, scanning the crowds around them. No attention to spare for small talk, apparently. This was a very different Leyton from the jovial, easy-going brawler Kyle had first encountered on Frysworld.

Without warning, the big man came to an abrupt halt.

"What is it?" Kyle wanted to know.

"Nothing. This way." He headed off at a right angle to their previous course, stepping up the pace even more.

Kyle scanned the crowd, trying to see what had spooked him, but all he saw was a mass of bobbing heads. He thought he spotted them the second time, though; a trio of smartly dressed men moving in their direction. They were definitely looking for something, and paid far more attention to the people around them than to the stalls and their wares. Shopping seemed to be the last thing on their minds. Kyle didn't think that he and Leyton had been seen as they ducked down a narrow alleyway between two rows of stalls bristling with clothes and bags and knick-knacks, but he wouldn't have wanted to bet his life on it, while suspecting that might be exactly what he was doing.

"Are they after me or you?" he asked.

"Trust me, at this point, it really doesn't matter."

Probably true. Kyle was beginning to think he would have been better off taking his chances with Low. As reprieves went, this was hardly ideal. None of which stopped him from shadowing Leyton's every move. The man offered his best chance of coming through this in one piece, whatever 'this' might be.

They dodged and weaved their way to the edge of the marketplace, where the crowds began to thin. Kyle was just starting to think they might be in the clear when a blast of air and a thunderclap of raw sound picked him up and flung him from his feet.

Explosion. Heat washed over him, shrapnel stung both his cheek and his hands, instinctively raised to protect his face.

Suddenly he was back in the War, a young engineer experiencing his first firefight; the heat, the noise, the juddering impact that jerked his arms where he was clinging on for grim death, afraid of being tossed around the engine room, the vibration from their ship's response, from heavy guns chattering and missiles belching forth into the void. Then the explosion – the thing he'd been most afraid of – fire and heat blasting across the room, catching one newly-met colleague full on, shredding clothing and skin before the poor wretch even had time to scream. No way of knowing whether this was the end, the ship in its death throes, or something more localised – perhaps their own machinery rupturing in the face of the constant concussion – before he was knocked from his feet and into oblivion. Only to feel hands lifting him up, to regain consciousness and recognise boots and uniforms and know that he was still alive, to be overwhelmed by the blessed relief of survival, closely followed by the guilt of knowing that others hadn't been so lucky, that there were friends he'd never see again.

"Come on, Kyle, move that sorry arse of yours!" Leyton's voice dragged him back to the here and now. His ears were buzzing. The voice sounded muffled, distant.

He blinked away dust and felt a sharp pain down his left temple. "Leyton?" For the second time in a matter of minutes, the other man was helping him up.

"Yes. Who were you expecting, a choir of fucking angels?"

Smoke and dust drifted in the air. People were screaming and shouting. Leyton was pulling, urging him onwards, not giving him time to think. He glimpsed bodies.

A small child, a girl in a pink and white polka-dot dress, stained white ribbon in her blonde hair, sat amidst the rubble and half-buried limbs, her face contorted into a parody of fear and grief as she wailed her distress. No one seemed to be paying her any attention. A darkly bearded man stumbled across their path, hand held to the side of his head, blood flowing from between protective fingers, as he stared around, with the look of someone struggling to make sense of it all.

Leyton eased the injured local impatiently out the way, while still gripping Kyle and dragging him in his wake. "Got to put distance between us and the explosion," the big man muttered.

"What was it?" Kyle asked.

"A bomb. Don't ask me who or why. Could be local terrorists stirring things up or it might have been intended for us, but either way it's going to draw attention, and we can't afford to be around when the authorities arrive and start asking questions."

Morbid curiosity remained a constant, no matter what star a person is born under; disasters and accidents can always be counted on to draw a crowd. At first the two of them threaded a path through those still too stunned to move, but soon they were swimming against the tide, heading away from a scene that everyone else was anxious to get near.

"Good old human nature," Leyton muttered. "Where would we be without it?"

Kyle worried about the fact that they were doing the opposite to everyone else. Wouldn't people remember them because of it, wasn't this going to make them stand out?

A siren sounded. The first of many, no doubt. Whether this was police or ambulance, he had no idea, nor did he have any desire to find out.

Then the crowds in front of them parted, to reveal a figure, a woman standing in their way; tall, lithe, and wearing a dark blue one-piece suit that was probably designed to grant freedom of movement, but also showed off her compact, muscular figure. Bizarrely, for a garment that close fitting, the result was to make her look somewhat androgynous. Difficult to see her face, which was half-obscured by a tinted visor, but there was no mistaking her purpose. She stood with feet firmly planted and a bulky, mean-looking gun pointed unerringly towards Leyton – Kyle being a little behind his new protector.

"Hello, Jim. Long time no see."

"Boulton!" The name hissed through Leyton's clenched teeth like an unpalatable swearword.

Leyton moved before Kyle could even think of reacting, and the engineer found himself shoved hard, thrown to one side even as the larger man dived in the opposite direction. Energy spat from the woman's gun, searingly bright. Kyle shut his eyes immediately but was still left dazzled and temporarily blinded, making it impossible at first to tell if Leyton had been hit or not. The sharp crack of gunfire from the other man's direction suggested he was still alive at least. Kyle squinted, blinking away distracting afterimages, and was able to make out Leyton crouching behind an upturned barrow. It provided little protection as far as Kyle could see. The woman had evidently changed weapons, because a stream of bullets was rapidly destroying the flimsy wooden cart. Leyton threw himself towards something that promised to be a little more solid – a white, bulky block which might have been a commercial freezer unit. As he leapt, he returned fire at Boulton with a handgun.

Kyle felt relieved, both because Leyton was clearly all right and because nobody was actually shooting in his direction as yet. But the relief was short lived. A firefight in the aftermath of an explosion seemed guaranteed to draw the sort of attention they'd been zigzagging to avoid for the past ten minutes. Groups of serious-looking men were probably converging on this very spot right now, and Kyle had a feeling they'd be even less impressed by his arguments of 'wasn't me' than Low had been.

He wasn't carrying a gun, had never felt inclined to – seeing himself as more of a lover than a fighter – but he had a knife in his belt along with a laser-blade cutting tool that would shear through flesh and bone as readily as metal and carbon fibre.

All he had to do was get within arm's reach of this woman, presumably a professional, armed with an energy gun, a hand pistol and goodness knew what else. That was all. Yet the neck-prickling threat of anonymous men spurred him on, and, despite his previous protests, he knew he'd thrown in his lot with Leyton from the moment he had taken out Low and his goons.

So, against all better judgement, against all sanity, he started to crawl. Not towards the woman – that would have been suicide – but obliquely, in her general direction. He moved quickly, knowing that whatever he was going to do had to be done soon if at all; before Leyton got himself killed, before the anonymous men closed their tightening net. The plan was to outflank her, to come up behind the woman while Leyton held her attention. At first he scrabbled on his belly, but once he came to a stretch of tall stalls that were still intact, he pulled himself to his feet and ran, crouching low.

He circled, coming around in a rough arc. The sound of gunfire drew closer – louder, and more alarming – but at least that told him he wasn't yet too late.

Kyle hadn't seen the woman, not since Leyton had thrown him out of danger, hadn't raised his head for fear of giving himself away; his ears had been enough to guide him this far. She was close, he knew that: just the other side of this stall, if he was any judge. He drew his knife and gathered himself, feeling every bruise and cut and ache the last hour had dealt him, but putting all such concerns aside as he prepared to leap out and grapple the enemy. Just as he went to move, a section of the timber in front of him ripped apart and something slammed into his right arm a little above the elbow. Excruciating pain came a split second after he saw the blood.

He'd been hit. Even as the pain registered and his mind pieced together that unpalatable fact, a blue-clad form came flying over the market stall, slamming into Kyle and bowling him over. The woman. *How had she known he was there?*

He felt himself dragged, jerked from behind, more quickly than he could think to react. Agony lanced through him as the movement jarred his injured limb. An arm, a bar of solid bone and muscle, closed across his neck, prised itself beneath his chin with choking force. He felt the woman's taut, lean body against his back, as firm and unyielding as a sheet of steel, and the pressure of a gun nozzle at his temple.

"Leyton, I've got him," Boulton called out. "The man you came here for. The stupid prick thought he could sneak up on me."

The gun briefly vanished from against his head. She jabbed the barrel viciously against his arm, into the wound, catching him by surprise. He cried out.

"He's wounded, but not fatally so, not yet. Come out now or that'll change. Give yourself up and I'll let him go, you have my word."

Kyle had never seen himself as a hero, but he hated this woman with a vengeance; hated her for shooting him, for holding him now so helplessly, for prodding his wound merely to provoke a reaction, and for dismissing him with such contempt, for seeing him as no more than a bargaining chip to be played, tossed aside, damaged or broken as she saw fit.

Life had been a real bitch of late, and at that moment all of Kyle's frustration and resentment, at the bad breaks and the persistent unfairness of his lot, focussed sharply on this bitch in particular. If his time really was up, then so be it.

"Don't you listen to her, Leyton," he yelled out, defying the death grip at his throat. "Just kill the cow and be done with it."

She clubbed him then, with the gun, releasing him at the same time so that he went sprawling over; landing on his good arm, thankfully.

"Your choice, Leyton," Boulton called. "He's dead on the count of three."

Kyle looked up to see her crouching, holding the bulky, slightly awkward-looking gun in one hand. It was levelled at the bridge of his nose. He could see right up the smoothly turned barrel.

"One."

Her gaze darted from him to the direction Leyton had to be in and back. No sign or sound of a reaction.

"Two."

Kyle tried to clear his head. He shifted position, knowing it was too late to do anything but still determined to try. This was it, a corner of his mind realised. He was amazed at how calm he felt. He stopped moving and braced himself, eyes focused on the mouth of that barrel. He wondered if he'd actually see the bullet, just for a split second, the instant before it smashed into him and tore his life away.

"Th..."

It wasn't exactly a blur that slipped around and behind Boulton then. Kyle clearly saw a girl, or rather a young woman. Tall, lithe, athletic, with a tumble of dark hair and a pretty, perhaps even beautiful, face. The problem was that by the time he'd seen her she was already somewhere else. It was as if his eyes and his mind were having to play catch up. They couldn't report and interpret her actions as swiftly as she actually performed them.

He watched her glide, dance, slip behind Boulton. The older woman stopped speaking, the fatal count incomplete. Her eyes widened and no longer seemed to be focused on him. Then he noticed the brown-red line that circled her throat. She started to topple, to fall sideways. His most immediate reaction was relief that at least she wasn't going to fall on top of him. As she fell, her head came loose, separating from the body to hit the ground and bounce once, twice, rolling over and around, coming to rest with blank eyes staring straight at him.

There was no blood. Whatever had cut through Boulton's throat and neck must have cauterised the wound instantly. Laser blade, an analytical corner of his mind reasoned, like the one tucked into his belt, though his could never have done this.

It would take a weapon, an assassin's tool, to achieve what he'd just seen.

He stared up at the girl, who had stopped moving and so was clearly visible for the first time. She *was* beautiful, he realised, with large, dark eyes and otherwise petite, elfin features. He didn't say anything, stunned beyond the ability to speak, too shocked by what he'd just witnessed to even consider thanking her for saving his life.

All he could think was that *nothing* could move that fast. Nothing human, at any rate.

CHAPTER THIRTEEN

THERE WERE TIMES in recent days when Leyton could convince himself that he didn't miss his gun at all. This wasn't one of them. Confronted by another eyegee; or, rather, by someone who was *still* an eyegee, he immediately ran through all the things he would have done were the gun still with him. As things stood, with his being outmatched in terms of technology and firepower, all he could do was dodge and hide and hope that he got lucky, while Boulton had her gun to report his every move and guide her every shot.

Any delusions he might once have entertained about life being fair had been shattered long ago, but this really sealed the deal.

Kyle's effort came completely out of the blue. He would never have had the engineer down for that sort of bravery. Of course the gun saw him coming and of course Boulton was ready for him, but that didn't take anything away from the man's courage. After all, *he* wasn't to know how futile trying to sneak up on an eyegee was, or how much trouble it would put them both in.

Almost a shame, really, after a noble effort like that. Leyton saw no alternative but to abandon Kyle, to save his own skin and get the hell out of there before the other ULAW operatives or local security – whoever they might be – closed in. It meant the whole trip had been a waste of time, foiled by Boulton, but better that than it should cost him his own life or freedom to boot.

Then Kethi made her move.

No question; it was impossible to sneak up on an eyegee. Unless, of course, you could move like *that*.

Leyton watched the whole thing and still didn't quite believe what his eyes were reporting. She'd been holding out on him – he'd no inkling she could do anything like this. It wasn't simply a matter of her movements being fast, they were on a completely different level, as if for that brief period, time somehow travelled at a different rate for her. It was over in a split second. The gun wouldn't have had a chance to warn its bearer of the threat. Who or *what* was he allied with here?

Boulton's body crumbled, the head falling loose like a beach ball knocked from a tilting stand.

He watched her die, this woman he despised, this former colleague, this person he had once spent a violent night with, taking out his anger and frustration on her body even as she sated her own needs on his. Making love had never been a part of their equation, the chemistry between them was all about volatility and aggression. And the fact of her death brought him nothing but a savage sense of joy.

He was moving before Boulton hit the ground, vaulting over the lacquered wood and metal casket which had formed his latest defence and then sprinting to where Kyle still knelt, looking stunned, as if not quite able to accept that he was still alive.

Kethi was crouching down, doing something to Boulton's gun. He hesitated before speaking to her, but pushed the words he really wanted to utter to the back of his mind. That conversation could wait. "Careful of the grenades," was all he said, meaning the twin shells moulded to the gun's chassis.

"Thanks, but I know what I'm doing."

He didn't doubt that, but the comment seemed preferable to an awkward silence.

Kyle was trying to get to his feet. Leyton considered helping him, but reckoned he'd done enough of that for one day.

"Are you okay?"

The smaller man nodded, favouring him with a wide-eyed stare before his attention again focussed on Kethi. In shock, Leyton realised. Aside from that, he looked to be bumped and bruised but essentially sound. Perhaps they might yet salvage something from this trip after all.

In the corner of his eye he caught a bright flash from Kethi's direction and looked across to see her pocket something as she stood up, evidently satisfied. "Dead," she said, referring to the gun's AI brain.

"Good," Leyton replied, "because we've got company."

Dark suited figures were moving towards them. Two groups of three, though doubtless this was just the vanguard.

Leyton fired off a couple of shots, just to encourage them to keep their heads down. He wasn't about to get caught up in another gunfight and allow the locals to gather in numbers, which only left one option. They ran. Kethi led the way, not at any superhuman speed this time but still impressively quick. He brought up the rear, pleased to see that Kyle didn't need any help or motivation; the man was running for all he was worth.

Shouts came from behind them, demands that they stop or face the consequences. Leyton counted the seconds – both of them – before the anticipated gunfire; he was at the back after all, the one most likely to be hit, and felt the cold thrill of that knowledge shiver down his spine. He tensed as the first of a pair of staccato pistol rounds punctuated the slap of their running feet like a giant's handclaps, followed by a brief drumroll of automatic weapon's fire. Crockery on an abandoned stall to his left shattered, urging them on, but nothing hit him.

Then they were out of the market, pelting along a street surprisingly free of people. Evidently the prospect of an ongoing gunfight with stray bullets zipping around was less appealing than a bomb blast which had already done its worst. Solid brick now stood between them and the men behind, although that would only last until the pursuers reached the edge of the covered market. There was a corner directly ahead, but it was going to be touch and go.

Leyton ran hard but not flat out, conscious of Kyle's laboured breathing beside him. As a field operative he kept himself in peak condition, but presumably personal fitness hadn't been a priority for the engineer, who was already showing signs of struggling.

"You're doing fine," he assured him. "Just keep going for a bit longer."

Kethi had forged ahead. Leyton fervently hoped she had something a little more elaborate in mind than simply running. They needed a vehicle, a means of getting ahead of their pursuers long enough for a quick pick-up via a flitter.

He kept expecting to hear the sound of renewed gunfire at any second, but mercifully none came until they'd all but reached the corner. He was just daring to think they might have won that particular race when three shots sounded and bullets slammed into the wall beside him. Kyle cried out and at first Leyton thought he'd been hit; he had, but only by brick shards, shrapnel blasted from the wall.

Leyton bundled him around the corner, then turned to peer back. Three dark-clothed figures were closing in. He raised the gun and steadied his arm, part of him still listening for the voice he knew he'd never hear again, then squeezed off two rounds. The leading figure convulsed and fell, causing the two behind to throw themselves to the ground, but more were already issuing from the market. Leyton didn't wait around. Return fire peppered the corner of the building as he abandoned it, running after the other two, quickly catching up with Kyle, who was now visibly flagging. Leyton could only hope he'd bought them enough time. The engineer couldn't go much further.

"Kethi..."

"I know." She'd stopped before a building that looked no different from any other in the street, and was fiddling with the door. In the second or so it took him to reach her she managed to open it.

A building? Presumably there had to be a back way out, otherwise this was a trap in the making, surely.

She looked around, met Leyton's gaze and must have seen the doubt there. "Trust me." Then she ducked inside. Faces stared at them wide-eyed from the plate glass window of the shop front opposite – anxious to catch every detail to gossip to their friends about later, no doubt.

Trust her? It wasn't as if he had much choice at this point. Leyton followed Kyle into the building, but not before he saw dark figures charging around the corner towards them. Close; too close.

He followed the engineer along a dark and narrow hallway, their feet pounding on an unyielding floor formed by a checkerboard of tiny black and white tiles. The whole place looked and felt old, tired. Kethi was already disappearing up a flight of steps halfway along the hallway. The two men followed.

"I don't... think..." Kyle gasped, faltering partway up the first flight.

"Then don't think," Leyton advised. "Just move. We're nearly there." Kethi had to be making for the roof, nothing else made sense. "A little bit further, that's all. Come on, Kyle, don't give up on me now."

The engineer had stopped, leaning forward, hand resting on his knee, chest heaving to suck in breath. Leyton didn't want to leave him, not after all this, but at the same time he didn't fancy dying on his behalf either. "Come on, Kyle!"

At Leyton's urging the other man started to move forward again. Not fast enough though, not nearly fast enough. A dark shape appeared in the doorway behind them. Leyton didn't hesitate, firing immediately, and then backing up the steps. The shape disappeared, but return fire answered his single round, smashing into the steps as he abandoned them like a wave lapping remorselessly in pursuit of a bather's retreating feet.

The resumption of gunplay evidently inspired Kyle to find his second wind, because suddenly he was moving far more freely again. Leyton fired off a couple more shots at the vacant doorway to discourage pursuit and then headed quickly after him. They had made it along the short landing and started up the second flight before he heard the clatter of feet on the stairway below. Leyton stopped and waited.

The presence of landings meant no stairwell, no opportunity for those below to take pot-shots, at least until they acquired direct line of sight. He crouched at the base of the second flight of steps, listening as the pursuers drew rapidly closer and judging when they reached the top of the first flight. He was already beginning to squeeze the trigger as the first man emerged around the corner. The shot caught him in the leg, just above the knee, punching straight through in a shower of blood and shattered bone. The man screamed and went down. Leyton was already sprinting upwards, taking three steps at a time and rapidly catching Kyle.

The stairs went all the way up to the roof. How Kethi knew that, he had no idea. He was beyond being surprised by her. Somehow, despite Kyle's flagging energy, they made it to the top without the pursuing troopers or agents getting to grips with them; largely thanks to Leyton's dogged rearguard defence.

As they took the final few stairs he heard a familiar rumbling – a craft coming in. He just hoped it was one of theirs. Then they were out of the door, onto a rooftop covered in a mosaic of paving stones. A courtyard garden, complete with slender, brick-built flower beds and metal garden furniture, currently in the process of being flung haphazardly about by the arrival of the craft: a gleaming silver flitter. He watched as a chair was sent skidding across the paving by the downdraft, tipping over before it could plummet off the roof. Joss waved frantically from the flitter's pilot seat as the landing skids touched down and the hatch popped open.

Built for speed, Leyton wasn't even convinced this sleek arrowhead of a craft would take all three of them plus Joss, but who was he to argue?

He covered the others as they scampered across to the flitter, emptying what remained in his final ammo clip down the stairwell blind before sprinting for the gaping doorway. Kethi was clambering in beside Joss, while Kyle made himself comfortable behind them. Leyton wasn't familiar with the habitat's flitters and could only hope there was an empty seat beside the engineer. Thank goodness they hadn't brought anyone else on this mission. He leapt up the short ladder and into the hatchway, half falling on top of Kyle before settling into the vacant seat that was indeed there, and fumbled to strap himself in.

The hatch retracted and sealed even before he'd fully repositioned himself. Dark clad figures erupted from the stairway and bullets pinged off the flitter's hull as she started to lift.

"Hang on," Joss called back above the climbing roar of the engines. "They've got copters closing in and have also scrambled a couple of jets from the military base. So far they only seem to have in-atmosphere fighters, so I'm going to take us as high as I can as quickly as I can. This might get a little rough."

Good tactic. Joss's clipped briefing was exactly the sort of thing Kyle needed to hear, keeping him informed while offering reassurance that the person at the controls knew what they were doing. Initially, Leyton had been a little surprised to see Joss here, certain that she was still grieving Wicksy's loss; then again, he doubted the habitat's native pilots would have had much in-atmosphere flight experience, so her being here made sense. Sentimentality was something they could ill afford.

The craft lifted almost ponderously from the rooftop, or so it seemed to Leyton's adrenaline-pumped senses. Bullets continued to ping impotently off their hull, sounding like hailstones hitting a window. Finally the nose tilted upwards and Joss was able to pour on the juice.

G-force slammed against Leyton's chest, pressing him into

the seat. At the same time everything started to pale towards monotone. He knew what was coming, he'd been here before, which didn't stop him fighting it. He wondered how Kyle was coping beside him, but couldn't spare the effort to look. Concentration, that was the key; yet despite his every effort colour continued to leach from the surroundings and the world began to narrow, to close in, as peripheral vision shut down. He refused to accept the inevitable; there was too much going on. They weren't safe yet, he couldn't afford to black out; so he wasn't going to, not this time.

But he did.

COMING TO AGAIN was always the worst part. Muscles turned rebellious, as if they'd enjoyed their lack of supervision and gained confidence from his temporary loss of control. His head twitched and jerked, refusing to either stay still or perform the simplest of tasks such as turning, and his arms flopped uselessly. He felt like a marionette with half the guiding wires cut. Fortunately, the effect passed in a matter of seconds but Leyton hated it, that sense of not being in command of his own body.

Kyle was still out, though doubtless he'd be coming around at any second.

Outside, the sky had lost its blue and Leyton could see stars, so presumably Joss had won her race with the jet fighters.

From beside the pilot, Kethi looked around at him and smiled. "Back with us, I see."

He wondered whether she'd blanked out at all. Probably not, given what he'd seen her do earlier. The smile withered away, presumably in the face of what she saw in his eyes. The fact that he knew; knew who she was, *what* she was.

When they first met he'd thought the name Kethi sounded familiar, now he remembered why. The sadness in her expression as she turned towards the front was like a door closing; the implication being that she recognised his newfound knowledge and regretted it, which suggested that his opinion mattered to her. Interesting.

A groan from beside him signalled Kyle's return to consciousness. He watched, amused, as the engineer struggled to reassert control over his defiant muscles. Finally the other man shook his head and grinned across at Leyton. "I hate it when that happens."

They reached *The Rebellion* and slipped inside her without incident. Once out of the shuttle, Leyton cornered Kethi, grabbing her arm before she could slip away. "We need to talk."

She glared at him but then nodded. He read reluctance and resignation in her face as she said, "All right, just let me get us underway before ULAW can muster anything to send after us. I'll meet you in your quarters."

He could hardly object to that. "Fair enough." He let go of her arm. As she walked away, Leyton couldn't help but watch. She moved with such grace. He tried to analyse his feelings towards her and failed.

"So this is where you make your home these days, huh?" Kyle said, joining him. The man had a knack for jovial bonhomie that Leyton could only envy.

"Indeed it is."

"And I take it you're looking for an engineer."

"Good guess."

"Very flattering that you've gone to so much trouble, but I'm guessing there's a reason you needed me in particular."

Leyton didn't want to get involved in this, not now. "Maybe, but time for that later." He wondered where he could find someone to palm Kyle off onto ahead of his meeting with Kethi. Emily Teifer, who had grudgingly taken over engineering after the battle, seemed the logical choice, but he couldn't very well put Kyle to work the moment he arrived and, besides, engineering was a fair trek away.

"Look, let me show you the rec room," he said. There was

bound to be somebody around. "You can relax, have a beer or two, and we can take things from there."

"That sounds good to me."

The first person Leyton saw as they entered the room was Joss, sitting on her own, warming down after her timely retrieval flight. Perfect; someone Kyle had already met. Only as he went to leave the two of them together did he register the wounded look Joss gave him and realise that to her Kyle was little more than a direct replacement for Wicksy, a reminder she could doubtless have done without.

Cursing his own preoccupation, Leyton returned to his cabin to wait for Kethi. Maybe it wasn't such a bad thing after all. Life could be a bastard at times and you had to learn to roll with the punches. Joss was an integral part of the crew; the quicker she accepted what had happened and moved on, the better, for all their sakes.

Scant moments after he arrived at his quarters there came a double knock at the door.

"Come in. It isn't locked."

Kethi looked stern faced, as if determined not to be apologetic for anything; neither for what she'd done nor for who she was.

"Well," she said, "here I am."

Okay, the direct approach was fine by him. "Your name, it's not really Kethi, is it?" he said. "It's K-E-T-H-I. Kinetic Entity Twinned with Higher Intelligence. I've heard about it – knew the name rang a bell when I first met you, but couldn't quite place it. Now, having seen what you're capable of, I can. Kethi's an experiment, isn't it? One that was abandoned, or at least so I thought."

"Abandoned by ULAW perhaps, but never by us," she replied. "Those involved came to the habitat and have continued their work ever since. Not with universal success, it has to be said. I'm the one that worked, and they're still trying to figure out why."

Her eyes flashed with... what? Defiance, challenge, suppressed anger? Perhaps a little of all of them.

He tried to reconcile what he knew of the KETHI project with the beautiful, vibrant woman before him. KETHI had been an attempt to produce human-AI synergy – much like the Kaufman Industries project, which had resulted in the needle ships that had engaged and defeated *The Noise Within* – but it had approached the problem from the opposite direction. Whereas KI had been intent on linking a human mind with the AI of a ship, the KETHI project had sought to introduce a nascent AI into the brain of a human baby at the embryonic level, where it would grow and develop as the child did. The aim had been to produce a more natural gestalt of the two forms of intelligence. It sounded viable in theory but the problems of rejection and the complications that arose in physical and mental development proved insurmountable. At least so Leyton had always believed. Apparently others had persevered, overcoming the obstacles. No wonder Kethi was so brilliant an analyst. She combined the processing capabilities of an AI with the intuition and leaps of logic that only an organic mind could make.

"Your aunt," he said, "the one who died defending the habitat...?"

"Was lovely," she replied, wistfully. "She was a 'near miss,' no deformity or rejection issues but incomplete meshing of the gestalt. The AI part of her brain didn't develop fully. None of which stopped her from being a wonderful person."

Leyton nodded. "You mention deformity," he said, suddenly making a connection and wondering if it was valid. "Is Simon...?"

Her turn to nod. "Yes. His arm is only the most apparent legacy. He nearly died at birth and had an incredibly difficult childhood. Eventually they had to kill the AI part of his brain entirely, with no guarantee how that would work out, but he came through it. Simon's a lot tougher than he looks. I think that's one of the reasons he's always so cheerful, almost as if he takes every day as a gift that he came close to never enjoying."

"That could have happened to you," he said, wondering how many had suffered worse during the course of the project.

"Yes, but it didn't." She took a step closer, her eyes gazing into his. As she stood before him, beautiful, vulnerable but proud, he struggled to think of her as anything other than fully human.

"I am human," she whispered, guessing his thoughts. Her face had drawn very close now.

"Are you? Prove it." He had no idea why he said that. Yes, he did. It was an invitation, but an ambiguous one; deniable and open to interpretation, which left the onus on her to make the next move. If she wanted to.

Evidently, she did.

As her lips moved towards his, he was reminded of another cabin, another unexpected encounter. Boulton. Yet this was totally different. Kethi's lips felt soft, plump and surprisingly cool. When he thought of Boulton, he remembered a body as rigid as steel; with her it had all been about need and dominance, with no room for anything gentle or loving and certainly nothing as feminine as the feel of Kethi's body against his as she pressed against him, encircled by his arms.

She drew back a little, a twinkle in her eye. "Human enough for you?"

"It'll do." He drew her into another kiss.

After all too brief a time she pulled away, easing out of his grip. "Sorry, I have to go. Still on duty."

He stared at her, not believing she meant it. "Surely they can cope without you for a little while?"

She giggled – a very young, girlish sound which surprised him coming from her. "Don't be so impatient. Aren't I worth waiting for?"

"Yes, but..."

"Shhh." She stepped forward, running a dainty fingertip down his lips and chin. "This is all so... Look, one step at a time, all right?" With a final, coy smile, she turned and left.

After the door had closed behind her, Leyton stood for a few seconds and simply stared at the empty space where she'd been. He shook his head and couldn't help but grin. Yes, that seemed all too human to him. Only then did he realise that she'd said nothing to explain the time-defying speed she'd displayed in dispatching Boulton. Had the kiss been intended as a distraction, to prevent him from pursuing the subject? If so, it worked remarkably well.

CHAPTER FOURTEEN

THE FIRST SET of coordinates Lara provided them with proved to be a dead end, quite literally. It led them to an insignificant corner of Virtuality just off a main thoroughfare, a place that was never destined to be anything more than backdrop, the sort of thing programmers habitually filled in with repetitive bulk standard coding. This time around someone had clearly decided to be creative, and, at the far end of a stunted, brick-lined cul-de-sac, had added a distinctive flourish: a shallow, insignificant little alcove.

"One down..." Tanya murmured.

The second of Lara's 'possibles' looked more promising. The coding was integrated into the back wall of a club.

"I'm sensing a pattern here," Philip said.

"Either that or we're about to encounter another alcove or two," Malcolm added.

"I'm putting my faith in the name."

The place was called Veils and, had he been aware of it, this would have been the first place Philip would have looked even without Lara's recommendation, give the Byrzaens' apparent penchant for flowing lines and floaty things.

"I've never been in here before," Malcolm said, as if to defend his not thinking of the place without Lara's prompting.

That in itself was interesting. Philip had somehow assumed his father was familiar with every part of Virtuality. Evidently not.

Veils lived up to its name. The first thing that struck Philip was how different the whole vibe of the place was from Bubbles. The rhythmic thud of bass that underpinned everything might have been much the same, but here it was a little less frenetic. That was symptomatic of the difference, he realised. Bubbles had been all about high energy cranked up to the nth degree; the very atmosphere had crackled with anticipation. Here, while energy was still encouraged by the music and the drink, everything seemed less urgent, as if the designers had quite deliberately aimed for a more chilled and laidback ambience.

Then, of course, there were the veils.

Soft furnishings – padded sofas and curved corner units, chairs, bean bags, water seats, and even a few hover mats – were artfully scattered at the fringes of the dance floor in a manner that looked almost haphazard but which cleverly utilized the available space to its maximum. Around, above and within these seat arrangements were the veils. Floating, hanging, draping and wafting in the air currents created by the movement of patrons and the club's air conditioning, they were in a multitude of colours, though violets, blues and greens predominated.

Even the dance floor complied with the theme. Although clearly solid – at least to judge by the number of people confidently gyrating and quick-toeing their way around it – the surface looked to be anything but. Instead it seemed to consist of nothing more than a mass of swirling veils, twisting serpents of silken cloth which changed colour and definition constantly as lights beneath the flooring pulsed and transformed in time with the music.

Nor was this effect confined to the veils on the dance floor; many of those throughout the club pulsed in varying colours and brightness with perfect synchronicity.

Philip found his attention transfixed by one veil in particular, which hung immediately before him and dropped from somewhere high above, reaching almost to the floor. The veil writhed sinuously, despite there being no apparent breeze in this part of the club to stimulate it, and the purple, green and black patterning seemed to ripple and run up and down the material's length. It was as if the veil performed solely for him, and the way it swayed put him in mind of a woman – a wiggle of the hips and sway of the pelvis – dancing privately, just for him.

He reached out and grasped the veil by an edge, running the material through his hand. It felt silky and warm to the touch, almost as if it were alive. He let go, allowing the material to drop back into its undulating rhythm.

It was like walking through some surreal woodland – the club-goers their fellow explorers, sharing the discovery of this sacred realm. The further they went from the dance floor the more subdued the music, the accumulated mass of the veils acting as a baffle, muffling the sound.

"I don't get it," Tanya said as they continued. "Shouldn't we have hit the wall by now?"

"Definitely," Philip replied. Yet the forest of veils stretched on into the distance.

"This doesn't make sense," Malcolm murmured. "I looked at the coding myself before we set out, just moments ago, and there was nothing like this."

The music had faded to mere background, the number of people around them growing fewer and fewer.

"What does it mean?" Tanya asked, her voice as subdued as Malcolm's. Philip could understand why; somehow it felt wrong to speak loudly here, in what had developed into a tranquil, almost mystic place.

"It means that wherever we now are doesn't exist in Home's Virtuality, that somehow we've gone somewhere else," he said.

"Bollocks," she exclaimed, evidently unimpressed by any sense of mysticism. "Things around you two just keep getting weirder by the minute."

"You could always go back," Philip offered, not sure whether he wanted her to or not.

"Thanks, but no thanks. I've got my reputation to think of."

"Of course you have. Wouldn't want to put a blemish on your CV now, would we?"

"Cut it out, you two," Malcolm interrupted. "Save the bickering for later."

He had a point; it wasn't as if there was any shortage of things to claim their attention. The veils were changing, slowly and subtly; a gradual shift from what they had been to something less substantial. The sense of being in a vast forest was more pronounced than ever, but the solid trunks of the 'trees' were becoming ethereal phantoms, as if the three of them had somehow stepped across into the realm of faeries.

Philip was absorbed by the changing veils, watching them intently to try and see the actual shift of form, but it was too subtle. The effect was undeniable, however. "They're becoming pure energy," he murmured.

Curtains of light now stretched around them, where previously delicate cloth had hung. Pillars of coruscating energy had replaced the tumbles of vibrant cloth they'd been walking between mere moments before. Nor was that the only change.

"Listen," Malcolm said. "Can you hear that?"

The music was now barely audible, but a new sound had begun to supplant it. Indistinct, yet somehow comforting, a distant murmuring, as if they were approaching a large gathering, an auditorium in which a vast crowd had gathered, conversation bubbling throughout as they settled in anticipation of a performance. The sound was too indistinct, too quiet, almost buried beneath the lingering music from the club, yet it was enough to have Philip straining to hear, striving to sieve meaning from the garble.

"Where the hell are we?"

It was a while since they'd seen anyone else. Tanya's question was little more than a whisper.

"I think," Philip began, "that this is a link…"

"A bridge," Malcolm interjected.

"...between our Virtuality on Home..."

"...and the Byrzaens," Malcolm finished for him.

"You're kidding me," Tanya said. Then, when neither laughed, "You're not, are you?"

"Wish I was."

"But how is that possible?"

"Absolutely no idea," Philip conceded.

Without any discernable leap, just incremental drift, they found themselves somewhere that was undeniably alien. They were now tiptoeing through a landscape dominated by curtains of light that rippled and ran and receded and darted. Bright colours ran through the translucent veils like veins, pulsing, thickening and dwindling. As with the veil he'd held earlier, Philip couldn't shake the feeling that these shifting films of energy were organic in some way, that they might almost be alive, but he couldn't have offered any explanation for that impression.

The music had disappeared completely, only the faint hum as of distant conversation remained, though it had grown no clearer and it remained impossible to discern anything as intelligible as words.

"Noise..." Malcolm said.

Philip nodded.

"What about the noise?" Tanya wanted to know.

"The Byrzaens believe that the sounds of intelligence – communication and other sundry asides – enhance the brain's ability to think," Philip explained. "It seems to be one of their fundamental tenets."

"Great, so you two geniuses ought to be on top form right about now then."

Nothing in Philip's experience, not even his brief visit to the Byrzaen spaceship at New Paris, had prepared him for this environment of energy, which seemed unharnessed and yet, at the same time, restricted to the forms of the veils. It was a strange dichotomy that somehow felt right, part of the intended order. He couldn't help but question the earlier assessment that they were within some sort of link between human territory and Byrzaen. What if this wasn't a bridge at all, what if they'd already crossed into Byrzaen space? Could this landscape of shifting veils be as familiar to a Byrzaen as forests of bark-crusted trunks and leafy canopies were to rural living humans? But how could that be? How could life in their galaxy have evolved to be so dramatically different when nothing similar had been encountered in human space? The questions multiplied without any prospect of imminent answers.

A figure walked across their path, some distance ahead. At first Philip paid little attention, lost in his own convoluted thoughts and assuming this to be some reveller from the club out exploring, but almost immediately he realised how mistaken that assessment was. Hunched shoulders and long, gangly legs that gave the figure an almost heron-like gait...

"A Byrzaen!" Tanya exclaimed.

"Evidently." There was always the possibility that this was a human club-goer who had chosen to mimic a Byrzaen for his avatar, but, given the context, Philip wouldn't have bet on it. The figure had disappeared from sight, masked by intervening screens of energy. It gave no indication of having seen them.

All three of them quickened pace, hurrying forward to the point where they'd seen the Byrzaen, but it had vanished from sight.

Without any warning, Philip fancied he could hear words emerging from the background noise, so faint that he couldn't be entirely certain, but a voice seemed to say, "We mean you no harm." The words sent a chill coursing through him.

"Can you hear anything in the static?" he asked, as casually as he could manage.

"No," Malcolm replied. "Damned annoying, isn't it? I keep trying, but nothing."

We mean you no harm.

"Well, do we follow after the bird-man?" Tanya asked, sounding none too keen.

"I don't know about you," Malcolm said, "but I think I've seen enough."

"More than," Philip agreed.

"If that means we're heading back, you've got my vote," Tanya chipped in.

We mean you no harm.

They retraced their steps, a walk that seemed to take far less time than the outward trip. For the most part they did so in silence, though Malcolm said at one point, "Still don't understand why none of this shows up in the coding. It *has* to, somewhere."

We mean you no harm.

The message stayed with Philip, constantly repeated, never clear enough to convince him that he wasn't simply projecting a pattern into the chaos.

The music gradually swelled as they walked, swallowing the constant background babble and its insistent message, if such it were, which neither rose nor fell in volume but simply disappeared beneath the club's pulsing rhythms, while the veils around them slid craftily from energy to tenuous substance to material. Before Philip realised, they were back in the club itself. The atmosphere, which had struck him as tranquil and relaxing when they first entered, now took on a more sinister edge, as if the tranquillity was intended to disarm and seduce, to lure the unwary into a false sense of security. None of their party seemed inclined to linger. They made their way across the floor and were soon exiting Veils into the bland simplicity of the street beyond.

It felt to Philip as if they had narrowly escaped the jaws of a cunningly concealed trap. Before he could comment to that effect, something flashed towards them. Philip only caught a glimpse in the corner of his eye and, but for Tanya, wouldn't have registered the presence of the flash at all before it killed him. Her hand shot out, interposing itself between Philip and whatever he it was. Later, Philip would recall what Catherine had

said about Tanya's avatar being 'packed with countermeasures.'
Presumably this was one of them. Certainly he'd never noticed
her clutching a translucent disc before, which was what she
seemed to have in her hand now; a shield of some sort, which
he only really saw as the flash struck and the disc was limned in
pulses of silver fire. The fire died, its energies spent.

Tanya's hand was blackened as she lowered it, charred, with
wisps of smoke rising from fingertips and palm, but she didn't
seem to notice. She was already in motion, sprinting in the
direction the flash had come from, towards a figure that appeared
to have been cast from polished chrome or perhaps silver, light
glinting from its skin and blank, featureless face. The assassin
– for that was all Philip could think this must be – crouched in
preparation. For a bizarre moment its silver hide reflected the
onrushing Tanya, making it seem that she was charging towards
an imminent collision with a warped version of herself.

As she ran, she swept out a hand and flung what appeared
to be a fistful of glowing embers at the mirrored assassin,
except that the embers raced ahead of her and zeroed in on
their target. Philip thought he caught a glimpse of tiny winged
figures within these fiery motes, but couldn't have sworn to the
fact. The motes converged on the faceless figure, which began
to pulse with light, before flaring in a manner that reminded
Philip of the flash Tanya had intercepted. The dazzling nimbus
formed a bubble upon which the embers dashed themselves, to
flare briefly and magnificently as they died.

Tanya was almost upon the assassin, who sprang away at the
last minute, as if afraid to grapple with her. Clearly deciding
discretion to be the better part of valour, the silver figure
turned and threw himself at the building behind, scurrying
up its wall like a monkey up a tree. Tanya skidded to a halt
and produced a gun with her left hand, raising it and firing
even as she slowed. Visible energy leapt from the muzzle in
a continuous stream, bridging the gap between the weapon
and the fleeing figure. Despite the very real threat and the rush

of fear, Philip couldn't help but wonder why he could see the beam. Surely there was no need for lethal energies to cross into the visible spectrum; in fact, it seemed inefficient to even think of designing a weapon that way. It reminded him of something from a game – souped up and vivid, perhaps, but even so... he recalled Catherine referring to Tanya as an experienced gamer and wondered if this was a result of that – Tanya's visualisation in some way finding form in Virtuality.

The assassin had frozen, and now began to lose definition, flickering in and out of existence, until it winked out entirely. Still Tanya kept firing, as if to make certain the silver figure wouldn't return.

Evidently satisfied, she holstered the gun and strode back to where Philip and Malcolm waited. "Damn! So much for hoping that this assignment would be a free ride."

"Why did you charge him?" Philip wondered. "I mean, if you had a gun, why not just shoot him and be done with it?"

"To put myself between you and the assassin, obviously," she replied with a toss of her blonde hair.

Obviously.

"The time it would have taken me to draw a gun and take aim is time he could have used to take another shot at you. This way, I kept him occupied and didn't give him clear sight of his target."

"Thanks," Philip said, lamely.

"Ah, glad I'm here now, are you?"

One thing Philip couldn't help but notice was how *hot* she looked right then, but, judging by her tone, he guessed sex was still off the agenda for the immediate future.

"If he was an avatar, why did he run? Why did saving himself matter so much?"

"He wasn't running," Tanya said. "He went up the building to remove me from the equation and get a better angle for a shot. That's why I had to take him out before he reached the top or before he could even stop partway up and turn."

"Oh." That possibility had never occurred to him.

"What happens now?" Malcolm wanted to know. "Won't he just come back for another try?"

Tanya shook her head. "I've set hounds to burn up his back trail and hopefully trace the avatar to its source, though I wouldn't count on the last bit. Doubtless they *will* try again, but not right now, not by simply rebooting that avatar, at any rate." She frowned. "The corp behind the avatar will know some of my counters next time, though, so I'll have to install a few upgrades. Expensive stuff." She flashed them a grin. "Just glad it won't be me that's footing the bill."

"Have you done this sort of thing before?" Philip asked, curious about how readily Tanya seemed to be taking events in her stride and wanting to gain some context.

"No," she replied. "Not really; not in Virtuality at any rate." She lifted her hand, the one that had been charred in the initial attack; not that you would have known it now. The hand was unblemished. "Same principles apply though, in here or out there. Show an enemy your moves and then let him walk away and you'd better learn some new moves fast."

Philip pondered her words, the nonchalant implication that she was some sort of hot-shot bodyguard in the corporeal world, and wondered whether that were true or a touch of bravado for his benefit. You never could tell in Virtuality.

Tanya flexed her fingers, balled her fist and smiled at Philip, evidently satisfied. "Now, unless you two boys want to hang around for anything else, shall we get out of here?"

"Good idea."

She sashayed past them, took a few steps and then paused to turn and blow Philip a kiss. "See you later." With that, she disappeared, stepping out of Virtuality. Philip looked at his father, who raised his eyebrows and shrugged. Where in the universe had Catherine found this woman? Not on Kaufman Industry's payroll, surely?

* * *

LEYTON LAY THERE in the dark, listening to the breathing beside him. He could tell she was no more asleep than he was and wondered if he should say something.

She beat him to it. "Can't you sleep either?"

"Not at the moment." He raised his voice a fraction. "Lights, minimum illumination."

A soft glow suffused the room and he looked at her, still questioning the wisdom of letting this happen, of wanting it to happen. Was he really over Mya, finally, after all these years? She'd only left the ship a matter of days ago, and here he was in bed with someone else.

"Is it Mya?" Kethi asked.

"No," he lied. "It's nothing. I've just grown used to sleeping alone. It's a little strange having someone beside me."

"I could go back to my own quarters."

"No," he said quickly.

She smiled, and then rested her head against his chest.

A corner of his mind doubted though, was afraid that this was still all about Mya. He really didn't want it to be a rebound thing. Kethi deserved better than that.

"It's not because of what happened on Arcadia, because you now know what I am?"

"No," he said again, and at least knew that to be wholly true. He gently lifted her head to gaze into her eyes. He'd never seen such vulnerability in her before, would never have dreamed it existed. "Of course not." He leant forward and kissed her – a chaste pressing of lips to lips. Hers were soft, warm, and dry.

"Good. I'm different, I know. I can do extraordinary things, but then, so can you. Doesn't mean you're not human."

"I know."

"What I do..." She drew a deep breath. "I can raise and lower my metabolism at will, crank up the whole pace my body functions if I need to – muscles, nerves, thoughts, the whole caboodle." She obviously wanted to talk, and he was happy to let her. "So that to me it seems as if I'm moving normally while the whole world around me slows to a crawl. It seems to everyone else I'm moving impossibly fast. I don't do it very often because..."

You don't like to be reminded of how different you are, he filled in the unspoken words. "How does your body cope with the speed, though, with the extra strain that has to come with it?"

"It's designed to, it *grew* to.. The AI part of my brain has been shaping my body's development since birth, sculpting my physiology so that I can handle the extremes required."

He didn't react, didn't draw back, because the prospect didn't bother him, but the fact remained that, despite her protestations, Kethi was a lot less human than she seemed – a lot less like *other* humans at any rate; not less in the sense of inferior, just different, as she said. In fact, *superior* in many ways, perhaps even a new evolutionary step. A different form of transhuman from the Kaufmans senior and junior, but a step forward none the less, so he continued to hold her, and said, in part to lighten the mood a little, "It is a neat trick, though, the speeding up; must make you a demon on the z-ball court."

"I don't use it, *wouldn't* use it when I'm playing. What would be the point?"

"Well, I suppose the point would be that you'd win."

"Exactly. Every time, without anyone else ever getting a look in. Sort of takes the fun out of things for all involved, don't you think? Besides, how many people do you imagine would want to play me a second time?"

"Ah, so that's the real reason."

"No, it isn't!" she flared, pulling away. Then, seeing his grin and presumably realising that he was winding her up, she added quietly, "Bastard," and mock-hit him on the chest before snuggling up to him again.

"One thing, though," he said. "Surely when you *do* win, fair and square though it might be, folk on the losing team must sometimes wonder."

"Maybe, sometimes, but I hope most of them know me well enough to realise I wouldn't cheat like that."

Leyton wasn't so sure. He'd watched Kethi play z-ball and had seen for himself how good she was. He could well imagine that in the heat of the moment someone on the losing team with a strong competitive streak might wonder whether she'd used her abilities, just a little bit. Still, if any such resentment did linger, he'd never noted it in the crew's reaction to her.

He snorted laughter at a sudden thought, jostling her head as his chest lifted.

"What?"

"Oh, nothing. I was just thinking that your friend Simon is going to hate me when he finds out about us."

She groaned. "Please, don't even go there, not right now." She hugged him tighter. A few seconds of silence followed before she said, "Are you still wide awake?"

"Yes."

"Good, me too. So, why don't you put the lights out again? We could maybe work on giving Simon even more reason to hate you."

He didn't need asking twice.

THE HOUR WAS late, but Catherine's partial, Cath, made no reference to the fact and didn't attempt to forestall him. Instead Malcolm found himself ushered into Catherine's presence with only a minimum of delay. Her hair was down, falling in platinum strands around her face, and she wore a light, pearlescent nightdress, so either his arrival had roused her from bed or disturbed her preparations for getting into it.

"Sorry," he said.

She waved the apology aside. "Don't worry, I realise you only have limited opportunity to slip away from Philip."

Good, which meant he could get straight to the point. "I take it you've heard about what happened today?"

She nodded. "I've spoken to Tanya and studied her report."

"So, where does this leave us?" He wasn't talking about the bigger issue – the Byrzaen landscape spilling out of the club, Veils – which could keep for another time. He was talking about his son.

"Under siege," she replied. "Viral attacks on Virtuality have increased significantly since you two returned from New Paris, and I don't think that's a coincidence. We've bolstered the already robust defences with KI expertise and that's held everything out so far – which is why, I suspect, they resorted to using an avatar – but there's no guarantee that'll last forever."

Malcolm realised that. He was desperate not to lose his son again, but at the same time didn't want Philip's new life to be dominated by fear and paranoia, which was why he was sneaking off to see Catherine like this, to shield the lad from the full implications of the situation if at all possible. He felt certain that Philip's assassination was linked to the Byrzaens and their presence in Home's Virtuality, where they had no right to be. The timing was too convenient otherwise. The only way to safeguard his son in the long term was to get to the bottom of whatever was going on. Understanding would make clear their alternatives, might even give them some leverage. Until then they were shadow boxing, fighting an opponent they couldn't actually see.

"Do you want me to arrange more bodyguards?" Catherine offered.

"No, Philip wouldn't stand for it. He's accepted Tanya. He doesn't like what she is, but he's accepted her presence as necessary, especially following today's events. I don't see him putting up with a whole squad of Tanyas, though."

"Really? I seem to recall him having quite an eye for the ladies. He takes after his father in that regard."

Malcolm smiled. "True, but you know what I mean. Besides, you've got the rest of the board to think about."

"Pft... them!" Catherine gave a dismissive wave of her hand. Her glib gesture didn't alter the fact that if she squandered too many of KI's resources on keeping them alive, questions would be asked. Not that Catherine Chzyski had ever been found wanting when it came to appropriate answers, but at the same time Malcolm felt it important she keep the realities of their situation in mind.

"One aspect that none of us have really discussed yet, something that bothers me..." Catherine said, a little awkwardly.

"Go on."

"Well, there's no question in my mind that there is some heavy intrigue being played out within the government. Things that are illegal, immoral, and dangerous for everyone. However, I've yet to see any evidence that the Byrzaens are involved in any of it. All right, their arrival has sparked off all the nastiness, but so far everything we've seen has been human against human, just like the War."

"I know what you're saying," Malcolm agreed. "We've all been very quick to cast the aliens as the villains."

"When they might be nothing more than innocent bystanders. Exactly. Our culture, our ways, are all going to be new to them. They could just be standing back letting humans be humans, oblivious to the backstabbing and violence going on behind the scenes, or maybe assuming this is simply how we do things."

"They *could* be," Malcolm agreed.

"But you don't think so."

"No, to be honest, and nor does Philip. Don't get me wrong, I'm willing to be proven wrong, but for now let's go forward on the basis that they *are* involved. Then we'll have all the bases covered."

"Fair enough."

Malcolm was about to leave, when Catherine said, "You do realise, don't you, that despite all that we're doing, whoever's behind these attempts might still get through to him?"

"I know," Malcolm replied, and he did; but what more could he possibly do?

CHAPTER FIFTEEN

RAIN SPLATTERED THE pavement. Droplets darted across the pools of illumination cast by the streetlamps in serried ranks like swarms of migrating insects. Night fell early, here in the tropics. Terri Gilkes pulled up her collar, hunched her shoulders, and tried to walk faster without lifting her eyes from the section of sidewalk immediately in front of her feet. On the whole, Terri didn't mind the rain. Prior to this deluge the air conditioning might have protected her from the afternoon's oppressive humidity but she'd still known it was there. She could feel it bearing down on her when she ventured outside at lunchtime, as if some giant hand were pressing all the moisture out of the sky. No, rain was fine by her – it held the promise of relief, of cooler, fresher air to come. But why, with all the day to choose from, did the rain have to fall now, when she was walking home? She was tired, damp, too warm, pissed off, and thinking of applying for another job. Oh, she knew she'd never match the current salary, but there were more important things in life than money. Actually *having* a life, for example. She hated shift work, hated her job, and hated the honeycomb.

As a rule, she *didn't* hate the fact that she lived outside the towering complex – only those of real importance had quarters within the building itself – since at least she got to escape once work had ended. Although today she might have made an exception.

Her waterproofs were doubtless working, but they could

easily have been porous for all the good they were doing. Heat and humidity had never been her favourite combination, and perspiration was taking care of what the rain couldn't. You'd think in the age of artificial intelligence, shimmer suits and interstellar flight *someone* would have come up with a cheap and simple system of clothing that let sweat out while holding the elements at bay, but apparently not.

She didn't see the collision coming and was both startled out of her wits and almost knocked from her feet by the jarring impact.

"What the f...?" Somehow her bag had been dislodged from her shoulder and went spinning to the ground. She watched in horror as its contents spilled out onto the sodden pavement. "Shit, shit, shit!" She could have sworn the bag was closed.

"I'm so sorry," said the woman, a slight thing who'd been hurrying in the opposite direction, apparently as oblivious to her surroundings as Terri was. They both crouched down and started scrabbling to gather Terri's escaped possessions. The woman grabbed her bag, was holding it out to her. She snatched it back ungraciously. It was on the tip of her tongue to bawl the girl out, to tell her to watch where she was going in future, but in fairness Terri was probably as much to blame as the stranger, so she contented herself with a grunt that was neither a complaint nor thanks, as her belongings were unceremoniously shovelled into the bag, soaked through, all of them.

God. Despite any earlier thoughts to the contrary, she hated the rain.

Without further ceremony Terri forced the bulging bag shut, stood up and continued on her way, with home now only a short distance ahead. Her shoulder throbbed painfully and would almost certainly bruise by the morning. It was difficult to believe that such a slight thing as that woman could have hit her so hard. She must have been running. Stupid cow.

*   *   *

MYA CLUNG ON for dear life, limbs splayed, keeping her body as flush to the ceiling as possible, all the while praying that they didn't look up. Smart boots and gloves held her in place, the tips of toes and splayed palms infiltrating the very fabric of the ceiling, but it was her own muscles and willpower that kept her flat, that prevented her bum from sagging downward. A few things worked in her favour: the two men currently walking below her were deep in conversation, their concentration elsewhere; they weren't alert; and this was a high ceiling. None of which guaranteed a damn thing, but it gave her cause to hope. She held her breath as they passed, felt the sweat gathering, trickling through her hair, and hoped fervently that they'd be gone before the first drop fell. She gritted her teeth as her muscles burned – the legs and thighs were the worst. Smart pads at her knees would have made things a whole lot easier right now. Why hadn't she thought to wear them?

Because she hadn't expected to be hanging from the ceiling, that was why.

Finally they were past, their banal conversation mercifully cut short as a door swung shut behind them. She dared to move again, allowing her body to relax as she prised one foot free and then the other, moving them closer together and bringing both hands in as well. Like some clumsy lizard she made her way to the wall and eased herself a little way down it before dropping to the floor. Only then did her muscles report anything approaching relief.

Mya was still a long way from optimum condition but she was getting there. Both strength and fitness were improving daily, thanks to a rigorous exercise regime and proper diet. No, she wasn't quite there yet, but close enough. She had to be.

Terri Gilkes' ID card, cloned in a split second via a sleight of hand as she helped the woman gather her things from the rain-sodden pavement, had done the first bit, enabling her to penetrate the building's outer skin, but it could only take her so far. The honeycomb never slept. This vast complex of a building, which nestled partially underground and thrust towards the heavens in a pillar of tinted glass, concrete and metal – was the nerve centre of ULAW's intelligence services and covert operations. Human space never slept, at least not all at the same time, so nor did the honeycomb. There were, however, periods when the building was quieter than others, dark hours when whole sections of the place shut down while others remained busy as any hive of insects. Mya had chosen her moment carefully, timing her intrusion to coincide with a quiet*er* period while avoiding the quiet*est*. It was a trade off, as so many things in life tended to be: the fewer people around to see her the better, but while there still remained *some* people wandering the corridors she didn't have to worry about under-floor pressure sensors or motion alarms.

Her legerdemain and the brazen bluffing that followed had played their part but she was now well beyond the point where Gilkes' ID was of any use at all. The woman – a lowly clerk in Media Analysis – would never have ventured into the areas of the honeycomb she was currently invading, would never have gained access to them had she wanted to. All Mya had at her disposal from this point on were her own wits and skills. Hopefully, they would prove enough.

Her goal lay towards the very crown of the honeycomb, the penthouse apartments reserved for the VIPs. The roof was out, unfortunately, even though it was a great deal closer to her target than the ground floor access she'd used. Being the most obvious place from which to infiltrate, the honeycomb's roof was a mess of alarms, cameras and automated weapons placements. Attacking that way wasn't impossible, but doing so quietly was.

Methodically and efficiently, Mya wormed her way into the building, walking boldly at first, but as she steadily infiltrated the more rarefied areas she took to avoiding people and their awkward questions, clinging to walls or ceilings when required, twisting nimbly around infrared beams and dodging cameras as necessary. She daren't wear a shimmer suit – its use would trigger every alarm in the building the second it was activated – and the hi-tech visor linked to her intelligent gun might be denied her, but the goggles the habitat had provided served their purpose, seeing clearly into the infrared.

Finally she stood before the door. A plain, unimposing slab that mimicked wood but was actually built of steel plate sandwiching layers of polycarbon fibre, it was loaded with alarms and even the odd nasty surprise to deter unwanted visitors. But she knew this door, knew how to placate its dormant defences and how to sidestep its impressive lock; knew how to open it so that the sensors wouldn't even register that anyone had passed through.

Less than a minute later she was easing the door open and slipping inside. Darkness here, but light spilled from the open doorway at the far end of the hall, as did the soft strains of music. Nothing she recognised, something orchestral and light. She padded forward, confident that no one suspected her presence and intent on getting some answers. Up until this point, Mya had kept a lid on her emotions, battening them down in order to concentrate on the demanding business at hand, but now, as she trod on the soft carpets, having all but reached her goal, she relaxed control just a little and allowed her feelings to boil forth; a heady cocktail of extremes, with anger chief amongst them.

He stood with his back to her, contemplating the view from the window the night, with its stars and mystery, the glow of streetlights and uncurtained windows far below. His left profile was bathed in an orange glow from the totally convincing yet wholly false fire that burned in the hearth, while his right side reflected the steadier light from the single wall lamp. He always had liked subdued tones and radiance.

She drew her gun slowly and pointed it at him, realising that she could kill him where he stood and he'd never know who was responsible, wouldn't even have a chance to recognise that he was dead. Perhaps he deserved such a fate... but perhaps not.

Instead, she stepped into the room, knowing that her movement would be mirrored in the window he was staring out of.

He turned around sharply and on cue, and smiled as if this were the most natural thing in the world, as if he'd been standing there just waiting for a psychotic woman to enter his room and threaten him with a gun.

He looked no different. He was just as confident, suave, and maturely handsome as ever, his brown hair showing the same degree of grey at the sides, while the crow's feet around his eyes conspired to be gentling rather than aging. Somehow, after all that had happened to her, she felt that he ought to look different, older perhaps, but he didn't. It was the same disarming smile that greeted her, the same Pavel Benson who stood before her and said, "Hello, Mya."

So calm, so composed, as if he was the one in charge here, despite the fact that it was her holding the gun.

"You bastard!"

Now the expression changed, to sorrow, remorse, perhaps even anguish. Yet she knew him to be the consummate politician, had seen him show the full gamut of emotions without ever being fully certain which, if any, were genuine.

"I'm so sorry. There was nothing I could do," he said, hands outstretched with palms towards her, beseeching. He took a tentative step forward.

"Don't!" She raised the gun a fraction and he froze. "You know what they do there, don't you? At Sheol. You let them do that to *me*."

"I know, and that's something I'll always have to live with. I did what I could. I let the rebels know about Sheol and about you, made sure they learnt how important you were."

"What?"

"I realised there was a leak, although I didn't know it was the habitat – we'd forgotten all about them – but someone was being fed information. We kept the leak open to learn more and for the potential it offered to disseminate false intel in the future. I doctored an outgoing info package, made certain it contained enough hint and detail to lead them to you."

She shook her head, knowing how devious he could be, not sure whether to believe him. "Why? What were you expecting to achieve?"

"I don't know... a public exposure of Sheol, a rescue... *something*." Another shuffled step forward.

"Crap, all of it. The habitat had never shown their hand before, why would you think they'd do so now?"

"It worked, didn't it?"

"Only because they wanted to buy Jim Leyton's loyalty. If not for that, I'd still be rotting in that stinking piss hole."

"Maybe, maybe not. Things are moving fast, Mya; the gloves are off. People are having to be bold just to stay alive. I think the habitat might well have made the move to gain you, irrespective of Leyton. You're one hell of an asset in your own right, and if that hadn't worked, I'd have come up with something else. I would never have abandoned you, not to Sheol, not anywhere. You know that."

She wanted so badly to believe him. This was the man who'd mentored her since she was first recruited, who'd looked out for her through her entire career. If she couldn't trust him, who *could* she trust?

He was suddenly there, standing directly before her with his chest resting gently against the muzzle of her gun.

"If you're going to kill me, Mya, do it now. Shoot."

For a tortured second she nearly did, feeling the muscles in her finger tighten as the urge to twitch that trigger finger vied with so many other considerations and came close to winning. She almost surrendered to the moment, could see in her mind's eye the bloody hole punched through the torso of the man who had betrayed her. Almost, but not quite.

The gun felt abruptly heavy. Her arm sagged and the barrel slipped downward. He reached up to hold her wrist and gently move the hand and the weapon it held to one side.

He took a deep breath. "For a moment there, I thought you were actually going to do it."

"For a moment, so did I."

His hands reached up to stroke either side of her face. "I'd never abandon you," he repeated, as if by saying it often enough he could make her believe him. Perhaps he was right.

His hands reached behind her, drawing her to him, his lips lowering to meet hers, and she clung to that firm body, dropping the gun and responding to his kiss as all the grief and the hurt and the need rose up, threatening to overwhelm her. Mya felt herself picked up and carried into the next room, wondering if he'd always been this strong or if she'd lost more weight during her ordeal than she realised. Gently he lowered her onto the bed and she felt him lie on top of her. They were still clothed but she wished they weren't as she opened her legs and wrapped them around him, her heels pressing against his buttocks, drawing him onto her, into her. He shifted again, pulling back so that he could remove his top, revealing a toned body and near hairless chest. Her arms reached out to either side of her, opening herself to his mouth, his lips, his hands, as their clothing slipped away. She clasped at the black silk bed sheets as his tongue found a nipple, the same sheets she had clung to in the deepest recesses of her mind when Sheol unleashed its worst; her haven, her retreat. None of that seemed important anymore. All that truly mattered was here and now.

CHAPTER SIXTEEN

KYLE FELT SURE there was an old saying about frying pans and fires that would have fitted his current situation perfectly. *Byrzaen engines?*

He hadn't seen much of Leyton in the past couple of days, nor of Joss, the pilot who'd pulled them off the rooftop in Arcadia and whom Jim had subsequently dumped him on in the rec room. She was an odd one, Joss. He couldn't quite make out whether she liked him or despised him. For all her outward politeness she treated him with a reserve that bordered on distaste at times, as if afraid that he was going to infect her with some hideous disease. Perhaps she simply resented the fact that she'd had to put herself at risk to rescue him. There was definitely some issue. All of which he found intriguing. She wasn't the sort of woman he usually went for – not that she was ugly as such, but he certainly wouldn't have called her pretty. More homely. There was a warmth to her, though, a passion that showed sometimes in her smile, her humour. The fact that he felt excluded from that passion and warmth much of the time galled him, offending his male pride.

He hated to admit it, but he was beginning to think of Joss as a challenge.

Most of his time since coming aboard had been spent with Emily Teifer – a stocky, solidly built rock of a woman whom he wouldn't have cared to face in an arm wrestle. He'd expected her to resent him for arriving out of nowhere and taking over her position, but nothing could have been further from the truth. So much for his expertise in women. He'd never seen anyone more relieved to relinquish responsibility and pass it on to someone else. Then he got a look at the ship's engines and began to understand why.

The energy veils were instantly familiar, though the engine units they fed into were less so – not Kaufmans, that was for sure; the fruit of some other line of development. That aside, he could easily have been back aboard *The Noise Within*.

"Gods in heaven," he said. "Byrzaen technology. They don't seriously expect me to work with *this*, do they?"

"'Fraid so, lover man," Emily replied. He'd made the mistake in an off-guard moment of referring to some of his previous sexual exploits and she'd taken to calling him 'lover man' since. "That's why they chased halfway across the galaxy to find you: 'The Man Who Works with Hybrid Engines.'"

He opened his mouth to say something and closed it again; thought for a second and then had another go. "I tinkered with the engines on *The Noise Within*, that's true, but that was *all* I did: tinker! I haven't a clue what to do about this." He gestured to where the shifting, multi-coloured veils that led to or from the drive units were clearly damaged. There were no pastel shades in the veils, the ever changing patterns were depicted in dark greens, royal blues, deep purples and burgundy reds – gothic silk that never stopped flowing, shifting, mutating. Except where the silk was torn. For some reason the energy didn't simply flow over the rents, closing them as if they'd never been; the tears remained, as if the veils genuinely were a type of material with defined form and boundaries. Yet clearly, they weren't. Energy shouldn't behave that way, not in this universe. Around the damaged areas the shifting colours slowed, as if the rents formed a choke point, and the edges of the holes themselves were jet black; blockages around which the energy could flow only sluggishly.

"Tinkering is more than most of us have done, Kyle," Emily said. "It still makes you the expert."

"Haven't you tried to fix this?" he asked in desperation, certain that others here must know far more about these energy fields than he did.

She guffawed. "Oh, yes, I've tried... sort of. Did bugger all good, though."

"What do you mean 'sort of'?"

She shrugged. "Well I didn't want to make things worse."

In other words she'd looked at the problem from a dozen different angles before deciding to leave things well alone. He could understand that. In fact, he sympathised entirely, which was why he said after a moment's consideration, "I need to talk to the captain."

"You could do that, of course."

"But?"

"Look, the captain's a busy lady, with a hundred things on her mind. If you asked to see her, she'd make the time, I'm sure she's that sort. Then you explain to her that you don't really think you're up to the job. Bearing in mind that she took the ship all the way across ULAW space and then risked her own neck to extract you from some backwater world, all just to get you here, what do you reckon she's likely to say?"

He sighed. "Give it a go anyway."

"Exactly. So why not cut out all the bits in between and just go straight to the giving it a go part? If you're as unsuccessful as you seem to think you'll be, *then* go and trouble the captain."

"That's certainly a plan," he conceded. Actually, even though he hated to admit as much, it was a pretty good plan.

So instead of approaching Kethi or even Jim Leyton and pleading his ignorance – not incompetence, no, he'd never admit to that – he decided to take a closer look at things for himself, starting with the most familiar element, the drive units. Outwardly, they looked similar to those he remembered from the war, but as he began to delve beneath their shiny metal cowlings he soon realised they were a far cry from anything he'd ever seen before. These were no Kaufman drives jerry-rigged to accommodate the Byrzaen energy fields as on *The Noise Within*, but had been purpose-built to utilise them.

"They had to adapt what they learnt from the Byrzaen derelict into a more familiar form," Emily explained. "No one could fully understand the mechanism of the alien drive units themselves, still can't as far as I know. It's one of the things they keep working on. We suspect our version isn't as efficient as the original, but who cares? It works."

Energy from the veils was drawn in through intake valves, he could see that much... computerised regulation, as precise as any he was used to... He summoned up instructions and 3D schematics, which scrolled across a virtual screen and hung suspended in the air before him, enabling him to compare the details in the manual to the physical reality. He rotated the schematic, studying every intricacy, freezing the image in place and crawling under the drive unit, pulling himself out to squint at the diagram once more before going back again, as he traced the flow of energy. Gradually, the whole process began to fall into place.

Then, once he was confident that he'd mastered the principles and mechanics of the drive units, he took another look at the energy veils, and realised that he still knew absolutely nothing.

"This is hopeless."

"Hey, don't be so defeatist," Emily said. "You're doing great."

"Yeah, until it gets to the difficult bit."

He frowned and stared at the tattered veils for the hundredth time. It still made no sense whatsoever – how energy could behave like that. One rent in particular claimed his attention, for good reason; it was getting bigger. When he first arrived, the tear reached perhaps a third of the way across one of the central energy curtains, it now stretched across at least half. What would happen when the veil tore all the way across was anyone's guess, but Kyle was willing to bet it'd be nothing good.

For the moment, *The Rebellion* hung in an anonymous part of space, going nowhere very slowly indeed, Kethi unwilling to risk another jump with the energy fields in their current state. Nor could Kyle blame her. In fact, the only detail he had a problem with was the bit where he was the one expected to fix things.

Suddenly he raised a finger and smiled, as if struck by sudden inspiration. "I know what I need to solve this."

"What?" Emily asked, all eager.

"A beer."

"And you really think will help, do you?"

"Of course; stimulates the old grey cells. It's a well known fact."

Emily shook her head. "Come on then, lover man, let's go to the rec room and feed those grey cells of yours. Maybe we can even get them tipsy enough to spark an answer, preferably before the engines pack up for good."

Who was he to argue?

KYLE WALKED AROUND the engine room. There was no one else there. Emily had hit the sack an hour ago and he should probably have done the same, but he was restless and felt compelled to come back here to do... what exactly? He wasn't sure.

Joss hadn't been in the rec room and he didn't really know any other crew that well yet, so after Emily left he just sort of ended up back here again.

There was a new wall in place, where the old one had been holed and melted in the attack. Gun metal grey, like all the rest. If Emily hadn't told him he might never have known about the damage. The wall looked no different, no newer, than any of the others, apart from the fact that a patch of flooring in front of it was blackened in a streaky, irregular pattern. Evidently the cowling to one of the drive units had also been partially warped and blistered, but again that had been replaced before he arrived, and Emily had taken care of any slight glitches in the drives themselves. He'd run a diagnostics first thing, and the engines were purring along nicely, which just left those damned energy veils to worry about. Problems only arose when the ship initiated a jump. Kyle had seen it for himself. The engines' performance dropped drastically, and there was no mechanical reason for that. It was the veils. During a jump they became stretched, pulled towards the drive units, the flow of energy around the tears interrupted. Damaged as the veils were, the feed wasn't constant, and the rents grew a little wider each time, causing performance to drop a little lower still. Eventually, the engines would fail completely, starved of energy, and if that should occur in mid-jump... There were rumours of ships which had suffered that fate. Only rumours, because no one had ever come back to give an actual report.

Kyle knew that if he didn't find some way to fix the damage soon Kethi would risk one more jump, back to a base somewhere deep in uncharted space, where *The Rebellion* would be pulled out of the action until her engines were given a full overhaul. Personally, Kyle couldn't have cared less whether that happened or not, but, although he was still new around here, he didn't want to let these people down. They were looking to him, hoping he could pull off some sort of miracle, and if he failed he'd always be remembered for failing, whatever he did after that. Professional pride took care of the rest. One way or another, he was going to fix these damned veils.

If he could fathom how they worked, then at least he'd be in with a shot. He understood engines, always had done, an affinity that enabled him to feel when something was out of kilter and sense what adjustments or repairs were needed. Nothing taught; it was something that went beyond all the training he'd received. There'd never been an engine yet that Kyle couldn't get a handle on. But these were proving elusive.

The ship's database held plenty of explanation and discourse on how the drive units operated and what the veils were, all of which he'd trawled through, yet none of which seemed to really get beneath the surface. The more he studied the information which the habitat's experts had accumulated, the more convinced he became that none of them truly understood what they were playing with here.

There were tools, many of which he recognised, while some were unfamiliar, and these he was highly dubious about. He clasped one of them now, weighing it in his hand and scowling. There was a plasticky feel to the handle that he instantly mistrusted. It seemed more like a toy, something lifted straight out of a child's play kit, totally inadequate for purpose. However, he was new to all this, and willing to put his doubts to one side until they were proven or otherwise. So he took the toy with him as he stepped beyond the drive units and between the energy fields.

Whatever Kyle's reputation might claim, on *The Noise Within* his tinkering had been restricted to the Kaufman units themselves; he'd never needed to interact with the energy veils – a detail he felt it politic not to mention, bearing in mind the trouble everyone had gone through to get him here. This was as much virgin territory for him as it would have been for anyone else on board. And yet there was something here, something he felt drawn to, which he couldn't even begin to explain.

When he'd encountered these veils aboard the pirate ship they had unnerved him. He'd imagined a machine or a presence lurking beyond them, just out of sight. The sense of presence remained, but this time around much of the fear was gone and he felt able to look directly at the veils and where they emerged from. According to the habitat's records, the veils were part of another universe, a completely different state of being. They provided a radically new breed of energy which enabled the habitat ships to punch holes in the fabric of space and initiate jumps without relying on pre-existing wormholes.

All fascinating stuff, but at the same time a little confusing. On New Paris, Kyle had been intrigued by talk of the Byrzaen stardrive, which apparently utilised zero point energy to effect jumps. It promised to open up a whole new avenue of science, but there was no sign of anything like that here, no suggestion of massive energies released by the localised collapse of space from false vacuum to true vacuum, just the siphoning of energies from another brane. Impressive in its own right, no question, but light years away from zero point energy.

Either the habitat were relying on outmoded Byrzaen technology – possible, bearing in mind their drives were based on those of an ancient derelict – a whole form of tech which the Byrzaens had since abandoned, or the aliens were lying through their teeth; assuming they had any. Bearing in mind that what he'd encountered on *The Noise Within* bore such a striking resemblance to what he's found on *The Rebellion*, Kyle's money was on the latter. It seemed to him that the Byrzaens had created a dazzling yet tantalisingly feasible myth about their engines to avoid explaining the true nature of the tech involved. It suggested they had no intention of ever sharing with human kind, which suddenly cast them in a whole new, sinister light.

All of which made Kyle wonder whether the 'false' Byrzaen he'd encountered in Virtuality not long after leaving New Paris might not have been the real thing after all.

Right now, though, he had to focus on repairing these energy fields and saving them all from being stranded in the back of beyond. He could quite go for the idea of becoming part of spacefaring folklore, though preferably not as crew on a vanished ship, thanks all the same.

Kyle squatted down beside one of the veils – minor damage only, a hole towards the top of the flow – no point in tackling one of the big boys until he was confident he could actually achieve something.

The tool was shaped a little like an adjustable wrench, moulded from shiny grey composite as if trying to convince the wielder this really was metal, with two open jaws opposing each other at the business end. The jaws were lined with black spongy pads that looked like rubber but were actually made from a stiffer polymer. Kyle opened the jaws to maximum extension and slowly inserted them into the veil, either side of the hole. He steeled himself, half-expecting to feel a tingle of current or receive a jolt. None came, of course, which was presumably why the tool was cast from non-conductive material rather than metal.

Once in position, he gently closed the jaws, using a ratchet built into the handle. To his surprise and great delight, the pads seemed to catch on the edges of the hole and pull the energy with them, until finally they met. For long seconds he held the tool in place, trying to keep his hand steady, and then he slowly pulled it clear.

Bugger! It worked! Where the jaws had met, the energy now flowed freely, with no indication there had ever been a breach. Typically, he'd gone for the centre of the hole, which was bigger than the jaws, and that now left two smaller gaps, one above and the other below his repair, but they were quickly fixed.

That had been easy. Why couldn't Emily have done this, at least fixing the smaller breaks? Maybe she'd tried and botched the job, or perhaps she'd simply shied away and left it for him to deal with. Much as he liked Emily, she struck him as a reluctant mechanic at best.

Now that he had the knack, Kyle swiftly moved around the veils, forgetting all about their nature, forgetting all about the peculiar otherness that he was working so close to. Before long, he'd fixed all the minor tears that the little wrench – which he now fully accepted as being useful and well designed – was capable of dealing with.

He had no idea what the time was and didn't care; he was buzzing. Yet all the he'd done so far would make only a slight difference. The real problem wasn't these small nicks and holes, but the larger rents. He toyed with the idea of going to bed and tackling the rest in the morning when he was refreshed, but only briefly. Buoyed by success and adrenaline, he determined to try at least one of the bigger bastards now, and that meant using the bow.

Light, moulded from the same composite as the wrench, the bow resembled a large stylised hacksaw but with the blade missing. It looked like some artist's tool rather than anything a mechanic might use. Kyle picked the bow up by its centrally positioned handle and wafted it through the air a few times as if this were some exotically shaped sword.

Unlike the wrench, the bow was powered. Again, he'd seen its use demonstrated via the ship's databank, but was even less convinced than he had been by the wrench. Still, he wasn't proud; he'd be perfectly happy to be proven wrong a second time.

Avoiding the largest rent, he approached one of the other damaged veils, braced himself and switched the bow on. Nothing visible, but in theory energy should have started flowing between the two tips, forming an intangible blade. Trusting that it was, Kyle slowly pushed the open end of the bow into the veil, directly beside the tear. Immediately the 'blade' became visible – a pale bright line within the dark primaries. He very deliberately drew the bow sideways, pulling the blade like a windshield wiper across the tear. As before, the energy moved with it, reaching out to bridge the gap, but just as Kyle dared to hope this was going to work, the solid block of energy following the blade began to fray and tatter, so that only thick strands and threads arrived at the far side. For a second he thought that might be enough, as the strands seemed to bond with the energy as they made contact, but they thinned and weakened almost at once and then snapped back, disappearing all together.

Frustrated, he tried again. Thinking that perhaps the first attempt had failed due to his own unsteadiness, he decided to hold the bow with both hands. He would later blame what happened next on tiredness. He knew there was a sharp, rough bit at the very top of the handle – as if the bow had been connected to some sort of frame or bracket in manufacture and snapped off once completed, the residual bump of the connection still sharp. In order to accommodate the second hand, he adjusted his grip without thinking, dragging the tip of his thumb across the sharp edge. The sudden pain almost made him jerk the bow away from the veil, but somehow he had the presence of mind not to, pulling the injured hand away instead. He couldn't believe how sharp that was, it had cut his thumb.

As his hand jerked away, a drop of blood arced from the injured digit. Kyle watched in frozen fascination as this ruby bead of his own life stuff sailed towards the veil. It struck just behind the blade, which was already partway across the rent.

He had no idea what to expect. The whole area around the impact pulsed. Had he caused some irreparable harm? The drop of blood hadn't sailed through the veil or splattered against it; instead it seemed to have been absorbed, to become part of the energy. A crimson stripe appeared in the wake of the blade as Kyle continued to draw it across the tear, one that flowed outward until it covered most of the energy being pulled by the bow. Surely that wasn't his blood? After all, colours were shifting and swirling the whole time within these energy curtains, and it had only been a single drop. Yet he couldn't escape the feeling that this *was* the result of his blood. The blade completed its journey. No tatters this time, no fraying. The tear had sealed.

Kyle flopped down onto the floor and sat cross-legged, staring at the veil and sucking on his injured thumb. One thing was certain: there'd been nothing about this in the bloody manual! He giggled at his own pun, proof positive that he was overtired.

As he watched, the veil seemed to pulse, very faintly but constantly, like the pumping of blood through veins, and at one point he fancied he could hear something – a multitude of voices all speaking at once; nothing intelligible, just a distant murmur, soothing as the babbling of a mountain brook.

He shook himself, realising that he'd been on the verge of falling asleep. Time for bed. No way was he going to finish this now, much as he'd have liked to. As he took his leave, Kyle stopped and gazed back at the veils. Funny, but as he was drifting off to sleep back there, it had almost seemed to him that these curtains of energy were in some way alive.

CHAPTER SEVENTEEN

"THIS IS UNLIKE anything I've ever seen before," Lara said. Her attention was focused on the screen suspended in the air before her, rather than on her visitors – real or virtual. Catherine Chzyski provided the former, while Philip and Malcolm constituted the latter.

The room was sparsely furnished – a single black upholstered flexiseat currently configured as an upright office chair sat in an apparently random position on the biscuit coloured carpet; a slick chrome drinks dispenser with twin nozzles, one for ice cold water and the other set for scalding black coffee, stood against a wall; a tall spear-leafed plant emerged from a pebble pot sunk into the floor near the far corner, by the window, with a bubbling water feature beside it which blended seamlessly with the pebbles from the plant pot. Other than these there was a single small glass shelf holding an exquisite statuette of a long-legged woman dancing – one knee crooked, toes pointed, every line sensuous – a pair of academic awards which Philip hadn't even realised Lara had earned, and, even more of a surprise, some sort of trophy for martial arts. The most striking feature of the room, though, stood directly opposite the door: a wall-to-wall, ceiling-to-floor picture window, providing an impressive view of the city's towering skyscrapers and lower rooftops.

Minimalistic, tasteful, but unmistakably an executive's office; sure sign of how much Kaufman Industries valued Lara's capabilities and of how swiftly her star had risen since Philip embarked on his galactic sightseeing jaunt and relinquished control of KI to Catherine. A silent rebuke to him, albeit unintentional. He probably should have acknowledged Lara's worth long before this, but he'd been so caught up in bringing the project to a successful conclusion that perhaps he'd been guilty of taking others involved for granted.

Catherine's presence emphasised that this wasn't merely Lara conspiring with them, that she did so with the backing of Kaufman Industries, which he and Malcolm might have had at their beck and call once, but not any more.

Lara's office boasted plain off-white walls, presumably pattern-free so as not to distract from details on the virtual screens they frequently provided a backdrop for. She stood before the largest stretch of blank wall now and, foregoing the chair, brought another screen into being with deft and precise hand movements – the second screen apparently budding from the primary in response to her gestures, as if it were some tame protozoan.

Once he and Malcolm had told her about their experiences at the Veils club, Lara had a better idea of what to look for and had set about doggedly studying the coding that underpinned that particular corner of Virtuality. She must have discovered something, or at least so Philip presumed. He very much doubted she'd invited them here for the pleasure of their erudite company. At one level, he was impressed at how quickly Lara had found something once they'd narrowed the search for her. At another, he wondered why someone of her much vaunted expertise hadn't spotted it in the first place.

Lara spoke with an authority that belied her apparent youth and with a confidence that surprised Philip, despite the years they'd worked together.

"Deeply encrypted," she went on. "It was a real so-and-so to isolate and identify; strands of code wrapped around other coding, like ivy snaking around a tree. Very clever, very tricky. Worth all the effort, though."

Philip had the impression that their presence was all but superfluous to Lara, that she would have been poring over the code sequences whether they were there or not – pulling one detail after another onto the secondary screen for closer scrutiny. However, no sooner had that observation crossed his mind than she looked away from the screen for a moment, to regard them sternly, as if to ensure they appreciated the gravity of what she was telling them. Philip was astounded. The Lara he recalled was quietly efficient but would rarely speak unless asked to. She really had blossomed. "It's as if this goes *beyond* mere code," she said.

"How do you mean?"

She shook her head. "I don't want to sound too melodramatic, but it's almost as if this is the coding for existence itself."

"What?"

"I don't mean *our* sort of existence," she said, "but the more I study this the more astounding and complex it becomes... and I'm increasingly convinced that this intricate and..." – she paused, searching for words – "...incredibly *detailed* system of code is underpinning the very fabric of a universe, of another brane. Some of the subsystems even appear to be self-organising, and that would seem to suggest..."

"Life," Philip said.

"Exactly. This is the code for an entire other universe."

"One in which human space and Byrzaen space converges," Malcolm murmured thoughtfully, "and the distance between becomes an irrelevance."

That would certainly fit with what they'd encountered at Veils.

"Right," the girl confirmed, clearly relieved that they were still with her, or at least someone was. "In a sense it's like Home's Virtuality, which anyone on the planet can access and instantly find themselves involved with someone from half the world away. This brane seems to link anywhere in the universe in similar fashion."

"Or at least our neck of the wood and the Byrzaens'," Philip interjected, feeling that Lara was making too big a conjecture based on what little they knew.

We mean you no harm. The repeated phrase hidden within the static came back to him. He hadn't mentioned it to anyone. He didn't trust that message, assuming it had been anything more than a product of his own imagining.

"Okay," he said, "let's assume for a moment that what we found at Veils *was* a new universe, one where energy proliferates in sheets, which I'm still not entirely convinced by, how did both races first happen to stumble upon this brane, or invent the math to access it?"

"Convergent science?" Malcolm suggested.

"Seems incredibly unlikely."

"I agree," Lara said. "This is far too intricate. One must have discovered the brane first and then led the other there."

"So we're no further forward than we were before," Catherine said. "We've still no idea what the touchstone was, what first brought humans and Byrzaens into contact with each other."

"But does that really matter anymore?" Malcolm wondered.

"It does if we want to put a stop to this. Or does it? Lara?"

"Depends on what you mean." Her voice was guarded, suspicious.

"Could you come up with something that would disrupt this code, subverting its whole structure so that it would never fit together again?"

She frowned. "You're talking about a pretty nasty virus, something that would affect this permanently at a fundamental level, tearing up the very ground rules it's built upon."

"Yes."

She chewed at her bottom lip for a second. "Possibly, but are you certain you really want me to try?"

"Why wouldn't we?"

"This is more than just messing around with code, Philip. If I'm right, we're talking about disrupting the very fabric of another universe."

"Not an issue. As far as we know this universe only exists to accommodate interaction between the Byrzaens and us. If what you're proposing can stop alien interference in human affairs, the collateral damage is more than worth paying."

"What about the self modifying subsystems I found? What if there really *is* life in there?"

We mean you no harm. He deliberately pushed that nagging message to the back of his thoughts. "We don't know that, and we don't know what level of life even if there is any. It could be amoeboid or bacterial. This is something we can debate and even look into once we have the virus. Until then, it doesn't matter."

Lara held his gaze for a moment, as if she wanted to say more, but then her eyes dropped and she said, "All right. I just want to make sure everyone appreciates what's being proposed here. I've no concept of what else the Byrzaens might tap this brane for or how our tampering with it could affect their capabilities."

Philip was growing impatient. "Exactly. None of us have any concept, and for all we know there won't *be* any other affects, so let's proceed on that basis for now, shall we?" He never imagined Lara had such an acutely developed social conscience, particularly not when the society in question wasn't even human. The responsibility of science had been drummed into Philip almost from birth, but he *was* being responsible; to his own race, his species.

"Fair enough," she said. He could only hope she meant it.

KYLE SLEPT WELL, but not long. He fell asleep thinking about the veils and woke up itching to get back to them. For all he knew his dreams in between probably centred on them as well. Kyle rarely remembered his dreams.

By the time Emily turned up he'd succeeded in repairing each and every tear. At first he had put the events of the previous evening down to his own tiredness and perhaps one too many beers in the rec room before wandering back here, but, try as he might, he couldn't get the bow to seal the really big tears. No matter how slowly and steadily he moved the blade across the gap the energy frayed before it reached the other side. Only when he (very deliberately this time) pricked his thumb and added a drop of his own blood to the mix did the energy adhere properly to the blade, enabling him to heal the rift.

Why blood should make such a vital difference, he had no idea, but, once he stopped questioning the logic of the process and merely accepted it, things moved swiftly. Again he felt a connection with the veils, a sense that there was something organic about them rather than pure inanimate energy. It was as if, damaged, they'd needed the introduction of new living material to heal themselves. The noise, too, hovered at the edge of perception, that background hum as of a million whispering voices, just beyond his hearing. It was trying to entice him, he concluded, to lure him into the energy fields and away from the world he knew. He closed his ears, refusing to be tempted, and before long the noise dwindled into insignificance. The great darkness from which the veils emerged – a space clearly not confined within the walls of *The Rebellion* – had resumed all the brooding menace he remembered from *The Noise Within*. He very determinedly shut such concerns from his mind, concentrating on the drive units and the veils immediate to them. That way, he could continue with his work.

In surprisingly short time every shimmering veil stood resplendent and whole again. Although he could spot the swirls of crimson patterning that hadn't been there before, marking where drops of his blood had apparently blossomed and stimulated the energy fields, he doubted anyone else would. Kyle felt elated and pretty damned pleased with himself, despite now having a couple of very tender fingers and thumbs.

On hearing Emily approach – in conversation with someone, a man's voice – he quickly ran through a series of nonchalant poses, settling on jauntily leaning against the cowling of one of the drive units, the bow held casually in his free hand, one foot cocked over the other, toe to the ground.

His reward was a greeting that dribbled into stunned silence as she took in the scene: "Hi, Kyle, what are you looking so smug a...?" and a look of complete disbelief.

Simon, one of the bridge crew who appeared to be a friend of both Emily's and Kethi's, entered the room behind her. He seemed equally impressed. "Well I'll be blowed!"

"Not by me you won't," Kyle assured him.

He found it hard not to stare at Simon's crippled hand. On most ULAW worlds you'd have to be destitute and raised in the back of beyond to reach adulthood with a deformity like that, and he couldn't work Simon out. Why hadn't the habitat corrected this?

Emily clapped her hands and grinned broadly. She followed that up by coming over to slap a kiss on his cheek. He could think of people he'd rather be kissed by, but beggars can't be choosers and adulation was always welcome from whatever quarter.

"You can tell the captain that in another day or so, her ship's engines will be ready to go," Kyle said. Actually they were probably ready there and then, but he wanted a day's leeway just to be certain his repairs didn't fall apart again.

"You can tell her yourself," Emily replied. "After all, you're the senior engineer around here."

He made the call. Kethi was on the bridge. His news brought her straight down to the engine room. She stared intently at the veils, as if looking to see the seam or perhaps discover a trick. Then she turned to Kyle.

"Congratulations," she said. "This is impressive. Do you mind me asking how you did it?"

Kyle shrugged. "Well, for the larger tears, I used the bow."

Kethi laughed. "You mean to say you actually got that thing to work?"

"Yes, I mean the manual says..."

"Oh, I know what the manual says," Kethi assured him. "I know what the bow's *supposed* to do, but I don't know of anyone who's actually managed to get it to work as advertised. Do you, Emily?"

"No," Emily replied cheerfully. "Tried hard enough during school training sessions, but the veils just tattered, no one could ever make the stupid things stick."

Kethi gazed at him as if seeing him in a new light. "It seems Jim was right. You really are a miracle worker."

"Just doing my job," Kyle assured her, though his chest puffed up a little when he said it. He didn't mention the blood, didn't see the need to. After all, miracle workers should never reveal the tricks of their trade.

WORD OF THE engine's repair soon spread around the ship, and Kyle's popularity soared accordingly. By the time Simon regaled a small group in the rec room with the tale of how he and Emily had entered the engine room to find Kyle leaning against the drive cowling, job done, Kyle had already heard it a half dozen times. He probably ought to have grown bored with it by then, but the truth was he hadn't. Particularly as Joss was sitting directly opposite him.

Being praised so enthusiastically by somebody else without any encouragement on his part could only be a good thing.

"Well," he said as Simon finished the anecdote, "I just did what I could. I mean, I can't help being a genius." He grinned, to show that he was at least partway joking.

Joss had been staring fixedly at her drink as Simon spoke. She now looked up, her gaze briefly meeting Kyle's, just long enough for him to see the hurt in her eyes.

"Yes, we're all so damned lucky you joined us, aren't we?"

With that, she pushed her chair back, stood up and stormed out the room.

Kyle stared at her retreating back. "What... what did I say?"

"It's not you, Kyle," Simon assured him. "It's Wicksy."

"Who the hell's Wicksy?"

"He was her closest friend, more than a friend. Part of the engineering crew; he was one of those we lost in the attack."

"Oh." All of Kyle's euphoria evaporated. No wonder Joss had been so ambivalent towards him since he arrived. "I... I didn't know."

But the person those words were really meant for had already left.

KETHI DIDN'T LIKE having the ship idle for so long. Fortunately there was plenty to keep the crew busy. Repairs were always easiest when the ship was in dock, but they didn't have that luxury. After the destruction of the habitat and the recent ambush it was clear that their network had been compromised. She had no idea how extensively, but she wasn't about to risk another stop to pick up intel, or even to find proper docking facilities. Instead, she simply parked the ship in deep space and assigned everyone who could be spared to ensure the patched up repairs they'd put in place after the ambush were as robust as possible, which meant replacing some parts and reinforcing others.

One thing an upbringing in the habitat gave you was a familiarity with zero g, leaving her with no shortage of personnel to deploy outside the hull as well as within. The added risks of EVA work brought their own headaches, but fortunately there had been no reports of serious mishaps to date.

Filling her own time was no problem whatsoever. When not with Leyton in the privacy of their quarters or monitoring the progress of the repairs, she could be found sifting through the information they had received, of which there was a considerable amount. The fact that they wouldn't be getting any more for a while made her all the more determined to wring every useful scrap and nuance from what they did have. Nor did her efforts to understand what was going on within

ULAW end once the screens were off. She questioned Leyton remorselessly. She felt obliged to. After all, he was the only resource available with any insight into how the government functioned. Though, as he pointed out to her, the eyegees were hardly part of the regular ULAW structure. He seemed to take her interrogations with stoic amusement, and they even became part of their lovemaking, with her teasing him by refusing to perform a given act unless he produced an answer she was satisfied with. The manner in which he accepted her obsessive questioning, without any sign of rancour, went a long way to reassuring her that she meant more to him than simply a rebound fuck.

By the time Kyle produced his miracle with the energy veils, she had pretty much exhausted the potential of the available info and was feeling increasingly frustrated. She'd learnt a lot, and could intuit a great deal more. There was a pattern emerging, but it wasn't complete, and there weren't sufficient clues for her to fill in the remaining blanks. One more parcel of intelligence might have given her the missing pieces, and she was tempted to reverse her previous decision by mounting a snatch and grab rendezvous with one of the beacons. However, she didn't underestimate the dangers in doing so. It was a real quandary, and one which she decided to discuss with Leyton as they lay in bed.

He listened patiently before saying, "You know, yours isn't the only network available to us."

"What do you mean?"

"I have contacts and snitches all over the place, people I've used for information gathering, equipment sourcing, local knowledge."

She sat up and stared down at him, but the sudden hope disappeared as quickly as it had formed. "A nice idea, but it's no good," she said. "ULAW must be aware of all those contacts from your mission reports. They're as compromised as our own network."

"Maybe, but the difference is we're talking about living, breathing people here, not impersonal beacons floating in the depths of space. People I know, most of whom I'd avoid like the plague right now, granted, but there are one or two."

"Who?" she demanded. "Who out of all of them would you trust the most?"

After a moment's pause he said, "Billy. If I had to, I'd trust Billy."

CHAPTER EIGHTEEN

THEY TOOK A shuttle in under a false name and with false registration details, though in the event they probably needn't have bothered. Security at the port was all but non-existent. Kethi plugged into the local net at the first opportunity, even before they had landed. She uncovered a welter of conjecture, debate and information about the Byrzaens, enough to keep her occupied for hours. This seemed safe enough to Leyton. After all, there must be millions of people on the planet curious about the aliens. It would be a logistical nightmare to monitor and check up on all those conducting searches on the Byrzaens.

She also tracked down a few conspiracy theory sites, which had plenty to say about the aliens and their relationship with the ULAW government. This struck Leyton as a little riskier, but Kethi insisted it was necessary and that she was being careful. In fairness, if this were to trigger a flag it was likely to be a low level one, and they intended to be long gone before anyone had a chance to follow up.

Billy was one of Leyton's most reliable contacts and also among the more amiable. The former eyegee had never needed to intimidate Billy, their relationship conducted on a comparatively civilised basis of mutual respect and understanding. He also had a more flexible working environment than most, which made approaching him less of a risk. Any form of premeditated trap would require a lot of coordination, manpower and resources. Billy worked the city's pubs, clubs and bars; a dozen of them, at any rate. All different, all popular, all noisy enough to make conversations difficult to overhear, with exits that were easily accessible.

Leyton opted for Flappers, a bustling midtown retro bar which claimed to emulate a bygone age from old Earth. As far as Leyton's cursory examination could determine, it actually drew inspiration from several bygone ages, but he wasn't about to quibble.

"Ready?" he asked the two ladies.

"Won't be a minute," Kethi replied. "I've just got to change."

He stared at her. "You brought a change of clothes?"

She grinned. "Well, a girl has to be prepared." So saying, Kethi slipped away to the back of the shuttle.

Leyton stared at Joss, who shook her head and shrugged. He considered his own clothes, which were typical of the sort of thing he tended to wear when casual: comfortable trousers, a leather belt with various slit-pouches in which all sorts of useful things could be carried, a shirt that was loose enough not to restrict movement, and a similarly comfortable jacket worn primarily to conceal his gun. Joss looked much as Joss always looked: hair slightly spiked, patterned short-sleeved top – blue and white – narrow belt and dark blue trousers with black flat-heeled shoes.

Then there was Kethi, who came forward again to join them a surprisingly short while later.

She had added a touch of makeup – something she rarely bothered with on duty. It was subtle but effective, emphasising her high cheekbones and spectacular eyes while not looking incongruous against her naturally pale complexion. She wore her hair down, tumbling around her shoulders in long dark tresses. Her top was sleeveless and figure-hugging, her skirt short and beautifully tailored, making the most of her legs, which Leyton knew she regarded as her best feature. Put simply, she looked stunning.

It struck Leyton that here was a woman dressed to kill, who didn't want to *look* as if she were dressed to kill.

He summed all this up by saying, "You look nice."

Her answering smile suggested that she already knew as much, but was pleased that he'd at least noticed.

"Wow!" Joss said. "Have I got time to nip out and buy a new outfit?"

"How do you want to play this?" Kethi asked as they approached Flappers.

"Split up, work the room separately and find out what we can," Leyton replied, "I'll hang by the bar until Billy shows up. Is that okay with you, Joss?"

"Fine."

"The important thing is that we keep this low key. We go in, mingle, find out what we can, make contact with Billy and then leave, without anybody even noticing we were there," Leyton said. Kethi and Joss both nodded. "One thing that concerns me," he added, "is money." Something he should have considered before this. "If Billy does have anything for us, he'll want paying for it." They all had a bit of ULAW currency for buying drinks, but nothing significant. "We're going to have to get hold of some cash, and somehow I don't think it's a good idea to call on my own credit lines."

"Leave that to me," Kethi said, with an enigmatic smile.

Leyton would have liked to quiz her on that a bit, but they'd arrived at the twin dark wooden doors with the word 'Flappers' emblazoned in white flowing script on their glass panes. He pushed one of the doors open and held it as Kethi and Joss entered.

Inside, everything was much as he remembered. A gently curving bar of polished rosewood dominated the far side of the room, in front of which stood padded seats that more resembled long-legged chairs than barstools. The staff wore uniforms of white trousers, checked shirts and red neckerchiefs. One was in the process of mixing a cocktail, which naturally became a performance, as he flipped a bottle from behind his back and caught it with a flourish, before pouring out a stream of amber liquid.

The place was already busy, with more than half the tables scattered across the polished wooden floor occupied. At one of them, a card game was underway. Beams criss-crossed the vaulted ceiling; *they* had to be cosmetic, while Leyton knew that the old upright piano which stood against one wall wasn't entirely. It looked acoustic, authentic, though of course it might have been designed that way. Leyton had heard it played on occasion, though he couldn't recall much beyond the fact. Elsewhere, framed photographs of dour looking women in fulsome skirts and men with outlandish hats and heavy moustaches adorned the wood-panelled walls. These glass-fronted images were flat, two dimensional, and completely immobile, adding to the establishment's retro feel.

Several long-legged, ever-smiling women minced between the tables, flirting with the patrons; all bobbed or tight-curled hair, glossy lipstick smiles, feather boas, pearl necklaces, and patent leather high-heeled shoes. The infamous Flappers' Slappers. They were there for decoration, to encourage the punters to relax, have a good time, and buy more drinks. The girls would even offer to fetch from the bar if needed. Towards the end of a really busy night these girls might be persuaded, with sufficient financial inducement, to take off their shoes and perform a high-kicking, skirt-waving dance on the bar top, accompanied by one of the check-shirted staff on the piano.

Leyton expected and sincerely hoped that their party would be long gone before that particular spectacle became a possibility.

As he had suggested, they separated once through the door. Kethi went to sit at one end of the bar and soon drew the attention of several male admirers, who set about vying with each other to see who could buy her the most expensive drink. Joss gravitated towards a rowdy group of spacers occupying a far corner of the room. She was soon laughing with them and swapping anecdotes.

Leyton fell into conversation with a pair of office workers, one male and one female, who were both several drinks ahead of him. Unfortunately, they were too intent on comparing notes regarding their various sexual conquests to discuss much else. The man was bisexual, which added a certain spice to the burgeoning rivalry, as each tried to out-shock the other, but Leyton realised he'd learn nothing here and began looking for a chance to extricate himself almost immediately.

"You mustn't breathe a word," the man said, drawing both Leyton and the woman, Gail, closer into a huddle, "but you know Martin in accounts and his wife, Sian, in exports? Lovely couple," he added for Leyton's benefit. "She's got fabulous tits. Well, anyway, for the last couple of months I've been screwing both of them without the other having a clue!"

"You've never!" Gail said, with a look that said she was scandalised and loving it.

Leyton made his excuses and stood up, certain they wouldn't even notice him go. He suddenly realised that Kethi was no longer at the opposite end of the bar. He looked around and saw her at a table with three men. She'd joined the card game. *Kethi played cards?* There seemed to be money involved, and Leyton sincerely hoped Kethi knew what she was doing. One of her admirers was still hanging around at her shoulder; the others had clearly recognised they were wasting their time and given up.

"Oh, I've had him!" said a familiar male voice from behind Leyton as he moved away from the bar to observe the game.

He'd never actually seen real playing cards before, and watched, fascinated, as the dealer sent the wafer thin boards of layered polymer skidding across the table top, to land in front of each player in turn. The back of the cards bore a uniform design of interwoven strands, with a starburst at the centre, all depicted in a monotone washed-out red. He wondered if there was any significance to the motif, whether it might be a copy of a classic design or some such.

Since one of the reasons for their being in the bar was to talk to people, he asked the man standing beside him, who proved to be a bit of an authority on the subject.

"Sort of," the fellow explained. "The designs on the backs of playing cards used to be unique to each manufacturer, you know. These days you just take your pick from a selection of standard templates, but the templates themselves are based on classic designs. So, in a sense, this one is significant. Don't ask me which manufacturer the deck is based on, though. I'm not *that* old."

Leyton drifted back to the bar, bought another drink and chatted to the young man who served him. Finally, here was someone full of curiosity about the Byrzaens, though he had nothing new to offer on the subject. The fellow who then came up to join them partway through did, though Leyton rather wished he hadn't.

"I know for a fact," said the man – tall, in his fifties, his complexion sallow and his face framed by ginger stubble peppered with grey – "that these Byrzaens don't exist. They've been manufactured by the government."

The barman chuckled. "How do you know this then, Burt?"

"Friend of mine helped design 'em," he explained. "The spaceships, everything. All very hush-hush."

Leyton couldn't resist. "So what are the government hoping to gain by inventing these aliens?"

Burt lifted a grubby finger and tapped the side of his nose. "Just you wait and see."

Leyton left Burt and the barman to it and wandered back to the card game. He wasn't the only one watching. Quite a crowd had begun to gather around the four players. He noted too that Kethi's modest stake had grown considerably since he was last here.

Once he took the trouble to stand still for a while and observe her at work he began to see why. Not only could Kethi *play* cards, she was either an expert or a hell of a quick learner. She didn't win every hand, but she did win more than her share, including nearly all the ones that mattered, while ducking out of those she couldn't win early enough to avoid getting burned. Slowly but surely, her winnings accumulated, while the funds of her opponents dwindled accordingly, in a form of skewed osmosis which seemed to dictate that funds should flow inexorably towards the greatest concentration of cash rather than away from it.

Joss came over to join the growing crowd, standing at Leyton's elbow. After a few hands she said, too quietly for anyone except Leyton to hear, "Isn't this a little unfair?"

He was momentarily startled by the comment, which suggested that Joss knew about Kethi being different. He caught his surprise almost as it was forming and strangled it. Of course she knew. Kethi's nature was apparently common knowledge among the habitat, and Joss had been with them a lot longer than he had.

"Not really," he replied. "Anyone who goes into a game like this has the odds stacked for or against them courtesy of their own speed of thought, their memory for the cards, their understanding of the odds and other factors involved, not to mention their ability to think clearly under pressure. Kethi just has a bit more going for her than most."

"You can say that again."

The stakes and intensity crept upwards and the game became the focus of the room, sucking in attention as a sponge draws in water. Conversations slowly died away, surviving only as murmurs in the farthest corners.

Naturally it was only once the tension reached this sort of peak that Leyton saw the figure he'd been waiting for saunter in through the door. He left Joss watching the cards and strolled back to the bar, ordering a further drink without looking at the short, solidly built man who eased onto the stool beside him.

"You're taking a heck of a chance coming here, aren't you?" said a high pitched, nasally voice which at the same time managed to sound gravelly, as if the speaker was forever on the verge of a coughing fit.

"Life's one big risk, Billy," Leyton replied, "you know that."

"Had some hard-assed woman leaning on me a while back, government type, wanting to know everything about you. I'm supposed to call a certain number if I ever see you again."

"Nice to know I'm so popular."

"I won't be calling, of course. Lost the number."

"Shame."

As the barman presented Leyton with his beer, the former eyegee ordered a double Rellian brandy.

"Ah," said Billy, sniffing the golden brown liquid appreciatively before lifting the glass in salute. "I'm touched that you remembered."

"How could I forget? You're the only bastard I know who can drink the stuff without your eyes watering."

"Helps soothe my throat." Billy said. He watched until the barman was busy serving someone else. "Now, what can I do you for?"

"Information; anything you've heard about the Byrzaens, ULAW, that sort of thing."

"Ha! Are you sure you want *anything*? 'Cos that'll take a week, what with all the crazy talk flying around at the moment."

"Thanks, but I've heard more than enough of that already. Cut the wildest stuff and what are we left with?"

"Not much. Perhaps if you told me exactly what you're after?"

Leyton paused, wondering how much to trust Billy with. Eventually, he said, "Let's just say that any hint, rumour or speculation about the Byrzaens being around prior to New Paris would be particularly welcome."

"Ah, really? Interesting." He looked at Leyton, as if waiting for him to say more. Leyton didn't. So Billy continued, "Okay, yeah, I have heard the odd rumour. Come and find me tomorrow afternoon, at Jacey's. I'll see what I can dig up."

"Thank you." Leyton picked up his beer and went to step away from the bar.

"Ehm, aren't we forgetting something? I mean, I know it's been a while since we last saw each other, but I do still have overheads to meet."

Leyton glanced around at the stocky man's 'office.' "Yeah, I can see that." He smiled. "Don't worry, Billy, you'll get paid." With that, he headed back to the card game.

Two of the men Kethi was playing against seemed to be taking their losses with good grace. In fact, one of them, a portly fellow who was sweating profusely, chuckled at each disastrous hand, as if he considered it an honour to be beaten by such a young and lovely woman. The third opponent, however, the skinny runt sitting directly opposite Kethi, seemed less impressed. He had a face like thunder.

By the time Leyton worked his way to a vantage point where he could see what was going on, the other two players had folded, leaving just Kethi and the skinny runt in the game. The latter watched Kethi like a hawk, as if convinced she wasn't playing fair and determined to catch her out. Leyton began to appreciate her choice of top: no sleeves, which eliminated one obvious method of cheating. He recalled the length of time she'd spent scouring the net when they landed; had she researched Flappers at the same time? Had she noted they habitually had card games on the go? Had she *planned* this and dressed accordingly? He suppressed a wry smile. The young lady continued to surprise him.

The pile of money in the centre of the table grew steadily, as the two players raised each other again and again. The betting rose steadily until Skinny Runt had committed all his remaining funds to the central heap. The two opponents locked gazes. Then, with a defiant glare at Kethi, he placed his cards face upwards on the table: three jacks and a pair of sixes; a full house. Appreciative murmurs arose from several of the watchers.

After only a slight pause, Kethi smiled and did likewise, to reveal a nine, a six... and then three more nines. Guffaws and exclamations went round the throng. "Four of a kind! Well I'll be," a man close to Leyton said, shaking his head. "Hell of a game," another muttered.

Joss took the opportunity presented by the crowd shifting and relaxing to work her way across to Leyton's side. "Don't like the look of that thin bloke," she murmured.

Leyton could only agree.

"Thank you, gentlemen, it's been a pleasure," Kethi said, nodding to each of her three opponents in turn. As she reached forward to haul in her winnings, somebody started clapping and a smattering of applause arose from all sides. She paused and smiled, acknowledging their appreciation, then returned to gathering the money.

A hand shot out, gripping her wrist before she could finish doing so. "Hang on a minute," said Thunder face. "You're not taking that. You cheated. No idea how you did it, but no one's that good."

The room had fallen deathly quiet.

"Take your hand off me." Kethi matched the man glare for glare.

"Come on, now," said the portly player who had risen and was standing beside his seat. "What do you think she was doing, hiding cards up her sleeves? The lady beat us fair and square."

"That's it," said Skinny Runt, his eyes darting between Kethi and the man. "The two of you are in this together, you bastards, cheating honest folks like me out of our money."

The fat man spluttered with laughter, his face reddening. "Don't be so ridiculous!"

"Calm down," someone else advised. This sparked a babble of comment: "Didn't see no cheating... just doesn't like being beaten by a woman... bad loser... she did have all the best hands, though..."

The atmosphere was turning nasty; people were shifting their feet as if ready to get involved. This was heading towards a brawl with the sort of inevitability Leyton had seen all too often before.

"How are you with your fists?" he murmured to Joss beside him.

"Fair to middling. I'm a real demon with my knees and elbows, though."

"Good, because I've a feeling we might be needing all of them."

He glanced quickly in the direction of the bar, but the stool Billy had occupied was now empty, the little man having sensed what was coming and scarpered.

Without warning, Kethi moved, lifting her free hand in the blink of an eye and smashing her balled fist down on the back of Skinny Runt's wrist with an audible *thud*. "I said let go."

He did, with a shriek of pain and a jerk of his injured arm, which he sat nursing, shock evident on his face.

Kethi stood up, leaving the money where it sat between them. She leaned forward, her hands pressed flat against the table, face flushed with fury, although her voice remained ice calm and steady. "I didn't cheat. I didn't need to and wouldn't know how if I'd wanted to."

Skinny Runt shrank away, visibly cowed, but he wasn't about to give up just yet. "Well you would say that wouldn't you?" he flung back, petulantly.

"I am now going to collect my winnings. If you try to stop me again, I'll break your hand. If you have a problem with this, I'll be happy to accompany you outside and whip your ass in a fight as thoroughly as I just did at cards." She raked in the money. There was a lot of it. Only the man's eyes offered further defiance. The watching crowd seemed to release a collective breath and the tension ebbed away as people relaxed.

Leyton had to admit he was impressed. There was no way he could have defused that situation and avoided a fight breaking out, yet Kethi had managed to do so in a matter of seconds. Winnings gathered, she strode up to the bar. Every eye in the place was on her. She took a couple of notes and slammed them down in front of a wide-eyed barman.

She then turned to address the room. "I've just put a hundred credits behind the bar. Drinks are on me until it runs out!"

So saying, Kethi slipped away just before the inevitable stampede and headed for the nearest door.

Leyton and Joss followed, joining her outside.

Kethi handed the money across to Leyton. "Billy's fee."

He took it without comment.

"That went well," Joss said as they walked back towards the port. "I don't think anyone noticed us at all, do you?"

CHAPTER NINETEEN

JACEY'S WAS A little more upmarket than Flappers, the ambience more sophisticated, with an interior that was all glass shelving and sweeping ferns in alcoves, dramatic arrangement and subtle uplighting. The floor was a harlequin mosaic of black and white tiles, while gentle muzak played in the background and cocktails were the order of the day.

There was no sign of Billy. Leyton strolled up to the bar and claimed one of the chrome pedestal stools that fronted it. The barman – slicked down black hair, black trousers with creases sharp enough to shave by, bright white shirt and black dickey-bow tie – stared at him a little oddly.

"Are you Leyton?"

He tried not to show his surprise or the jolt of fear that coursed through him. "Depends who's asking."

"Billy left this for you." The man held out a wric, one of the cheap and disposable knock-offs that kids on street corners tried to foist onto the unwary.

Leyton stared for a fraction of a second and then took it. The small display screen showed a photo. Of him, in profile, snapped at Flappers the previous evening, presumably as Billy was leaving. So this was how the barman recognised him.

Leyton thumbed the image away. A message appeared in its place – stark white lettering against a plain black background.

GIVE MONEY TO BARMAN

He smiled. Trust Billy to get the important part of the proceedings out of the way first. Leyton reached into his jacket and withdrew a slender opaque shrink-wrapped parcel. It contained most of the winnings from the previous evening. Most, but not all. He intended to use the balance to buy something for Kethi on the way back to the shuttle. It felt a little strange to be handling real money rather than credit; stranger still to be contemplating buying a gift for somebody.

He handed the package over to the barman, who then moved away, leaving him to thumb the wric to the next screen. As he saw the message revealed, he froze. Two lines, four words, a message and a warning:

VIRTUALITY
GET OUT NOW!

Leyton eased himself off his perch, nodded to the barman and strolled out of the bar, a study in nonchalance. He didn't hurry until he was in the street, where so many people were always in a rush to be places and he became just one more.

The wric he tossed into a disposal chute at the first opportunity. He then called Kethi. "On my way. Tell Joss to be ready." He closed the connection as soon as the words were out. It was a risk, that call, but a small one.

Billy's message had been long on import, short on detail. He trusted the little man's judgement but there was no way of knowing exactly how much trouble they were in or how much time they had. Clearly something had aroused suspicion – whether Kethi's little performance last night, her snooping on the net, plain bad luck, or Billy playing both ends of the situation and giving them away, Leyton couldn't be certain. It didn't matter. They had to be gone from this world as soon as possible.

Walking to the port would take him about twenty minutes, fifteen if he pushed it, but that might be too late. He decided to take a further risk and hail a cab – distinctive in their black and purple livery – and flagged one down almost immediately. The journey now took him only four minutes, despite city traffic. He kept an eye on the cabbie throughout, looking for signs of tension in the man's neck and shoulders, wary for any extraneous movements, but the brief ride passed without incident.

While sitting in the back of the cab, Leyton reflected on the fact that Billy's actual message had comprised of a single word: 'Virtuality.' Hell of an expensive word, in this instance. He could only hope it proved to be the key Kethi was looking for.

The cab's old but well upholstered seats had a whiff of fresh polish and detergent. Before he could spend too much time in unpleasant conjecture about what might have been on them recently that required such rigorous cleaning, they arrived at the port. Almost before the cab came to a halt he was climbing out, paying the fare, and hurrying to where the shuttle was berthed.

He breezed through customs, security failing to give him a second glance. Nothing struck him as obviously out of place as he strode through the port's various reception areas; everybody seemed as relaxed or preoccupied as they generally were, while there was no profusion of individuals loitering with suspicious lack of purpose. Although he didn't relax, Leyton did dare to hope that the danger might not be as pressing as he'd feared. Which was when he caught sight of the two dark-suited figures huddled around a desk at the far end of the vast terminal building, talking earnestly with one of the service staff. All right, they may have been asking for directions to the nearest loo or fast food dispenser, or have business relating to any of the other vessels currently landed, but Leyton wasn't about to bank on it. He moved past them quickly, making sure to keep people, kiosks, and every available object between him and the two suits.

Leyton didn't run – nothing was more likely to draw attention – but his gait was barely slower. Fortunately he was fully alert, or he might not have seen the man who lunged at him until it was too late. As it was, he caught a blur of movement in the corner of his eye and was able to begin his twist and turn before the half-seen form cannoned into his left side. Leyton's swivel effectively side-stepped the bone-jarring body-to-body impact the assailant had intended and instead turned the man's impetus against him. Only the left arm caught the former eyegee as he rolled out of the way, and he was able to get both hands on the man's back, shoving him forcefully while tripping him with his right leg, so that the would-be attacker hit the ground hard.

This seemed like a good time to run. Leyton sprinted for all he was worth. Shouts from behind, more than one voice, probably demanding he stop. Fat chance. They should have saved their breath for the chase. Would they risk shooting? There were people around, but not many, not enough to rely on for protection. A lumbering automated luggage transporter offered temporary cover. It hummed along like some giant segmented caterpillar, laden with cases and baggage, presumably fresh off a commercial flight. The thing was coming diagonally towards Leyton. He jinked his run, nearly colliding with a startled elderly couple as he zigged left and zagged right, now running with the transporter between him and those chasing.

A clear path ahead. He put his head down and gave it everything, arms and legs pumping, brain calculating how long until his pursuers would be free of the baggage train. About now, he'd reckon, and the corner that offered salvation was still a few strides away. Still, there was always the floor to consider... it was polished, slippery. He flung himself to the ground, just as a shot rang out, right on cue. Momentum sent him sliding forward. More shots sounded as he scrambled, rolled, was around the corner and back on his feet, running again.

The shuttle waited a short distance ahead, its door open and ramp down. He just hoped Kethi and Joss had understood his deliberately hasty message and were ready to take off. If not, presumably the gunshots would provide a clue. With relief, he realised that the engines were firing, ready to lift. A dark-clad figure appeared in the doorway and he felt a jolt of horror. Had the women been overpowered, the shuttle taken by ULAW? Was he running straight into a trap? No, almost immediately he recognised the figure as Kethi. She crouched in the entranceway, cradling an automatic weapon, and, as he charged up the ramp, she began to fire, covering his escape.

"Go!" he yelled as he took one final leap from the springy surface of the ramp and felt his foot land on the less forgiving floor of the craft proper, but the two women were ahead of him. Kethi drew herself back fully inside the door and slammed her palm against the control button while Joss began to take the craft up, even before he'd come to a stop against the far wall.

"This sort of thing's getting to be a habit," Joss called out from the craft's small cockpit.

Leyton was breathing hard. His legs might have stopped pumping, but the adrenaline hadn't. As he found a seat and activated the safety webbing, he voiced a whoop of joy. It felt good to be alive.

VIRTUALITY WAS A phenomenon Leyton was aware of but had never really ventured into. Most ULAW worlds had developed their own versions of the place, and he knew that many people, particularly teenagers, spent a great deal of time there. He'd always considered the virtual world an excuse for self-indulgent navel gazing, but when he gave the sparse content of Billy's message to Kethi she seemed thoughtful rather than disappointed, which he took as a good sign.

"Virtuality," she murmured, "I wonder..."

As soon as they were reunited with *The Rebellion*, Kethi hurried to the bridge with a distracted expression he was coming to know well.

Within the hour, she summoned Leyton and all the ship's officers to a meeting. The former eyegee noted that Kyle was also included. Of course, as head of engineering he would be, though he looked far from comfortable at being there.

Humility was not a quality Leyton necessarily associated with Kethi. As a rule she trusted her own counsel implicitly and was fully confident in her own judgement and abilities, but he was coming to realise that she didn't entirely discount the opinions of others, that once the deductive trail had taken her as far as it could she was willing to listen to options.

This meeting offered further evidence of this, as she outlined her discoveries and thinking.

"The internal troubles we've noted in ULAW flared up comparatively recently," Kethi explained. "Doubtless divisions existed beneath the surface before this, but something specific has now forced then to the surface. Some of the actions taken by factions within ULAW have an air of desperation to them, as if time is running out and events have required a violent response. It all seems to have kicked off shortly before *The Noise Within* first appeared and began her campaign of piracy.

"I'm increasingly convinced that the advent of *The Noise Within* and the subsequent appearance of the Byrzaens at New Paris are the catalysts that have sparked the internal bickering. They knew the Byrzaens were coming. Individuals and cliques have been jockeying to put themselves in the most favourable position to take advantage of the fact. In their determination to undermine the opposition, different groups within ULAW set about killing key supporters and operatives of opposing groups, hence the number of accidents and assassinations we've identified."

"The Byrzaens," Kyle muttered, beside Leyton, and gave an exaggerated shudder.

The reaction struck him as an odd one. Evidently Kethi overheard the comment and thought the same. "Did you actually meet one while you were on *The Noise Within*?"

"No, not there."

"Where then?"

"Well, it wasn't even a real one. At least, I don't think it was."

"Even so...?"

"In Virtuality," he said. "But, like I said, I'm pretty sure it was just someone pretending to be a Byrzaen, not the real deal."

"Virtuality." She nodded as if taking this as confirmation of something. "Yes, that would fit."

Kethi then continued to explain herself in a manner Leyton hadn't seen before, and which he couldn't help but admire. Such an inclusive approach was a sign of good leadership in his eyes, and something he'd experienced all too infrequently during his ULAW days.

"Despite this growing conviction, I was missing a piece. I couldn't pin down the link that connected humans to Byrzaens prior to New Paris. Until the recent trip planetside, that is. As Kyle just suggested, that link is Virtuality. What better route for clandestine contact than a hidden world which most people over a certain age dismiss as trivial, a playground for the youthful? I'm now close to certain that this is how ULAW has been communicating with the aliens... somehow. The thing is, I can't begin to envisage how such communication is possible. I know nothing whatsoever about the place."

Nor would anyone native to the habitat. Leyton knew from previous conversations that their own dabbling in the field had never gone beyond the occasional game and the odd training scenario.

"I'm open to suggestions on where we go from here," Kethi finished.

"I can't pretend that I'm all that familiar with Virtuality myself," Leyton said into the silence that followed her words, "but I know a man who ought to be an expert on the place by now. After all, he lives there."

Kethi slowly turned her head to look at him. He could see in her eyes that she knew exactly who he meant. "Philip Kaufman," she said. "Of course."

* * *

LEYTON DIDN'T MUCH enjoy the role of outlaw. He'd spent all his adult life hunting down and dispatching ULAW's enemies, and now he'd become the very thing he was trained to kill. Life at this end of the relationship was proving to be far more restrictive and claustrophobic than he could ever have imagined. Since taking up with the habitat, his home had been this ship, his world defined by its logically designed environment – metal corridors, uniform spaces and cramped rooms – and he didn't imagine this was likely to change any time soon. He'd been given a reminder of life beyond when they picked up Kyle and went after Billy, and he was about to be granted another, but these were no more than temporary reprieves. It was not what he'd envisaged at all.

The door shushed open, interrupting his reveries. Kethi stuck her head into the room.

"You ready?"

"Yes," he assured her. "I'm ready."

He took a deep breath and stood up.

"Good." She stepped fully into the room, her right hand behind her back, her face alight with a mischievous grin. "Only I've got something for you."

She slowly brought her right hand into view and held it out towards him.

He stared in disbelief at the familiar shape that lay across her palm. Smooth, curved handle, slightly bulky stock and a fatter barrel than you might expect. Some might think it ugly, cumbersome, but not him.

"My gun."

"Your newly sanitised, AI free gun," she corrected, and laughed.

He took the proffered weapon, opening and closing his hand around the grip and instantly noticing a difference.

"The AI's dead, but we've installed a simple computer chip to handle the switches from one function to another," Kethi explained. "Lacking the software ULAW had packed into your skull, we haven't yet perfected a voice operated system that's going to be foolproof in the noisy confusion of an all out battle, so for the moment you're going to have to live with a dial switch, but we'll sort out something on the voice front which doesn't involve wires and a face mounted mike as soon as we can."

A dial? And he thought the habitat was supposedly founded by scientific geniuses. He flicked the small wheel sunk into the gun's handle with his thumb, gazing at it to memorise which function was where. At least the action was smooth enough, easy to flick between the various settings. He ran the dial from one end to the other – *projectile, grenade, armour piercing, energy* – and then back again, wondering how easy it was going to be to accidentally skip one of those steps in the heat of a battle and fire an armour piercing shell when he wanted a grenade. Still, given the choice between this and any other hand weapon, he knew which he'd go for in a flash.

"Obviously this isn't going to provide the sort of intelligence support the old gun and visor combination gave you, but..."

Kethi seemed uncertain, perhaps disappointed at his lack of visible reaction. He smiled, and said as reassurance, "Thank you. Feels great to have it back."

Despite everything, it did.

LEYTON'S INITIAL REACTION to Catherine Chzyski was complicated. At first glance she had an open expression and a disarming, welcoming smile – the sort of kindly demeanour which, combined with her age, made you want to relax and suspect that she might be about to offer you a home-baked cake and a mug of hot chocolate. Look a little closer, however, especially at the eyes, and you'd see there calculation and a sharpness that suggested your first impression might be a trifle misleading. She was clearly well into her – what, seventies? – yet she moved with the vitality and confidence of someone half her age. No hesitant fear of brittle bones here, instead the assured confidence of someone at ease with herself and her age.

"So," she said, once he and Kethi were seated, "you're Jim Leyton; the man who was present when Philip Kaufman was murdered and who hunted down and killed the killer."

"I am," Leyton admitted.

"Pity about that last part, mind you. Who knows what we could have learned from the Cirese woman, had she lived?" Her smile only softened the implied criticism by a fraction. "Still, no helping that now."

"Indeed," Leyton agreed. "Particularly as it emerges that if I *had* taken her into custody I might well have been handing her over to the very people she was working for."

He said this to get a reaction, but Chzyski's smile gave nothing away. If his words came as a shock or surprise, Leyton couldn't read the fact, and he was trained to.

"Can I get either of you a drink?"

A cool one, no doubt about it.

"No, thank you," the two of them, almost in harmony.

They were taking a chance in coming here, but his gut told him the risk was worth it and Kethi agreed, though not without reservations. Kaufman Industries were one of the corporations that made ULAW tick. They had designed the engines that powered ULAW's starships and supplied the government with the needle ship squadron that ambushed *The Rebellion*... and yet... Philip Kaufman's assassination made them potential allies if Kethi's assessment was correct, and Catherine Chzyski was known to be staunchly loyal to the Kaufmans, going back to the time of Philip's father. This was an association that seemed set to continue, since both the transhuman Kaufmans had been taken on by KI as consultants.

It was that last that was the clincher, which persuaded them to gamble, relying on Leyton's wits and Kethi's skills to get them out of a scrape if it proved necessary. He felt increasingly confident, though, that it wouldn't.

"You do realise, I presume, how great a risk I'm taking in even having you here, Mr Leyton," Catherine said. "You're not exactly ULAW's favourite son at present. While you, young lady," she nodded towards Kethi, "don't even appear to exist as far as official records are concerned."

"True," Leyton agreed. "Yet here we are."

"Indeed, and one has to wonder why that is."

"As I explained to your... partial?" Leyton was aware that downloaded personality fragments were commonly used for what amounted to secretarial purposes on some worlds, but this was the first time he'd ever encountered the practice directly. Encouraged by Catherine's nod of confirmation, he continued. "We're hoping you can put us in touch with Philip Kaufman."

Catherine laughed. "Philip has the freedom of Virtuality. You could have contacted him from anywhere."

"Perhaps," Kethi said, sitting forward, entering the conversation for the first time, as if to emphasise that she was just as relevant to proceedings as Leyton. "But we wanted to make sure we had his attention."

"Oh, I think you can safely assume you have that," Catherine said. "The question is, why do you want it?"

This was the moment of commitment, when they either damned themselves by admitting what amounted to treason in front of one of the government's strongest supporters, or found a much needed ally. Kethi gave Leyton the shallowest of nods, relinquishing the floor to him. "We have evidence that Philip's assassination was part of a wider campaign of murders instigated by factions within the ULAW government and triggered by the appearance of the Byrzaens. Further, we believe that elements of the government have been in contact with the aliens prior to New Paris, and wish to explore the possibility that said contact was facilitated via Virtuality. We'd like to hear Philip's take on this."

He thought that put the situation pretty succinctly.

"I'll bet you would," said a new voice as two figures materialised beside the Kaufman Industries CEO.

"Philip." Leyton nodded towards the younger of the two. "I had a feeling you might be listening in. I presume this must be Malcolm."

"Indeed it is. Hello, Jim, good to see you. And Kethi, is it? Interesting name; I'd like to hear more about that. In fact, it sounds to me as if we've got a great deal to talk about all round."

CHAPTER TWENTY

KYLE TRIED TO talk to Joss about Wicksy several times. Finally a suitable opportunity presented itself. They were in the rec room, no one else at the table, when he attempted to express his regret at her loss and apologise for anything he might have said or done to make her feel worse. Strange, but when it came to light, witty banter with a woman – *any* woman – he had always found that words flowed freely. Now, when matters were anything but frivolous, he felt as if his tongue had been dipped in lead rather than the desired silver. The conversation went badly, with her snapping that she didn't want to talk about it before ensuring that others came over to join them. She might not have stormed off this time around, but she pointedly spoke to the new arrivals rather than him, with a forced cheerfulness presumably intended to convince Kyle that she was fine and there was no problem here at all.

He came away from the encounter feeling frustrated and a little embarrassed, wishing that he'd never bothered trying to explain himself in the first place. He also felt confused, not least about whether he was merely trying to win Joss's friendship or was hoping for something more. There were certainly prettier women on board, so why was he spending so much time and effort trying to get into the good graces of this one?

On the plus side, the energy veils had held up admirably, with no sign of tearing or damage following the two jumps since his repairs. Also, he continued to feel far more comfortable around the rest of the crew, as if they really had accepted him now. He began to wonder whether his previous sense of isolation was the result of a milder form of what Joss had shown him; that the crew as a whole had subconsciously resented his presence as a reminder of the friends they'd lost. If so, his success in fixing the ship's drives seemed to have overcome their reservations; in all bar one instance, at least.

Something that continued to surprise him was the lack of fatigue evident among his shipmates. Not in the sense of physical tiredness, but rather the simple wearing down of spirit that spacers usually suffered after being cooped up for so long within the confines of a ship. From what he'd been told, these people had been stuck aboard *The Rebellion* for an age, and yet he heard no real griping, not even when they learnt that Kethi and Leyton had escaped to the planet below while everyone else remained up here. He supposed this was to do with their culture. On any other ship, he felt certain there would have been muttered complaints on all sides.

He was on his way to engineering when he glanced down a branching corridor and saw Joss again. She was with someone – Simon – and she was leaning into him, hugging him. Joss looked up and saw Kyle at the same instant he almost stumbled. Then he was past and hurrying on towards his station, without a word spoken. *Joss and Simon?*

His shift went by in a blur, even though there was little for him to do. He couldn't get the image of Joss's head on Simon's chest out of his mind. Who'd been hugging whom? Had they both been hugging each other or was it only one way? Where had Joss's arm been? Was it around Simon or by her side? He tried to remember, tried to analyse the picture in his mind's eye, but the more he thought about it the less he trusted his memory and the more variations he could envisage.

Kyle was so wrapped up in his own thoughts that he missed the big news. Only when he dropped in to the rec room at the end of his shift did he hear. *The Retribution* had arrived.

Rumours were rife that she had brought a VIP with her, though if any of the off-duty bridge personnel knew who it was, they weren't saying. Kyle wasn't really in the mood for the animated gossip that was flying around the room and didn't even know the other two names which kept being bandied about – Nyles and Mya – so he decided to make an early night of it and headed for his quarters.

The way life had been slapping him around of late, he probably should have been prepared to bump into Joss at the rec room doorway, but he wasn't. She looked as embarrassed as he felt. None the less, he remembered his manners and stood back, ushering her into the room.

"Look, I wanted to explain about what you saw earlier, me and Simon..." she started to say.

He waved away her words. The last thing he wanted right then was an awkward conversation, and he certainly didn't need her pity. "No problem. You don't have to explain yourself to me," he assured her. "Have fun." With his best imitation of an unconcerned smile firmly in place, Kyle brushed past her and strolled on towards his room.

KETHI AND LEYTON were in transit back to *The Rebellion* when *The Retribution* arrived. Catherine Chzyski had offered to put them up at Kaufman Industries' expense, but they declined. Not because they had any qualms about trusting Kaufman Industries' CEO, but they decided it was safer to return to the ship, bearing in mind their rebel status and the fact that Home was not some backwater planet but a significant world deep within ULAW space. The meeting itself had gone remarkably well, with common ground apparent from the off, after which all parties were able to contribute information that the others lacked. The fact that both groups had reached similar conclusions independently strengthened their conviction that they were on the right track. A further meeting had been scheduled for the following day. Finding likeminded people was one thing, now they had to decide on what to do next.

Both Leyton and Kethi left in buoyant mood. It was hugely uplifting to realise they weren't alone, and that a corporation as powerful as KI was sympathetic to their cause.

The good mood didn't last long.

News of their sister ship's arrival came as no surprise – Kethi had ensured a coded message was left for Nyles informing him of their destination – but news of *The Rebellion*'s additional passenger did.

"You've brought *who* with you?" Kethi asked.

"I know, but things aren't always as clear cut as they might seem, Kethi," Nyles told her.

The tone Nyles habitually adopted when addressing Kethi never ceased to amaze Leyton: patronising, as if she were a child. He supposed it came from the man having known her since she was. Leyton for one didn't welcome the return of the habitat's leader. In his absence, Kethi had blossomed, growing into the responsibilities of command, and that tone had seemed light years away. Now, here it was again, in the very first communication between the two of them.

"Mr Benson has provided us with some fascinating intel and has convinced me that he's not our enemy. In fact, far from it," Nyles continued. "He, Mya and I will transfer to *The Rebellion* shortly, allowing Captain Forster to withdraw *The Retribution*. I don't like having two of our ships exposed like this so deep in ULAW territory. We can discuss the matter further when I arrive."

"Are you all right?" Leyton asked once the connection was broken. Their own shuttle was about to dock with *The Rebellion* and Leyton knew that once they were back on board she'd be too busy for any private conversations.

"Yes, I'm fine," Kethi replied, though her face suggested otherwise. "I'm just thinking about the reallocation of cabins all over again."

"Bullshit; that's just logistics. What's really bothering you? Is it the prospect of losing the captaincy now that Nyles is back?"

She smiled. "Maybe, a bit. I've enjoyed being captain, I have to admit, but it's more than that."

Of course it was. "Benson."

"Yes!" and she frowned, looking anxious, frustrated, and perhaps even a little angry. "I've spent so much time looking into all this, and it's been like chasing shadows. There are hints and half clues about the people responsible, but hardly ever anything concrete. They are adept at avoiding the limelight, these faceless kingpins. Identifying them with any certainty has been impossible most of the time. The one name that's emerged from the murk and shadows enough for me to point at and say 'yes, he's one of them' is Benson's. To me he's like some dark spider sitting at the heart of a web of manipulation, misinformation and conspiracy, pulling the strings and making his puppets dance, and now Nyles turns up with this man and presents him to us as an *ally*?" She shook her head and looked at him, as if seeking reassurance. "What do you think? Am I too close to this, reading too much into Benson's role? You know the man, you've worked with him."

"I don't know," he said. "To me Benson was the political side of what I did. He was the man who represented ULAW, who issued the assignments and told me what needed doing. I always viewed him as a bureaucrat, a politician; not exactly a figure of fun, but someone to be humoured, whose world moved in a completely different orbit from mine. Then he was put in charge of things at New Paris and I had to start taking him a whole lot more seriously.

"As for knowing him... no, not really. I don't think any of us ever did."

"But can we *trust* him?"

That was the question, of course, and he knew that Kethi was looking to him for the answer. "For as long as it suits him, yes," he said. "And there's no question that Benson could prove a useful ally. He's shrewd, perceptive, and knows a lot more about the inner machinations of ULAW than I do. The trick is going to be recognising the point at which his interests no longer coincide with ours. Then... watch out."

"That's what I thought," she said. "That's exactly what I'm afraid of."

KYLE TENDED TO sleep on his side much of the time. So when he came awake to the soft movements of somebody slipping into bed, he had his back to them. Even so, he reckoned the field of likely candidates was pretty limited. He lay there, not moving, not reacting, not wanting to spook her.

"You'd have liked Wicksy," she said softly.

"Yeah," he replied, "I'm sure I would have done."

She snuggled up against him – her thigh against his, the soft pressure of her breasts on his back, while her hand reached round to rest on his stomach. Joss was something special. He'd bedded many prettier girls in his time but none more beautiful. It seemed to him at that moment that all his previous conquests had been shallow, two dimensional, or at least his perception of them had been. There was a lot more to Joss than that, a greater depth, and he was delighted to feel all of her dimensions cuddling up against him right now. He sensed that this was all she wanted, at least for the moment, and that was fine by him; that was enough for both of them.

CHAPTER TWENTY-ONE

THERE WAS SOMETHING new between Kethi and Leyton. They did a good job of hiding it, of masking their body language, but Mya was an expert at reading them. She was also an expert at reading Leyton, and he was trying just a little too hard not to react to Kethi. Lovers, perhaps? It was all very touching.

She'd picked up on it the previous evening when she, Nyles and Benson had boarded *The Rebellion*. Not so much from Kethi, oddly enough, who'd been preoccupied with greeting them all and handing command back to Nyles, but from Leyton, whose gaze lingered just a fraction too long on the ship's erstwhile captain. The real giveaway, though, was his reaction to her. Nothing overt; he smiled warmly enough and hugged her in greeting, but he wasn't focussed on her with the sort of intensity he'd shown after she was liberated from Sheol. Mya no longer felt that she was the centre of his universe, which piqued her curiosity, not to mention her pride, and made her determined to discover who had usurped her: Kethi, it would seem.

Mya felt a small prickling of jealousy, which was ridiculous, and she experienced a flash of amusement at her own reaction. She ought to feel pleased for him, not proprietorial. The jealousy was followed by a sudden jolt of fear. What if he could read her reaction to Benson as clearly as she could his to Kethi? No, start getting paranoid about that and it was bound to lead to awkwardness and tell-tale behaviour. She just needed to relax and act naturally.

At least staring too much at Pavel hadn't been an issue. He was the centre of everyone's attention, with Nyles inviting him to explain to Kethi and Leyton why he was such a vital ally.

It was interesting seeing Jim and Pavel together – these two men who, Louis aside, had been the most important in her life. Leyton was powerfully built – not fat, all solid muscle, but nor was he some muscle-bound grotesquery. He possessed the sort of rugged handsomeness displayed by a wild coastline of sweeping cliffs standing defiant against the pounding waves. He moved with the easy grace of a dancer, but held the menace of a watching bull. Pavel was older and, despite being well-toned, seemed positively slight in comparison, although the two were roughly the same height. His features were softer, more sensitive, the artful touch of grey in his hair conspiring to make him look distinguished and wise. Pavel had poise and a real presence. He could command a room with a gesture and a few well chosen words. Here was a man who exuded authority and an aura of power that was pure aphrodisiac.

Considering the two of them now, Mya felt that Leyton had been the great love of her youth, when everything had been about energy and fierce excitement; but over the years her needs had grown more sophisticated and less visceral – technique and intelligence valued more highly than obsessive, unadulterated passion. She had matured, and found Pavel. If Leyton was the love of her youth, then Benson was the love of her life.

Their relationship had always been an intensely private one. For professional reasons they'd gone to great lengths to ensure that no one in ULAW suspected they were sleeping together, and it seemed natural to continue such discretion now. The last thing either of them wanted was for personal factors such as her previous relationship with Leyton to cloud the important issues.

Pavel had explained himself with typical charm and forthright sincerity, but Mya could sense that neither Kethi nor Leyton were entirely convinced. Now he would have to do the same all over again to the higher ups at Kaufman Industries, and she could only hope that they proved a more sympathetic audience.

The party that travelled down to Home's surface was a comparatively large one. In addition to the anticipated quintet – herself, Nyles, Kethi, Leyton and Pavel – Kethi insisted on including an engineer *The Rebellion* had picked up somewhere along the way, Kyle, as well as a pair of the ship's security officers.

The latter struck Mya as an affront, despite Kethi's explanation that the previous day's visit had been an 'informal one to test the ground,' while this time their intent was more official and therefore 'merits a proper escort.' It seemed more likely that the guards were there to keep an eye on Benson, and she was all ready to bridle on his behalf; but he took their presence with equanimity, forcing her to do the same.

She noted that Nyles didn't attempt to gainsay Kethi in this. During the time they spent together aboard *The Retribution*, Mya had sensed a deep weariness in Nyles, as if he were going through the motions of leadership because it was expected of him and *someone* had to do the job. The fact that he was willing to give Kethi her head now, despite his having nominally reclaimed the captaincy of *The Rebellion,* suggested an interesting shift in the dynamics of command.

Kaufman Industries had influence on Home. She supposed it was inevitable when such a vital civilisation-spanning corporation had all its executive power concentrated on a single world, but the ease with which their arrival was processed disturbed her. They bypassed official channels and were whisked through security checks and customs as if they didn't exist. In her former life as a ULAW operative, she would have flagged this and reported it as something that merited investigation. Despite recent experiences, she found her instincts were too deeply ingrained not to make their presence felt.

She didn't get a chance to see the KI building from the outside – their party was whisked straight into an underground car park via a side entrance – but she didn't doubt it was impressive.

She'd encountered partials before, but not often enough to prevent the manifestation of 'Cath' that greeted them from being of interest.

"Sorry I can't meet you in person," Cath said, demonstrating that aspect of these uploaded partials that Mya found vaguely disturbing; their habit of speaking as if *they* were the corporeal original, as if the two were somehow interchangeable. The partial then bade them accompany the fresh-faced young man who stood flanked by two chisel-jawed security personnel, which they did. He led them via an elevator to the plush conference room where Catherine Chzyski awaited them in person.

The security details waited outside. The rest of them were ushered in by the fresh-faced secretary, who then left. Catherine was much as Mya had expected, managing to combine the gravitas of experience with the vitality of somebody who still had things to achieve. It was the other two in the room who intrigued her: Philip and Malcolm Kaufman. No mere partials these; from what she understood they were far more than that. These insubstantial forms represented all that remained of two brilliant minds and the personalities that had animated them.

Unsurprisingly, Benson was given the floor. Philip had evidently met him before, on New Paris, and all present seemed aware of who he was.

"I've come here in the hope that we can act together to prevent a tragedy in the making," Pavel began. "As most if not all of you are aware, the government has been experiencing inner turmoil on an unprecedented scale in recent weeks. As yet the nature of the resulting divisions has been kept from the media, but that can't last. When the full extent of the self-inflicted wounds comes to light, I'm not sure the ULAW government can survive. Of course, the timing of this couldn't be worse. We're at a true turning point in human history: first contact with an alien civilisation. Ironically, the cause of the disunion is the very reason it can't be allowed to continue. Thankfully, the Byrzaens too have been kept in blissful ignorance of the petty squabbling their presence has sparked. So far. But the cracks are beginning to show, and it won't be long before they realise what a shambles the body governing our society is in. That can't be allowed to happen. The antagonistic factions within ULAW *have* to be reconciled so that we can present a united front to the Byrzaens, or we risk damaging our standing with them forever."

"Good speech," Kethi said. "Undermined only slightly by the fact that you've been up to your neck in the very intrigues and disruptive plots you're now advocating we should try to put a stop to."

"True," Benson held his hand up. "I can't deny it. Look, everyone has been using whatever resources they can call upon to advance or secure their own position, and I've been as guilty of that as anybody, but I was misguided. We all were. I've had a chance to stand back and take a look at the bigger picture, and I can see the harm we're doing. If the bickering doesn't stop, nobody will benefit and the whole of the human race will be the losers here. I know that now."

"You've expressed these views to your colleagues, I take it?" Catherine said.

"I've tried, of course I have, but they won't listen. They're all so involved in their petty schemes and their plotting that they can't see the wood for the trees. They don't or *won't* accept what all this is leading to."

Mya glanced around. It was difficult to assess people's reactions. The two transhumans were unreadable, and Leyton had adopted his granite face, which made him pretty much the same. Nyles, she knew, was already sold on Benson's sincerity, and she had a feeling that Catherine was at least swayed. The engineer, Kyle, she dismissed, still not certain what he was doing here in the first place, which left only Kethi as openly sceptical.

Kyle's inclusion remained an enigma until later in the morning.

"What you have to understand here," Benson was saying, "is that all the intrigue and killing that's been going on is a purely human affair. The Byrzaens are the reason it's all been happening, yes, but they're not in any way responsible. We've done all this to ourselves. I suspect the Byrzaens wouldn't understand these shenanigans if they *did* find out about them. As far as we can tell, they're above such things as political intrigue. I'm not even sure they're capable of dishonesty as we know it."

"Oh yes they are," Kyle said quickly and forcefully, taking Mya and, judging by their reactions, most of the others present by surprise. This was the first time the engineer had really spoken. The hint of a smirk which Kethi swiftly banished suggested that perhaps she wasn't quite as surprised as the rest of them. "They've lied about their engines," Kyle continued.

"How so?" Philip Kaufman wanted to know.

"They claim their drive technology is based on zero point energy and that's complete bollocks," Kyle said. "I've worked on the engines of *The Noise Within* and *The Rebellion,* both of which are based on Byrzaen tech, and there's nothing like zero point energy involved. It's a red herring, dangled in front of us so they don't have to reveal how their stardrive really works."

Ah. Now Mya understood what Kyle was doing here. She bet Kethi was loving every second of this.

"Even so, assuming what you say is true – and I'm not trying to suggest for one minute that it might not be," Pavel said, doing exactly that, "we can't be certain that it's the Byrzaens themselves who are perpetrating the lies rather than the human go-betweens, who are, let me remind you, employed by ULAW."

"I can," Philip cut in. "I've been aboard the Byrzaens' ship at New Paris, remember, and that's exactly how their drive was presented to me. No question, that deception was theirs. We've caught them out, thanks to Kyle."

Pavel didn't show it, but Mya knew this was a setback; one he would have to work hard to recover from.

Soon after, they broke for lunch. Philip and Malcolm left them, promising to return before the afternoon session began.

Mya had eaten many different things in many different circumstances, but she'd never had a meal quite like the luncheon that Catherine Chzyski then hosted. Two waiters – a man and a woman, both smart and formal in black trousers and brilliant white shirts – entered the room, each guiding a trolley. The two carts were laden with trays, which were all but obscured by compartmentalised chrome lids.

Mya and a majority of the others had taken advantage of the break in proceedings to stand and stretch their legs. As the waiters appeared, Catherine invited them to return to their seats.

The first trolley was pushed flush to the far end of the table, and the four trays it held started to move, gliding off the trolley and onto the centre of the table, as if travelling along a continuous conveyor belt. Mya stared, fascinated, trying to decide if the smooth movement was a product of the table top or of the trays themselves. Once the first trolley had emptied it was pushed aside by the attendant, allowing the second trolley to be brought up for a repeat performance.

The surface of the polished wood conference table looked no different either in front of or behind the strange sliding procession. Mya concluded the trays were the culprits. They came to rest in front of the guests, and Catherine invited each person to take one. As she lifted hers, Mya's fingers strayed underneath, but all they found was uniform smoothness.

Six gleaming chrome compartments occupied her tray – two rows of three – while a flap running lengthwise at the front lifted to reveal an array of cutlery, including ornate chopsticks and silver forks and spoons. No knives, she noted, perhaps to prevent stabbings amongst the dinner guests.

Mya had no idea where to begin with this, so watched Catherine for clues. The older woman was chatting amiably with Nyles, who sat beside her on the same side of the table as Mya, with Benson between them. Not pausing in her conversation, Catherine reached out to tap the top of the container occupying the upper left corner of her tray. The lid promptly crumpled.

Mya instantly tapped the corresponding container on her own tray, which did likewise, the lid folding back on itself, concertinaing into a narrow strip of material at the far edge of the dish. A draft of slightly chilled air struck Mya's face in the process; not frozen or even strikingly cold, just fractionally lower than room temperature.

She gazed at the contents. Two thirds of the dish was taken up by a leaf salad – predominantly green but shot through with curls of purples, red, and even a streak of blue. The remainder of the compartment contained small balls of white, waxy cheese, which proved to be far more than they seemed. When she bit into one it released a wonderful smoky taste that she couldn't immediately identify. There was a hint of garlic in the background, but the predominant flavour was of something almost nutty, perhaps a spice she hadn't previously come across. The salad leaves were tiny and varied, from peppery to sweet, all crisp and fresh and complimented by a light, lemony dressing which stopped just short of being piquant.

As she savoured the first course the two waiting staff returned with glasses and a choice of red or white wines. She opted for the white, which proved to be crisp, dry, and fruity, without being in the least acidic, exactly to her taste.

The next dish Catherine tapped was the one below the first, and Mya did likewise. Glancing around, she suspected that everyone present was following Catherine's example, and she'd bet the sly old fox knew it.

The second lid rolled back and Mya found herself assailed by a waft of heat and the mouth-watering aromas of soy and ginger. Within were two plump, ivory-coloured shellfish, each sitting in an open-palm half-shell surrounded by a small pool of soy and topped by the thinnest ringlet of red chilli.

Steam curled from the fish, which were cooked to perfection – succulent, piping hot and bursting with flavour.

Mya felt she was getting the hang of this now. The containers somehow kept each of the varied dishes at the perfect temperature and the serving system conspired to deliver it in tip-top condition, while the waiting staff materialised with quiet efficiency to top up her glass before it ever threatened to empty. Benson had barely touched his own wine, while Leyton, sitting diagonally opposite her, refused either bottle and opted for water. She never had understood his penchant for the stuff. To her the alcohol scrubber ULAW implanted in all the eyegees was a tremendous boon. She raised her glass in the direction of her former lover and smiled, before taking another sip.

The lid of the third container lifted to release a breath of truly chilled air, visible wisps of which dissipated to reveal the palate cleanser: three small pale balls of a citrus granita, elegantly decorated with sugar-dusted leaves to resemble a cluster of plump winter berries.

It occurred to Mya that this was by far the best meal she'd eaten since she was snatched and thrown into Sheol, and she had to admit that the sheer volume of food was becoming a bit overwhelming.

None the less, remembering the delicious smells that assailed her when she first unveiled the shellfish, she couldn't wait to reveal the fourth and presumably main course; nor was she disappointed. As the lid rolled back she was instantly engulfed in the rich aroma of braised beef, redolent with wine, garlic and herbs. The chunks of meat were tender, flaking beneath her fork, and the whole dish packed more flavour than anything she could remember eating in ages, managing to fully live up to the burst of savoury fragrance that had heralded it.

Despite the modest portioning of each individual course, Mya was filling up rapidly, and she viewed the two unopened dishes with more than a little trepidation. A few around the table had already progressed to the fifth, which evidently held a concoction of moist sponge, cream and chocolate. Doubtless it was lovely, but there was no way she could do justice to anything that rich right now.

Fortunately, she was saved from having to try.

Catherine abruptly stiffened. "Yes?" She seemed to be speaking into space and clearly wasn't addressing any of them. "What?" Implants, Mya guessed, since there was no evidence of earplugs – doubtless the whole room was programmed to respond to the CEO's voice. "Show me."

In the air above the table a scene materialised, presumably depicting the building's lobby. A veritable sea of black garbed figures filled the area. A few startled civilians stood aside, pressing against walls as if seeking sanctuary or simply frozen to the spot, gaping at the heavily armed troops in their midst. The soldiers ignored them, moving onward and inward. ULAW, and in force.

"Shit." The food was suddenly forgotten.

"Must have tracked us here somehow," Benson muttered.

"No shimmer suits," observed Leyton. "They want to intimidate and impress, not sneak in unnoticed."

"Shut down all the elevators," Catherine instructed. "Replay the moment they first entered the building." The scene vanished, to be replaced by an apparently calm lobby, smartly dressed receptionist at her station, the whole suddenly disrupted as the troopers burst in through the front doors. "Freeze image."

All eyes focused on the man leading the assault. Mya for one noticed the visor instantly.

"An eyegee!"

Catherine looked at Benson with blatant suspicion. "I thought you were in charge of the eyegee unit."

"I was. Evidently I'm not anymore."

"Patch me into their comms," Catherine said. "I want to talk to that eyegee."

"No!" Benson shouted. Catherine looked at him, startled. "It'll give the gun's AI a route into your systems, and you don't want that, trust me."

She glanced at Leyton, who nodded. "All right, scratch that. Give me an open channel to the lobby area instead."

Interesting, Catherine trusted Leyton ahead of Benson, even though she barely knew either of them. Pavel had clearly failed to make the progress he would have hoped to.

"This is Catherine Chzyski, CEO of Kaufman Industries, addressing ULAW forces. I insist that you cease this unlawful action and explain yourselves." Her words brought no visible response. "I suggest we stay calm here before anyone is hurt. If you are willing to wait in the lobby, I'll be happy to come down and discuss matters with your commanding officer."

She might as well not have bothered speaking. The soldiers kept advancing without any attempt to reply.

"Well, I tried," Catherine muttered. She remained calm and focused, issuing instructions as if born to it. "Initiate security protocol beta. All security personnel deploy to the stairways. The lifts are inoperative. Give me general office broadcast.

"All staff please remain in your offices or at your workstations. Do not venture out into the corridors under any circumstances. You'll be notified when it's safe to do so again. Thank you."

"Now that you've done that, it might be wise to turn all your systems off and lock them down," Benson advised.

She stared at him as if he were mad. "And why would I want to do that when we're under armed attack?"

"For the same reason you chose not to open a channel to the eyegee," Benson replied. "They'll subvert your own systems and use them against you."

"Not these systems they won't."

Mya glanced at Catherine, realising she meant it. She really was that confident of KI's security. There was a greyness to Catherine Chzyski, but it wasn't the grey of anything faded, rather the sheen of toughened steel. Mya had made a point of studying the woman's official profile *en route* and so was aware of Catherine's formidable reputation as a hard-assed businesswoman, but only now was she gaining an insight into where that reputation stemmed from. Mya couldn't help but admire her.

"More personnel to the south... Damn!" Catherine looked furious. "They've blocked communication. I can't get through to our security or anyone else."

Perhaps KI's systems weren't so formidable after all.

Leyton was studying the images of ULAW troopers spreading like a black stain through the building's lowest levels. "Can you bring up the building's schematics?"

Catherine did so, to hover in the air beside the soldiers.

"How robust are the defences between here and the ground floor?"

"Very," Catherine assured him. "Enough to slow them down considerably at least."

"Good." Two red beacons had started to flash on the schematics, clearly alarms. "Because it looks as if we've got more immediate problems. Two more incursions, both on this level."

He looked to Mya, who nodded once. Neither of them actually *said*, 'just like old times.' "I'll take the nearer one," she said.

Leyton smiled. "Okay, then I'll take the other."

The pair of them were moving immediately, each picking up one of the habitat's security detail on the way out. The two KI guards stayed on station, protecting their CEO. That didn't come as a surprise; Kethi tagging along with her did. If anything, Mya would have expected her to go with Leyton. Anyone would think that Jim's new lover didn't trust her. Not that she cared either way.

CHAPTER TWENTY-TWO

PHILIP WAS GLAD of the chance to talk to his father away from the others. "So," he said, "what do you think?"

"A politician," Malcolm replied. "I've known many like Benson in my time and never trusted any of them. I'm not about to start now."

Philip could only agree. There was something almost *too* sincere about the man. Rather like this place, the bar that Malcolm had elected to bring him to whilst the corporeals filled their faces. Couples sat and nattered at tables, sipping drinks from tall glasses. Soft lighting, art deco styling and retro ambience for the soundtrack; the whole place felt upbeat and relaxed, nothing unusual about it at all. Which was weird in itself, bearing in mind most of the venues in Virtuality that Malcolm had taken him to.

"So, what exactly is this place?" he asked.

"Just a bar," Malcolm assured him with studied nonchalance. "A singles bar, if you like, where people come to hook up if they're looking to experiment with virtual sex, most of whom probably aren't all that single, at least not out there."

Philip stared at his father. "You've brought me to a *pick-up* joint?"

The older Kaufman grinned. "What else are fathers for?"

"Hi, guys," a familiar voice said, right on cue.

Philip had wondered how long it would to take Tanya to track them down. He somehow suspected Catherine would have alerted her the moment they quit the conference room.

"Fancy meeting you two in a place like this," she said, dropping into a seat beside Philip.

"We were just waiting for you," Malcolm assured her.

"Of course you were." She grinned.

Philip was actually pleased to see Tanya, particularly after the intensity of the morning's meeting, but he wasn't about to admit as much.

"So, what does a girl have to do to get a drink around..."

Tanya vanished. Not just her, everyone at the tables around them simply blinked out of existence.

"What the hell?" Philip looked at his father.

"I'm not sure, but it can't be anything good."

"...here?" Tanya was back. They were *all* back. Everyone in the room had reappeared as if they'd never been away, resuming conversations and flirting, laughing, seeming completely unaware of the interruption.

"Guys, why are you looking at me like that?" Tanya asked. "Was it something I said?"

"Not exactly," Philip replied. "You disappeared. You and every other avatar here; vanished for a split second and then reappeared, resuming exactly where you left off."

Tanya looked aghast. "Shit!"

"A virus?" Malcolm asked.

"Yeah, probably. Almost certainly."

"Attacking the library files supporting the avatars," Philip said, catching on. Virtuality was a huge undertaking. There was room for very little redundancy in the systems and logical shortcuts were inevitably employed. Templates were used for just about every aspect. Individual avatars were unique, for example, but at the root of each was the same basic human design, however outlandish the embellishments. All of them stemmed from a very limited number of files, there to provide the bulk standard basics which could then be varied and built upon according to individual taste. Interfere with the library files and you'd affect every avatar within a given vicinity, possibly within the whole of Virtuality, depending on the scope of the interference.

The same held true of buildings, trees, wine glasses. It made no sense to invent the wheel a million times over. Once you had a wholly effective design which worked at all levels of authenticity, practicality, function, lock it in and use it as the template for every other generically similar feature.

The logic of the process was impeccable. The only time you could really question it was on occasions such as this, when the system came under attack. The lack of redundancy made the whole thing potentially vulnerable. When your very existence depended on this world, that was a sobering thought.

"That shouldn't happen again," Tanya said. "I've just written myself into the hard drive."

Really? There was more to this girl than met the eye.

The tables went next. Around the room there was consternation and angry shouts as drinks went crashing to the ground and couples who had been leaning on tables gazing lovingly into each other's eyes suddenly found themselves falling off their chairs. As before, the tables reappeared a split second later, in several cases materialising with legs and other parts emerging from startled people's bodies. It was a surreal sight which lasted only a split second before the affected avatars died and were kicked out of Virtuality.

"One thing," Malcolm said, his voice quiet amidst the confusion. "When all the avatars disappeared just now, I noticed that the guy in the blue shirt at the bar didn't."

Both Philip and Tanya turned to look, to see the man in question staring at them and smiling.

THEY RAN DOWN a deserted corridor, to take position at the next junction. The guard dropped down on to his belly, manoeuvring so that just his head and gun poked around the corner. He carried an efficient looking short-barrelled automatic. Mya didn't recognise the model, and guessed it was of habitat design. Kethi stood above him, half crouching, her own weapon levelled. Mya stood in the doorway of an empty office opposite, slightly more exposed, holding her gun right-handed and standing with her back to the office. She could only really target half of the corridor. That was fine. It was the other two's job to deal with the other half.

They didn't have to wait long. Half a dozen figures in full combat gear appeared at the corridor's far end. As with those currently storming the lobby they weren't wearing shimmer suits, the cowing effect of such a blatant military presence presumably considered of greater tactical advantage than the camouflage provided by shimmers. Nor did they execute their advance in accepted operational fashion – individuals checking each office, gun-muzzle first, while covered by their colleagues. They simply strode forward, ignoring the closed doors of offices on either side.

Mya could immediately see why. Leading them was an eyegee. She couldn't tell who it was at this distance, but knew that his gun would be whispering in his ear, telling him that all was clear. Surely the gun had to pick up on their presence any second now?

Kethi must have reached the same conclusion, because at that instant she fired. The man below her followed her lead and sent a stream of bullets down the corridor. Mya watched as the eyegee staggered, clearly taking a hit, but the body armour must have done its job, because he didn't go down. One of the troopers behind him wasn't so fortunate. His dark form crumpled in the centre of the corridor as his colleagues took cover in neighbouring offices. His unmoving form looked like some heaped mound of black rags, abandoned by the cleaning staff. Mya took careful aim and squeezed off a volley of shots, belatedly joining the firefight.

Return fire chewed up the frame of the doorway she was stationed in, forcing her to pull back, while the wall opposite was peppered with slugs. A cry from the far end of the corridor and another trooper went down.

Mya bided her time but she couldn't afford to do so for long. In the corner of her eye she watched Kethi and the guard. They were both fully engrossed in their efforts to stay alive, to kill the enemy before they were shot themselves. Good; this seemed as good a moment as any. Mya leant out to squeeze off a further round in the direction of the ULAW troops before swinging her arm around. With clinical precision she shot Kethi and then lowered her aim, shooting the habitat guard before he could react. Whereas Kethi dropped like a stone, the man was still moving, trying to bring his gun around. She shot him again, this time in the head, and the movement stopped.

She then crouched and pushed her own weapon out into the centre of the corridor before calling out, "Hostiles are down, repeat, the hostiles are down. It's Mya, and I'm unarmed."

Seconds later the three surviving troopers reached her along with the eyegee, whom she recognised as Tobias – a canny operative with a good reputation.

Tobias glanced at Kethi and the habitat guard. "Good work, they're both dead," he confirmed, relaying the conclusions of his gun's AI.

Mya nodded as she retrieved her own weapon. She glanced down at Kethi's body one final time but felt no regrets. Yes, Kethi had been responsible for rescuing her from Sheol, but not out of any sense of altruism. She had done so purely because it served her own agenda. The fact that her actions benefited Mya was merely happy coincidence. Mya had now removed Kethi for the exact same reason: it suited her to do so. Nothing personal. Expediency was king and gratitude didn't merit a look in.

As Mya led the way back to the conference room, an office door opened. She didn't hesitate but raised her gun and fired, without stopping to consider that had there been any sort of a threat the eyegee would have reacted before she did. She caught a quick glimpse of a young woman collapsing, a blossom of red staining her chest, and then she was past. There was no reason for this girl to die. She should have stayed where she was instead of putting herself at risk. Collateral damage.

Something Mya knew all too much about.

At first she hadn't believed it, hadn't *wanted* to believe it, but then she'd hacked ULAW's security systems and tracked down the recording of the mission. It had been taken via an eyegee's visor and stored by the gun's AI, as all missions were – an infallibly objective means by which to assess performance and effectiveness. Even afterwards she wondered whether the recording had been doctored, whether she was meant to find it, but that seemed ridiculously paranoid. This wasn't something that had been left lying around for her to stumble across, it had been filed and sealed under heavy encryption and a hell of an effort to get to. No, this was the real thing, she was sure of it; a recording of Jim's most recent mission. A triumphant success, of course. Except that at one point Jim had been forced to mow down two ULAW troopers in order to kill the man beyond them, who would otherwise have blown the mission wide open and killed them all. Collateral damage: necessary, unavoidable.

How was he to know that one of those troopers had been Louis, Mya's brother, the lynchpin of her existence?

Until she saw that recording she'd no idea that Jim was responsible or even involved, only that Louis was dead.

It wasn't Jim's fault; she knew that, logically. She'd have done the same thing in his place. Yet how could she possibly continue to love the man who had killed her only brother? She tried. Despite her hurt, her anger, the accusations she was desperate to scream at him, she tried. Never saying anything because her mind told her it wasn't his fault and because such a tirade would mean having to explain how she knew about the incident and likely lead to her losing her job. So she bottled everything up; the hurt, the pain, the fury. Instead she ended up yelling at him over other things, trivial things that didn't really matter but which gave her an excuse; until in the end she froze at his touch and couldn't bear the thought of being near him.

When it all became too much she left, without ever telling him why.

Tobias and the troopers hung back out of sight, leaving Mya to stride up to the conference room doors alone. The two guards must have heard the shooting; they were alert, with weapons drawn, but they relaxed subtly on seeing her and the muzzles of their guns didn't track her as she drew nearer. After all, they'd no reason not to trust her.

"Everything all right here?" she asked.

"Yeah," the one nearest her confirmed.

"Good," she said as she shot them both.

The conference room doors were locked. Tobias's gun, set to energy, had them open in no time. Within, they found Benson standing over the other occupants – Catherine Chzyski, Nyles and the engineer Kyle, all of whom were seated in a row, their hands placed on the table-top palms down. Pavel held a gun trained on the three of them.

"What took you so long?" her lover asked.

THE ODDS DIDN'T bother Leyton. Numbers were only relevant up to a point. His real concern was the fact that one of them was an eyegee. True, he had his gun back, but that was only half the story. Coming towards him now was the real deal.

He had one chance, and several lives including his own depended on his ability to take it. He needed to nail his former colleague before the gun's AI cottoned on to how well equipped he was. As soon as they realised he had an eyegee's gun, no matter that it lacked the usual guiding intelligence, all hell would break loose.

Leyton thumbed the dial round to energy and took aim. Before he could pull the trigger, a wave of heat washed over him, the section of wall just above his head catching fire and melting, while the habitat trooper beside him cried out in brief agony and collapsed, his uniform and skin burnt away to reveal a grotesque display of seared organs and blackened ribs. *The eyegee had used energy.* Either they'd sussed him out far sooner than he'd hoped, or this man wasn't taking any chances.

Something flashed through the air towards him. *Grenade!* Leyton flung himself to one side, reflecting on the fact that they must have upgraded the guns again. His grenades had nothing like this range. It was also a timely reminder that only the best of the best were selected for the eyegee unit. This guy had beaten him to the punch.

The shell exploded, buffeting him in mid-leap, slamming his body into the far wall. Shrapnel sliced a line of agony up one leg and he lost his grip on the gun. His head crashed against something – floor or wall, he couldn't be certain. Consciousness started to fade, but he clung to it doggedly. For a few dazed seconds he lay there, trying to focus. The gun rested on the floor just beyond his outstretched left hand. He sensed rather than saw people approaching.

What would the eyegee's visor be showing him as at the moment? An amber dot? Not red, technically he wasn't armed so didn't represent an immediate threat. Amber seemed most likely; but the moment he touched the gun it would flare up to red and the eyegee would react. He had to make this quick and decisive, or he was a dead man.

One more deep breath, allowing the enemy to come one more step closer; then he moved, snatching up the gun left-handed and firing. Body armour, clothing and flesh withered away as the deadly energies ripped into the eyegee at the front of the group. Even before the man had fully collapsed Leyton played the beam over the three soldiers behind him, taking all of them out before they could get a shot away. Only then did Leyton ease up, forcing his reluctant finger to lift from the trigger. Only then did he move, dragging his aching body into a sitting position.

He checked his weapon and cursed. The power was pretty much drained; he'd fired for too long. Projectile should still work and presumably the grenades – both of which were mechanical functions – but sonic and energy were denied him until he could recharge. He flicked the dial to projectile and fired an aimless round down the corridor, just to be certain. It worked. At least that was something.

Blood seeped from the gash in his leg but it was only a flesh wound. It would sting rather than disable. His ears were ringing from the force of the explosion, but that would fade with time, he hoped.

Having hauled himself to his feet, Leyton headed back to the conference room, conscious of how quiet everything was beyond the buzzing inside his own head. You'd never know there was a small war being fought in the building. The silence started to bother him. By now he ought to have heard the sounds from any other gun battle, at least on this floor, which meant Kethi and Mya's little skirmish must have ended; favourably, he hoped.

Evidently not. The two KI security men were lying dead. A pair of ULAW troopers now crouched in the open double doorway of the conference room, weapons raised, each covering an approach to the room. Pure luck that neither of them had been looking directly at him when he peeked around the corner. There was no point in hesitating, no telling who or what was inside that room. He stood flush against the wall, holding the gun two handed before him, pointed towards the ceiling. In his mind he held the image of the two soldiers, fixing their positions. Then he spun round, swivelling on his left foot, bringing his body round the corner and his arms level, firing twice in quick succession.

He was running before the two bodies hit the ground, leaping through the doorway, gun at the ready... to find himself staring down the muzzle of Mya's gun. Benson stood to one side, covering Kyle and the others. A further ULAW trooper stepped forward from behind the door, automatic weapon levelled. There was no sign of Kethi.

"Hello, Jim," said Benson. "We've been expecting you."

MALCOLM CONSIDERED IT to be something of an anti-climax when all the avatars vanished again. Except for Tanya and the grinning man at the bar, of course.

Tanya tutted. "Repeating himself already? I'd have expected a bit more."

"Why is he here at all?" Malcolm asked. "I mean, if this is a virus, why a visible manifestation in Virtuality?

"To taunt us, to show us how clever they are," Philip suggested.

"Yeah," Tanya agreed. "My guess is that they're showing us how they got the virus into the system."

"A Trojan horse," Philip muttered.

"Clever bastards. They sneaked it in wrapped inside an avatar, like sugar-coating a pill." Tanya said.

Malcolm suspected she hadn't understood his son's ancient historical reference. They were all three on their feet by now. Tanya stepped forward, to interpose herself between Philip and the stranger, as though anything in this pseudo-physical world was likely to help if a virus was busy wreaking havoc on the files that sustained them. Not that the stranger had made any overtly threatening move. Not yet, at any rate; just that smile.

Malcolm didn't doubt for a second that they were in trouble, though. He let part of his consciousness slip away, spreading out through the vast computer network of Home in search of a countermeasure while keeping the main focus here. Doing this took practice, skills Philip hadn't yet learned.

Should he urge Philip to dissolve his focus and flee to the furthest corners of every system on Home? No, that wasn't an answer. They were clearly up against a sophisticated weapon. If it found its way into the files supporting Philip, hiding would be redundant.

The man stood up. Tall, tanned, golden-haired – an angel without wings. He took a step towards them and, as he did so, the world altered. The walls and ceiling around them slowly faded away. The tables, the chairs, their drinks, all the accoutrements of a bar remained, but the building that should have contained them was gone. Not just this building either; they stood on a vast, flat, featureless plain with not a single significant structure in sight.

"Has it taken out the whole of Virtuality?" Philip said.

"A good chunk of it," Malcolm replied.

"That's some virus."

"Yeah, a nasty one," Tanya agreed. "This is already getting messy and loud and it'll have every geek and hacker involved in Virtuality out for the blood of whoever sent it, but I suppose if you've got enough clout that's not a problem. You must have pissed somebody off royally, lover of mine."

Philip gave her a sour smile, doubtless wishing that he *had* been her lover.

The grinning man took another step forward and everything else that hadn't already vanished did – the furniture, the drinks, the ornamental hat stand that had stood sentry by the door, gone like the buildings – leaving just the four of them.

"I would suggest we run," Tanya murmured, "But somehow I don't think there'd be much point."

"Besides," Philip added, "I get the feeling that's exactly what Smiley here wants us to do."

Their nemesis had paused after those first two steps, as if inviting them to react. Now that they hadn't, he stepped forward again.

"Screw this!" Tanya said at the first sign of renewed movement, and she whipped out a gun. Before she could fire, however, what remained of the world came apart at the seams. Literally. The ground beneath their feet started to shake and convulse, cracking and separating as if a violent earthquake had hit this corner of Virtuality. Malcolm struggled to stay on his feet as a vast fissure opened, with him on one side and Philip and Tanya on the other. It didn't end there. More convulsions sent him sprawling to his hands and knees and continued to eat away at the patch of ground around him. He found himself kneeling on a small irregular rectangle of concrete, surrounded by an abyss on all sides. Philip and Tanya were on another: Tanya still on her feet and Philip in the process of regaining his. Around them stretched a whole vista of cracks and broken ground.

"Don't give up, either of you," Tanya urged. "The AIs will be onto this by now, hunting the bastard down, working relentlessly to identify the unique coding sequence that constitutes the virus. It doesn't matter how clever this thing is, how many variants it transforms into or where versions of it have been hidden, once they identify that coding they'll find all the caches and erase every scrap of it."

All well and good, if the AIs were to be trusted, but Malcolm wasn't so sure about that. What if the AIs chose to turn a blind eye? Ultimately, those vast inscrutable brains were connected to ULAW, and who was to say that this virus wasn't as well? Nor did he buy the idea that what they were being subjected to here in Virtuality was mere window dressing, an act of bravado. It seemed a hell of a lot of trouble to go to merely to twist the knife. After all, if the virus succeeded they would all soon be dead.

Then he had it – the reason for this. Those responsible weren't doing it for *their* benefit at all but for his, at least primarily. A warning, to emphasise that if they wanted to they could come into Virtuality and finish him off whenever they chose, just as they were about to put an end to his son. Philip was the target here. As his father, Malcolm was little more than an incidental bystander, but one that those responsible for the virus were keen to impress.

Ahead of them, the ground seemed to gather, fractured segments of concrete pulling together and rising in a tall wave, a ground-borne parody of a tsunami. Riding the crest of this wave was the avatar, the virus' vector. It had adopted a splay-legged stance, like a surfer, and rode the rippling swell of concrete towards the island on which Philip and Tanya waited.

Tanya still had her gun in hand, and presumably the avatar simply made too tempting a target. She fired. The vector didn't simply disappear as any normal avatar might have done. Instead, it melted, face first. Its eyes slipped downward, the mouth drooped into the sullenest of frowns, the right eye dropping beneath the corner of its lips while the nose slipped sideways. Its clothing too began to lose definition. Like thickly applied paint sliding off a non-absorbent surface, all the colours ran together. Then the body started to open, from the crown of the head downward, splits appeared in the image, and the skin peeled open in three segments, as if this were a seed pod about to release its spore.

The analogy struck Malcolm as particularly apt once the black mist started to rise from the vector's shattered torso; a mass of roiling darkness that rose in a billowing cloud and immediately started to spread.

"Oh, come on," Tanya said. "Black is evil. We get it. At least be original"

They weren't trying to be original. If Malcolm's theory was right and all this was primarily to make a point, overt symbology was hardly a surprise.

"Nice shooting," Philip observed, "but I'm not exactly convinced it's worked in our favour."

"Thanks for the constructive criticism. All I'm trying to do is hold this thing at bay long enough for the AIs to do their stuff."

PART OF MALCOLM *was elsewhere, trying to attract the attention of human, AI or whoever was monitoring Virtuality. He might not entirely trust them, but a drowning man clutches at anything. Mind you, it seemed unlikely that anyone paying attention could possibly not be aware of such massive disruption. Malcolm was also searching for some form of countermeasure they could employ in their own defence.*

TANYA STILL HELD her gun and now fired into the seething mass of black. Perhaps this had some effect. Perhaps it destroyed some small segment of darkness. It was difficult to tell with there being so much of the stuff.

"Shit!" Tanya exclaimed. "How do I fight shadows?"

There was a defence against this, there was always a defence.

MALCOLM HAD TO find some way of stopping this. He scoured every circuit and memory storage he could access, determined to copy, clone and grab any defensive mechanism he found and drag it back to their besieged refuge. Yet almost all those he encountered were passive defences – barriers, buffers, firewalls – programmes designed to repel intrusion, and he Philip and Tanya were way beyond that. The virus was already inside. What he really needed were aggressors, hounds and hunters, programs that would relentlessly seek and destroy; but they proved to be more sophisticated, less easily reached and hacked. He found only one, a generic countermeasure, which he brought back with him, knowing even as he did so that it would never be enough.

TANYA FIRED AGAIN, with similarly ambiguous results. The black smoke had them surrounded and proceeded to close in. It did so slowly, as if to prolong their suffering. Malcolm couldn't help but wonder whether this was co-ordinated with the virus's attack on the files storing their actual essence. Did the proximity of the smoke signal the imminent destruction of those precious files?

Tendrils of darkness suddenly reached forward, wrapping

around Tanya. She waved her arms, as if attempting to beat it away, and kicked her legs, but to no avail.

"Hell!" was all she said as the blackness rolled over her. The single useful program Malcolm had found manifested as a compact, transparent gun. It looked to be made of plastic. A child's toy, a water pistol to combat a forest fire.

Philip had joined in, cursing and trying to pull Tanya out of the gathering black cloud, but there was nowhere to go. As yet, the smoke had ignored Malcolm. He didn't know whether to feel relieved or guilty. It seemed to validate the theory that he wasn't in any real danger this time around.

As the blackness reached her neck and left only her face visible, Tanya's legs stopped kicking and her arms ceased their frantic jerking. She gave up, or perhaps her limbs no longer responded, Malcolm couldn't be sure.

She looked at Philip, her face a caricature of anguish. "I'm sorry," she said.

Philip bent down to kiss her lips.

"Philip!" Malcolm warned

Philip looked across at him as his face lifted from Tanya's. "What does it matter, Dad? What does anything matter anymore?"

The 'Dad' mattered. That sort of thing always mattered. Tanya's blonde hair began to darken as the black coating closed about her head and finally her face. It seemed to have gained substance, losing much of its ethereal nature. Something about the way it flowed reminded Malcolm of mercury: negative mercury, black instead of silver. For an instant Tanya stood there, a glistening ebony version of the person they'd come to know, and then she disappeared, imploding as her avatar died, the blackness losing concentration and reverting to thick, oily smoke.

Malcolm raised his pistol, the only frail defence they had, but as he was about to shoot, he realised that he cared far less about his own survival than his son's. "Here." He called. "You have this," and he tossed the gun across to Philip.

He watched as Philip caught the gun, turned it towards the floor in front of him and squeezed the trigger.

"You don't seriously think this is going to work, do you?"

"No," Malcolm admitted, "but I've been wrong before."

Philip raised the gun and squeezed. A jet of liquid squirted out, bubbling and steaming like acid where it struck the smoke. It didn't matter. They were surrounded by far too much of the stuff for the token attempt at retaliation to make any difference.

Philip looked frustrated, furious, and anguished. He stared at his father, imploring. "I've died once, isn't that enough for anyone? What more do they want from me?"

"Dissipate!" Malcolm urged, "flee to the farthest corners of Virtuality."

Philip shook his head. "No, the virus has found me. I can feel it breaking down my structure, attacking the files that define me. Dissipating won't help."

Malcolm heard the words but had no further answers, could offer no comfort. The last thing he wanted to do was witness his son die again. He couldn't face that. Almost he stepped forward, to throw himself from his rocky plinth and into the chasm that surrounded him. He had no idea how terminal such a step would be but couldn't quite bring himself do it in any case. At the end of the day, he wanted to live, even in the face of his son's demise. The fact shamed him, but it was true.

He turned away, refusing to look at Philip, refusing to look at anything.

Behind him, he could hear Philip cursing as if from a great distance, a dwindling voice that he shut out, not bearing to listen. "Hope you choke on me, you black scum, hope I corrupt you beyond..." And then it stopped.

The silence that followed lasted an eternity. Once time resumed its sluggish course, Malcolm turned his perceptions outward again, opened his eyes... and found himself standing in that same corner of Virtuality, alone. Around him, the ground remained shattered, like some vast limestone plain in which the passage of time and water had combined to produce a fractured pavement. Philip, the back smoke, even the melted avatar that had concealed it, were gone.

The virus had done its job, killed its target and then either withdrawn or disassembled. Malcolm had been spared – not a target, not a threat, a mere irrelevance. Not worth killing. Unlike his son.

Malcolm wanted to cry, wanted to rail against cruel fate that had done this to him again, but wasn't certain his transhuman emotions were capable of such depth. He searched inside himself for the despair he knew had to be there, but found only emptiness.

AFTER A WHILE the world began to heal. No cataclysmic shaking or rumblings; the vast cracks in the ground simply disappeared, to leave unblemished concrete. The landscape started to fill up again immediately, as Virtuality set about repairing itself. The process didn't take long. Malcolm watched entire buildings materialise out of thin air, as sections of the program rebooted, returning to an earlier, undamaged state. The world soon began to look whole again, ready to move on as if recent events had never happened and no one at all had died here today.

At any other time Malcolm would have been fascinated to watch this happening in front of him, but not today. It seemed as if Virtuality and the minds behind it were trying to deny that Philip had ever existed.

Procrastination had never been something Malcolm advocated. He knew what he had to do. He'd been putting this off, afraid of what he might find, but no longer. Quick as thought, he sped through Virtuality, sped through the network of systems supporting this ethereal world. He wasn't circumspect, no longer caring whether he left a back trail or not – far too late to worry about bolting that particular stable door. Now that he'd committed to looking, he had to *know*.

Cath was waiting for him, in the small sparse pocket of existence where he had taken Philip to be copied, where their clones were stored.

He stared at her, wanting to hope.

"I'm sorry, Malcolm," she said.

Not that he needed the words. He knew the answer as soon as he saw her face. He'd failed. For all his cunning and all his effort, the virus had found its way here too.

Philip was dead.

LARA CAME TO with the memory of blackness still clinging to her skin – burning, suffocating – though the sensation vanished almost immediately. The knowledge that she'd failed didn't, though. *Shit!* Despite all her best efforts, Philip Kaufman was dead. She might not have actually seen him die, but the situation she'd left could only end one way.

She'd always had a bit of a crush on Philip, ever since she first joined the project and started working with him. She never said a word, of course, would never have done anything about it, especially not after she met Jenner and, besides, Philip hardly noticed her.

In Virtuality, though, it was different. There she could be everything she'd ever dreamed of being but wouldn't dare to be out here. She was going to miss Tanya; so confident, so brazen, so *sensual*. Dancing at Bubbles had been one of the most exhilarating moments of her life. She knew as soon as they hit the dance floor that Tanya had Philip Kaufman totally in her thrall, this man who barely even knew Lara Chinen existed. The sense of achievement, of power, had been intoxicating. Despite the frustrating way fate had cut that encounter short, she'd found the experience liberating, and afterwards had complete confidence in the Tanya persona, with no qualms about throwing herself into the role. Catherine subsequently assigning her to work beside Philip and Malcolm here in reality was a wonderful twist, while being entirely logical. She was the best at what she did and this ensured the cabal remained as tight as possible.

None of which had prevented their ultimate failure. She didn't doubt that Philip was dead, and presumably Malcolm as well. She'd left a delayed message for Malcolm, set to be delivered while she was still beside him as Tanya – an additional layer of subterfuge that had amused her at the time. Now it seemed that the message was destined to never be delivered at all.

Lara sat up, the flexiseat responding to her movements by raising its back, converting from a couch into a chair.

She gazed out the window, still not quite able to believe that this really was *her* window. Ever since Catherine had plucked her from the obscurity of Susan Tan's team and fast-tracked her promotion, things had been happening so quickly she was still trying to get her head around it. Not that she was complaining, and she would never *ever* tire of the view from this window.

Enough navel gazing. Time to make a call she really wasn't looking forward to.

She spoke into the air. "Priority call to Catherine Chzyski."

Nothing happened.

She repeated the instruction and then tried to call up a screen; both requests met with the same lack of response.

Something was clearly up, but she had to let Catherine know about Philip and Malcolm, even if that meant delivering the tidings in person.

Her mouth was dry after the protracted period in Virtuality. She stopped to grab a bulb of ice-chill from her deliciously retro dispenser, sipping at the pure cold water as she rehearsed what she was going to say to Catherine. The direct approach seemed best. Deliver the news and then explain the circumstances. Satisfied, she dropped the empty bulb into the machine's recycling chute and headed for the door. The biscuit of the office carpet was annoying her; it was too bland, too neutral. She reset it to crimson on the way out, which was far more in keeping with her mood.

Lara was so preoccupied that at first she didn't notice anything amiss. Only when the unmistakable sound of gunfire penetrated her thoughts did she register the unusual stillness around her. Okay, the exec level was never a bustling thoroughfare, but right now there was nobody else in sight at all. Until, that is, she had nearly reached the end of the corridor, at which point a figure in full matt battledress stepped out immediately in front of her, gun levelled at her chest.

To her own considerable surprise, she didn't hesitate. In Virtuality, Tanya would have multiple countermeasures to call upon, but all Lara had was her training and her skill. Jahainô was a fighting style which had been practiced for centuries. Its roots lay in an amalgamation of various disciplines that had been prominent on old Earth. Lara knew herself to be pretty damned good at Jahainô, but she'd never used it in anger before, at least not in the real world.

So this was new territory. The rules were much the same though. She swivelled and kicked, evidently surprising the soldier as much as herself. The sole and heel of her boot slammed into his gun, jerking it from his hands without the trigger finger even twitching to fire off a round. He was bigger than her and armoured, so she followed with an upward blow to the soft tissue under his arm and a kick to the knee. The latter was a little off target as he rolled, landing on his thigh just above the knee, but it was enough to cause him to cry out and to send him crashing to the floor.

She was off, sprinting for the stairs that led to the floors above. In the corner of her eye she registered the arrival of more soldiers coming up the stairwell, and she strove all the harder. Nearly there. Two more steps and she would be on the stairs, with a wall between her and the guns.

A voice yelled out, "Halt!" It was immediately followed by the crack of a gunshot and something punched her in her right shoulder. The impact sent her sprawling, crashing into the wall. Agony coursed through her body.

She pulled herself up with her left hand and looked back to where the soldier stood. She found herself staring down the muzzle of his gun. Behind the soldier holding it, others moved, tending to the one she'd felled, but they were no more than dim shadows. The soldier's finger seemed to move in slow motion as it squeezed the trigger, giving Lara time for regret, time to mourn the future which was about to be cruelly snatched away. Her final thoughts before the bullet punched a hole through her skull and tore her life away were of Jenner, the man she loved; the man she would never be able to say that to again.

CHAPTER TWENTY-THREE

"No." LEYTON WAS adamant, his face fierce, the anger and hurt for once plain to see in his usually granite countenance.

Mya wasn't fooled, though. She knew that he was in denial, refusing to face up to the truth she'd just hit him with. She had no idea why it had all come tumbling out, why she suddenly found it so easy to tell him about Louis and what she'd discovered about his death, when it had been impossible to do so before. Perhaps her relationship with Pavel gave her the strength, or maybe it was simply the passage of time. Either way, when he'd stared at her and at the gun she held and asked, 'Why, Mya?' she felt compelled to explain. Once the words started to flow they became a torrent, and with their release something inside her eased, a knot of tension she hadn't even realised was there. She made no effort to hide the tears that trickled from the corners of her eyes.

"There's no reason you should have known." She snivelled, wiping her nose on the back of her hand, decorum forgotten.

"Of course I'd have known," he said. "If I ever killed one of ours, I *always* made a point of knowing. I don't take what we do for granted, Mya, I never have, and I know for a fact that I didn't kill Louis."

"You did, Jim. You did."

"Mya, it never happened."

"Liar!" She screamed the word, shocked at her own loss of control. She steadied the gun and determined to keep a tighter rein on her emotions.

"You know me better than that. This recording you saw must have been doctored. To make you hate me, to break us apart. You *know* the official line on operatives getting involved with each other."

"Don't listen to him, Mya," Benson cut in. "He's just saying whatever it takes to save his own skin. Focus on what's real, on what matters."

"Of course the recording was hard to get to," Leyton continued, speaking calmly, ignoring Benson. "They knew you'd smell a rat if they made it too easy for you, but they also knew that you'd find a way, that where Louis was concerned you'd never give up until you discovered what had happened. Your psych profile would have told them that much."

"Shut up!" she yelled, hand pressed against her head, to push her tight dark hair backwards along her skull. It was all too much; everything was a jumble of hurt and pressure. Her head ached with it.

He took a step towards her.

"Don't, Jim." She raised the gun a fraction.

"It was a set up," he said, not coming any closer, "intended to break us apart."

Could he be telling the truth? Pavel hadn't said anything more, wisely giving her space, doubtless confident she'd believe him, but did she? Mya knew better than anyone just how cunning and manipulative Pavel could be. He hadn't been put in charge of the eyegee unit by accident. Had he been playing her all along? No, what they had was real. It might not be as deep or as bells-and-fucking-whistles wonderful as what she once thought she had with Jim, but that was in the past. Pavel was her here and now, and they both knew where they stood and what they wanted.

"Don't let him confuse you, Mya," Pavel said.

He was right. They'd come here for a reason: to stop this interference in the smooth acceptance of the Byrzaens by humanity as a whole. An inevitability that would see Pavel rise to the very pinnacle of government, with her at his side. She couldn't let anything sway her, not now.

So why was she crying? Why did she feel so wretched as she focused the muzzle of the gun on Leyton's forehead? She tried not to look at his eyes, but couldn't help herself. There was no fear there, no pleading; just the same implacable acceptance of whatever life might bring that she'd always found in them.

"I'm so sorry, Jim, really" she said through the tears, and pulled the trigger.

KETHI RAMPED UP her metabolism, taking it from one extreme to the other far quicker than she'd ever dared try before. How much time had passed? For her, a single heartbeat, but for the universe in general...? She had no idea. That was the problem with slowing her metabolism to this extent – enough to fool anyone into believing she was dead – there was no gauge for measuring the normal flow of seconds and minutes, any of which were likely to be vital at present. She could only hope her judgement was more or less right, that she hadn't left it so long that whatever drama was set to unfold had already run its course in her absence.

She shut down blood flow around her wound and dampened the pain receptors in the vicinity. The bullet hadn't hit anything vital, and doing this, the pain became tolerable. Grabbing her gun from the floor, Kethi ran, quick-timing all the way. As she approached Catherine Chzyski's office, she slowed, rejoining the normal world. A single guard outside the open door sent her ducking back around a corner, and she heard voices. Mya's screaming, and Jim's quiet, reasoning, sounding completely unfazed. She wasn't too late. If not for the guard she would have sobbed with relief. Instead she concentrated on listening. There seemed to be a pause in conversation, which struck her as ominous. As Mya started to form an apology, instinct told Kethi it was now or never.

She ramped up to her highest tempo and sprinted, brushing past the guard; it must have felt like a battering ram. She was in the room, focused on Mya, not daring to risk a shot, not with such a small target. Instead she ran straight at the other woman, slamming into her and pushing the gun hand away. She felt the impact jar through her, but knew that the blow would be worse for her target. Her bones were bound to shatter. The gun went off but the bullet flew harmlessly into the wall. Kethi didn't hesitate, swivelling to shoot the next most immediate threat – the eyegee – followed by the two ULAW troopers. Headshots, all three, straight in the face. They would have died even as their brains were processing the need to react. Benson wasn't armoured. Kethi shot him in the shoulder. Only then did she slow, breathing hard but not yet craving food or feeling desperately weary, thanks to the adrenaline still coursing through her body. She knew both reactions would come after she'd drawn so much from her systems in such a concerted burst, but not right now.

Catherine Chzyski stared at her in open astonishment, which she reckoned was quite an achievement. Jim moved in on the injured Benson, dragging the man's arms behind his back, which brought a stifled cry of pain.

"Now," he growled, his mouth close to Benson's ear, "you're going to call off the rest of your men, or I will kill you, slowly, you piece of shit!" He prodded the injured shoulder, which produced a further gasp.

At Kethi's feet, Mya stirred. The small woman looked frail and crumpled, reminding Kethi of when she'd first seen her, the gaunt figure they'd rescued from Sheol station such a short time ago. The fingers of the hand that had been holding the gun were twisted at improbable angles, like in a child's drawing, and her crumpled chest rose and fell raggedly, as if breathing was hard and not bringing enough oxygen to fulfil her body's needs. Blood ran from her mouth. Kethi didn't need to be a doctor to know that this woman's body was badly broken inside.

"Jim..." The voice was barely louder than a whisper. It

induced a fit of harsh, blood-burbling coughs. Her head never rose from the floor. "I really, really am sorry…"

Leyton wasn't listening. Kethi alone was there to hear Mya's final words. Her chest stopped heaving, the eyes remained frozen open. Only the blood continued to flow, pooling around her head to form a devil's halo.

IN THE HOURS following the ULAW forces' withdrawal, as the shock of what had happened began to sink in, Malcolm visited Benson in his cell – a small room without windows, commandeered for the purpose and hastily cleared of the equipment it usually stored.

Malcolm arrived without fanfare or warning, but if he'd expected the government man to be nonplussed by his sudden appearance he was disappointed. Benson might almost have been expecting him, for all the reaction he showed.

"Well, well, the great Malcolm Kaufman," the prisoner said. "The inventor of the Kaufman drive, not to mention, of course, *The Sun Seeker*, here to visit me in my humble little cell. I'm honoured."

"Let's cut the bullshit, shall we, Benson?"

If there were any justice in the world this man would be dead, his memory disgraced, but the universe paid no heed. While the corpses of many more worthy men and women grew cold, Pavel Benson received expert medical treatment and lived on, albeit for the moment in somewhat reduced circumstances.

"Whatever you say. I am, as you can see, entirely at your service," he said.

Malcolm felt tempted to dispute that, to voice his conviction that Benson had never really been at anyone's service but his own, not even ULAW's. Instead he concentrated on what had brought him here. "First off, let me stress that this meeting is off the record. I've ensured that no recording is being made and that no one need ever be aware that I've visited you."

"Oh?"

Gods, this man was calm. No hint of contrition over his actions or fear for his own safety, just an air of resignation tinged with a heavy hint of cynicism. "After we've had this little chat, I'm going to persuade Catherine Chzyski to let you go."

Not even this news brought a discernable reaction. Benson was good, no question about that.

"Seems to me that she's going to have little choice in the matter, in any case," he said. "If she doesn't free me, ULAW will level this building and everyone in it."

"Nice try, but that's a load of crap and we both know it. If this was an official ULAW action they'd have slapped us down hard by now, made demands KI couldn't ignore, and reclaimed you. They haven't. In fact, we've yet to hear a peep from any official channels. This is you, acting in your own interest, which makes your position a lot weaker, don't you think?"

"Semantics. I'm a ULAW official who brought the forces at his disposal to bear..."

"Without official sanction," Malcolm interrupted. "I thought we'd agreed to cut the bullshit."

Benson's smile was a thin one. "Very well, let's assume for the moment that you're right, that the action in question doesn't have the full weight of the government behind it... *yet*. Why would Catherine Chzyski or anyone else feel inclined to let me go?"

"Because you represent the only chance of getting ULAW off our backs."

Benson chuckled. "Really, is that what you think I am?"

"Indeed I do. You see, you're going to persuade the government to leave everyone involved in this alone. No assassinations, no recriminations, no persecution of any sort."

For the first time Malcolm saw a glimmer of reaction in Benson's grey-blue eyes. He could imagine the thought processes. *Malcolm Kaufman isn't an idiot. He must have something up his virtual sleeve, but what?*

"And why would I want to do that?"

"Because if you don't, I'm going to personally bring your world crashing down around your ears. Not just you; ULAW, the Byrzaens... all of you."

Now he had him. Malcolm could see the curiosity. "And exactly how are you going to manage that?"

Malcolm smiled.

He had been astonished to receive the message. It arrived anonymously and he felt certain that any attempt to trace the source would prove devilishly hard, but there was no need to. He knew who this was from: Lara Chenin. News of her death had been one more blow in a day of so many. Then this had arrived, a message from beyond the grave. She must have sent it not long before the attack, setting delivery on some form of time delay for reasons of her own. The message was terse, containing just one word. Four fateful letters: 'Done.' Not much as final words went. However, attached was a parcel of data code. He didn't open it immediately, didn't interfere with the parcel in any shape or form, not until he was sure of his own security. He knew what this was, what it had to be.

Lara had perfected the virus.

Malcolm absorbed that fact slowly, allowing its import to permeate his consciousness by steady osmosis. Here was the trump card that might just get them all out of this mess, but it needed to be played carefully.

The moment to do so had now arrived.

"I've done a little research into you, Pavel Benson," he said, "and I discovered something very interesting: you have an eidetic memory. Not computer enhanced or reliant on technology in any way; genuine photographic recall. That's an incredibly rare gift, in this day and age, and I can only imagine how useful it's been to you over the years. Well, now it's going to prove useful to *me*."

A line of coding appeared in the air between them.

"Memorise this, Mr Benson, and, for everyone's sake, make sure you get it right."

"What is it?"

"I'll tell you once you've memorised it."

Benson scanned the coding sequence for a couple of seconds, as if to make sure he had it, then he nodded.

The line of code vanished.

"What I've just shown you is the first fragment of an incredibly intricate piece of code, a virus. It was written by a lady called Lara Chinen, a rather brilliant young woman whom you've just caused to be murdered – an incidental death during this little 'action' of yours. As for what the virus does... It's a doomsday weapon, if you will. It's designed to destroy a whole universe, a place we refer to as the realm of veils, though you doubtless have your own name for it.

"If this virus were ever released, it would completely disrupt the fabric of that brane, restructuring it in such a way that it would become incompatible with the physics of our universe, impossible to access or to utilise for you, for us, for the Byrzaens. Am I painting a clear enough picture?"

Benson nodded. All of a sudden the slimy weasel didn't look quite so composed.

"What you're going to do for me," Malcolm continued, "is this. You're going to return to ULAW and show both them and the Byrzaens that snatch of coding. It's only a small scrap of the whole, but it should be enough for your experts to confirm that I'm not bluffing, that this virus is real.

"Now let me tell you what I did before coming here. I cloned myself. Not once, not twice, but a score of times. Already those clones are in the realm of veils. Each of them is loaded with this virus, and they're just the start. I'm going to keep cloning myself. You gave me the idea for this, by the way. I suppose I should thank you for it. If you hadn't sent the assassin virus after my son sheathed within an avatar, I might never have thought of this. Forgive me if I'm not too grateful, though, won't you?

"As for my clones, pretty soon they'll find their way into every Virtuality on every human world that has access to the realm of veils, which, I'm guessing, is pretty much all of them. You can send in your agents and your assassins and your viruses, but you'll never get all of me, and should I catch a hint of anything like that going on, I'll release the doomsday virus immediately."

Benson was visibly shaken. "You're bluffing."

"No, I promise you I'm not. And it's very important that you appreciate how tempted I am to trigger the damn thing right now. *You killed my son!*"

Benson licked his lips and then said, slowly, "Have you any idea what this would do?"

"Some. It would crash the network of communications you've established secretly via Virtuality. It would negate the Byrzaens' stardrive…"

"It would do a hell of a lot more than that. Their whole technology is based on siphoning energy from that brane."

Benson was more shaken than Malcolm had anticipated. He must have been to let something like that slip.

"All the more reason for them to co-operate, then. Let me make myself clear. If anything happens to me, to Catherine Chzyski, to Jim Leyton or any of the habitat folk involved in recent events, the virus will be released. Never forget, you've murdered my son. *Twice.* Do you really think I give a damn about the fate of the Byrzaens or any of your precious schemes and intrigues? Push me on this at your peril. *Am I being clear enough*, Mr Benson?"

The other nodded. "Perfectly."

"Good." A question occurred to him, one which he was unlikely to ever find an answer to elsewhere. "Can I ask you something?"

"I'm not exactly in a position to refuse you."

"First contact. How did it *really* happen?"

Benson sighed. "No harm in telling you, I suppose. I wasn't there and officially this is still need-to-know only…"

"Unofficially?"

"Unofficially, and uncorroborated, it happened courtesy of a crystal."

"Excuse me?"

"I'm told it was an attempt to discover a new energy source. ULAW scientists directed AIs to build a particularly complex crystalline structure in Virtuality. Once completed, it proved to be identical in every detail to a crystal the Byrzaens had already built and were using to process energy from the other brane."

"Resonance!" Malcolm said.

"Something like that."

"Structures *that* identical are the same... the same object existing simultaneously in two different places. Quantum physics allows that this would open the door to communication between both locations, and maybe more. That's incredible."

"Isn't it just?"

"What I don't understand is why this constant draining of energy from another brane hasn't destabilised it. Presumably the brane is vast and the amount being taken infinitesimally small in the scheme of things but even so... And that begs another question: where does all the energy come from in the first place?"

Benson shrugged. "I'm no scientist, so not my field." Nor, evidently, his interest. "Now, when exactly did you say you were going to get me out of here?"

MALCOLM'S NEXT CALL was not one he was looking forward to, even though it was to his oldest friend. He knew she wasn't going to like the idea. He was right.

"Are you serious? That man is responsible for so many deaths, Malcolm," Catherine pointed out, "most likely Philip's included, and you just expect me to let him go?"

"What else were you planning on doing to him? He's a ULAW official. How do you think they'll react to his summary execution?"

"Who said anything about execution? You know better than to underestimate me, Malcolm. A renegade faction within the government mounts an illegal raid on Kaufman Industries head office, killing KI personnel in the process. Do you really think anyone at ULAW is going to kick up a fuss if some of those responsible, including the primary organiser, get killed during our perfectly legitimate attempts to defend ourselves? I'm about to lodge a strongly worded complaint about the whole incident. I'll be amazed if ULAW want to take on KI over this, no matter how many bodies turn up. In fact, I'm going to be pushing for financial compensation and a public apology."

Knowing her, she'd probably get them, too.

"Catherine," he said, "I would never underestimate you. It wasn't the corporation's welfare I was concerned about. Trust me, releasing Benson will ensure not only yours and my safety but that of everyone involved."

She snorted. "Which still sounds like you're underestimating me." Catherine pursed her already thin lips and glared at him. "You're asking a lot, Malcolm. I'm not going to enquire what sort of a deal you've struck with that arsehole. I can guess the leverage you employed. Just tell me this much: is it real?"

"Yes."

She took a deep breath. "God bless Lara. What a tragic loss."

Malcolm could only agree. He refrained from reminding her that the tragedy didn't end with Lara. There was no point. Catherine knew that only too well.

At length, she said, "There's not another soul in the universe, corporeal or virtual, I'd trust to this extent. You do know that, don't you?"

"Yes."

"On the other hand, what's the point in employing a genius if you don't listen to their advice? Very well, I'll do as you ask. Benson can go free – after he suffers a few choice words from me – and I'll even smooth out the matter of his release with Leyton and the habitat folk."

"Thank you."

"You'd better be right about this."

"I am," he replied, and hoped his conviction was justified.

"One more thing. Your concern for my welfare is all very touching, but I've lived a long life in an environment that's as cutthroat as they come. I'm a tough old bird, Malcolm, not that easy to get rid of. Don't you forget it."

He smiled. "How could I ever do that?"

THINGS HAD CHANGED. *The Rebellion* had long gone, having disappeared back to the habitat's final refuge, an outpost known as Far Flung. Leyton had no idea where this was, nor did he wish to know. He and Kethi had new identities and were part of a network of habitat personnel scattered across the ULAW worlds.

They stayed in touch through Virtuality, utilising the realm of veils even as their enemies did. Both sides must have been aware of the other's presence, but they ignored it, adhering to the fragile peace of stalemate.

He and Kethi saw a fair bit of Malcolm Kaufman, or at least versions of him. There were more clones of Malcolm than Leyton cared to think about, and that bothered him for some reason. He didn't really know Malcolm Kaufman, and to have so many versions of this acknowledged genius in virtual form struck him as unnatural and vaguely dangerous, though not for any reason he could justify.

As yet, the Byrzaen influence on human society had been as minimal and benign as promised, though Leyton didn't trust that and still felt this smacked of invasion through the back door. For now, the habitat watched and waited – something they were well versed in. Leyton, on the other hand, wasn't, and he chafed to be doing something more proactive. He knew that Catherine Chzyski had some hold over Benson, but she refused to specify what it was, and his ignorance on the subject was a further frustration. Leyton's biggest fear was that, while they might have the upper hand for now, the faction within ULAW that Benson represented wouldn't be taking their reversal on Home lying down. If the habitat and their allies remained passive for too long, Benson would find some way of outmanoeuvring them.

In her new identity, Kethi had helped establish and was vigorously promoting a pressure group demanding greater transparency in all dealings with the Byrzaens. Their lobbying had caught the media's attention and it was producing results, all of which Leyton applauded; he just wished they could do more. Anything that might keep ULAW and the Byrzaens off-balance he would have jumped at.

Kethi's ongoing analysis of events suggested that the 'accidents' and murder of key individuals had stopped, which was something, at least; although Leyton wished they could be certain this wasn't due to the assassination programme having been completed rather than anything else. That was the problem. There were so many unknowns; too many for his peace of mind.

He was on his way to a meeting with Malcolm, a new version only recently cloned, who would have the latest intel on ULAW activities, which Kethi was anxiously waiting on. The clone might even have something productive for Leyton to do. Unlikely, but he could always hope.

MALCOLM HAD BEEN keeping himself busy. He was increasingly called upon in his role as 'consultant' for Kaufman Industries. He was enjoying his involvement in his old firm enormously, having been starved of such diversions during Philip's time as CEO. In the meantime, cloned versions of him had spread to every corner of human space, just as he'd warned Benson they would. Odd, but he still thought of himself – the Malcolm Kaufman that remained on Home – as the *real* Malcolm, and suspected that every other version felt the same about themselves. Was his point of view any more valid than that of the others? This line of thought held the potential for an introspective spiral of philosophical pointlessness, so he determined not to go there.

The snippet of coding he'd revealed to Benson was next to nothing. It had to be. He didn't want ULAW or the Byrzaens perfecting a countermeasure before the virus was ever deployed, but at the same time he'd needed them to take him seriously. A delicate balance, but one he felt he'd got right. Malcolm was nothing like the coding expert Lara Chenin had been, but nor was he a novice. Now a Sword of Damocles hung suspended over both civilisations. A situation that couldn't last forever perhaps, but it would hold everything in check for a good while, hopefully long enough for the two races to learn to work together, and for Malcolm that was enough.

Ever since he transcended, he had been fascinated by his own emotional responses. In his former corporeal self, the levels and balance of specific chemicals were key in determining his mood. In his subsequent uploaded state, these had been replaced by the triggering of analogous coding. Superficially, his emotions felt the same as they always had, but the more he studied the issue the more convinced he became that this wasn't strictly true. His feelings were a great deal simpler and clearer than they had been in the physical world. It was something he intended to examine in more detail at some point. The real question, of course, was whether or not this less complex emotional palette was desirable. Did it make him any less human, or was it a welcome improvement – did it facilitate less confused and therefore more efficient responses?

Excitement was always an intriguing one. He'd rarely experienced that particular emotional state since adopting a virtual form. He'd been intrigued and perhaps a *little* excited by the advent of the Byrzaens and the opportunity to study an entirely new form of science, to discover an alien culture.

He'd enjoyed no end the time spent recently with Kyle as they stripped down one of *The Rebellion*'s off-line drive units. They did so in order to study the technology involved in converting the radically different energies of the veils into something that could propel objects between the stars. But not even these had excited him in quite the way that he remembered.

Yet now, as he waited on the arrival of the latest ship from New Paris, he was closer to that tingling, can't-wait, cat-on-a-hot-tin-roof fidgetiness that he could recall from his corporeal days than he'd been in a long while. Malcolm kept telling himself that he needn't feel guilty. He hadn't actually *lied* to his son. His only sin had been one of omission – he'd failed to correct an assumption. It was perfectly logical for Philip to have supposed that Malcolm had left a clone of himself on New Paris, but he hadn't. Not of himself.

"Hello, Malcolm," the latest arrival from New Paris greeted him.

"Hello, son," he replied. "Welcome home."

BEING FRESH FROM New Paris, Philip had none of his predecessor's knowledge or experience, though he'd picked up a few things along the way. Malcolm had to teach him a lot of stuff all over again, which brought with it a poignant sense of déjà-vu, as he repeated many of the same lessons and shared similar moments. Not that he begrudged a single second. After all, time was hardly an issue, and it wasn't so long ago that his son wouldn't have allowed him to get close at all. Besides, the repeat performance enabled Malcolm to exercise more discretion and be selective about what was taught and what was omitted.

He studiously brought Philip up to speed on most things, but not quite everything. He firmly believed that a father had a duty to protect his son. The least he could do was spare Philip the burden of the doomsday virus. Malcolm suddenly realised that *this* Philip had never even met Lara Chenin, or indeed Tanya, who hadn't reappeared since Philip's 'death' and presumably wouldn't again, her services no longer required. Both had been impressive and formidable women in their own way.

As far as Malcolm could see, there was no reason Philip should ever be aware of the question that haunted his father's thoughts more often than not: *to use or not to use*. No, the responsibility of deciding the fate of two civilisations would remain Malcolm's alone. After all, the universe only needed one god.

ACKNOWLEDGEMENTS

I'VE HAD GREAT fun writing the two *Noise* books – just as well, considering they represent an investment of a year and a half of my life – and can only hope that people enjoy reading them. Writing is often described as a solitary vocation, sitting alone staring at a screen and tapping away. True enough, in as far as it goes, but this series, for one, wouldn't have happened without support from a number of people who merit recognition.

First and foremost I owe a huge debt of gratitude to Helen, who accepts being a keyboard widow with grace and understanding, and is more supportive than I have any right to expect or deserve. Then there is Ian Watson, whose advice and input have been invaluable, especially with the first book. It was Ian who suggested naming the pirate vessel *The Noise Within*, for example, effectively providing the novel with its title. A debt of gratitude is also owed to Andy West, whose technical input for this second volume has helped me avoid making an even greater fool of myself with aspects of Virtuality. More thanks are due to the members of the Northampton SF Writers Group, who workshopped assorted chapters of both novels (three from the first, two from the second) and made a number of useful criticisms and suggestions.

I'm deeply indebted to George Mann, Mark Newton and Christian Dunn of Black Library, who were brave enough (feel free to replace with either 'farsighted' or 'foolhardy,' depending on your opinion of the books) to commission two novels from a debut novelist based on a sample chapter, a synopsis, and a history of short story sales, to literary agent John Jarrold for facilitating the deal, and to Jonathan Oliver and Jenni Hill at Rebellion for seeing the process through to its conclusion.

Thanks to Dominic Harman for coming up with such bloody brilliant cover art, and, finally, to all those who have blogged, reviewed and emailed to say how much they enjoyed *The Noise Within*. Such feedback and support means a heck of a lot. After all, without readers, writing really would be a solitary existence.

Ian Whates
August 2010

JAMES LOVEGROVE'S *PANTHEON* SERIES

THE AGE OF RA

UK ISBN: 978 1 844167 46 3 • US ISBN: 978 1 844167 47 0 • £7.99/$7.99

The Ancient Egyptian gods have defeated all the other pantheons and divided the Earth into warring factions. Lt. David Westwynter, a British soldier, stumbles into Freegypt, the only place to have remained independent of the gods, and encounters the followers of a humanist freedom-fighter known as the Lightbringer. As the world heads towards an apocalyptic battle, there is far more to this leader than it seems...

THE AGE OF ZEUS

UK ISBN: 978 1 906735 68 5 • US ISBN: 978 1 906735 69 2 • £7.99/$7.99

The Olympians appeared a decade ago, living incarnations of the Ancient Greek gods, offering order and stability at the cost of placing humanity under the jackboot of divine oppression. Until former London police officer Sam Akehurst receives an invitation to join the Titans, the small band of battlesuited high-tech guerillas squaring off against the Olympians and their mythological monsters in a war they cannot all survive...

THE AGE OF ODIN

UK ISBN: 978 1 907519 40 6 • US ISBN: 978 1 907519 41 3 • £7.99/$7.99

Gideon Coxall was a good soldier but bad at everything else, until a roadside explosive device leaves him with one deaf ear and a British Army half-pension. The Valhalla Project, recruiting useless soldiers like himself, no questions asked, seems like a dream, but the last thing Gid expects is to find himself fighting alongside ancient Viking gods. It seems *Ragnarök* – the fabled final conflict of the Sagas – is looming.

 WWW.SOLARISBOOKS.COM

Follow us on Twitter! www.twitter.com/solarisbooks

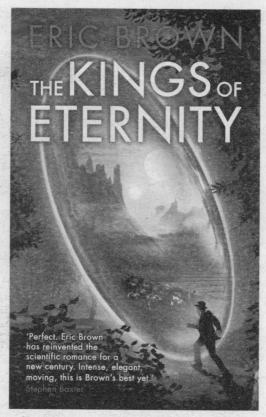

ERIC BROWN

THE **KINGS** OF **ETERNITY**

'Perfect. Eric Brown
has reinvented the
scientific romance for a
new century. Intense, elegant,
moving, this is Brown's best yet.'
Stephen Baxter

UK ISBN: 978 1 907519-71-0 • US ISBN: 978 1 907519 70 3 • £7.99/$7.99

1999. Novelist Daniel Langham lives a reclusive life on an idyllic Greek island, hiding away from humanity and the events of the past. All that changes, however, when he meets artist Caroline Platt and finds himself falling in love. But what is his secret, and what are the horrors that haunt him?

1935. Writers Jonathon Langham and Edward Vaughan are summoned from London by their editor friend Jasper Carnegie to help investigate strange goings-on in Hopton Wood. What they discover there will change their lives forever.

What they become, and their link to the novelist of the future, is the subject of Eric Brown's most ambitious novel to date. Almost ten years in the writing, *The Kings of Eternity* is a novel of vast scope and depth, yet imbued with humanity and characters you'll come to love.

 WWW.SOLARISBOOKS.COM

Follow us on Twitter! www.twitter.com/solarisbooks

XENOPATH

A BENGAL STATION NOVEL

ERIC BROWN

UK ISBN: 978 1 844167 42 5 • US ISBN: 978 1 844167 43 2 • £7.99/$7.99

Telepath Jeff Vaughan is working for a detective agency on Bengal Station, an exotic spaceport that dominates the ocean between India and Burma, when he is called out to the colony world of Mallory to investigate recent discoveries of alien corpses.
But Vaughan is shaken to his core when he begins to uncover the heart of darkness at the centre of the Scheering-Lassiter colonial organisation...

 WWW.SOLARISBOOKS.COM

Follow us on Twitter! www.twitter.com/solarisbooks